Jayci Lee writes poignant, sexy and laugh-out-loud romance every free second she can scavenge. She lives in sunny California with her tall, dark and handsome husband, two amazing boys with boundless energy, and a fluffy rescue whose cuteness is a major distraction. At times, she cannot accommodate reality because her brain is full of drool-worthy heroes and badass heroines clamouring to come to life.

Because of all the books demanding to be written, Jayci writes full-time now and is semi-retired from her fifteen-year career as a defence litigator. She loves food, wine and travelling, and, incidentally, so do her characters. Books have always helped her grow, dream and heal, and she hopes her books will do the same for you.

Joss Wood loves books and travelling—especially to the wild places of southern Africa and, well, anywhere. She's a wife, a mum to two teenagers and slave to two cats. After a career in local economic development, she now writes full-time. Joss is a member of Romance Writers of America and Romance Writers of South Africa.

OFF LIMITS ATTRACTION

JAYCI LEE

HOT HOLIDAY FLING

JOSS WOOD

MILLS & BOON

First Published in Great Britain 2020
by Mills & Boon, an imprint of HarperCollinsPublishers,
1 London Bridge Street, London, SE1 9GF

Off Limits Attraction © 2020 Judith J. Yi
Hot Holiday Fling © 2020 Joss Wood

ISBN:978-0-263-28011-1

1220

MIX
Paper from
responsible sources
FSC™ C007454

This book is produced from independently certified FSC™ paper to ensure responsible forest management.

For more information visit: www.harpercollins.co.uk/green

Printed and bound in Spain
by CPI, Barcelona

OFF LIMITS ATTRACTION

JAYCI LEE

To Dad. Thank you for passing on the writing gene.
Your amazing talent and love of writing has been
an inspiration for me. I love you.

One

Jihae Park nodded even though she couldn't hear a word Rotelle Logistics's CEO and CFO were saying over the din of the helicopter. The two men were fighting to put an arm over her shoulders to lead her away from the gales blowing from the propellers. Ultimately, they both grabbed a shoulder each and rushed her into the building.

She huffed impatiently as the two men continued to fight for her attention. Her father's people behaved so ridiculously around her. What would they do in the presence of the almighty Chairman Park? They would probably freeze and pop out an egg. Or they would throw out their backs, bowing so low that their noses bumped their knees. The second option was a definite possibility, but the first one was so much more amusing to imagine.

In Los Angeles, she was more than the daughter of Rotelle Corporation's chairman. She was the hardworking and competent vice president of Rotelle Entertainment, and was respected by her employees. She wasn't *just* the chairman's daughter.

She exhaled and drew back her shoulders. She shouldn't get herself worked up. It wasn't worth it. She was probably jet-lagged from her flight to New York last night, and the helicopter ride to New Jersey had been a bit bumpy.

"It's a tremendous honor to have you with us, Vice President." The CEO spoke in Korean once they were inside, bowing ninety degrees at the waist. *Well, what a nob.* The bowing was fine, but the CFO, a US native, clearly didn't speak Korean.

"I'm glad to be here," Jihae replied in English, giving Mr. CEO a pointed look.

She generally didn't mind these visits to various subsidiaries of Rotelle Corporation. It gave her a chance to show them that their contributions mattered. What she did mind was the fact it took time away from her work at Rotelle Entertainment. Luckily, she had competent employees who could cover for her during her trip.

But her father might not be as fortunate with Mr. CEO. He'd been transferred to the New Jersey office from Korea and would sit as the CEO of Rotelle Logistics as long as he remained in her father's good graces. Unfortunately for him, her father couldn't care less about Jihae or her opinions, so the ass-kissing was wasted on her.

Rotelle Corporation had been founded by her great-great-grandfather soon after the Korean War. Its revenue, reputation and political power had grown exponentially until it had become what it was now—one of the biggest conglomerates in Korea with businesses in various industries including food, pharmaceutics, biotechnology, entertainment, media and logistics. She probably missed one there. Yes. Home shopping. She didn't know why she kept leaving that one out.

"Would you be amenable to a quick tour of our office, Miss Park?" Mr. CFO bowed repeatedly to her with prayer hands like a Buddhist monk.

Why do people do that? Jihae wasn't even certain where the custom originated. Did it belong to a country or a religion? She'd only seen the prayer-hands-and-bow thing during yoga and at Buddhist monasteries. When people randomly bowed to her that way, she felt mildly confused and quite offended by the caricature of Korea's culture of bowing at the waist, which was a show of respect used to greet others or to thank them. And it didn't involve bowing ten times at once like an unhinged marionette.

With a resigned sigh, Jihae smoothed her hands over her pristine white suit and schooled her expression into a polite smile. The two men were irritating her to an inch of her life, but there was no need to let on.

She survived the office tour led by the two bickering executives and ate an overpriced meal that didn't come close to filling her up. After acknowledging their hard work and their important contributions to Rotelle Corporation, she bid them farewell.

Despite her assurances that she could find her way back to the roof without assistance, both the CEO and CFO followed her up to say their goodbyes. The CFO repeated his frantic bowing and the CEO held his ninety-degree bow the entire time it took her to board the helicopter. Once the helicopter took flight, they switched to waving so enthusiastically that their hands blurred. They soon disappeared from sight.

Jihae sighed and settled back in her seat, relieved to be finished with her latest heiress duties. The flight back to her hotel in New York City wasn't long, but she had a hard time staying awake. The remarkable view that revealed itself as they approached the city saved her from falling asleep, and possibly drooling, in the pilot's presence. That would've been very unheiress like.

The helicopter came to a smooth landing on the hotel roof, and Jihae rushed to the privacy of her room. By the time she let herself inside the presidential suite, she was exhausted and starved. After kicking off her snake-print stilettos, she made a beeline for the hotel phone.

"Yes, Miss Park." Her butler picked up on the first ring.

"Could you send up a double cheeseburger with extra jalapeños, some curly fries and three bottles of ice-cold lager?"

"Do you have a preference for a specific brand of lager?" he asked with his usual fake not-so-British accent.

Jihae had lived in the UK for close to a decade and it was obvious her butler never had. But she would never burst his bubble. If he got a kick out of using a British accent on the job, then by all means, why not let him speak with a fake accent?

"Anything local is fine. Surprise me."

She hung up the phone and took stock of her evening. Her schedule was gloriously empty. Since she didn't need to leave her suite until tomorrow morning, she headed for the bathroom for a proper hot soak. The food wouldn't arrive for at least thirty minutes, and she was dying to scrub off her makeup and let her hair down. Literally.

Princess Jihae, as the Korean media called her, hadn't been born into this world. She'd been meticulously created by the Park family's PR specialist and stylists when the real Jihae was about seventeen. Her parents needed a persona worthy of being a part of their pseudoroyal family—the almighty *jaebul*. She had preferred the prior seventeen years of neglect by them compared to the constant reminders of her responsibilities to her family and the importance of maintaining a perfect image.

By then, she'd already been tall, close to her current five foot eight. They couldn't work the lovely, delicate-flower image on her, so the team decided she would be presented to the world as the picture of aloof elegance. Other than when she was home, Princess Jihae always wore her hair up in chignons, buns or elaborate updos befitting the occasion. And her entire wardrobe consisted of finely cut clothes in various shades of white—all selected by her stylist during the private shows that fashion designers hosted for her family. She'd fought tooth and nail for her right to choose her own shoes as long as they were appropriately upscale.

People probably thought she wore a billowy white nightgown with a chignon to bed. *Ha!* She plopped down on the couch in her French terry joggers and a baggy T-shirt, and draped one leg over the arm of the sofa. Tonight, she was dressed from head to toe in pink. Unsurprisingly, her home-alone clothes were the colors of the rainbow. And her hair was falling freely over her shoulders, brushed but damp.

She grabbed the remote and raised it toward the TV when a familiar "British" voice said from the hallway, "Your dinner, miss."

"Please leave it outside the door. I'll serve myself when I'm ready. Good night, Timothy," she said in rapid succession. He couldn't see her out of character.

After a slight pause, he replied in a slightly miffed tone, "Very well, miss. Please let me know if you need anything else. Anything at all."

"Okay. Thank you."

When she heard his receding footsteps, she scrambled off the sofa and rushed to the door to listen for the ring of the elevator. She waited ten more seconds before opening the door a sliver to check the hallway. All clear. There were only three other suites on the floor, but she couldn't be too careful.

Once she grabbed the cart, she headed straight for the couch and TV, and opened her first bottle of beer. She closed her eyes and took a long swig of beer. *Heaven.* With one hand, she clicked until she found the channel showing *The Bachelor*, and grabbed the burger with her other hand. The first sloppy bite of the juicy, oozing cheeseburger was probably the best thing that happened to her all day.

By some miracle, she finished her burger without getting any of it on her clothes, and leaned back on the sofa with her second bottle of beer. Her favorite part of watching *The Bachelor* was the commercials. American commercials were so different from the Korean ones. She loved the outrageous humor in many of them.

"Tomorrow on *Hollywood Insiders*," the voice-over bellowed from the speakers, "does Sandy Lim have a new suitor? The mystery man with his arm full of Sandy has been identified as an up-and-coming film producer, Colin Song. We'll tell all…tomorrow."

Jihae set down her bottle on a coaster and lowered the volume. She reached for her laptop and powered it up. A film producer dating an actress always made her a little wary, but she didn't jump to any conclusions. After all, love conquers all.

Oddly, her heart was doing an intense HIIT workout behind her ribs, and she couldn't figure out why. Maybe it was the film producer. He was by far the most beautiful man she'd ever seen. But that was nonsense. She'd only had a passing glimpse of him on the screen. She was just excited about getting back to Rotelle Entertainment business.

They had been making connections in Hollywood and getting a decent lay of the land, but there was still so much to learn. Rotelle Entertainment had some clout in the in-

ternational film industry through Cannes and other inter-
national film festivals, but she was the first to admit that
they were newbies in Hollywood.

They'd been searching to partner with a US-based production company to even out the handicap. Ego had no
place in business, so she'd asked for help where help was
needed. Producing and distributing a successful Hollywood film was not child's play, and Jihae was determined
to do a damn good job, which meant she had to find a
damn good partner.

Could Colin Song be a potential candidate? Just thinking about the handsome producer made soft trembles
course through her body. He was so gorgeous. *Gah*. If a
glance at him on TV did this to her, she might spontaneously combust if she met him in person. She would never
be able to work professionally with him. He would be too
big of a distraction.

But what if his production company was exactly what
she was looking for? She should look him up. It would all
be for business, of course. She couldn't discount him just
because of his good looks. That wouldn't be fair.

Springtime in Los Angeles was a ridiculous streak of
one beautiful day after another, and today was no exception. It set the perfect scene for the conversation Colin
Song was having with the author Jeannie Choi at a cozy
little coffee shop filled with fresh flower arrangements.

"I know you could option your manuscript to another
production company or even a studio for much more
money, but I believe in your story and your vision," Colin
said, his voice rising with excitement. He always got this
way when he spoke with Jeannie about her book. "I want
you to have maximum creative control of the script and
you will benefit from a higher percentage of revenue from

the box office, DVD, TV, merchandise and the works. You just have to trust CS Productions and be a little patient for the payout."

"Colin, we've chatted a few times now, and I know we're on the same wavelength," Jeannie said with laughter in her voice. "Honestly, you had me at 'maximum creative control.'"

"You won't regret this." He held her hand in both of his and shook it vigorously. "Thank you for trusting CS Productions."

"I'm taking a chance on *you* personally. I don't want anyone else leading this production. I want you to remain my main contact person until the end. Are we clear on that?"

"Crystal." Colin grinned broadly. He liked Jeannie. She was funny, fair and sharp, and she also had that no-nonsense-mom thing going on. She had three little boys, so she probably couldn't help it. The woman laid down the law and accepted no half-assed crap. He was delighted to work with her. "We'll need to partner with a studio for the film's theatrical release, but I will always be your point person."

"That's what I like to hear," she said with a wink.

They walked out onto the sidewalk and said their goodbyes. It wasn't even noon yet; they'd had to meet before Jeannie's kids got out of school. *Talk about starting the day off on the right foot.* This was a huge win for CS Productions, a company he'd been dreaming of starting since he was a high-school kid. With this option, more opportunities would open up for the company, and the momentum could move CS Productions out of obscurity.

Founding CS Productions hadn't been an easy road for Colin Song. His first business had been a nightclub in LA called Pendulum. He'd started out working there as a server during college. Soon after graduating with an economics degree, he went on to become a manager. When the owner decided it was time for him to retire, he decided to become a silent partner and gave Colin a chance to buy out a small share of the business.

Colin had sold off most of his belongings and emptied his savings account to buy in to the business. He worked his ass off to grow the business, and bought Pendulum outright by the time he was twenty-three.

His grandmother, the formidable Grace Song of Hansol Corporation, had allowed him to become a nightclub owner without censure—not because she approved of his plan, but because she always stood by family. She didn't approve of his choice, but she'd understood why he wanted to branch out on his own, and succeed through hard work, not through his name and connections. He wanted to be a self-made man who never needed to depend on anyone but himself and prove that he was nothing like his father.

His father was the proverbial trust-fund baby who'd never done an honest day's work. He was too busy burning money on expensive cars and women, and jetting all over the globe. His grandmother, and his uncle and aunt—before she'd passed away from cancer—had raised Colin. He had grown up with his cousins, Garrett and Adelaide, who were more like an older brother and a little sister to him.

He now owned several popular nightclubs in Koreatown and West Los Angeles, and business was flourishing. He didn't exactly have a party-animal reputation, but it was his business to ensure that the real party animals had a good time. That didn't make Grandmother very happy with him, especially since he was running his clubs rather than working at Hansol. But his clubs had allowed him to save up enough money to open CS Productions.

His grandmother, the family matriarch, hadn't given up on Colin's joining Hansol one day. So far, she had him on a long leash, but he didn't know how long she would let him go on like this. No matter how hard he tried to distance himself from Hansol and the Song family name, she found ways to hold on to him. In a way, he appreciated that. He avoided all association with Hansol Corporation in public and kept his identity a tightly held secret, but he loved his family and needed to be a part of it.

He revved his engine and drove out of the café's parking lot with a cheek-cramping grin on his face. Jeannie Choi had optioned *Best Placed Bets* to CS Productions. He could hardly believe what had just happened. They only had three employees so far, including him, but they were a tightly knit group. They had a critically acclaimed TV series under their belt, but this would be their first full-length film. He couldn't wait to tell his team members about the news.

Colin had set up the company in a small office in West LA, and he got there in about forty minutes from the suburbs where Jeannie lived. When he opened the office door and entered like a superhero, Kimberly and Ethan jumped up from their desks and ran to him.

"You won't freaking believe this," Ethan said before Colin could open his mouth.

"Rotelle Entertainment is looking to partner with a US production company for their first Hollywood venture," Kimberly blurted as soon as the words left Ethan's mouth.

"This could put CS Productions on the map." Ethan was practically bouncing on his feet.

"Totally!" Kim shouted. Then she clenched her hands into fists, and her expression hardened in steely determination. "We have to lock this in."

Colin still hadn't gotten a word in. He had very mixed feelings about working with Rotelle Entertainment. Even so, he didn't want to dampen morale, so he added his good news to the excitement. "I have something that could help with that."

Both his employees turned to him with blank eyes, as if they'd forgotten he was even there.

"What was that?" Kim said with a confused frown.

Colin chuckled, shaking his head. "Do you remember where I was this morning?"

"Where you were? You never tell us where you're going—" Ethan gasped. "Jeannie Choi."

"Spill it, Colin. You can't keep us in suspense any longer." Kim looked at him like a puppy hungry for a treat.

"I was keeping you in suspense? You guys wouldn't let me get a word in edgewise."

"Come on, boss," Ethan said. "Stop teasing us."

He sighed in resignation. Hyped up, Ethan and Kim were an unstoppable duo. "She agreed to sign an option with us for *Best Placed Bets*."

Much screaming and a group hug ensued. Colin extracted himself and got down to business. "All right. Give me the coherent version of Rotelle Entertainment's search for a partner. Are they looking in their capacity as a studio, or are they planning to coproduce the film, as well?"

He ran his fingers through his hair and listened to Kimberly's recap of Rotelle Entertainment's search for a production company with whom to coproduce a film, which they would then distribute in theaters nationwide. It was a golden opportunity for CS Productions, but goddammit, why Rotelle?

The Song and Park families had a troubled history. The chairman of Rotelle Corporation and his grandmother had arranged for his daughter, Jihae Park, to marry Colin's cousin, but the engagement was broken when Garrett married the woman he loved instead. In retribution, Rotelle had orchestrated a corporate espionage scheme against

Hansol, nearly causing Garrett to lose his CEO position *and* his wife, Natalie. Colin wholeheartedly despised Rotelle Corporation for that.

But he couldn't put his personal grudge ahead of his duty to his company. CS Productions deserved this chance. Ethan and Kimberly deserved it. Unfortunately, from what he'd heard, Jihae Park was the creative head of Rotelle Entertainment. Perhaps he'd luck out and find that she'd stayed in Korea and sent her second-in-command to the United States.

"What's the catch?" Colin said.

Maybe the Rotelle name made him paranoid, but the deal sounded too good to be true. With a great story like Jeannie's *Best Placed Bets*, and the clout of a well-funded production company and studio, it meant they really had a chance at coproducing the best romantic comedy out there.

"There isn't one. Their VP, Jihae Park, has great ambitions for Rotelle's Hollywood debut, and she wants a production company that knows the lay of the land," Kimberly said with a shrug.

So much for his wishful thinking. If they got the partnership, he would have to work closely with Jihae Park. And often. *Hell.* That was going to complicate things. But that was his problem to deal with.

"We should move quickly on this," he said, heading toward his office. "I want our proposal in front of Ms. Park before the end of the week."

"Consider it done," Ethan replied, high-fiving Kimberly. "We got this."

Colin closed his office door and leaned his head on it. No one knew that he was Grace Song's grandson. He had no social-media presence other than for his businesses, and he only attended private family affairs. He shouldn't have to make an exception for Jihae Park and reveal his relationship to the Song family. His family had nothing to do with CS Productions, and he wanted to be judged for who he was, not whom he was related to.

However, if Jihae Park found out who he was, it could jeopardize their project. She would probably misunderstand, and believe that he had deliberately kept his identity a secret from her. People like her believed the world revolved around them, didn't they?

Wait. If he was already taking a risk—why not take another? The partnership could give him an opportunity to find new evidence about Rotelle's role in the espionage. Garrett had had their PI investigate Rotelle when they first got wind of foul play, but there were only suggestions of their involvement. It wasn't enough to prosecute them, especially since their pawn had disappeared to God knew where.

Colin sat heavily on his chair and ran his hand down his face. His meeting with Jeannie Choi felt like ages ago, and the elation of that win had faded into a faint sense of accomplishment. One thing was clear—he wanted CS Productions to partner with Rotelle Entertainment for its success and growth, and for the opportunity to repay his family for all they'd done for him. But he dreaded the partnership for himself. He had no wish to spend long working hours with a spoiled, conniving heiress, and the idea of spying on someone made his skin crawl.

He had a feeling this partnership—if they got it—was going to be a dream come true and a complete nightmare.

Two

"So how many interviews do I have left this week?" Jihae asked in Korean to June, her right-hand woman and a trusted friend.

They were sitting side by side on Jihae's office sofa and having a much-needed cup of coffee.

"You'll be interviewing Colin Song from CS Productions today, and Green Grass Productions on Friday," June said.

Jihae's heart immediately switched into high gear at the mention of Colin Song's name. It turned out the handsome producer and his production company were a good fit for Rotelle Entertainment. Even so, she was hesitant about approaching him because of her obvious attraction to him. But before she could decide what to do, CS Productions had applied for the partnership of their own accord.

She still couldn't help but feel conflicted about the whole thing. CS Productions was a strong candidate. But... why did the man have to be so unreasonably attractive?

Just don't be biased one way or another. Looks had no bearing on a business decision.

"Just two more to go?" Jihae yawned behind her hand to hide her sudden flush. "Thank goodness."

"You're pushing yourself too hard," June said, eyeing her with concern. "Even for you."

"I know. I know." She rolled her eyes then affectionately bumped shoulders with her friend. "It's just that I've been dreaming of this for so long, and we're finally here in the States, living it. It's hard not to be excited."

"Sure. Fine. Be excited. Just slow down a little. You could still be excited working eight to nine hours a day instead of eleven to twelve."

"Maybe you're right." Jihae noticed for the first time that June had dark circles under her eyes that even her flawless makeup couldn't hide. "Oh, my goodness. You've been working those hours with me all this time. How thoughtless of me. I'm so sorry, friend."

"Don't worry about it. You weren't asking me to do anything you weren't doing yourself. I say that's fair."

"Let's cut back to a sane eight hours a day once the interviews are finished."

"Promise?" June stuck out her pinkie, and Jihae shook it with hers.

With their coffee break over, they went back to work like proper workaholics. Her team had sifted through stacks of proposals and narrowed it down to ten production companies to interview. A few were lackluster and some were promising, and now Jihae was down to her last two interviews.

Her earlier glimpse of him on TV had given her mixed feelings about Colin Song, but she wasn't about to judge him based on a snippet of entertainment news. She would do her utmost to be completely fair. Maybe he wouldn't be as handsome in person. *Yes.* He was probably just very photogenic and looked like any other man in real life.

Her phone rang and brought her wayward thoughts to a halt.

"Yup."

"Mr. Colin Song is here to see you," June said.

"Thanks. Please send him in."

"He's level-ten yummy," her friend whispered almost inaudibly.

"Stop that," she said, fighting a laugh.

Jihae hurriedly replaced the receiver in its cradle and wiped the goofy grin off her face. She walked around her desk with her professional half smile on, ready to greet her guest when he came in.

Her office door opened and all the oxygen was sucked out of the room. Colin Song in the flesh. The video clip hadn't done him justice. He took long strides into the office and stood in front of her before she could get a proper breath in. He wore a sharp suit in a perfect shade of gray with a white dress shirt that showed off his athletic physique. His shoulders were so broad, she wondered if he had all his suits custom-made. She should've said hello about three seconds ago, but he was so beautiful she forgot how to speak.

Oddly, he, too, stood transfixed in front of her, his mouth slightly agape. *Oh, bloody hell.* She must seem completely bonkers staring at him like a goldfish of little brain. She shook herself out of whatever spell held her hostage and extended her hand.

"Mr. Song, it's a pleasure to meet you."

His big, warm hand enveloped hers, making her mind go stark white. Then her knees turned to gelatin when he said in a smooth, deep voice, "The pleasure's all mine."

"I'm Jihae Park. I work here," she offered helpfully.

God. When he uttered the word *pleasure*, it sounded like it was dipped in copious amounts of butter. So decadent.

"Yes," he said with laughter twinkling in his eyes. "I'm well aware of that."

"Well…yes." Jihae gave herself a mental forehead slap, and forced herself to focus on business. It was her comfort zone. She had to stop acting so weird. "Please have a seat."

"Thank you."

He folded his long form onto a sofa, and watched her with quiet eyes as Jihae picked a seat across from him. The coffee table between them created a much-needed barrier for her brain to function somewhat normally.

"I was impressed by CS Productions's proposal. It was articulate, and it got straight to the point without flowery, superfluous posturing. I appreciated that. And I quite enjoyed reading *Best Placed Bets*. It was endearingly funny, romantic and heartfelt," she said, relieved that she sounded sufficiently professional. "But I want to hear more about your vision for the story."

"Everything aside, I want this film to be a funny, uplifting rom-com that makes the audience giddy—the kind of movie where everyone walking out of the theater has a spring in their step," he began with a smile that exponentially increased his attractiveness. "I'm also excited about the Korean-American main characters, and the cultural elements they bring to the story. I believe the Asian-American audience will be able to relate to the quirks and humor in those scenes."

Before Jihae could respond, her cell phone trilled from her desk. She shot up from her perch and hurried to turn off her phone. When she reclaimed her seat, her cheeks were burning. "I'm so sorry for the interruption. I must've forgotten to put my cell on silent."

"It's not a problem. We've all done that."

"Thank you." She paused to gather her thoughts. "To continue with our discussion, there have been Korean films, including Rotelle Entertainment's, that have been released in the US. So seeing Asian actors as leading characters isn't as rare as it used to be."

"Those films are stunning works featuring Korean culture, but what we want is to represent Korean-Americans as Americans, not as foreigners who live in this country. Films set in Korea obviously don't accomplish that goal."

"I see your point," she said, nodding slowly.

The passion in his words created a spark of excitement inside her. She would need to research and think further on the issue, but she would love to be part of the movement Colin envisioned.

"This film could add the Asian-American voice to the majority's dialogue. Our journey, the same but different, is part of American life, too. It's like this—the French *mirepoix* and the Creole holy trinity are only one ingredient apart. Both of them have onions and carrots, but the *mirepoix* has celeries and the holy trinity has red bell peppers. They are more similar than different, and the difference isn't a bad thing. They're equally good," Colin said, his hands punctuating his words. She liked his analogy, which she readily understood thanks to her many cooking certificates. "I don't know where that analogy came from, but I'm going with it."

She laughed. "No, it makes complete sense."

"*Best Placed Bets* could be a film that takes America one step closer to acceptance without being heavy-handed and didactic. Nobody wants to be lectured, but I believe everyone wants to understand. This film has the potential to be a dynamic, pivotal work in the industry. And with Rotelle Entertainment's influence and resources, the change could be far-reaching."

Colin Song's energy and intelligence made her pulse pick up speed. His dark eyes glowed with intensity, and he sat forward in his seat, bringing his gorgeous face closer to hers. He had lovely, faint laugh lines in the corners of his eyes. He was someone who laughed often, and suddenly she wanted to hear what his laugh sounded like.

She wished she knew some funny jokes. *Wait. Full stop.* She was acting like a tween with a hard crush—thoroughly awkward and dorky. Even her palms were sweaty. This was blooming ridiculous. She surreptitiously wiped her hands on her pants as she leaned forward to show that she was listening with great interest.

When he shifted in his seat, a waft of his cologne drifted her way, and her eyes nearly fluttered shut. Fresh and woodsy, like he'd hiked through the woods to come to the meeting. It took Herculean effort to keep her eyes from drifting to the muscular thighs that filled his slacks.

Oh, Lord. Her mind did not just go there. Her body was already warm and hypersensitive from his proximity. She had to rein in her attraction. Jihae's reputation was built on her unshakeable professionalism and acute business sense. Lusting after the head of a partner company could tarnish that reputation. Without the respect she garnered, performing her job as well as she had been would become impossible.

Moreover, if this attraction led to…something, her father could take the one thing that helped her survive his scorn and her lonely existence—Rotelle Entertainment. Her work was everything to her. She couldn't forget that. Ever. As long as there was a chance of them working together, Colin Song was off-limits.

"Thank you, Mr. Song," she said in a cool, level voice despite her unsteady breathing, and rose to her feet.

"Thank you for your time, Ms. Park." He extended his

hand and she put hers inside it, trying and failing to feel indifferent to his touch.

She released a soft wavering sigh, and his eyes shot to her lips and lingered. *Bloody hell*. This attraction might go both ways. A secret part of her rejoiced at the realization, but the sane part of her shivered with apprehension. It doubled her temptation to test out their attraction, but she wasn't a mindless body. She was the vice president of Rotelle Entertainment.

"I'll be in touch in the next couple days," she said, gently withdrawing her hand.

"That sounds perfect. I look forward to hearing from you." He released her hand and blinked rapidly as though he was trying to get his bearings. Could he tell how attracted she was to him?

With a curt nod, he walked out of her office. As soon as the door closed, Jihae plopped back down on the chair she'd been occupying and pulled her shirttail out of her slacks and flapped it rapidly. What in the world just happened to her? She had never been so attracted to someone at first sight. It was a crazy, instant chemical reaction, and she could swear he'd felt it, too.

She shot up to her feet and paced the floor. The temptation to explore these newfound feelings was overwhelming, but her willpower had to be greater. Jihae was excited about what CS Productions brought to the table, and she was very much interested in working on *Best Placed Bets*. But did she have the discipline to make certain that she wouldn't act on her attraction?

Partnering with CS Productions would provide a great opportunity for Rotelle Entertainment's venture into Hollywood. Partnering with Colin Song could mean trouble for her. Big trouble.

* * *

Colin was back at CS Productions but he wasn't getting any work done. His mind was too busy replaying his meeting with Jihae Park. He dragged his hands through his hair and leaned back in his chair.

Her beauty had taken him by surprise. He had no business thinking it, but it was undeniable...she was beautiful. He couldn't breathe for the first few seconds in her presence. Her hair had been pulled into a low knot, revealing her long, graceful neckline. Her fair, heart-shaped face looked like cool porcelain, with an expression to match—placid and aloof. Dressed in an all-white pantsuit, she'd seemed almost celestial. Like the elves in *The Lord of the Rings*.

When she spoke with a sexy-as-hell British accent in a warm, husky voice, his libido had spiked like it had been hit with a shot of adrenaline. If that hadn't been enough to throw him off, there was the matter of her shoes. She'd worn a pair of nude, patent-leather stilettos—he was a sucker for women in gravity-defying heels—with rock studs imbedded in a *T* shape over her feet. It was edgy and hot. Were her shoes—so different from the rest of her—a glimpse into her true personality? And...he was analyzing her shoes.

"What the hell is wrong with you?" He wearily wiped a hand down his face.

It was all Colin had been able to do to focus on the meeting. But Jihae had conducted the interview with frank professionalism and respect, listening to what he had to say with genuine interest. What had stunned him the most about her was her embarrassment and regret at having her cell phone ring during the interview. The blush on her cheeks couldn't have been feigned, and she'd apologized profusely. That didn't seem like something an entitled, self-absorbed woman would do.

Colin was confused and enthralled by Jihae Park. Dislike and suspicion were the only emotions he'd felt toward her before the meeting, but his first impression of Jihae Park now warred with what he'd assumed her to be. If he didn't know about the espionage, he would've seen her as a colleague he could respect and come to like. Since they might end up working together, having some professional respect for her wasn't all bad, but it made spying on her even more distasteful.

In all honesty, his plan to spy on her had never been pleasant. The idea of sneaking around and gleaning information from someone through subterfuge made him mildly nauseous. Besides, he had no idea how to go about gathering intel or even what kind of information would help rekindle Hansol's investigation against Rotelle. All he had to fuel his plan was his loyalty to his family, and his desire to do what was right by them.

Was he willing to put the film in jeopardy for his family? This partnership would be a huge step forward for CS Productions, and it would open up many more doors in the future. Opportunities like this didn't come along often, and Colin wanted to make the most of it. He wasn't about to unnecessarily risk the partnership if it could be helped.

But if he found concrete evidence of Rotelle Corporation's involvement in the espionage against Hansol, he would have to inform his family. He would do everything in his power to minimize the risk of being exposed and see the project to its conclusion, but he would always choose his family in the end. Even over the film. He just hoped it wouldn't come to that.

A knock sounded on his door, and he smoothed the frown off his face. "Come in."

"Am I interrupting something?" Ethan asked, poking his head in.

"Not at all." Colin sat up straighter in his chair, giving himself a mental shake. "What can I do for you?"

"I think we might be able to sweeten the deal even more for Rotelle Entertainment."

His stomach lurched with excitement and dread. "I'm all ears."

Colin was excited for CS Productions, but the thought of being another step closer to spying on Jihae Park started a throbbing pain behind his eyes. He just hoped his inconvenient attraction to her wouldn't cloud his judgment in this precarious situation. One thing was for certain: under no circumstances could he act on his attraction her.

They would be business associates and any other relationship between them would be unprofessional. It could adversely impact the partnership and stifle the film's potential. That alone should be enough to nip any interest he had in her. Moreover, she was an enemy of the Song family. He shouldn't be swayed based on a single meeting with her. It wasn't worth the complications.

"You know the screenwriter Charity Banning, who wrote the screenplay for *Never Again Maybe*?"

"Of course I know her. She's immensely talented and her comic timing is perfection. Are you telling me that we have her?"

"Sort of." Ethan adjusted his red-framed glasses when Colin cocked an eyebrow. "She's very interested in *Best Placed Bets*, but after her success with *Never Again Maybe*, her pay rate should reflect that. It would be a stretch to hire her on our budget, but a partnership with Rotelle Entertainment should make things like budgets a nonissue."

"Charity Banning would be a fantastic choice." But Colin wasn't sure if Charity Banning would be a big draw for Jihae Park. She might not have even seen *Never Again Maybe* yet. "Is the movie still playing somewhere?"

Ethan quickly typed into his phone and looked back up in five seconds flat. "Most of the mainstream theaters pulled it last week, but the Shadow Cinema in Santa Monica is still playing it a couple times a day."

"That should work. Thanks, Ethan." An idea formed in Colin's mind. It was bad for his sanity, but good for CS Productions. "Good job getting Charity Banning's interest in *Best Placed Bets*."

"You're welcome," Ethan said with a beaming smile, and returned to his desk.

Colin pulled up Shadow Cinema's website on his computer and purchased two tickets for an evening showing.

His hand hovered over the phone for several seconds. Then, with an impatient flick of his head to get his overgrown hair off his forehead, he snatched up his phone. He listened to the dial tone for two deep breaths, then punched in Rotelle Entertainment's office number.

"Rotelle Entertainment," said the singsong voice of Jihae Park's assistant. "How may I assist you?"

"Ms. Park, please. This is Colin Song."

"Hold, please."

Colin caught himself fidgeting in his seat and stopped himself. He was not some awkward teenager asking a girl out on a date.

"This is Jihae Park."

Her sultry voice hit him in the gut, and he was momentarily out of breath. "Hello, Ms. Park. This is Colin Song and I have news that might interest you."

"Do go on. Please." He grinned when he heard the curiosity in her voice.

"We found the perfect screenwriter for *Best Placed Bets*, and she's interested in working with CS Productions."

"Oh? What's her most well-known work?"

"*Never Again Maybe*. It's a recent release, just fading from the big screens."

"*Never Again Maybe*?" Jihae's laughter, pitched slightly higher than her speaking voice, rang across the line and raised every hair on his arms. She sounded so carefree and young in that moment. "I love that title. So adamant then…not so much. But I'm afraid I've never heard of or seen the movie."

"That's not surprising since you have so many films to keep track of in multiple countries. I assure you it's great, but you don't have to take my word for it. I found a theater still playing it, and have taken the liberty of getting us tickets for tomorrow night at eight twenty."

"For us? At the theater?" She sounded stunned, and Colin frowned. Did she think he was asking her out on a date? *It couldn't be.*

"CS Productions would like to persuade Rotelle Entertainment to work with us. I believe seeing *Never Again Maybe* will convince you that a perfect story with the perfect screenplay could be ours if you say yes to the partnership."

"Let me have the name of the theater and I'll meet you there at eight o'clock sharp." Her voice was poised and professional once more. "Will that work for you, Mr. Song?"

"Absolutely. It's the Shadow Cinema in Santa Monica. I look forward to seeing you tomorrow."

Colin hung up his phone and placed his face in his hands. He could barely handle a phone call with her without getting hot and bothered. How was he going to keep it together sitting beside her in the dark?

By remembering what a coldhearted, vengeful woman she was.

Jihae Park had planted a corporate spy in Hansol and endangered their partnership with Vivotex, a multibillion-dollar venture. Not only that, but she'd also chosen a spy who had been Natalie's college boyfriend to cast the blame on her, and put Garrett's marriage in jeopardy. How could Colin forget what Jihae had nearly done to his cousin and Natalie? What she had almost accomplished with Hansol Corporation?

No, he could never forget that. Not only would he not forget it, but he would also get this partnership any way he could and get hard, cold evidence of Rotelle Corporation's culpability in the Hansol affair. Somehow. That was what tomorrow night was about—making sure CS Productions secured the partnership for its future and finding justice for his family. He wasn't in any way motivated by his attraction to her.

His argument was so convincing, he almost had himself for a second.

Three

Jihae felt glued to the spot and none of her limbs obeyed her. Had she just agreed to go to the movies with Colin Song? It certainly wasn't a date. People wanted to wine and dine her all the time. This was no different. He was only trying to get in her good graces so she'd partner with his company.

But Jihae had never even been to the movies at a public theater. She'd been sequestered to watch movies in her family's private theater or at the office. It would've been a lonely, isolating experience, but the movies always transported her out of there. She couldn't imagine how wonderful the experience would be with a room full of people. She was beyond excited about going to a real theater. Their home theater served five-star meals and beverages, but she wanted nothing more than some popcorn and a Coke. She wanted to experience the movies as they were meant to be, enhanced by the shared excitement of the other viewers. It was going to be amazing.

She couldn't tell June. She wasn't trying to keep it a secret from her friend. After all, it was nothing. But she didn't want June to blow things out of proportion and call it a date. That was unacceptable. It was a casual business meeting to determine the quality of the screenwriter's talent. It was necessary for her to make an informed decision.

After a short knock, June walked into her office, and Jihae stared at her with wide eyes, not saying a word.

"I've done more research into Colin Song and his production company, and everything comes up squeaky clean and up-to—" June stopped both talking and walking when she looked up from her tablet. "What the heck is going on here? What's the matter with you?"

"Nothing," Jihae replied in a tiny voice.

"Don't even go there. I want you to spill it in five seconds." She began counting off on her fingers. "One. Two. Three. Four—"

"I'm going to the movies with Colin Song," she nearly screamed then clapped her hand over her mouth. When she resumed, her voice was at the right decibel. "It's a business meeting."

"Whoa." June ran the rest of the way to Jihae's desk and sat on a guest chair that faced her. "Is that why he called? To ask you on a date?"

"Are you out of your mind, woman? It isn't a date. He called to let me know that he had something to sweeten the deal. He'd found the perfect screenwriter for *Best Placed Bets*. On that note, I want to know everything you can find on Charity Banning."

"Got it. Now go on."

"I told him I'd never seen anything Ms. Banning has written. He said there was a theater still playing her latest film and offered to take me to watch it. He wants to convince me how perfect the film could be with someone who could masterfully transform the story into a great screenplay."

"All I hear is 'blah, blah, blah.'"

"I'm serious, June. This is not a date. I can't risk my professional reputation by having people believe that I have a personal relationship with Mr. Song. Can you even imagine what would happen if my father found out?"

Her parents would accuse her of being naive and frivolous for dating a colleague, and put her under complete lockdown and take Rotelle Entertainment from her. Sadly, she wasn't exaggerating at all. When her father had agreed to let her work at Rotelle Entertainment, he probably thought she was seeking a fleeting distraction. He didn't believe she'd excel at her job and become recognized as a successful businesswoman. According to him, it made her bigheaded and fed her rebellious nature. He would jump at the chance to remove her from her position over the slightest mistake, but she hadn't given him the opportunity so far.

As for her rebellious nature, she had smothered it to ashes after her one flailing leap for freedom. When she'd finished her last term at Oxford, she had disappeared into the countryside instead of attending her graduation. Both of her parents had *prior arrangements*. Couldn't they have made an effort to *care* for once? After all, her college graduation was a huge milestone. Their absence had made Jihae furious and reckless.

Even though she'd lived in Oxford for nearly eight years, Jihae had never been allowed to travel around Europe on her own. She decided if she didn't take a chance then, she would never be able to be on her own, even for a few months.

She'd relied completely on the cash she'd saved up, and had taken Eurail to go from city to city, mostly staying in hostels. It had been the most freeing, exciting few months of her life. She had returned to the UK and settled down at a little inn in the Lake District when her father's men had tracked her down. They'd escorted her home immediately, and she had never been out of her family's and the security guards' sight again.

After years of denying her entreaty to expand Rotelle Entertainment to Hollywood, her father's sudden order for her to travel to the US was a godsend. Her parents' unreasonable expectations and constant scorn had become unbearable to live with. Especially when her engagement to Garrett Song had come to an end. Jihae had been secretly overjoyed by the cancellation of her impending arranged marriage, but her parents blamed her for the broken engagement. For bringing shame to their family. They told her Garrett Song broke the engagement because he'd somehow found out about her selfish, wild nature. Just one, single rebellious incident as a college kid had permanently marked her as the family's black sheep.

"I just wish you could have some normal moments in your life," June said with somber understanding. "You're like Rapunzel trapped in a tower. Even an ocean away, your father controls your every action. Why can't you go on a freaking movie date?"

"Someday, but not with this man. Getting involved with a business associate is unprofessional and improper enough to give my father the excuse he needs to remove me from Rotelle Entertainment."

Jihae reached out and squeezed her friend's hand. It meant so much to have someone who understood that she wasn't living a fairy-tale dream. She was grateful for the privileges she had, but being a *jaebul* heiress meant isolation and loneliness. It was like being imprisoned in a golden cage, tightly leashed at all times.

"Okay. Fine. Then you better make sure no one construes your outing as a date, either. You did mention him being on *Hollywood Insiders*."

"That was because he was with Sandy Lim." She'd almost forgotten that he might still be dating her. Yet another reason not to get involved with him. He wasn't available. "I doubt they'd follow him around when he's not with her."

"You know there are Korean media plants tracking you in the US, don't you?"

"Bloody hell. Should I just cancel the stupid thing?"

"No. The paparazzi don't get to dictate what you do. It's enough your father has so much power over you. You just have to make sure you look the part of a businesswoman."

"Do I ever not?" Jihae sighed wearily. "But I know what you're saying. I'll make sure and wear one of my pantsuits, not even a dress suit, and low-key shoes. And I'll shake his hand when we meet and as we part. Those will make good, boring pictures."

"You're a pro. But can you try to have a little fun? Just a little bit. Deep inside."

Jihae burst out laughing. "I adore you."

"I adore you, too."

The next evening, Jihae smoothed down her jacket and made sure she didn't have a single strand of hair out of place before she stepped out of her cherry-red Corvette. It was a bit showy, but there was no rule that said she had to buy a white car. When she was in Korea, she happened to be driven around in white cars, but it had never been specifically discussed with her PR specialist.

She was lucky enough to find a spot in the tiny parking lot behind the equally quaint theater. Her sensible, white wedge heels clacked against the sidewalk as she strode toward the ticket booth, and it took all her strength not to stop and gawk at Colin Song. He'd ditched his jacket and tie, and he wore a pair of khaki pants and a white button-down shirt with his sleeves rolled past his forearms. Manly, veiny forearms. *Gah*. That multiplied his sexiness tenfold in her book.

Without breaking stride, Jihae came to a stop in front of Colin and extended her hand to him. She braced herself for impact. Even as a frisson traveled down her spine, she kept a polite smile on her face and maintained direct eye contact. But she forgot to withdraw her hand, and Colin didn't seem to have any intention of releasing it. Unable to feign calm a second longer, she took a hasty step back and her hand dropped to her side when he let go.

"I hope I haven't kept you waiting," she said in a steady voice. She was a freaking rock star. No one would be able to tell she wanted to climb all over the man in front of her.

"Not at all. You're right on time. I just got here a few minutes early."

"Did you say you already purchased the tickets?" she asked, not sure about the right protocol for their casual business meeting. It should be fine if he already bought the tickets. He could expense it.

"Yes, I have the tickets," he said, extending his hand toward the entrance. "Did you want anything from the refreshment stand?"

She nodded a little too eagerly. She would finally get to try all the movie-theater goodies. "Yes, but I'll get them myself."

"By all means. I'll stand in line with you."

Colin stood beside her, keeping a respectable distance between them. Very businesslike. Soon Jihae was lost in the wonderland of choices. In the end, she ordered a small popcorn, a Coke slushie and some peanut M&M'S. She peeked over to where Colin was ordering, curious about his selection. He only had a bottle of water and some red licorice. She must look like a junk-food glutton.

Oh, screw it. It might seem a bit unprofessional, but this was her first time at a public movie theater. She was going to live a little.

"Are you ready?" Colin asked, coming up to her. He was obviously holding back his amusement at her bounty.

"No, I'm not done ordering. How are the nachos?" she said and snorted at her own joke. Then she gasped in horror. *Oh, Lord.* She instinctively lifted her hand to cover her mouth, but she was holding her Icee, so she stuck her straw in her mouth and took a long sip. Her public persona had slipped way off at the wrong time in front of the wrong person. She was grateful she didn't get a brain freeze in front of him on top of everything.

"Horrible, but the pretzels aren't half-bad," he answered in a level voice, though he was grinning from ear to ear.

"Shall we?" She arched an eyebrow and bit hard on her cheeks to hold back her answering smile.

"Yes, we're in theater three. There are only three theaters here, so it's easy to get around." He quickly reined in his smile, but his eyes still sparkled with humor.

He led them to their seats in the center aisle and several rows back from the screen. It was perfect, and it was all she could do to contain her excitement. It wasn't until they were seated and the lights went out that she noticed how close they were sitting. He definitely wasn't man-spreading, but he was a big man and his leg grazed her knee when he shifted in his seat. *God, it felt so good.* She really was a sad, lonely woman to get turned on by an innocuous brush of his thigh against her leg.

Before she could spiral into one of her self-pitying moods, the previews filled the screen. She couldn't help but critique the trailers, but she promised herself she would lose herself in the feature film, let herself feel the full impact of the screenplay.

She drank half of her slushie, and ate almost all of her M&M'S and popcorn before the movie started. She hadn't eaten dinner, so she only felt a little guilty. Colin extended his box of red licorice to her, and she took one with a sheepish smile. She was doing a horrible job with her Princess Jihae persona. Was she trying to get him interested in her? No. Not possible. She wasn't hard up enough to risk Rotelle Entertainment for a man. Definitely not *that* hard up. She ripped off a piece of her licorice with her mouth and chewed vigorously. This attraction. It would fade. She would just book a date with one of her vibrators. Some good solo fun would do the job.

When the feature film started, all thoughts of lust and dirty fun were replaced by joy, tears and laughter.

In the name of all things holy...
Jihae was so close to him that he could feel the heat radiating off her body. She smelled fantastic, and that laugh of hers was doing strange things to his heart rate. And the cracks in her icy demeanor did nothing to cool him down.

It struck Colin that he was sitting beside an actual human being with a sense of humor, empathy and dedication to her work. He couldn't fit her into the spoiled-villainess role he'd created in his mind. Of course, he still didn't trust her, but it had been the idea of her that he'd despised, not the real woman. He wouldn't go so far as to say that he liked her, but he would be lying to himself if he said that she still made his skin crawl. The problem was she made his skin feel tight and sensitive with awareness. He couldn't have those feelings toward her.

His smiles and charm weren't exactly feigned, but he had the partnership in his mind. He had to make that happen in order to earn her trust, and have her drop her guard around him. He cringed inwardly at using her that way, but this was the path he'd chosen. Hopefully, she would let something useful slip.

Colin wasn't going to seduce her—he would never do something that abhorrent—but he would befriend her if necessary. She'd only moved to the United States several months ago and couldn't have made many friends with her famous workaholic tendencies. Besides, he wouldn't be acting based purely on his ulterior motive. If all went well and they ended up working together, they needed to get along to be the most efficient and productive team they could be.

That was why he watched her more than he watched the movie. He'd already seen it and knew Charity Banning was the one, but he wanted to learn about Jihae Park. For research purposes.

Unlike the professional mask she'd worn during their meeting yesterday, her face was an open book. Her smiles brightened up the darkened room, and the tears falling down her cheeks made his chest squeeze tightly.

At the end of the film, Colin knew he had her. She'd watched the movie with undivided attention and reacted exactly as intended in every scene. Rotelle Entertainment wasn't what it was now because of her lack of good taste. Jihae knew Charity Banning was golden. He gave her some time to wipe her tears and gather her armor around her—because his gut told him that was what her ice-queen demeanor demanded—then spoke quietly to her.

"Ready?"

She nodded and he gave her his hand to help her up. He didn't know why he did that, since she obviously didn't need help to stand from her seat, but she was too polite to refuse and put her hand in his again. Maybe he was getting addicted to the sensations that flooded through him whenever their hands touched. Her long, delicate fingers wrapped around his palm—her hand was as soft as silk and just cool enough for him to warm up in his bigger, rougher hand. As usual, her eyelashes fluttered in response to his touch, and he felt his blood rush south.

Colin quickly dropped her hand and berated himself for the impulsive move. But he felt less panicked once they were out in the brightly lit lobby.

"So how did you like the movie?" he asked, already knowing the answer.

"It was just how a perfect rom-com should be. The jokes didn't take away from the tender poignancy of the movie, and the dark moment didn't shrivel up my soul, but made me empathize strongly with both main characters. It's a very well-written, acted and directed movie. Thank you for introducing me to it."

"Don't forget," he said with a teasing smirk. "I have ulterior motives."

Her eyes widened for a second, then she awarded him with a small but genuine smile. "I have to admit you're very convincing. I'm going to consider your proposal very carefully."

"Why not say yes now?"

"That would be very impulsive of me, wouldn't it? If we work together, you'll learn that impulsivity isn't one of my flaws."

"Is impulsivity always a flaw?"

"Yes," she said with a frown, as though she couldn't believe he had to even ask.

"Hmm. I disagree. Sometimes impulsivity can make life more fun." Colin wondered what Jihae would be like if she let down her guard and let spontaneity rule. He definitely wanted to see that. *No, you don't, idiot.* Why did he keep forgetting his objective when he was with her?

"I never considered that a possibility." She cocked her head and studied him with a bemused purse of her lips.

"Of course, being impulsive wouldn't be a good business move, but I think trusting your gut instinct is something else entirely."

"Do you think my gut instinct is telling me to say yes?" she asked in a contemplative voice.

He must've been crazy, because he could swear there was a double entendre in her question. One that turned him as hard as iron. "Hell, yes."

She raised an eyebrow and a *Mona Lisa* smile appeared and disappeared from her face. "I like your confidence, Mr. Song."

"Thank you. And please call me Colin."

"Colin," she said slowly as though tasting his name on her tongue. Said in that low, sexy voice of hers, it was a miracle he didn't groan out loud. "I'll take that into consideration, Mr. Song."

"Oh, yes. You don't want to be impulsive. Right, Ms. Park?"

"No. No, I don't."

Colin woke up the next morning, bleary-eyed and agitated. He'd dreamed of Jihae Park all night and was now painfully hard. She was one of the most beautiful and intriguing women he'd ever met. But he couldn't let his inconvenient attraction to Jihae Park cloud his judgment when it came to the partnership and his duties to his family.

He scrubbed his hands over his face and threw back his covers. He took a cold shower to get his head on straight. Once he was ready, Colin visited two of his clubs and met with his staff. His clubs were well-oiled machines, but becoming comfortable with the status quo wasn't an option. He worked continuously with his managers to move the clubs to the next level.

By the time he checked his watch, it was close to noon. He wasn't someone who flustered easily, but his stomach churned as he waited for Jihae's call. After how she'd reacted to the movie last night, she had to say yes. But she had a shrewd business mind and he couldn't take her acquiescence for granted. The more he thought about it, the more unsure he became about the outcome.

Sitting around and fidgeting wasn't his style, so he headed for Pendulum next. It was the first nightclub he'd owned, and its success had made all the other clubs possible. It was Pendulum that had allowed Colin to move out of his father's house, where the decor had gotten more hideous with each new wife he married, and get CS Productions off the ground.

Twenty-five minutes later, Colin pulled into his parking space at the club and walked inside. He sighed with relief when Pendulum—his place of solace—welcomed him home.

"Hey, Tucker. How's it going?" he greeted his manager, walking farther into the club.

"Everything's going smoothly, As for me, I would like a month paid vacation," Tucker replied, following Colin into his office.

"You and me both."

"What brings you in? I wasn't expecting you until Saturday."

"I needed to relax," Colin said with a rueful smile, delivering the truth like a joke.

For a brief second, Tucker frowned, as if he wanted to say something. Colin's longtime employee and friend knew something was up, but he chuckled instead, giving

Colin the space he needed. "Well, you go ahead and do that while I run your nightclub."

Once Colin was alone, he logged on to his computer to get some work done. The distraction would do him some good. When the lights clicked off in his office, he waved his arms to alert the sensors. He was so focused on the clubs' marketing plans that he must have been sitting like a boulder for the last twenty minutes. When the lights came back on, he rolled his shoulders and returned his attention to the screen.

After his office plunged into darkness for the fifth time, Colin stood up and gave in to the urge to pace. It was late afternoon. Maybe she didn't plan to call him today. But he'd been so certain she was close to a decision last night.

"Damn it," he muttered, frustrated with himself and the whole situation.

Colin continued to disappoint his grandmother by refusing to work for Hansol Corporation, but his love and loyalty lay with his family. They already knew that, but he wanted to do what was right. To protect them and redress the wrong done to them. And, of course, the partnership opportunity would be a giant leap forward for CS Productions. That had to be why he felt so impatient to hear from Jihae Park. His impatience had nothing to do with his desire to hear her voice again. None whatsoever.

His cell phone rang as soon as he finished his thought, and he picked it up on the first ring, barely registering the caller ID. "This is Colin."

"Mr. Song, this is Jihae Park." She sounded slightly winded and his gut tightened with worry. Was she okay? Was she nervous about telling him bad news? But that didn't make sense. Why would she call him to deliver bad news? That was what emails were for. He took a deep breath through his nose and waited. "Rotelle Entertainment has decided to offer a partnership to CS Productions for *Best Placed Bets*."

"That's amazing news. CS Productions accepts the offer. We're thrilled to work with Rotelle Entertainment." His heart was beating hard enough to bruise his ribs, and he couldn't stop the smile that spread across his face. "With the partnership sealed, we can lock in Charity Banning as the screenwriter. We're going to make one hell of a film."

"We certainly are," she said. Her voice held a hint of a smile. "I'll have my assistant email over the contract once we're off the phone. Let's make it official."

"Thank you, Jihae," Colin said in an unintentionally low voice. "Would it be all right to call you by your first name now that we're partners?"

"I believe that's perfectly appropriate, Colin."

He didn't know where his blood was rushing to—south or north—but he was light-headed with pleasure at hearing her say his name. He'd pierced one layer of her armor, and was one step closer to her.

Four

Jihae had followed her gut instinct and partnered with CS Productions. Colin had sounded so relieved and happy to hear the news that she wasn't able to hold back her smile. And calling Colin by his first name had felt as intimate as a lover's touch.

"Bloody hell," she muttered as she pushed away from the desk.

Jihae had endlessly second-guessed her instinct to agree to the partnership, questioning the consequences of such a decision. A partnership with CS Productions was exactly what Rotelle Entertainment needed, so it was a smart business decision. But their "business meeting" the night before had confirmed that their attraction to each other wasn't a fluke. It flared to life whenever they were close, and was almost tangible in its intensity. To make matters worse, it wasn't one-sided, which would've made it far easier for her to quell. Knowing he felt the same pull as she did made her helplessly drawn to him.

Helpless. She didn't like the sound of that. Losing control was an unknown to her and she had no interest in going down that road. Considering the potential of the partnership, she'd decided to ignore whatever chemical reaction was brewing in her body to work together with CS Productions. But her phone call with Colin had set her heart racing, and her confidence in her self-control turned a bit wobbly.

Regardless, the decision was made and there was no going back. She ended any chance of exploring their attraction for the privilege of producing *Best Placed Bets*. It was the best decision for Rotelle Entertainment, so it was the right decision for her.

"June," she said into her phone. "When you send over the partnership agreement, could you also schedule for the CS Productions team to meet with our team? They're going to be working closely together. Let's get them introduced sooner rather than later."

"Sure thing. Will you be attending the meeting?"

"No, I don't think I will, and neither should Colin. The two teams should get a chance to know each other in a comfortable environment without their bosses breathing down their necks. It's meant to be a casual meeting where they discuss their visions for the movie, and get excited about producing it."

"Should I make it a lunch meeting? I'll book one of our conference rooms, and have it catered."

"That's a great idea. Thanks, June."

"Anytime. That's what I'm here for."

Jihae replaced the receiver with a smile on her face. Excitement for the partnership bubbled up inside her. *Best Placed Bets* was the first romantic comedy that she would be working on, and she loved the humor, love and heartache the story held. She couldn't wait to see it come together as a feature film—a larger-than-life realization of Jeannie Choi's love story between two Asian-American characters.

Having the honor to work on *Best Placed Bets* came with the heavy responsibility of making a film worthy of bringing the spotlight on the importance of representation. It had to capture the hearts of the viewers and convince Hollywood that they wanted—no, needed—more diversity in the industry. She would work with Colin to make *Best Placed Bets* a long stride in the right direction for his cause, and create momentum for more Asian-American films to come.

Jihae was up for the challenge. So, yes. She'd made the right decision for Rotelle Entertainment and herself. All she could do was hope for their attraction to fizzle out. And soon. Keeping herself in check was only going to get harder the more time she spent with Colin.

Jihae wore a white jumpsuit with elegant silver embroidery across the bodice and on the hem of her pants. Colin stood at her side in a sharp, blue suit with a slim white tie as they smiled and posed for the cameras. They were at an awards ceremony to support Charity Banning's nomination for best adapted screenplay for *Never Again Maybe*, as well as utilize the ceremony to publicize Rotelle Entertainment and CS Productions's partnership.

It was Jihae's first time attending this casual, laid-back awards ceremony held on a beautiful stretch of Santa Monica beach. This was one of the things she liked about working in the United States. It wasn't all about glamour and glitz, but sometimes about down-to-earth fun where the celebrities connected with their fans in a closer, more intimate setting.

After smiling until their cheeks cramped, Jihae and

Colin retreated to the huge tent where the ceremonies were being held. She was acquainted with many of the beautiful people, but there were plenty she hadn't been introduced to. It would be unbecoming of Princess Jihae to fangirl over her favorite actors and actresses, but that didn't mean Jihae wasn't sorely tempted to.

"This isn't the kind of awards ceremony that you're used to, right?" Colin asked, leaning close so he could be heard in the crowded venue.

"Everyone seems so much more approachable and relaxed. I feel like I could walk up to just about anyone and talk to them."

"Then do it."

"Don't be silly," Jihae said with a small smile. "We'll say hello to the people we need to and possibly make some advantageous connections as necessary. Remember, I'm the great Chairman Park's daughter. I'm not allowed to gush over stars. That would be undignified."

"That must suck sometimes." Colin looked steadily at her. "Including nights like this."

"It's hardly an inconvenience. I'm quite used to it."

Jihae was surprised and grateful for his empathy, but she didn't let it show on her face. She refused to act the part of the poor little rich girl. "But feel free to mingle. Don't hold back on my account."

"I won't," he said, but he made no move to leave her side.

She was embarrassed at how glad she was that he stayed with her. She needed to stop acting like a fool. Jihae reminded herself that he might be involved with someone else.

"Is Sandy Lim attending tonight?" she asked.

"Sandy?" Colin cocked his head, wearing a quizzical frown. "I have no idea."

"Oh?" Her heart skipped to a happy beat against her will. She didn't care whether he was with Sandy Lim or not. "I saw some speculations about you being her new boyfriend."

"Oh…that." Colin scratched the back of his head with a sheepish smile. "She's a good friend. She needed help keeping her real boyfriend—well, actually her fiancé now—a secret until they were ready to make their engagement public. I was what you would call her decoy arm candy."

"Decoy arm candy?" Jihae laughed. "Well, congratulations on your performance. You obviously did a good job of distracting the public. How long will she need you to play the part?"

"Well, she just walked in with her forever arm candy on her arm, so I guess I'm free of my decoy duties."

"They must be making things public tonight." Jihae turned around to see the beautiful actress walking into the tent with a handsome, glowing man beside her. "They look so happy together."

"Yeah, he's a great guy," Colin said. "They deserve each other."

He almost sounded wistful, as though he was envious of their happiness. Just as she was. Jihae really needed to get herself under control before she built a fairy-tale story for her and Colin.

He didn't have to stay beside Jihae like her bodyguard. It was obvious she was perfectly comfortable in her environment. She greeted her acquaintances with grace and warmth, and introduced herself to new people with poise and confidence. It wasn't because she *needed* him, but because Colin *wanted* to stay by her side. It was as though he was caught in her gravitational pull.

Just as at the movies, he found himself spending more

time watching her than the awards ceremony. In the darkened theater, he'd been able to enjoy all her changing emotions without effort. Tonight, out in the open, her serene face hardly changed at all. But he could see the subtle differences in the light of her eyes and the curve of her lips. The ever-changing, dynamic current under the calm surface of her demeanor held him captive.

"Charity Banning."

He heard the presenter intone as though from far away, but when he saw Jihae bounce ever so slightly in her seat, he realized what had just happened.

"Yeah, Charity," he yelled, clapping furiously for the talented screenwriter.

Jihae clapped beside him, her face as placid as ever, but he knew she was as excited as he was for Charity because she was sitting on the very edge of her seat. When the crowd quieted down, she leaned toward him and whispered, "So well-deserved."

"Yes, and imagine what she can do for *Best Placed Bets*."

"I know. I so hope she will decide to work with us."

"We're close," he assured her.

Colin's blood hummed with excitement. Charity Banning was a gem, and she was going to transform a beautifully told story into an addictively entertaining script. His and Jihae's partnership was already proving to be an amazing match. And he was dying to pull her into his arms in a bear hug, but he didn't think he could handle it.

The rest of the ceremony passed in fast-forward mode as many films received the recognition they deserved and others were passed over. Colin's high remained until the end, and he couldn't wait to brainstorm with Jihae about their joint project.

"Let's go," he said.

He tugged Jihae to her feet, hoping he could convince

her to have dinner with him. Her hand felt so right in his that he held on to it for a second too long.

Jihae gave him a soft smile, gently freeing herself. "I feel like I could talk the whole night away."

His eyes shot to hers. He wanted to kiss her so much in that moment that he couldn't breathe. But more than that, he wanted to share his ideas and excitement for *Best Placed Bets* with her. He wanted to know what she was thinking and hoping for. He wanted to know her.

"You want to grab some food?" he asked in a voice much huskier than the question warranted.

"Yes, please," she said, and glanced at her watch. "We need to find someplace that stays open late."

"You've been to Pink's, right?" he said as he got into his car.

"Nope. I've never been." Jihae grinned at him from the passenger seat. "And I don't want you to pass out or anything, but I've never even heard of them."

"Seriously?" Colin shot her a sideways glance, his eyebrows hovering near his hairline. "How long have you been in LA?"

"Eight months or so."

"You've been missing out. Pink's is a Los Angeles institution and you can't call yourself a true Angeleno until you've had a hot dog there."

"Well, we can't have that. Let's go get some dawgs."

They lucked out and snagged a parking spot right outside the hot-dog stand. He'd deliberately chosen the least romantic place he knew—he needed help to keep himself in check—but he didn't want to make Jihae walk for miles in her heels.

"Oh, wow! Is that the line?" Her jaw dropped when she saw the line of people down the street and around the corner. "Must be some hot dog."

Colin grinned at her wide-eyed wonder, proud he was responsible for it. Her excitement didn't cease even after the forty-five-minute wait.

"Ready to order?" the cashier asked when they finally got to the counter. She gave them a friendly smile despite the never-ending line.

Colin turned toward Jihae, who waved him on to order first. Even after studying the menu for nearly an hour, she wasn't ready to decide on her first Pink's Hot Dogs experience.

"Two Planet Hollywood dogs, onion rings and an Orange Crush." Then he turned to her with a raised eyebrow.

"A Martha Stewart dog and a root beer," she ordered in a rush as though she was afraid she might change her mind if she didn't hurry.

"Good choice," he said.

"I hope so." She still sounded nervous about her decision.

"You really can't go wrong with them."

They sat down at one of the white plastic tables with aluminum fold-up chairs and waited for their order. His mouth watered as he watched the other patrons devouring their dinners. It was an elbows-on-the-table, talk-with-your-mouth-full kind of place. He hadn't been sure if Jihae would appreciate a restaurant like this, but there was no doubt she was thrilled to be here. A genuine smile danced in her eyes, the shuttered look of her business persona nowhere to be seen. God, she was breathtaking.

Their dinner arrived and her eyes widened at the sheer size of their hot dogs.

"That's a lot of food." She sounded more delighted than worried.

Without further delay, they dug in. *Damn.* It was heavenly.

"So? What do you think?" Colin waited expectantly for her response.

But she'd just taken an enormous bite—her cheeks expanded like a chipmunk's—and could only nod enthusiastically. After swallowing, Jihae grinned dreamily at him. "Oh, my goodness. The last twenty-seven years of my life have been a total waste. What was I doing when there was food like this to inhale?"

She continued to surprise and enchant him. She took another bite of her loaded hot dog, leaving behind a dollop of sour cream on the corner of her lips. Without thinking, Colin reached across the table and grasped her chin. To his great pleasure, her lips parted on a soft sigh as he gently brushed the pad of his thumb at the corner of her mouth, and her eyelashes fluttered like butterfly wings. He quickly withdrew his hand and leaned back in his seat as though he'd touched fire.

"Sour cream," he choked out.

"Oh." Jihae flushed a bright pink as she grabbed her napkin and scrubbed at her lips. "Thanks."

"No problem," he said with forced nonchalance.

Jihae recovered from her brief embarrassment, and he managed to drive out his lusty thoughts. Barely. They ate in amicable silence, and quickly cleaned off their plates. She ate like she meant it. He liked that.

"*Best Placed Bets* is going to be amazing. I can feel it," she said as soon as they'd cleared the table.

"Charity is going to do an incredible job with Jeannie's beautiful story."

"I know." Jihae sighed happily, then asked in a slightly hushed voice, "Who do you think should play our heroine? I think Sandy Lim is a good candidate."

"Sandy's great, but I think finding someone new and fresh might be the way to go."

"I hear what you're saying, but there are some risks involved there."

"There are risks to everything," he countered with a shrug. He was grinning broadly because he even enjoyed disagreeing with her. The slight tension and the anticipation of how she would respond made adrenaline rush through his veins.

"Of course there are, and taking the *right* kind of risks is essential to good filmmaking." She smiled back at him, seeming to enjoy herself as much as he was. "But maybe we're getting ahead of ourselves. Our future director might have something to say about the matter, too."

"True, and I want us to be closely involved in the location scouting," he said. "There are some scenes in my head that I see so clearly that anything different will feel off."

"I hope our visions are aligned because I have several scenes that are dear to my heart, as well."

They grew silent as they gazed at each other, and their smiles waned. She felt it, too. The electricity hummed between them. This was merely the start of their partnership, and they were going to spend much more time together. They couldn't let every lull in their conversation become charged with desire. *But how do you stop something this instinctive and fierce?*

He coughed into his hand and broke the silence. "We have a lot of work to do tomorrow."

"Yes," she said emphatically, her business face back in place. "Why don't we call it a night? We're going to need all our energy to get this project off to a proper start."

And they were going to spend half that energy just to resist each other. Colin prayed fervently that their attraction was a fleeting thing...not believing for a moment that it was.

Five

With an impatient sigh, Jihae scrolled through her never-ending emails. It was close to six o'clock, the new close-of-business she'd promised June. She had cheated a bit by starting her day at seven, but her friend didn't need to know that.

She pushed away her mouse and leaned back in her chair, drumming her fingers on her thighs. There was no use trying to concentrate with only five minutes left until quitting time. She logged off and stood from her desk. Unsure of what to do next, she paced her office in an agitated to-and-fro. She couldn't understand her peculiar mood. It wasn't only her disquiet at how much of a distraction Colin Song was promising to be, but for the first time, work hadn't been enough to fill her day.

Jihae was discontented and restless. That was why she felt so off. She'd gotten a taste of freedom through her "business meetings" with Colin, and remembered how much she used to long for it—to lead a normal life outside the range of her parents' censuring eyes.

She would indulge in just one more adventure to get the restlessness out of her system. What was something she'd never done before? There were so many things she'd missed out on… What could she do? Then one bright idea lit up in her head.

"June." Jihae peeked out of her office, and motioned for June to come inside. "Psst, psst."

"Quiet. You're making a ruckus," June said, deadpan, not looking up from her computer. Her friend didn't stand from her desk until she'd typed a quick succession of words on her keyboard. Then, and only then, did she stride into Jihae's office. "Now, tell me. Why are you flagging me down like a crazy woman?"

She burst out laughing. June loved teasing her about her reserved manner at work. But her friend would be surprised to know that Jihae felt far from reserved right now. She was craving fun and excitement.

"I want to go to a nightclub."

"You set up a meeting at a nightclub? Why would you do that? Don't those sleazeball businessmen usually take other men to those places to have 'hostesses' sidle up to them and pour their drinks? Ew."

"I never said I had a meeting. I want *you* to go clubbing with *me*," Jihae said rather clumsily. She'd never uttered the words *go clubbing* before. "Not to a Koreanized club. That'll be too risky. More people are likely to recognize me there. I want to go to a hot, American nightclub."

"You—you want to go to an American nightclub? A 'hot' one?" It took June a couple seconds to close her gaping mouth. "Who are you, charlatan, and what have you done with my bestie?"

"Oh, shut up." Jihae blushed, regretting her impulsive

request. This was so unlike her. "Never mind. Forget I said anything."

"Oh, no, you don't. You can't back out now." June rushed to her and wrapped her in her arms. "I can't believe you waited until you're close to thirty to rebel against your father a little."

"Hey, I'm only twenty-seven. Besides, I'm not rebelling…" Wasn't she? Was she captivated by a newfound hunger for adventure, or was she lashing out against the punishing rigidity of the life that her father forced on her? *No.* She had found peace with her life, and she counted herself lucky to have a job she loved. "Really, I'm not. I think I'm bored of working nonstop. Of work being the only thing in my life."

"You're finally talking sense. Work should never be your everything. You need to let your hair down and get a bit sloppy once in a while. Where is the fun in being so flawless all the time?" Her friend stood back and studied Jihae from head to toe. "I know the perfect place for tonight. All the staff went clubbing a couple weeks ago—it was your treat, of course—and we had such a great time. I think you'll love it, too. Alas, I can't let you just walk into a club looking like Princess Jihae."

"But all my clothes look like these. Or there are the floor-length dresses. I don't want to draw attention to myself, especially not as a weirdo wearing a white ball gown to a nightclub. My other alternatives are purple, pink or baby blue sweat suits. Even I know that I won't get past the bouncers in those."

"Are you forgetting how filthy rich you are? Your stylist isn't here, but you don't need her. Instead, you'll have your best friend pick you the hottest, tiniest dress you've ever worn. Rodeo Drive is only twenty minutes away."

They rushed to the parking structure and hopped into

Jihae's flashy sports car. As soon as her seat belt was secured, June scrolled through her phone until "Oh, Pretty
Woman" blared from the speakers.

"You're like Julia Roberts except you don't need a man
to pay for your clothes," June shouted over the music.

"Girl power. Woo-hoo," Jihae hooted, and sped toward
Rodeo Drive. Everything around her looked sharper and
even the air tasted fresher. It was the taste of freedom.

As the theme song of *Pretty Woman* played in a loop
in Jihae's head, she tried on every outrageously seductive
dress that June piled onto the salesperson's loaded arms.
She felt like she was living a different person's life, and
it felt wonderful. But distress niggled at the back of her
mind. If she loved someone else's life so much, what did
that say about her own?

June wouldn't let Jihae look in a mirror until she'd poked
and prodded her for an hour. Thank goodness she was used
to being poked and prodded for hours by her stylist. Otherwise, she might've shoved her friend to the ground and
run to the streets screaming for help. She couldn't breathe
properly in the shimmery silver mini dress they'd chosen,
and her butt cheeks were asleep from sitting in the same
position for too long.

"There. Go 'mmm,'" June said, smacking her lips together. Jihae did as she was told, hoping that was the last
of it. "You're all done, and you're welcome."

"Thank God. I can't feel my bum." Jihae stood from
her seat and opened her friend's closet door for the full-
length mirror. Her reflection made her breath catch. "I look
smoking hot. I'm so glad you sat in on so many of my styl-
ing sessions. I think you're even better than my stylists."

June laughed as Jihae twisted this way and that to see
all of herself. Her simple, spaghetti-strap dress clung to

her curves like magic water, transforming her rather narrow, slender body into a delectable, curvaceous one. Her dramatic cat's-eye makeup and bloodred lipstick made her look bold and mysterious. But her favorite thing about herself right now was the long, jet-black waves that flowed down her back and shoulders. This—this was no princess. No, the woman staring back at her was the mistress of her own life. She did as she wanted and no one could stop her.

"I'll get ready fast, then we'll go clubbing," June said, ducking into her bathroom.

Jihae nodded distractedly and turned her gaze back to herself. She felt as though she had shed a layer of her skin and revealed a hidden side of her. Perhaps her true self. The one that matched her red, patent-leather stilettos—the only thing on her that she'd already owned before tonight. But Jihae knew who she was. Whenever she was alone, she could be as sloppy and goofy as she wanted. But a sudden rush of melancholy hit her. Maybe the real her wasn't a silly side character in her persona, but a powerful, vibrant woman that shouldn't be hidden.

Enough feeling sorry for yourself. This version of her might have some aspects of her true self, but she had to acknowledge that Princess Jihae also held parts of her. Her drive to succeed and her search for perfection had never been feigned.

Her friend stepped out of the bathroom looking beyond gorgeous in her black sleeveless dress. "Let's go party, babe."

With a resolute nod, Jihae straightened her spine and let a wicked smile spread across her face. "I'm ready."

Colin buried his head in work all day, but it didn't do much to distract him from thoughts of Jihae. Immobilized by his conflicting dread and excitement about the partnership with Rotelle Entertainment, he barely finished half of the tasks he'd set out to get done.

He pulled his hand down his face then eyed his left-over dinner with a grimace. The turkey club and fries had long gone soggy, which was just as well since he didn't have much of an appetite. He couldn't figure out why he was so twisted up.

His door cracked open and Kimberly peeked into the office. "Staying much longer?"

"No, I'll probably follow you out in a few," he said, rubbing his temples. "You're here late."

"I was finishing up my research and presentation for tomorrow."

"I'm looking forward to it. Selecting the right director is an essential part of our project."

"Would it be unprofessional to say 'Duh'?" She smiled cheekily at him. "Of course it is, and I'm excited to share my thoughts with you. So go rest up. I want you sharp to-morrow."

"Yes, ma'am."

And just as he promised, Colin logged off his computer and closed shop for the night. It was already past ten, but he needed a drink to wind down, so he decided to head over to Pendulum.

The pressure in his chest eased a bit as he drove his car onto the road. He was letting his emotions get the best of him, and that wasn't like him when it came to business. He hadn't made millions by his midtwenties by being wishy-washy. He laughed wryly at the cocky observation. His confidence hadn't hurt, either.

But now he questioned what was up and what was down. Was Jihae a spoiled villainess or was she a brilliant businesswoman with the allure of an angel? Who the hell knew? He certainly didn't. *No.* No, that wasn't true.

Colin stubbornly tipped the scale toward villainess and quelled his doubts. He had to keep his crap together if he was going to get anywhere in his investigation.

By the time he parked his car at Pendulum, he'd almost convinced himself of Jihae's culpability. All the evidence, albeit circumstantial, pointed to her involvement in the Hansol espionage. Her arrival right at the onset of the suspicious activities, and the targeted attack on Garrett and his marriage, implied that she had been seeking revenge against his cousin. With long, impatient strides, he walked into the club and headed straight for the bar. He planned to down a double cognac then take another into his office to enjoy more leisurely.

"Hey, Tim," he said, waving down the bartender. "How's your evening going?"

"Like a pretty typical weeknight. It's just busy enough for it to be fun, but not enough to make me sweat."

"Then you won't mind if I trouble you for a drink."

"Not a problem. Double cognac?" Tim asked.

"You know me so well," Colin said with a grin.

Something about the music made him turn his head toward the stage and his suspicion was confirmed. Tucker was mixing the songs. He got the complete picture when he spotted the regularly scheduled DJ nursing a beer at the bar.

"Hey, Dan. Did Tucker beg you to sit out for a bit?"

"He's this huge, intimidating dude, right? But he does a damn good puppy-dog look." Dan shrugged sheepishly. "I can't say no when he pulls that on me. It also doesn't hurt that he's the manager."

"You did good. He misses being up there, and it helps him let loose a little. Managing this place isn't an easy job."

"Yeah. I totally get that." The DJ sipped his drink as his eyes drifted to the stage. He whistled under his breath, shaking his head. "Those two women have been dancing like crazy for the last hour or so, and they're distracting as hell. In a way, I was relieved to let Tucker take over, so I could stare at them properly. They look like goddesses but dance like unoiled automatons."

With a wry smile, Colin turned toward the direction of Dan's gaze and froze. June from Rotelle Entertainment was dancing with a woman who bore a striking resemblance to Jihae Park. The woman was wearing a dress that looked like liquid metal poured over her. It hugged her curves and moved sinuously against her body as she danced. Her dramatic eye makeup and her red pouty lips made her look sultry and enigmatic at the same time.

Whether he could believe his eyes or not, she was indeed Jihae. She was so far outside her brand that she was nearly unrecognizable. He didn't like surprises but he could definitely live with this one. He wondered if this seductive, bold Jihae was closer to her real self than the armor-wearing businesswoman. This side of her made Colin's desire spike even higher.

Goddesses who dance like unoiled automatons. He chuckled under his breath. Jihae and June weren't the best dancers, but they made up for it with enthusiasm. He admired their complete disregard for what people might think of them, focusing on their joy instead. Shaking their heads, jumping in place, waving their arms…everywhere. Their sheer abandon made them shine, and Jihae glowed like a multifaceted crystal, too mesmerizing to look away from.

When Tucker dragged down the tempo and transitioned into a slow, sexy number, Colin shook himself out of his stupor. He welcomed the break from their dancing. His tongue was on the verge of unrolling out of his mouth, and his heart was already doing its damnedest to shove itself out of his chest. He was turning into a freaking cartoon wolf.

But as he swiveled back toward the bar, he caught a glimpse of Jihae and June stepping closer together. *Oh, hell no.* He swung his stool back to face the dance floor and lost the battle to keep his mouth closed. It was completely innocuous. They were hugging each other and laughing as they swayed from side from side. But the problem was, they were *touching*. No matter how innocent and playful they were being, watching two beautiful women dance and touch was too much to handle. Colin's eyes were threatening to pop out of their sockets.

"Damn," Dan said, and whistled quietly by his side.

Colin had forgotten that he wasn't their only audience. A low growl started at the back of his throat, but he swallowed it with supernatural willpower. He wanted to punch the drooling DJ off the barstool, which was ridiculous since he'd been doing the same thing a second ago. Even so, he wanted the younger man's eyes off Jihae.

"Dan, go relieve Tucker," Colin said in a deceptively casual voice. "Playtime is over."

"But…"

The protest died on his employee's lips when he saw Colin's expression, and he hurried toward the stage. The unexpected surge of possessiveness left Colin unsettled and on edge. He'd dated his fair share of women, but he'd never been the jealous sort. But it was different tonight. He didn't like other men looking at Jihae that way. At all.

After downing his glass of cognac, he strode to the dance floor with deliberate steps. He braced himself for their shock at coming face-to-face with him on their night out on the town.

"Jihae," he said, drawing her attention. "What an unexpected pleasure."

June slowly stepped away from Jihae and stood beside her in a protective stance. Jihae lowered her eyes to her shoes as a lovely flush spread onto her chest, neck and cheeks. After a few breaths, she shifted her gaze to his face, and he couldn't find a trace of her shyness or surprise.

"Colin." She nodded her head in a regal manner that Colin couldn't reconcile with the playful, happy woman he'd seen a moment before. The carefree Jihae was disappearing and he wanted to hold on to her before she could hide away completely.

Possessed by an inexplicable urgency, he stepped close to Jihae and pulled her into his arms. "May I cut in?"

He glanced briefly at June, who exchanged a look with Jihae, then shrugged. "By all means. I'll be at our table."

Jihae watched her assistant—who was obviously a close friend—walk off the dance floor, and met his eyes again. She placed one hand near his collar and drew it slowly down to his shoulder. Then she offered him her other hand, which he wrapped up in his own, and cradled it to his heart. Colin gulped audibly as he placed his free hand on her back and pulled her a little closer. Her soft body fit so perfectly against the hard planes of his own.

"Well, this is rather awkward. It was supposed to be my secret night of debauchery," Jihae said in an even voice that didn't reveal a hint of nerves, whereas he was trembling inside. Did she have the slightest idea what she was doing to him? Maybe he was too late and she'd gone back inside her armor.

"Was it?" he replied in a slightly rough voice. Because he could certainly oblige and assist her with the debauchery. "Well, I think it's a perfect chance meeting to celebrate our partnership."

"By dancing together at a nightclub? Besides, we already celebrated our partnership at the awards ceremony." Her dismissive laugh did something to him, and he pulled her flush against him. Her aloof demeanor changed to one of surprise…and awareness. Colin's lips curled in triumph. Her voice was a husky whisper when she said, "This is not exactly how I usually conduct business."

His shoulders tensed at the thought of her dancing with other men, looking the way she did tonight. He blew out a breath through his nose and deliberately drew his shoulder back down. It was none of his goddamn business whom she danced with.

"Like I said, sometimes impulsivity leads to the best sort of fun." Taking on a life of its own, his thumb drew soft circles on her lower back. "How else would we have had this great opportunity to build rapport?"

"Now it's rapport-building?" She held his eyes and her lips lifted into a *Mona Lisa* smile. "This keeps getting better and better."

With their heads bent close to hear each other, the sexy-as-hell hint of whiskey on her breath was driving him wild. He lowered his head imperceptibly to breathe in her scent, and she shivered in his arms. She felt the magnetic pull, too, and it was damn hot. When her eyes searched his, he slowly angled his head until their lips were mere inches apart.

Both of them drew back as though lightning had struck them. They were dancing in the middle of a crowd. They couldn't do this. Breathing roughly, they gazed at each other in wonder and panic, not quite knowing what to do next. Then a look of stubborn determination filled her face, and Jihae slowly rose to her toes, shocking the hell out of him. She was so bold and true to her feelings. He respected her and wanted her exponentially more. And he wanted to kiss her full, red lips. So badly.

But he jerked himself back at the last second and eased her into a spin. When they faced each other again, he held himself stiffly apart from her. No matter what happened, he wouldn't seduce her. What had compelled him to nearly kiss her had nothing to do with his plans to earn her trust, but the end result would be the same. He couldn't use her that way.

"Yes, rapport-building," he continued as though there hadn't been a sizable lapse in their conversation. "This is definitely more effective than a company retreat."

"I trust you're as discreet as you are professional." Her determined expression was replaced by a hint of mortification. *Damn it.* He hated making her feel rejected, but it was the honorable thing to do. "Jumping around and dancing like a crazy woman doesn't meld with my business image. Neither does dancing in the arms of my partner. I don't intend to repeat either of these activities."

"I'm not the gossiping sort if that's what you're asking," he said, hoping to ease her concern. "But this is hardly a matter that requires discretion. We're two adults sharing a dance. Not exactly top gossip material. Besides, I don't think anyone here recognizes you, and my presence here is expected."

"So you're a regular here?" She leaned back in his arms to look at him. "Should I assume you're something of a party animal by night and a businessman by day?"

"I'm a businessman day and night." He allowed himself a small smile, anticipating her surprise. "I own Pendulum."

She didn't disappoint. She gasped sharply, her eyes becoming wide saucers. Nightclub Jihae was the perfect amalgam of sexy and adorable. "What do you mean you own Pendulum? Wait, forget I just said that. That was a silly question. Of course I understand what you're saying."

"You're right to be surprised. Not everyone runs nightclubs on the side while growing a production company. It's not a well-known fact, especially in the film industry. I'm just known as the new kid on the block."

"Did you say 'nightclubs'?"

"Yes, I own three others, but I started with Pendulum." To his regret, the song came to an end, and he let his arms drop to his sides, sadly bereft of her warmth. "She's something special."

"Well, then." Curiosity saturated her face, as they arrived at her table to find June's rapt attention on them. "It was nice running in to you, Colin."

"Yes. It was very nice," he said, extending his hand to her. The jolt of electricity made his body hum again. His body was even more aware of her after having held her in his arms. He quickly withdrew his hand, breaking contact. He had to walk away this minute because he was barely holding it together. "Good seeing you, June."

"Mmm-hmm." June didn't exactly roll her eyes, but he sensed her attitude nonetheless. He must have looked like an eager pup, panting after Jihae. He had to stop being so obvious, so he furrowed his brow to look more serious. Because, well, he was an idiot. He probably looked like a ridiculous caricature.

"Well, then. I hope you ladies enjoy the rest of the night, and your drinks are on the house."

"You don't need to—"

"Thank you, Colin," June said cheerily, cutting off her friend's protest.

He smiled his approval at her, then inclined his head to both of them. "Good night."

Jihae bit her bottom lip as though she wanted to say something but simply said, "Good night."

Colin sighed in relief. He didn't think he could handle her company much longer without doing things that could jeopardize their partnership as well as his personal objective. The woman was sinfully alluring and he was no saint.

He went back to the bar, walked behind it and grabbed himself a half-empty bottle of cognac and a glass. Tim acknowledged Colin's little indulgence with a wave of his hand and shooed him out of his space. After throwing a smirk over his shoulder, Colin went inside his office and closed the door.

He intended to drown his lust in liquor so it wouldn't be able to resurface too soon. Yes, it would resurface. Colin was never one to deny the inevitable. He just wanted to delay it.

Six

She was fully encased in her Princess Jihae armor as she waited for her elevator. She needed it more than ever as she headed to her meeting with Colin. It'd been a couple of weeks since they'd run in to each other at Pendulum, but she still felt raw and exposed when she thought of how she'd behaved.

Jihae had no excuse or explanation for her impulsive actions that night. She'd just done what she wanted to for once. She hadn't cared about anything but being in his arms. Being pressed against him. And wanting to kiss him.

Remembering how Colin pulled away from her made her blush with mortification, but she also felt another, more troublesome emotion. Regret. Despite everything, she wished she'd kissed the hell out of him, and the ferocity of her desire scared her. She'd had a couple of discreet affairs before, but she had never felt the thrill she experienced with Colin.

Did she regret the partnership with CS Productions? No. The project was proceeding like a dream and her excitement grew every day. It was worth the physical and mental toll of denying her attraction to Colin. He'd asked her to come to his office, which probably meant he had a presentation ready for her. She was looking forward to the meeting.

But it would be a shame to be indoors on such a beautiful day. And…that was the strangest thought. When had she ever spent a workday enjoying the outdoors and the sun? The answer was never. Unless she was scouting a location, but she would be too focused on what she was doing to appreciate the experience. *Wonky.* She gave herself a mental shake.

After tasting a bit of fun, she craved it like an addiction. Well, enough of that. Today was going to be a day of air-conditioned offices, dimmed lights and PowerPoint presentations. But she was still excited to find out about prospective directors. She had a few ideas of her own, but Colin had the insider knowledge.

As she drove toward his office, she decided now was a great time to enjoy some sun and rolled down her top, uncaring about what the wind would to do her low chignon. Maybe she could wear her hair down today. Go bonkers. She laughed and let the breeze carry it away. What kind of life was she living when she couldn't even choose her own hairstyle? But the sun was warm on her neck and arms, and the breeze was cool without being too cold. She didn't feel like she was a prisoner in her own life at the moment. She felt free and vibrant.

Jihae briefly regretted her impulsivity when she parked at Colin's office and checked her appearance in the rearview mirror. She had loose strands of hair framing her face and falling down her back, and her cheeks were as red as spring blossoms. Her princess armor had gone askew. She gave up trying to fix her hair and got out of her car. No one was going to notice a bit of windblown hair.

When she walked into the office, she was immediately greeted by an eager, fresh-faced young man. "Hello, Ms. Park. I'm Ethan. It's a pleasure to finally meet you. And this is my colleague Kimberly."

"It's nice to meet you," Kimberly said.

"I'm so glad to meet CS Productions's team members. I think we're going to have an amazing time working on this film together," Jihae said, shaking their hands.

She was subtly scanning the open-plan work space and wondering where Colin could be when he strolled out of his office with a messenger bag strapped across his shoulders. He was in a casual button-down shirt, rolled up to his elbows, and a pair of khakis. He looked tanned and athletic. She, in her usual white dress suit and python heels, probably looked boring and anemic beside him.

"Come on, Jihae," he said, leading her to the exit by a gentle hold on her elbow. "We have to go."

"Where are we going?" she asked, waving hastily at Ethan and Kimberly. "I thought we were having a discussion about the potential directors."

"We are," he said, not bothering to elaborate. He was up to something, and she was dying to find out what it was.

She lengthened her strides to keep up with Colin as they left the office "Then where are we going?"

"To the zoo."

"The zoo?" She skidded to a halt, a few feet from what she assumed was his car. "Whatever for?"

"I think better when I'm walking, and the zoo is a great place to walk. It's never too crowded on weekdays and it's quiet."

Jihae's heart flipped. Another adventure. She glanced

at the easy grin on Colin's face and felt her heart melt a little. Doing business didn't mean you couldn't have fun. She appreciated and admired his way of thinking and his easygoing manner. She could get used to working with him in this new way. Much too easily, in fact.

"Well, what if the lions roar and drown out our conversation?" she joked, her heart beating faster.

"Nah. California lions are way too chill to roar." He walked a few steps to his car and held open the passenger door. "Besides, they're too cool for school, so they stay inside their caves most of the time."

She sat down and buckled her seat belt, and bounced the tiniest bit in her seat. She had actually been to a zoo in Korea when she was a child, but it was before the zoo was open to the public. It was just her, the zoo administrator and her tutor in the spacious animal park. The grounds had been shadowed in the early morning light, and the animals had seemed too sleepy to play.

Visiting a zoo in daylight with Colin by her side filled her with giddy anticipation. But, of course, this was still a business meeting and they had work to get done. She shouldn't forget that or think that he was doing this for her benefit in any way.

"So how often do you go to the zoo to work?" she asked.

Colin shifted in his seat and coughed into his fist. "Not often enough."

Hmm. Was he embarrassed about being a regular at the zoo? "Where else do you go to think?"

"Um…the museum," he blurted. "The museum is another great place to walk and think."

Jihae absolutely loved museums but she hadn't had an opportunity to visit the ones in Los Angeles yet. "Oh, that sounds lovely. I've been wanting to go to LACMA and the Getty Center."

"We could have our next meeting at the Getty Center."

She nearly clapped her hands and cheered. But she held herself in check. "Perhaps."

He shot a glance at her and smirked like he could see right through her. She turned up her nose at him and held her answering smile in check. They drove the rest of the way in comfortable silence with random observations here and there, but anticipation wound up her stomach.

The zoo looked like a wonderland in the glorious California sunshine, and Jihae felt her spirits rise even higher.

"Ticket for two adults, please," said Colin, reaching for his wallet in his back pocket.

God, how do you get an ass that perfect? Before she got too entranced by his backside, Jihae spoke up. "Hey, you don't have to wine and dine me anymore. We're partners. I'll pay for this."

"But it was my idea…"

"And it'll be my treat," she replied, handing over her card.

Colin grumbled under his breath but didn't protest any further. His mood lifted as soon as they walked into the park to be greeted by neon pink flamingos.

"They smell horrible but they are such a lively sight," he said in a nasally voice. He was breathing through his mouth, as she was.

"I agree to both observations."

"Let's find an animal we could breathe better around, and we could chat about some of the ideas my team and I came up with."

Jihae's shoulders drooped a little at the mention of business. Just for a moment, she'd imagined them to be simply enjoying each other's company. Such silliness. "Good idea. I have some ideas of my own."

The next animals they visited were the giraffes. They

were quiet and still except for munching leaves in their mouths. Their heads were so high up, she didn't have to worry about them eavesdropping on their production plans.

"Kimberly did a very thorough job of researching and weighing the pros and cons of each of the directors she selected for my preliminary review. I've chosen five of them for you to consider. I have my favorite but I won't tell you until you share your thoughts."

"Who are they?"

"Stella Merles, Edward Stein, Ken Park, Cora Huang and Mateo Sanchez." Colin counted off his fingers.

"Mateo Sanchez?"

"Yup."

"He's done some amazing work," she said, excited to have a director of his caliber on their list. "I think he would be sensitive to how we want to treat diversity."

"But Cora Huang did an incredible job with her last two films," he said, pushing back from the railing and motioning for her to walk with him. "I was blown away by how she portrayed the female protagonists to be both strong and vulnerable, and to grow with all the clumsiness and faltering of real people."

"All your picks have their own special strengths. I could narrow it down to three at best, but from there on, I wouldn't know who to pick. I would be thrilled to have any of them."

Colin chuckled and said, "You know, the choice isn't entirely up to us. Those directors are hot commodities. They may turn us down."

Jihae lifted her chin and gave him her haughtiest look. "If I set my mind on something, I don't take no for an answer."

It was true. She was relentless. Of course, she didn't

always get what she wanted, but it wasn't for not giving it her everything. Some things were worth fighting for.

Colin was quiet for a while as he led them to their next animal. She glanced around and took in her surroundings, and sighed a little wistfully. She couldn't deny that she enjoyed these easy moments with him.

He stopped in front of the elephants and rested his hand on the railing. When Jihae stopped beside him and saw the baby elephant standing by its mama, she couldn't hold back her *aww*. Colin turned and awarded her with a wide grin, and she smiled back happily. The mama and baby elephants were the cutest sight. She stepped closer to the railing and held on with her hands, wanting to be near them.

She inadvertently brushed her pinkie against his, and pulled back as a tremor traveled down her back. She glanced at him from under her lashes, pretending to watch the elephants. Her hand looked pale and small next to his darker, bigger one. An image of their intertwined fingers seared itself into her mind, and she wanted it to be real. She could almost feel the warmth of his hand and the heat burning through her veins.

As though reading her mind, Colin placed his hand over hers and laced their fingers together. Neither of them said anything. They both looked down at their entangled hands with quickening breaths. Finally, his eyes, full of gentle yearning, sought hers out, and she fell into their depths.

"Come with me?" he asked with a soft squeeze of her hand.

"Yes."

His steps weren't hurried as he led them down the miniature streets of the zoo. But he picked up speed when they arrived at the entrance of a small aquarium. A narrow, dark hallway led them inside and continued into a semicircle as it opened up into a round aquarium that hugged the outer walls. The blue light emanating from the water gave the interior an otherworldly vibe. And it was deserted.

Colin didn't stop until they walked into another dark hallway leading into what she presumed was another exhibition. He maneuvered her back against the wall and ran his hands up and down her arms, making her shiver with anticipation.

"I shouldn't do this," he said in a rough, low voice.

"Neither should I." She wrapped her arms around his neck. "Kiss me?"

"God, yes," he said, crushing his mouth against hers.

Jihae let herself melt against him with a content sigh. When his tongue gently outlined her bottom lip, she parted her mouth and flicked her tongue against his. That earned her a sexy growl from Colin, and his hands pressed against her back, bringing her even closer to him.

Her curious hands traveled down the length of his firm, muscular arms and came to rest on his narrow waist. First her thumbs drew circles on his stomach, then she boldly grabbed his shirt and tugged it out of his pants. She didn't stop there. She couldn't. She wanted to touch him. To feel him.

He hummed under his breath and pressed his torso into her hands, so she followed her instincts without hesitation. Her fingers traveled over his stomach, delighting in every muscled groove. Then she moved her palms onto his hard, broad chest. It was so smooth. So hot.

Meanwhile, he kissed her like a man starved, but kept his hands planted firmly on her back. He was holding himself in check—trembling beneath her hands—to give her control of how far they would go. They were semihidden in the darkness of the hallway, but they didn't exactly have privacy. This shouldn't go far at all, but she wanted it to last just a little bit longer.

"Goddammit." Colin suddenly pulled back to her bewilderment. "Sorry. It's not the kiss. It's not you. I just have a call I need to return."

Then in the recesses of her mind, Jihae recalled the subtle ringing of a gong. It must have come from Colin's phone. He walked through to the other side, his phone against his ear. She stayed behind to give him privacy and to take a moment to gather herself. She realized she was shaking, as well, and she breathed deeply in and out. After straightening her suit, she finally followed Colin into the next room.

The lights were even dimmer in this section, shining purple, blue and pink to exhibit the multicolored, glowing jellyfish that filled the various tanks. The firm line of Colin's lips and the frown creasing his forehead looked out of place in the beautiful setting. Soon he ended his call and turned to her, his expression transforming into a regretful smile.

"I'm sorry. I'm afraid we need to leave," he said.

"Leave?"

"I'll drive you back to your car."

"My car?" She knew she was repeating everything he said, but she didn't understand. They'd just shared a passionate kiss, and he was going to dump her at her car. Shouldn't they go someplace to talk? Or kiss some more?

"I'm so sorry," he said again. "We'll talk later."

His grandmother had uncanny timing.

He was beyond frustrated by her interruption, and… grateful. He'd lost his head. No, he'd known exactly what he was doing, and he hadn't wanted to stop. Jihae had tasted improbably like a summer day—like the warm sun and a soft breeze. Then she'd sucked him in like a sultry, tropical night. Her soft, cool hands exploring his body, and her sweet, wet lips kissing him with a hunger to match his own. No, he'd never wanted to stop.

But Grandmother's call had been like a bucket of ice-cold water thrown at his face. A much-needed wake-up call. He couldn't kiss Jihae forever. He shouldn't have kissed her in the first place. Not only were they business partners, but he was also a Song. His cousin had broken their engagement, and she had sought revenge against him. They had quite a sordid backstory, except Jihae didn't know yet. What was worse was that he planned to spy on her. He couldn't risk having her become emotionally attached to him. He had no intention of breaking her heart. Ever.

Their drive back to his office had been tense and silent. Was it regret that had clouded her expression? His gut clenched. *Hell.* He couldn't believe that he felt disappointed at the thought. Was he kidding himself that the kiss was a mistake that he never intended to repeat?

Before he could dissect his jumbled thoughts, he arrived at his grandmother's Pacific Palisades home. He parked in the driveway and jumped out of the car. He was glad he could escape his confused emotions. And he had other things to worry about. He was quite positive that his grandmother had found out about CS Productions's partnership with Rotelle Entertainment.

"Hello, beautiful," he said when Liliana, the Song family's housekeeper, opened the door.

"Hello, handsome boy," Liliana said, laughing, and tousled his hair. "Mrs. Song is in her study. What trouble have you gotten yourself into today?"

His mind immediately flashed back to the darkened halls of the aquarium with Jihae sighing and arching into his body. He shook his head and flashed Liliana his dare-devil smile. "What have I *not* gotten myself into is the question."

Despite his flippant words, he walked down the hall with solemn steps. He thought he'd prepared himself for this, but one could never be fully prepared to face off with Grace Song. After taking a deep breath, he knocked on the study door.

"Come in," she ordered.

He opened the door then closed it behind him. Despite his instinct to hightail it out of there, Colin walked up to his grandmother and bowed. "Hal-muh-nee, have you been well?"

"I had been rather well, but I'm not so sure at the moment," she said with a slight downward turn of her mouth. "Are you ready to explain yourself?"

Damn. She was pissed off. She usually began her interrogations with complete stoicism. The tension in the corners of her mouth didn't bode well for him. Was he ready to explain himself? *No.* "Yes."

"What in the world prompted you to partner with Jihae Park? After what she and her family tried to do?"

"Jihae Park and I aren't partners. I don't seem to have the romantic luck that Garrett and Adelaide have," he quipped, but quickly turned down the humor when his grandmother's eyes narrowed with impatience. "CS Productions entered into a promising partnership with Rotelle Entertainment. It has nothing to do with us personally."

"And who might this *us* be?"

"Jihae and me."

"*Jihae* and you are an *us* to you?"

An emotion between fear and doubt churned through him. "Grandmother, you're playing word games with me. If you think I've forgotten what Rotelle tried to do to Garrett, then you don't know me at all. I'm not only looking out for CS Productions's interests but those of our family."

"You're not altogether wrong about me being a little

unreasonable right now," she conceded with a sigh. "But we almost lost Natalie and the baby because of the Parks. Well, them, and Garrett behaving like a complete fool by pushing Natalie away like that. All in all, it's not something I could easily forget or forgive."

"And that brings me to my second motivation for entering into a partnership with Rotelle Entertainment." Colin sat forward in his seat. "Jihae Park doesn't know that I'm your grandson, since we've made sure that only our family and our oldest friends know."

"Go on."

"I could earn her trust and find evidence of Rotelle Corporation's involvement in the espionage attempt against Hansol."

"While you work with her on a project that will benefit CS Productions? Do you think that wise? Or honorable?"

"Honorable? They're the ones who started the war. I only mean to end it with justice."

"Technically, Garrett began the war by refusing her hand. I have to take partial responsibility for that, as well."

"Are you defending them now?" Colin couldn't understand his grandmother's reaction. Didn't she want the Parks brought to justice?

"Not at all. The only one I care about in this twisted farce is you, my child." Grandmother sighed, shaking her head slowly. "You've told me, and shown me, how much CS Productions means to you. You are putting your company at risk by this stunt you're intending to pull. What happens to the partnership if she finds out who you are? What happens when she finds out you've set out to betray her and her family from the start?"

"Jihae is a brilliant businesswoman. I don't believe she would jeopardize the film because of a personal falling-out. She wouldn't. I know her." But Colin also knew that Jihae would never forgive him for intending to spy on her.

"Suk-ah," his grandmother said, her tone softening with the use of his Korean name. "Listen to yourself. You believe Jihae Park to possess integrity. If what you say of her is true, then I find it hard to believe that she was involved in the corporate espionage. Perhaps she's in the dark about what Rotelle Corporation did. Or perhaps your objectivity has already been compromised. Either way, if you keep pushing yourself to spy on Rotelle Corporation through her, I'm afraid you'll only be harming CS Productions and your conscience."

Colin realized that she was right. The more time he spent with Jihae, the harder it was to believe that she was involved in her family's attempt to sabotage the Hansol-Vivotex partnership, not to mention Garrett's marriage. What he knew of Jihae did not fit such subterfuge. But maybe he was allowing his attraction to her cloud his judgment. He refused to let that happen.

"I apologize for not agreeing with you, Hal-muh-nee. The partnership with Rotelle Entertainment will put CS Productions on the map, and working closely with Jihae will allow me to bring Rotelle Corporation to justice."

"Rotelle *and* Jihae, you mean?"

"Yes," he said through clenched teeth.

"Rotelle Corporation should pay for their crime, but I don't want this bad blood to affect your future. The espionage attempt was ultimately a failure, and Garrett and Natalie are happy as can be," Grandmother said, searching his face. "I understand and accept your professional judgment in forming a partnership with Rotelle Entertainment, but compromising your integrity to bring someone else to justice could bring you down to their level in a blink of an eye."

"If you're worried about me losing my way, please don't. I know exactly what I'm doing." *Ha.* He was so conflicted and lost. He needed his grandmother's guidance more than ever.

"You have always been the most stubborn child," she huffed. "Despite what you believe, I am happy that you are doing so well on your own. It is true I would be happier if you were thriving in Hansol, but you did not disappoint me. There is nothing to make amends for or repay. We are family, and I am your grandmother. Do not let a false sense of gratitude or guilt persuade you to harm your conscience or integrity."

"Thank you for your reassurance, Hal-muh-nee." A suffocating weight lifted off his chest at his grandmother's words. He had no idea how much he needed to hear that. "And I will take your advice to heart."

Grandmother was right. He wasn't convinced of Jihae's guilt as he had first been, and the thought of actively gaining her trust just to betray her made him sick to his stomach. Besides, he wasn't getting anywhere with it. He hadn't even been able to take the few opportunities he had to steal a glimpse at Jihae's computer because his conscience got in the way.

He would continue to be alert and on the lookout for information about Rotelle Corporation, but he would focus on producing the best film he could and take a step back from the amateur sleuth business.

Seven

Well, two could play at this game. If Colin wanted to pretend that nothing happened between them, then she would happily oblige. *Maybe not happily, but still.* Her willpower had proven to be shamefully weak when it came to Colin Song. It wasn't that she had forgotten why she couldn't be with him, but when she was with him, it all seemed so distant and…trivial.

What harm could a brief fling do? She knew how to be discreet in her affairs. No one had to find out. Then what was holding her back? *You're afraid of wanting more. That's what.* Colin Song's pull on her was something she'd never felt with anyone else. And the spirit she'd hidden deep inside her to appease her parents flared back to life in response. Wanting him, having him, could mean the unraveling of the precarious balance she had forced on her life.

And she didn't think she wanted to lose that balance. She was…content with the little bit of freedom she found in the United States, and working on *Best Placed Bets* was a longtime dream finally coming true. She just needed to get lost in her work. That was her safe place. She was confident when she worked and was damn good at what she did. She never had to doubt or second-guess her business instincts. Jihae could not let a man make her falter.

She had been summoned to do her father's bidding—through the impersonal email of his executive assistant—for yet another affiliate. The brain-numbing job of smiling and reassuring Rotelle Chemical that Chairman Park was pleased with their work and dining on tiny, expensive meals should keep her busy for the day. Then it was on to two other facilities for the opening of their factories. Spending a week away from LA, and Colin, would do her good. It would slow down her libido from hyperdrive. And when she returned, she would focus 100 percent on her job.

Jihae returned to LA after a week away, but focusing 100 percent on her job was turning out to be a pipe dream. She'd missed the darn man during her entire trip, and now that she was back, their kiss refused to leave her head.

"You're doing it again," June said, barely glancing up from the TV.

It was their weekly movie-bingeing night. It really was part of Jihae's job, but watching the movies with June made it a lot more fun. But then again, her best friend was being massively irritating at the moment.

"No, I'm not," Jihae insisted, making sure she wasn't wearing the slightest smile or frown on her face. In other words, she slid on her Princess Jihae face.

"Remember, your ice-princess mask doesn't work on me, dummy."

"Will you just stop it?" She took a huge bite of her pizza.

"I'm just saying." June shrugged and munched on her

own slice. "That kiss wasn't just a lapse in good judgment, like you insist. You get that sparkling Disney princess face every time you daydream about it. Then, you turn all red and blotchy, and get psychopath-eyed."

"Shut up. Please." It was true, so Jihae didn't want to hear it.

"He still hasn't called you?"

"No," she said, sliding her plate away from her. Her ravenous appetite had vanished like magic. Instead, she reached for her red wine and took a healthy gulp. "Kimberly is lining up the interviews. She's been keeping you posted, right?"

"Right. So you're avoiding direct contact with him, as well?" June rolled her eyes. "You guys are so juvenile."

The week spent away from LA and Rotelle Entertainment, and pretending that nothing had happened between her and Colin, had not made Jihae forget the kiss they'd shared in the dark, glowing hallways of the aquarium. His taste, his warmth, his smell. Her body heated up by several degrees every time she remembered their kiss. It wasn't just the physical pleasure of the encounter, but the connection she'd felt with him. He'd made her feel safe and cherished, like she'd never felt before. And more than anything, she wanted to feel that again despite all logic dictating against a repeat of their kiss.

But then, he'd just up and left. Acted as though nothing had happened between them. And as June pointed out, he hadn't said a word to her since he'd dropped her off at her car that day. She felt bewildered and indignant…and she just wanted to hear his voice. So much.

This foreign need inside her to yearn so desperately for someone both frightened her and made her feel more alive. When it came to business, she never hesitated to reach for what she wanted. Why did this have to be any different?

Certainly, there were risks and obstacles, but weren't risks and obstacles present in everything worth having in life?

She tried to convince herself that it was her lady parts doing the thinking. That if she'd wanted a chance to be with Colin Song, she shouldn't have partnered Rotelle Entertainment with CS Productions. But it was no good. She wanted the partnership *and* Colin.

It was a relief to finally admit to herself that she wanted Colin Song. And she was going to win him over. No man had ever made her feel the way he did, and maybe no other man ever would. She needed to take this chance to explore her attraction to him.

But would a personal relationship with him impact their working relationship? She and Colin were mature adults and professionals. They would be able to keep their personal life separate from their work. Besides, how different could it be from their current situation? She already thought of him constantly and discreetly ogled him when he was around. She just had to remember not to make her infatuation obvious to everyone around them.

She was a smart woman. She knew how to be careful and neutralize risks. Even her father had never found out about her other lovers. Well, there were only two of them, but she had chosen men who hadn't come from money, men her father wouldn't have approved of. Men she respected. If her father had known, he wouldn't have looked the other way. There was no reason she couldn't keep her personal interactions with Colin a secret. *But what if you want something lasting with him? Something real?*

The thought came unbidden, and she had no answers. As far as she knew, he didn't come from a well-known, wealthy family. Her father would frown on such "lack of pedigree." Was she willing to oppose her father to be with a man her family wouldn't accept? Would she be willing to give up Rotelle Entertainment for Colin? *Never mind all that.* She would cross that road if she ever got to it.

"I wasn't allowed to be juvenile even when I was a child. I'm not going to start acting like a child as a grown woman," Jihae announced to a startled June, who thought she'd had the last word.

"Okay, then. Are you going to call him?"

"Nope."

"For God's sake—"

Jihae cut her off before she could resume her nagging. "I'm going to see him in person."

"Right on," June said, raising her palm in the air.

She high-fived her friend and stood up. "Right now."

Her decision made, Jihae felt bold and determined. She rushed to the parking structure and pulled out onto the street before voice-dialing Colin.

"Hello, Jihae." He picked up the phone just as she was about to hang up, and his tone was oh-so-casual.

"Hi." Had he been busy or was he contemplating not answering her call? "Are you working late tonight?"

"Yes, but not for CS Productions. I'm catching up on business at Pendulum."

Bingo. "Were you able to make things official with Charity Banning?"

"I was planning to email you about that tomorrow. We reached an oral agreement, and Ethan will be communicating with June to draw up a formal contract."

"Excellent news. I'm glad I got to hear it tonight."

There was slight hesitation on his end. "Is that why you called?"

"That was part of it."

"And the other part?" he asked in a low, coaxing voice.

Was he flirting with her? If he was going to be like this, why hadn't he just called? He was the one who had rudely cut short their kissing session. Her indignation suddenly rose again. She wasn't going to make this easy for him.

"I actually can't recall the other part. It must not have been very important," she said archly. "Good night, Colin. Congratulations on Charity Banning."

"But—"

She hung up, cutting off his protest. *That felt good.* Hanging up on him gave her some immature satisfaction. Now she was going to invade his home turf and show him exactly what the other part was about.

Traffic was moderate and she made good time to Pendulum. She checked her reflection in the rearview mirror. Her eyes were bright and her color heightened. Adrenaline. Pure, natural makeup. She was wearing a white sleeveless mock neck and a pair of wide-legged white slacks. She wasn't exactly dressed for a nightclub, but she wore her hair down and a swipe of clear lip gloss made her adequately presentable.

Jihae got past the bouncers without a hitch and approached the host. "Hi, I'm here to see Mr. Song."

"Is he expecting you, miss?" the gentleman asked, giving her a perfunctory once-over. She seemed to meet his approval.

"We spoke on the phone only a few minutes ago."

"Then let me escort you to his office."

"I don't want to disrupt your duties. Pointing me in the right direction is all I need."

"Very well. Go down that hallway and turn left. You'll see one door marked *Employees Only* and an unmarked door across from it. That's his office."

"Thank you so much, Mr...."

"Tucker. Just Tucker is fine," he said with a smile.

"Thank you, Tucker. I'm Jihae."

"Nice to meet you, Jihae."

With a wave, she strode toward Colin's office. But once she got there, her nerves faltered for a moment. Then, with an impatient shake of her head, she knocked smartly on the door.

"Come in."

His voice was clear but he sounded a bit distracted. He was probably immersed in his work. But when she stepped inside, he was staring down at his phone, his thumbs at rest.

"I remembered the other reason I called," she said softly.

Colin's head shot up and the intensity of his gaze stole her breath. He pushed back from his desk, making his chair spin wildly, and took three long strides to come stand in front of her. Her heart pounded bruisingly against her ribs, and all her confident resolve seemed to melt.

"Care to share what it is?" he said in a low growl.

She swallowed and gathered her wits about her. "Your urgent business at the zoo that day? Were you able to take care of it satisfactorily?"

"Satisfactorily? No. Far from it," he said, his eyes dropping to her lips. "All I managed to do was feed the fire."

"Kiss me." Her breaths came in short puffs.

"No."

"No?" Her shock overshadowed her hurt at his rejection. He was trembling in front of her, his eyes near manic. He wanted her as much as she wanted him. "Why ever not?"

"We work together. You have built up this image of yourself as the untouchable ice queen. If word gets out that we've slept together, it could taint your image. This industry is brutal. They would use any weakness to undermine you."

"Who said anything about sleeping together?" Jihae said with exaggerated surprise. "I thought we could make out a few more times, and maybe have some oral fun. You're getting way ahead of yourself."

Colin looked at her like he wanted to rip off her clothes and take her against the wall twice. Jihae sucked in a quick breath and continued, "Besides, there's no reason anyone needs to know. We're both intelligent adults. I'm sure the two of us will find a way to keep whatever we do completely discreet."

"Don't do this," he said, his eyes pleading. He was almost hers. "You don't know what you're getting yourself into."

"I always know what I'm getting myself into." She closed the distance between them and tugged him roughly by his collar. "And just to make myself clear, I'm doing this. Very thoroughly."

She crushed her lips against him and moaned in relief when Colin met her lips with possessive heat. She'd been dreaming of kissing him again and she wasn't going to waste any time. She parted her lips and slid her tongue against his bottom lip, then lightly bit it.

"God," he moaned.

When he opened up as she'd wanted, Jihae took full advantage of the situation and plunged her tongue inside the warmth of his mouth. He groaned deep in his throat and the last of his reserve seemed to shatter. He spread his hands wide against her back and brought her flush against his body. Then he overtook the languid sweeping of her tongue and plunged his into her mouth again and again.

She whimpered and pressed her hips into him, needing to be closer, and felt his hard length dig into her pelvis. Satisfaction flooded her and she was gripped by power. With fumbling hands, Jihae pulled his shirt out of his slacks then smoothed her palms over the firm ridges of his stomach and slid them up to his broad chest. He jerked beneath her hands and ground his hips into her. She couldn't help it. A low, sultry laugh escaped from her lips. She was high on the power she held over him.

"You like that, do you?" His voice held a hint of danger, and a thrill ran down her spine.

"Oh, yes. Very much."

He groaned in answer and spun her to press her back against a wall. His hands slipped to her bottom and squeezed, and her eyes nearly rolled back in her head.

"Colin."

"Jihae. You're so beautiful."

He hiked her leg around his waist, and rocked his hips against her center, making her moan low and long. Colin clapped a hand over her mouth, and kissed a trail of fire down the side of her neck. The hand that had been holding her hip released its hold, and came to rest right below her breast. His thumb moved slowly back and forth on the bottom curve and she arched her back, giving him permission to explore farther.

"Shh," he warned before removing his hand from her mouth.

Returning his left hand to tightly secure her leg around his waist, he worked his right hand under her top. He smoothed his hand across her stomach, reclaimed her lips and murmured words of sweet adoration against them. With excruciating gentleness, he slid his hand up, cupped her breast and twirled his thumb over the lace of her bra.

She wiggled against him and pushed into his hand. With a sexy, arrogant laugh, he bent his head and licked the mound above the bra like it was the most decadent scoop of ice cream. She shivered against him with a lusty sigh as he continued to torture her. Unable to handle any more, she reached to tug down her bra and thrust her peak against his lips.

With a guttural groan, Colin succumbed to her will and tasted her nipple, twirling his tongue around it and pulling it deeply into his mouth.

"Colin," she whimpered as her frantic hands reached for his belt. She needed him inside her. Now.

Colin was so turned on he could hardly see straight. Her creamy, pink-tipped breasts tasted as sweet as honey, and her skin slid beneath his hands like warm silk. He was so hard that it almost hurt, and when she cried out his name, he thought he was going to lose it in his pants.

He was so lost in her that it didn't register in his brain what her hands were doing. When she freed his belt and unbuttoned the top of his pants, he finally understood. For a split second, he wanted to succumb to her siren's call. He was dying to feel her soft, warm hand on his aching dick. Then he remembered why he shouldn't kiss her, much less make love to her.

"Don't," he ordered in a ragged voice, grasping her wrists to stop her from going any farther. She stilled at his command, her whole body going stiff against his. He mourned the loss of the languid warmth of her aroused body. But no. He couldn't do this. He shouldn't. "We need to stop."

Slowly, he righted her bra and tugged down her shirt to cover her glorious bare skin. Then he stepped back, tucked his shirt into his slacks and buckled his belt. He couldn't meet Jihae's eyes. He hadn't meant for things to go so far, but when she'd walked into his office, he knew he was going to kiss her. Her boldness and sweet vulnerability were his undoing. But now, he'd pushed her away, and the last thing he wanted to do was hurt her.

He finally looked up to find her staring right at him.

He wasn't sure what he'd expected to find—maybe embarrassment and regret—but it certainly wasn't cold fury.

"That's it?" she asked. "Are you going to avoid me for months now? Are you going to pretend this never happened, too?"

"Jihae, that's not—"

"I am not a fragile porcelain doll that you need to protect. Even if I were fragile—and I certainly am not—it isn't your job to protect me. I can take care of myself. If you offer me your bullshit about protecting my reputation again, I will kick your skittish ass."

"It's not that simple—"

She cut him off again. "This is the last time I offer myself to you. You want me, but you're too afraid to take a chance. Well, listen very carefully. I will have you on your knees before I ever let you lay a finger on me again. On. Your. Knees."

That was the sexiest angry speech he had ever heard. He definitely felt like he'd been put in his place, but it was so incredibly hot. Since thinking of pleasurable ways to get on his knees for her wasn't conducive to getting his body under control, and Jihae needed to leave his office before he lost all willpower, he decided to just keep his mouth shut. He couldn't think of what to say at any rate. Other than *wow*.

She arched a perfect eyebrow when he didn't offer any more excuses, then tsked impatiently. "I'll see you next week for the director interviews. Good night."

With that, she opened the door and walked out of his office with her head held high. Colin was relieved that their last two kissing sessions weren't going to affect their business relationship. He wasn't surprised, though. Jihae was a true professional and she wouldn't let her personal life interfere with her work. If he'd liked and respected her before tonight, he was in awe of her now. She was spectacular in every way.

He'd been doubting his initial belief that Jihae had been involved in Rotelle's espionage scheme. After tonight, he couldn't believe that she'd been a part of it. Despite her impenetrable ice-queen image, Jihae was frank, honest and fair, and was an incredible partner to work with. She had such innate integrity that she gave praise and credit where it was due, and wasn't afraid to admit when she was wrong.

Could such a person have participated in such subterfuge? Colin's gut instinct told him no. And he would never hold her accountable for the depravities of her family. Rotelle was still the prime suspect for the espionage attack against Hansol, but he wouldn't wrap Jihae into it anymore. Maybe he could even trust her enough to ask her outright if she knew anything about the espionage. No, that would be crazy. He couldn't do that without revealing his connection to the Song family. While she didn't allow her personal life to interfere with her work, working with her ex-fiancé's cousin would probably be too much, even for her. And, more importantly, Jihae wouldn't betray her family.

Despite the guilt nagging insistently at him, he had to keep his identity a secret for the sake of the production. He didn't want to be a constant reminder of her broken engagement and her injured pride. Jihae was as invested as he was in the project. He couldn't ruin things for her by putting her in such an impossible position.

Colin swiped his hands down his face. Preparations for the production were going into overdrive soon, and he would have to spend a lot of time with Jihae. Hopefully, she didn't hate his guts after tonight, and they could go back to being good colleagues.

The thought of being "good colleagues" with the most

alluring woman he had the pleasure of meeting plunged him into a black mood. A platonic relationship with Jihae was as appealing as climbing a rocky mountain with bare feet. The lust blazing inside him was likely to burn him to cinders, but he had no other choice.

He had to protect Jihae from himself, find justice for his family and make a damn good movie.

Eight

Jihae was a strong-willed woman. She didn't regret throwing herself at him, but she was most definitely not going to give in again. She'd meant every word she said. He would need to beg to have her after that spectacular rejection. She'd spent a lifetime playing the role of Princess Jihae. While it took monumental willpower not to touch him, she was able to exude cool professionalism on the outside.

With the director and screenwriter selected, they were moving on to casting. The director, Cora Huang, already had the lead actors in mind and reached out to them. She would be working with a casting director for the remaining roles. Jihae and Colin had brief phone calls and exchanged emails, but hadn't seen each other since they interviewed the directors together. Both of them acted as though they were business partners and nothing more.

But wasn't that the truth? They *weren't* anything more than that. Sure, they'd shared two passionate kisses, and

Colin looked at her like he wanted to tear off her clothes whenever he thought she wasn't watching him—she smiled smugly at the thought—but that didn't mean there was anything between them.

Jihae gnawed at her lip. She wasn't a woman who opened up easily, and physical acts weren't meaningless to her. Those kisses had meant something to her and it irked her that Colin was able to ignore them so casually.

When she heard a knock at the door, she shook her head to clear it.

"Come in."

June stuck in her head. "Hey, boss. I'm taking the team out to dinner—on you, of course—to show them how much you care."

"That's great, and I do care. Too bad it wouldn't fit my image to join you guys. Besides, if I come along, the staff will be so tense, they'll probably get indigestion," Jihae said, only half joking.

"Hey. You could come if you want," her friend said with gentle sympathy. She understood Jihae's isolation and loneliness.

"No, I've got work to do. You guys go and have fun," she replied with a forced a smile.

"Are you sure?"

"I'm sure. Now go away. I really have to work."

"Fine. Do you want me to lock up for you?"

"No, I'll lock up on my way out."

"Okay. See you tomorrow, friend."

When the door clicked shut, Jihae had the sudden urge to run after everyone. *What happened to cool profession-alism, Princess?* She was in an odd mood and blamed it on Colin Song. Jihae wouldn't be feeling so lonely if she'd never known how warm and cherished she felt in his arms. She tsked impatiently. *Stop being unreasonable.* Pushing Colin from her thoughts, she turned her attention to her inbox.

Confidential: Top Priority jumped out at her from the top of her unread emails. It was from her father, which startled her. He usually left emails and such to his executive assistant. With trepidation, Jihae clicked open the email, and what she found inside befuddled her.

Introduce Yami Corporation's CFO to one of your contacts at NAM.

That was it. The terseness was expected but the content made no sense to her. She'd never heard of Yami Corporation. If she had to guess, they were an apparel company. She might've seen a bus-bench ad featuring a model wearing their jeans.

She wasn't directly involved with Rotelle Corporation's businesses, but she had some knowledge of which companies they did business with. Yami wasn't one of them. Besides, fashion was one of the few industries that Rotelle didn't dabble in. Why would Father want her to introduce Yami Corporation's CFO to a talent agency?

None of it made sense. She checked the time and calculated that her father might be awake. He was something of an insomniac.

"Father," she said when he picked up after a few rings as expected.

"What is it?"

"Your email. It doesn't make sense."

"It's not your job to understand but to do as I instructed you," he said dismissively.

She forged on despite his tone. "Since when did Rotelle do business with Yami Corporation? Isn't that an apparel company? We don't do apparel."

"You don't know everything. Far from it."

"I don't *want* to know *everything*. I just need to know why Yami's CFO wants an introduction to NAM."

"How the hell should I know? Just do as you're told and stop wasting my time with incessant questions." His terse tone warned her that she didn't have much time.

"My connection to the talent agency is important for my job. For Rotelle Entertainment. I can't jeopardize it by pushing a stranger on them for reasons unknown."

There was a brief pause as he considered her words, and Jihae's grip on her phone tightened.

"You can deal with the details of the introduction directly with Yami's CFO. If she tries to ask you questions relating to Rotelle Corporation, tell her you don't know anything. Which is the truth. You're merely my representative." He sighed quietly. "I need someone I can trust to handle this."

Her father sounded so weary that her heart constricted. "I understand, Father. I'll take care of it."

"Good."

"Father…" She hesitated, wanting to ask him if he was okay. The line went dead before she could say another word.

While she doubted there was any information, Jihae searched the internet for any connection between Rotelle and Yami. Not surprisingly, she found nothing. What she did find left a bad taste in her mouth. Yami Corporation had competed against Hansol for a partnership with Vivotex. The mention of Hansol still brought with it a twinge of humiliation even though she had cheered on Garrett Song in her head. He had been brave to marry the woman he loved rather than marry the woman chosen for him by his family. She closed the browser window resolutely. She didn't care what Yami had to do with Hansol.

* * *

The office was empty but the door was unlocked, so there was someone still there. Colin hoped that someone would be Jihae. He'd assiduously avoided her since the director interviews—he had Ethan and Kim deal with anything that required direct contact—but he knew that this cowardly tactic couldn't last forever. He and Jihae were partners. They needed to work fluidly together without a middleman.

No matter how much her presence tempted him, he had to keep his attraction to her separate from CS Productions business. With the director selected and the casting underway, it was past time to discuss their future direction and to prioritize what had to get done. He told himself that was why he'd rushed to her office after hours, as he stood in front of her door.

Just as he was about to knock, he heard the murmur of her voice. He turned away thinking she was in a meeting or on the phone. But her next words froze him to the spot.

"Since when did Rotelle do business with Yami Corporation? Isn't that an apparel company? We don't do apparel."

After a moment's pause, she continued, "I don't want to know everything. I just need to know why Yami's CFO wants an introduction to NAM."

Colin couldn't hear the other side of the conversation, which meant she was on the phone. His heart pounded against his chest, and sweat sprung out across his hairline. Yami Corporation wanted an introduction to NAM? And Jihae was supposed to do the honors? Why?

"My connection to the talent agency is important for my job. For Rotelle Entertainment. I can't jeopardize it by pushing a stranger on them for reasons unknown," she said.

For reasons unknown. The sudden elation caught him off guard. Blood pounded in his ears, and his chest rose up and down as he fought for his breath. Jihae knew nothing. His gut instinct hadn't steered him wrong. She hadn't been involved in the espionage. Colin had been worried that his judgment was compromised by his desire for her, but now he had proof of her innocence. The relief made him lightheaded.

"I understand, Father. I'll take care of it."

Then trepidation washed over him. Was Rotelle scheming again? Her father was instructing her to meet Yami's CFO, and she'd just agreed. She might not know anything yet, but the meeting might get her involuntarily involved. He didn't want her taken down with her father just because the conniving snake decided to embroil her in the mess now. But the Jihae he knew would balk at any shady business. Her honesty and integrity wouldn't allow her to do anything she felt was wrong. He trusted Jihae. She would be smart about it, and keep herself safe.

And Rotelle Corporation would be taken down. After running into dead end after dead end, the investigation was about to get a fresh start. After tugging his cell phone out of his back pocket, Colin typed in a quick text to Garrett.

Found new lead on Rotelle. Yami's CFO might be their contact person. Have PI shadow her.

Then he turned his phone to mute. The professionals could handle the rest. He'd carried out his duty to his family, and he could stop scrounging around for evidence. A part of him whispered that he still might need to keep an eye on Jihae, but he hushed the nagging voice. His belief in Jihae's innocence hadn't been wishful thinking born out of his interest in her. She truly was innocent. He didn't need to feel guilty for having feelings for her—the Song family's enemy—anymore. His careening thoughts came to a screeching stop.

Did he have feelings for her? *Yes.* Colin cared about Jihae. He'd been suppressing his feelings and calling it lust because caring for her would've been a betrayal of his family. But now, with proof of her innocence, he could let himself admit his feelings for her. And maybe even act on them.

Colin took a deep breath, then knocked softly on Jihae's door. He was being either brave or stupid, but he didn't want to hold back. Not anymore.

"Come in?" she said after a brief pause.

"I hope I'm not interrupting anything," he said as he walked into her office, closing the door behind him.

"Colin." His name left her mouth in a breathy whisper, and her wide eyes revealed her pleasure at his unexpected appearance. But it disappeared with a blink. Her damn armor was back in place. "What are you doing here?"

She looked pristine in her white Princess Jihae attire, but her cheeks were stained with color and loose strands of hair framed her delicate face. He had never seen a more beautiful sight. Her expression exuded confidence and a hint of tightly controlled curiosity, but her eyes greedily roamed his body. Despite his rejection and subsequent in-attention, Jihae miraculously still wanted him, but it was going to be difficult to have her admit it again. What was it she'd said?

I will have you on your knees before I ever let you lay a finger on me again.

With the last traces of his suspicion gone—freeing him from any guilt he might have felt over betraying his family by wanting her the way he did—he saw her with clarity for the first time. Her intelligence, her integrity, her beauty, her courage to experience new situations with curiosity and joy. He respected her. He desired her. And he wanted to do much, much more than lay a finger on her.

She'd come to stand in front of him as he stood glued to the spot, gazing mutely at her. With her within arm's reach, her exquisite scent hit him, jerking him out of his paralysis. He wanted to kiss her so badly a shiver shook his frame. But if he wanted to kiss her, he had to get on his knees. She was quite clear on that, and he intended to obey her explicitly.

His expression must have shifted because her eyes widened and she took a hasty step back. Her retreat snapped the last of his control, and he stalked her step by step until she was backed against the wall.

"I asked what you're doing here," she said with the slightest catch in her voice and lifted her eyes to meet his. "I don't believe we have any urgent business at the moment."

"Oh, you're wrong about that," he growled. "I have *very* urgent business with you."

Her pink lips parted on a gasp before she stood up straighter. "And what business is that?"

He lowered his head, gaze darting over her lovely face, until her eyes fluttered shut. But rather than claiming her mouth, as he was badly tempted to do, he brought his lips close to her ear and whispered, "Come with me."

Before she could answer, he leaned back and took her hand in his own. When he walked toward the door with single-minded determination, Jihae came willingly until she stopped short. Colin's stomach dropped to his feet. He didn't know if he could handle her rejection tonight.

"Wait," she said softly. "I need to get my purse and lock up for the night."

He nodded jerkily, both relieved and impatient. He freed her hand so she could lock the door, but placed his hand possessively on her lower back. Once she was finished, he reclaimed her hand. He couldn't bear not touching her for even a moment.

"Where are we going?" she asked when he settled into the driver's seat beside her.

"My place." He was amazed that he could still get words out. His heart was hammering against his chest and his hands trembled as he backed out of the parking space.

"Your place?"

He gave a curt nod and kept his eyes on the road. Jihae didn't voice any objections and settled into her seat, turning her attention out the window. Her face was carefully expressionless, so he couldn't guess what she was thinking, but Colin was grateful that she was coming with him.

By the time they arrived at his condo, his hands were shaking so badly that he had trouble unlocking his door. This was a bad idea, but he was all out of willpower.

"Would you like a drink?" he asked as casually as he could once they were inside.

"What have you got?"

Jihae reached down to remove her heels, bracing a hand on the wall. He couldn't help noticing how shapely her calves were. He had groveling to do before he could let his thoughts go anywhere near there. He snapped his eyes back to her face, but it wasn't much help because it was also distractingly beautiful.

"Everything," Colin said with a wry grin. "My cousin is an amateur mixologist and insisted I needed a full bar for when she visits."

"Is she good?"

"She's an amazing cook but her cocktails taste like fruit-infused diesel fuel."

Laughter trilled out of Jihae as he led her toward his wet bar. To his surprise, she removed her suit jacket and handed it to him, and began rolling up the sleeves of her silk shirt.

"You don't seem like a harsh critic at all," Jihae said with a mischievous smile. An odd ache came and went in the recesses of his heart at her playfulness. He liked this side of her so much. "Well, no matter. I do love a challenge."

"You're an amateur mixologist, too?"

"Actually, I'm a professional." She laughed at the shock on his face. "I took a crash course in bartending and have a certificate to prove it. I actually have a shoebox full of cooking, baking, flower-arrangement, you-name-it certificates. I snuck in bartending as my little rebellion against my parents' will to domesticate me before my wed—"

Before her wedding. The thought of her having almost married Garrett made his jaws clench. But not wanting her to feel flustered, he quickly redirected their conversation. "So are you planning to wow me with your skills?"

"Depends. Can I raid your fridge?" she said, her relief evident in her smile.

"Be my guest. I have to warn you, though. There isn't much in there."

He followed her into his kitchen and leaned against the island as Jihae searched for ingredients.

"Aha," she said, straightening up with a basket of blueberries and a serrano chili pepper.

"You're using those blueberries?" he asked with his forehead furrowed in consternation. "Are they still good?"

"A little dry, but perfectly edible. They'll do fine for my needs. But…" Her eyes darted around the kitchen counter.

"Do you need something else?"

"You don't happen to have any basil, do you?"

He actually had a miniature herb garden. Another gift from Adelaide. She claimed that even if he couldn't cook worth a damn, adding some fresh herbs into premade sauces did wonders.

"Um…this way, please."

Colin showed her to the little alcove where his garden of basil, Italian parsley and thyme flourished under artificial sunlight.

"You have an herb garden?" she said with an incredulous smile.

He scratched the back of his head and shrugged. "It's here to help me with my abysmal cooking skills."

"Aww, I think that's rather sweet." She reached out and gently grazed the herbs with her fingers.

"Really?" he said, breaking into a wide grin. "I'll take that."

Once they were back at the wet bar, Jihae got to work. With quick twists of her wrist and fast-moving hands, she muddled the basil with some blueberries and a splash of simple syrup, then poured the mixture into the shaker. Then she added measures of fragrant gin and elderflower liquor into it, and topped it off with ice before she shook the shaker with easy efficiency.

A glint of mischief entered her eyes, then she bumped the shaker from elbow to elbow before throwing it and catching it behind her back. It was an exciting finale. Simple and elegant. Especially when done with her intoxicating half smile. She added a slice serrano chili into two martini glasses and poured the concoction into them.

It was hot. She was hot. *Damn.*

She pushed a glass toward him and raised hers in the air. *"Gun-bae."*

"Gun-bae." While the salutation meant "bottoms up" in Korean, Colin took a much more careful sip of the drink. His eyes widened and he gawked at Jihae. "Why aren't you out there selling this stuff? How about if I buy the recipe from you for my clubs?"

"Is that what I'm doing here? Having another business meeting?" She took out the sting in her words with a teasing smile.

"Dammit. Sorry. No."

"Relax, Song. My claws are officially withdrawn," she said, raising her curled fingers toward him like little paws. "Besides, I just made the drink up on the spot, so there is no recipe. I'd probably forget it in like two minutes."

Colin gave her a pained look. He didn't want to sound like a haggling businessman tonight, but it would be a travesty for the rest of the world to never try her cocktail. He didn't know what to do, so he bit his lip and stayed quiet.

Jihae's laughter filled his living room as she took him out of his misery. "Give me a pen and paper. I'll jot down what I remember."

He patted his pants for a piece of paper and found a receipt, then grabbed a pen. "Here."

She turned over the receipt and bit the end of the pen. Then she wrote out the recipe for him. She paused, worrying her bottom lip, then smiled as she scribbled something on top. She handed him the receipt with a look of anticipation in her eyes.

"Once in a Blue Moon," he read, and looked up to smile at her. "Clever."

"I figured I won't be coming to your condo to create brilliant cocktail recipes very often—"

"No," he blurted, cutting her off in the middle of the sentence.

She cocked her head in question. "*No* what?"

"No, I want you to come to my condo often—very often—and mix as many amazing drinks as you'd like."

"I don't understand."

"Be with me, Jihae."

Nine

"Colin, I..." Jihae couldn't continue because he pressed his index finger against her lips.

Slowly withdrawing his finger, he came around the bar and clasped her hand, then tugged her toward his couch. She couldn't breathe. What was he doing? Well, she had a vague idea he hadn't brought her to his condo to talk business, but she wasn't sure what exactly he wanted.

"I want you, Jihae."

With gentle pressure on her shoulders, he settled her on the couch then he kneeled in front of her, spreading her legs to get as close to her as possible.

"But..." She didn't know what she meant to say as the heat in his eyes sucked the air out the room. All she could recall was that she'd told him he would need to get on his knees if he wanted to touch her again. And here he was. On his knees. She was going to have a heart attack.

"May I kiss you?"

"I don't know. Why now? What's changed?"

Colin blinked rapidly as though her question had touched a nerve. Before she could wrap her mind around it, he replied, "Me. I've changed. I want you, and I can't hold back anymore."

He wanted her and he was finally admitting it. Sweet victory. A triumphant smile rose to the surface, and she wet her already tingling lips. "So...you want to kiss me?"

"Very much."

She had no patience left to gloat because she wanted to kiss him very much, too. Jihae wrapped her arms around his neck and lowered her face toward his. She dropped a chaste kiss on the corner of his mouth. "Like this?"

"More," he growled, his hands spanning her waist.

With a whisper of contact, she moved her mouth from one corner to the other. "Like this?"

"More." His fingers tensed around her waist.

"Show me," she commanded into his ear.

He moved so fast that she gasped against his lips as they crushed against hers. His kiss wasn't gentle or teasing. It was Colin's desire bared raw. Their teeth clacked as his tongue danced with hers, demanding that she match his passion. She had zero problem with that. His hands traveled to her hair and made quick work of undoing her bun. When her hair was free, he tangled his fingers into the long strands and tilted her head to expose the column of her neck.

His hot breath and wet lips drew a line down to her collarbone and the hollow at her throat. He licked and blew into the sensitive spot, and she moaned helplessly.

"Colin."

He hastily captured her lips again as though to swallow her small sounds of pleasure, his name on her lips. She scooted farther back into the sofa and lay down, pulling

Colin on top of her. When all of him covered all of her, he groaned his approval.

She wanted him naked. She wanted him to fill her. She whimpered and writhed under him when his thumb brushed the tip of her aching breast. He pushed up her shirt and her bra, exposing the hard tip, and sucked it into his mouth. She nearly screamed and knew she was close to losing all control.

"Wait," Jihae gasped, pushing against his shoulders.

"Wait?" Colin immediately raised his head and looked her in the eyes with heavily hooded lids. *Gah. Sexiest bedroom eyes ever.* She almost pulled him back against her breasts, but she took a deep breath instead. Or at least she tried.

"Yes, wait. Please," she said, barely managing to get the words out.

She was so turned on, and so was he. Colin sat up on the couch and pulled her onto his lap as though he couldn't quite break contact with her. He smoothed her hair out of her face and said, "Tell me. What is it?"

"You and I… We're both doing this against our better judgment. True?"

"True," he replied with a bemused curl of his lips. Then he kissed her temple with such tenderness she wanted to melt against him. "Continue."

"To ensure we don't regret this, I think we should set some ground rules." When Colin nodded for her to continue, Jihae placed a kiss on his jaw. "Rule One, this—us… We have to be discreet. I don't want this to affect our professional reputation in any way. And I absolutely don't want my father to find out. This has to stay between us, and us alone. Okay?"

"Okay."

His eyes had turned watchful at the mention of her father, and she cringed in embarrassment. Bringing up her father while warm and horny in Colin's arms was not the sexiest of maneuvers.

"Rule Two, no matter where this leads, I want us to finish our project together. I won't sacrifice *Best Placed Bets* for anything."

"Agreed."

"Rule Three, no promises. I want us to take this one day at a time. Let's just be two adults, enjoying each other."

Jihae knew herself. What she felt for Colin wasn't commonplace. Not for her. If she slept with him, she might give too much of herself to him. She couldn't allow that to happen. She wasn't even in the States permanently. Once their project was finished and her father summoned her home, she would have no choice but to return to Korea. To return to her family and her duties.

"No promises," Colin said solemnly while he quietly searched her face. Afraid of revealing her vulnerabilities to him—and how much she wanted promises—she buried her face against his neck. "May I add something?"

Surprised, she pulled away to look at him again. "Of course."

"While we take this day by day, I want all of you for every day we have together. I don't like to share."

She sucked in a sharp breath at the possessive note in his voice and nodded rapidly. "Okay. And same goes for you."

"Oh, don't worry about that. You will have my complete and undivided attention while we're together. There won't be room for anyone or anything else."

Hot damn. She wanted to fan herself. He said "complete and undivided attention" with such intensity, she could only imagine what making love to him would be like. But ironing out the rules made things suddenly seem so real that Jihae was overcome with shyness.

"So, um, what should we do now?" she asked. She wanted to palm herself in the forehead. It sounded like "should we shag now?" She truly wasn't trying to be suggestive.

"I have an idea or two," he said in a low voice that sent shivers down her spine.

All shyness forgotten, she took his face in both of her hands and kissed him until they were both out of breath but hungry for more. Desperate to be closer to him, Jihae straddled his lap and pushed herself against him, delighting in the pressure of his hard chest against her aching nipples.

It wasn't enough. She shifted back just enough to get her hands between them and began unbuttoning her blouse. Making a noise of frustration, Colin pushed away her fumbling fingers and undressed her himself. Once the blouse was pushed down her shoulders, he reached around her and unclasped her bra. After he'd thrown that on the floor, he immediately took a hard, sensitive peak in his mouth. Moaning with exquisite pleasure, she instinctively ground her hips against his hardness.

"God, Jihae," he said as he freed one nipple and moved on to the other. "You're killing me."

"Perfect," she replied in a small puff of breath, giddy with relief and joy.

"Oh, is it?" He pulled back to grin wickedly at her, and she squirmed in her seat so he could go back to what he was doing so beautifully. "I'm going to get you back for that."

"What—"

Before she knew it, Jihae was lying on her back on the sofa with Colin kneeling at her feet. "I'm going to make you come so hard, you'll scream."

Jihae wasn't sure if she was excited or a little alarmed. Probably both. She was already so wet and aching, she didn't know if she could take any more. When he parted her thighs, nestling his head between her knees, her hands fisted in his hair.

The first lick and hot breath had her whimpering, "Please."

Other than a low, rumbling chuckle, Colin didn't stop to respond. He licked her center with slow, sensual attention until she was a mass of desire. When he added a finger, then another, she ground against his hand and tongue without self-consciousness. Only want. She was so close that she could see white sparks beginning to go off behind her lids. Somehow sensing she was about to fall off the edge, he pulled her into his mouth and gently sucked.

"Colin." His name left her lips in a sharp scream and her hips lifted off the sofa.

He pushed her hips firmly against the cushions and brought her down torturously slow, his palm lightly massaging her sensitized core. Once she could see straight again, Colin rewarded her by removing his shirt and pants in swift succession. When he was gloriously naked, he took a foil packet from his wallet, tore it open with his teeth and sheathed himself.

His eyes looked out of focus and heavy-lidded with need as he smoothed the hair out of her eyes. "You okay?"

"Yes, I just need you inside of me," she said, biting her bottom lip. "Please."

His gaze not leaving hers, he plunged inside her, deep and heavy. She felt herself stretching to accommodate him.

"God. You feel so good," he said.

"So do you." But it wasn't enough. She swerved her hips to get used to the feel of him.

"Wait. Don't do that," he groaned. "I'm close to losing it just being inside you. I want to take it slowly."

"Colin, I've been wanting this from the moment I saw

you," she said, shifting in the other direction, and was rewarded with his hips jerking involuntarily against her. "Screw taking it slowly."

With a helpless groan, Colin pulled himself out and buried himself to the hilt inside her. Then out again and deeper still. She matched him thrust for thrust until all semblance of a smooth rhythm broke down and they jerked wildly against each other, each seeking a climax so close within reach.

"Yes. God, yes." She fell apart, with him close behind, pumping wildly into her before shouting his own release.

Colin collapsed on top of her, but shifted slightly to the side on his elbow so he wouldn't crush her. Her limp legs hung over his back and one of her arms hung loosely off the side of the couch.

"My God," she whispered in a raspy, awe-filled voice. "That was brilliant."

"Anytime, sweetheart," he replied, his voice muffled, his shoulders shaking with laughter against her. After a moment, he raised his head to look into her face. "It was my absolute pleasure."

That was the most amazing, mind-blowing sex she'd ever had, but he managed to make her want him again with just a crooked smile and a few husky words. She wanted this after-sex warmth to last, but realized they would soon have to untangle their limbs and get off the couch. Then what? Would he expect her to leave right away? No, he wouldn't be that callous; he'd said he wanted this to be a real relationship, at least while it lasted.

So, putting aside her trepidation, she simply asked, "Do you want to watch a movie?"

"Absolutely," he said as he shifted his weight off her.

"Perfect." Jihae must've sighed in relief because a

knowing grin spread across Colin's face. "I mean, good. I'm glad."

"Here." He handed her the remote control, then began picking his clothes up off the floor. "You choose the movie and I'll pop the popcorn after I clean up."

Colin was sweet and considerate, and she sighed dreamily. She wasn't going to hope for an unattainable future, but would enjoy the here and now to the fullest. Because the here and now was pretty fantastic.

Colin had been wearing a stupid grin on his face all day. He and Jihae were dating. It was a secret, and it belonged only to them. *Hell.* He was a grown-ass man, acting like a giddy high-schooler. If he hadn't been buried in work, he would've been drawing heart curlicues on his notepad. Fortunately, the sheer size of his workload prevented him from making an even bigger fool of himself.

To be discreet, they hadn't appeared in public together more than once a week, and they were even more careful about spending time at each other's places. They took advantage of as many chances as possible to see each other in their business capacity, but it was a far cry from spending time alone with her. The curtailed opportunities for privacy were frustrating, but it made each meeting all the more precious.

The script was close to being finalized—it was even better than his highest expectations—and the auditions were scheduled to commence in the next month or so. Other than relaying the author's suggestions to the director, he and Jihae would be relatively hands-off in the initial creative process. They trusted Cora, and the casting director she brought on board, to do an amazing job.

But they definitely wanted to be present when the candidates for the female and male leads did their readings. In a romantic comedy, the hero and heroine's chemistry was crucial to whether the movie worked or not. They wanted sparks coming off the lead actors when they were together on screen. Cora had some strong favorites she wanted to work with. He and Jihae also saw great potential in her choices, but they wouldn't know for certain until they saw the candidates read together in person.

He leaned back in his chair and stretched out his stiff neck and shoulders. The clock on his monitor told him it was already past seven thirty in the evening. *Damn.* He'd wanted to mix business with pleasure with Jihae tonight, but she might already have had dinner. He sat upright and texted her, his pulse picking up speed.

Hungry?

Her response was almost immediate. I'm starving, baby. He choked on a laugh even as his shifted uncomfortably in his chair. He loved her sexy sass.

I could fix that. What about for food?

Hungry for that, too.

Then allow me to fix that, as well. Where should we meet?

Somewhere that serves cheesy, decadent pizza.

He gave her the name of the perfect place for her craving. She was a bit closer to the restaurant than he, so he only had time to write one more email before he closed shop. That minuscule act of discipline made him feel a bit more in control of himself, and he was able to stop himself from running to his car.

Despite his attempts to slow down, he arrived early at the restaurant. He always came before Jihae. Not that she had a habit of running late, but he simply enjoyed the anticipation of waiting for her arrival, with his heart pumping a little faster each passing minute.

When she finally walked into the restaurant, his stomach clenched in a visceral reaction to her presence. She was wearing a white pantsuit with a pale, off-white blouse. Her patent-leather, nude stilettos completed her signature look. She exuded aloof sophistication and ice-cold detachment. He couldn't believe how well she carried off her public image when he knew how contrary it was to her true personality.

"You look lovely," he said softly into her ear while pulling out her chair.

"Thank you." Her expression remained carefully neutral but a splash of pink stained her cheeks.

"This place has the best New York-style pizza you'll find on the West Coast." He took his seat across from her and opened up his menu.

"Yum. I'm starving."

"So you've said," he drawled, staring pointedly at her perfect red lips.

"Now behave." She arched an eyebrow at him. The subtle twitch at the corner of her lips betrayed that she was holding back a smile.

"When have I not?" Other than tugging her into a stairwell the last time they'd met to kiss the hell out of her only to find the door locked behind them. They'd had to climb five stories to find an open door. And that other time... Now that he thought of it, he'd misbehaved quite a lot.

Jihae gave him the subtlest eye roll in the world. Actually, he only recognized it as an eye roll from spending so much time with her. Her every emotion and expression was subdued to the point of stoicism in public, but he soaked up her barely there smiles and the teasing twinkle in her eyes that were meant only for him.

As dinner progressed, however, Jihae's subtle smiles and gentle teasing grew dim, and her eyes took on a distracted, faraway look every time there was a slight pause in their conversation.

"Hey," Colin said, reaching across the table to touch her hand. But he hastily withdrew as soon as he realized what he was doing. PDA was not a risk they wanted to take. "Is everything all right? You're hiding it well, but you seem distraught. We could talk about it in private later, if you'd like."

"No, everything is fine. I'm fine. I'm just knackered." She looked down at her pizza and pulled off a pepperoni to pop in her mouth. "I had a three-hour meeting with the Korean production team on one of our celebrity reality shows. They're a well-oiled machine but it was a lot to catch up on."

"That must've been draining." She was hiding something from him, and nausea rose in his throat. Was it about her meeting with Yami Corporation's CFO? He hadn't heard back from Garrett about the PI's progress, and it'd been weeks. "Once you finish your pizza, we'll get out of here. Okay?"

"That'll be nice. Thank you." But again, her smile fell short of reaching her eyes.

"Should we go to your place, so you don't have to go out again?"

"No," she said in a rush. "I mean… I'd like to go to your place tonight."

"Sure. We'll do that."

They were quiet on the drive to his condo, each of them lost in their own thoughts. What was she hiding from him?

More than ever, he believed her innocence. Throughout the film production, Jihae was always the first to ensure that everything was aboveboard. If there was ever the slightest doubt, she would err on the side of being shortchanged rather than injure the other party. The Jihae he knew would never involve herself in any unethical behavior, much less corporate espionage. But something had happened today and he wanted to find out what. Was it about Yami Corp.?

Once they were inside, he helped Jihae out of her jacket and hung it in the entryway. She stepped out of her heels with a sigh and plopped herself down on the sofa like a limp doll. He couldn't fight the smile that pulled at his lips. He loved it. He loved how she just let go and relaxed when she was alone with him.

He followed her to the sofa, pulled up her legs onto his lap and gently massaged the ball of her foot.

"Mmm. You're good at that," she said, her eyelids fluttering shut.

"I'm good at a lot of things," he joked, moving on to the arch.

"And ever so humble."

He tickled her for that response and nearly got kicked in the jaw. "Whoa, watch it. You could've broken something."

"Sorry. I seriously could have," she said, breathless from laughter. "I'm really, *really* ticklish."

"That doesn't sound right." He ran his hand up the back of her legs. "I've touched you everywhere and you haven't reacted like this before."

"Just on my feet. I'm only ticklish there."

"Thank goodness. Otherwise, I'll get a good beating every time we make love."

"Aw, poor Colin. Did I scare you? We could take a break tonight if you want."

"Not on your life," he growled, pouncing on her. "I already don't get to have you often enough. I wouldn't stay away from you even if you were covered in sharp needles."

She giggled and pretended to push him off her, but he made quick work of trapping her arms above her head. "Can we at least go to your bedroom tonight? I feel like we rarely make it that far before we rip each other's clothes off."

"As you wish."

He stood from the couch, lifted her into his arms and carried her into his room. After laying her down on the bed, he unbuttoned and shrugged out of his shirt as Jihae watched with rapt attention. As he unclasped his belt, a familiar ringtone sounded from his back pocket. Garrett. And all his trepidation from earlier in the evening rushed back to him.

"God, I'm sorry," he said, pulling out his phone. "I need to take this."

"Go right ahead. I'm not going anywhere."

Colin left the bedroom and walked into his study, making sure to close the door behind him.

"Garrett."

"Hey, little cousin. What are you up to? You sound a bit out of breath. Did I interrupt your workout?"

"In a manner of speaking, yes. So, what's going on? Any news on the lead?" Colin deliberately exhaled when he noticed that he was holding his breath.

"As a matter of fact, there is, but I thought we might exchange some social niceties like normal people first."

"Since when do the Songs engage in small talk over the phone?"

"I guess you have a point." Garrett chuckled on the other end.

"So tell me. Was there any movement from Yami Corporation?"

"Yes. Yami's CFO, Sylvia Taylor, finally met with Jihae Park at a coffee shop this afternoon."

Colin's heart drummed against his ribs. "Did we have ears on them?"

"Our PI had someone planted a couple tables away."

"What—what did they talk about?" he asked, both eager and afraid to hear the answer.

"The conversation was convoluted and brief. Taylor asked Jihae Park about how her father was doing and whether Rotelle was running smoothly. Park effectively shut her down and asked for the reason she wanted an introduction to NAM."

"Then what?"

"Taylor said her father owed her, and Park should just do as she was told."

Colin almost laughed. Jihae would not have liked that. "What happened next?"

"She told Taylor in no uncertain terms that there will be no introductions to the talent agency unless there were legitimate reasons for it."

Atta girl. "So, did Taylor succumb and tell her everything?"

"Basically, but nothing of use to us. She wanted Park to pressure executives at NAM to have their big-name stars endorse Yami Corporation's apparel. Be seen wearing it and share how much they love it on social media. All for free."

"That's ridiculous. Jihae would never ask for something like that from NAM. She values them as colleagues."

"I guess Taylor thought NAM would rather do Park's bidding than lose Rotelle Entertainment's goodwill."

"That may very well be true, but Taylor wanted to take advantage of NAM. It's far from a fair deal. Jihae would never stand for that."

There was a short pause. "You sound pretty confident about that."

"I am." Colin clenched his fists, ready to defend Jihae if his cousin questioned her integrity.

But all Garrett said was "Huh."

"What is that supposed to mean?"

"It means *huh*. Why does it have to mean anything?" There was a smile in his cousin's voice. Was Colin that obvious about his feelings for Jihae? "Anyway, the only information that we gleaned from their meeting was that Sylvia Taylor believes Chairman Park *owes* her. Just more circumstantial evidence."

"So how did the meeting end?"

"Park told Taylor to go pound sand, and Taylor left in a huff, threatening that her father won't be happy about this. Maybe Taylor has something on Chairman Park and is pressuring him for favors. But could she be so foolish as to anger the chairman? If she was, then she was playing with fire. The bastard might humor her for now, but he will bury her for daring to pressure him." Garrett's sigh communicated his frustration across the line. "But again, it's all speculation and conjecture. We got nothing, which means we're back to square one."

"We did get something. This meeting proves that Jihae Park is innocent. She obviously doesn't know what Rotelle Corporation's connection to Yami is about. She was forced to play the middleman, but she walked away."

"Again, it's all just conjecture at this point, and it isn't Park's innocence that we're trying to prove but Rotelle's guilt."

But it wasn't conjecture. Jihae could've inadvertently been pulled into the espionage scheme, but she'd distanced herself from the situation. She was innocent but the situation reeked of her father's guilt.

"So what's next?" Colin dragged his fingers through his hair, pacing his office.

"We need to continue keeping an eye on Sylvia Taylor and Jihae Park."

"On Jihae? She's not a part of this."

"We don't know that for sure. She may even be the key to solving this case."

Colin blew out a frustrated breath, not liking the idea of Jihae being watched. It could also reveal their relationship, but he would deal with that later. He needed to protect Jihae from being under the PI's surveillance.

"Look, Garrett. I'm sure Grandmother has relayed to you that I'm working with Rotelle Entertainment while keeping an eye on Jihae Park. From everything I've seen so far, I believe her innocence. But if she ever diverges from that, I'll be there to see it. Jihae is already under casual surveillance by her father's people. Following her would only risk the PI's cover and expose our investigation."

"I see your point. Then we'll leave Jihae Park up to you and focus on Taylor." There was a slight pause on the line. "Colin, I appreciate you doing this for the family, but be careful. You don't need to risk your dream for us or Hansol. If things get too hot, I want you to stop and focus on producing your film. Is that a deal?"

"Deal." A small smile quirked Colin's lips. Garrett was like an older brother to him, and he appreciated how he always looked out for him. "Thanks for the advice, *hyung*."

The weight on his shoulders feeling significantly lighter, Colin walked back to his bedroom. Jihae was asleep exactly where he'd left her. She slept with her hand tucked under her chin like a child. He could imagine touching her skin and finding it hard and cold as porcelain, she was so perfect in her sleep. Then her pouty lips blew out a soft breath that sounded like *puuuu*.

He wasn't quick enough to cover up his snort but managed to hold back his laughter with his hand over his mouth. He loved that sound. It was so adorable. She always did that—blew out puffs of air like she was trying to extinguish a row of birthday candles—when she was especially tired.

Still laughing softly, he tiptoed to the dresser and searched for a blanket, since she was sleeping over the duvet. He pulled out a soft knit throw and laid it gently over Jihae's sleeping form. He badly wanted to climb into bed with her and hold her as she slept, but no alarm would wake him if he got that cozy. Frustratingly, sleepovers weren't allowed in their secrecy pact, so he would need to wake her up in a couple of hours to send her home.

Colin walked to the kitchen and got some coffee going. He would stay awake and catch up on some work. Then he would provide Jihae with the most erotic and satisfying wake-up service she'd ever had.

Ten

"Sylvia Taylor is trying to leech off NAM and their clients. I'm not a brainless pawn you can push around," she said in a commanding tone she'd never used with her father. "I know I haven't been a perfect daughter to you, but if you see me as an intelligent human being, you have to let me make my own decisions."

"You have always been too soft. And stubborn. If you are aware that you've disappointed your mother and me, you should obey me without question."

It didn't come as a surprise that her father would take a hard line with her. But that didn't mean she was going to take it lying down.

"Why are you so set on helping Ms. Taylor?"

"Who says I'm set on helping her? You don't need to know anything other than the fact that I want you to do this favor for Taylor. I am keeping you in the dark for your own good."

"No. I refuse to do it." Jihae's heart pounded so loudly she was afraid she wouldn't hear her father's response. She had never outright defied her father except for her rebellion after college.

"Then I will remove you from your position at Rotelle Entertainment effective immediately." It wasn't an idle threat. He wouldn't hesitate to take away what was most important to her. Unless it wasn't in his best interest.

"I'm in the middle of a production with a partner company. If you remove me now, the partnership and the production will suffer, as well as the film itself. I know my company and my teams better than anyone else. Are you willing to gamble with Rotelle Entertainment's success after everything I've built up? How happy do you think the shareholders will be at my sudden dismissal? You can't deny that Rotelle Entertainment is one of Rotelle Corporation's most profitable branches."

"You overestimate your value. Rotelle Entertainment is profitable because it's a part of Rotelle Corporation. But I am too busy to deal with finding your successor right now." That was his way of capitulating without giving her credit. He knew that Rotelle Entertainment would falter if he removed her before the film was complete. "I will allow you to remain as the head of Rotelle Entertainment for the time being, but don't fool yourself into thinking your disobedience will go unpunished."

"Oh, no. I would never doubt your ability to hold on to a grudge." Jihae gasped behind her hand. She couldn't believe her own recklessness.

"Such impudence! How dare you speak to me this way?"

She needed to appease him if she wanted to hold on to her position at Rotelle Entertainment. Jihae had to keep her promise to Colin and see *Best Placed Bets* to its completion with him.

"I'm truly sorry, Father. Please forgive me. The stress of being on bad terms with you has made me hysterical. I still can't introduce Yami Corporation to NAM, but please let me keep my current job. I only want the best for Rotelle Corporation."

He took a huffing breath on the other end of the line. Jihae smiled bitterly. Her groveling had done its job. With his ego stoked and her pride in tatters, he was going to give her an inch. "Like I said, you can remain in your position for the time being. But what happens after that depends on how you deal with Yami Corporation."

And that was the end of the call. She listened to the dial tone for a blank moment before sluggishly putting down her phone. Production was going smoothly, and so was her relationship with Colin. It was going so well that she sometimes forgot Rule Three—no promises—and dreamed of more. The call with her father was a rough intrusion of reality. She would be returning to Korea sooner rather than later. That much was certain. Her defiance in the Yami situation had cemented that outcome. But she would never change her mind about the introduction. What Yami intended to do was contemptible and she would have no part in it.

Her father was hiding something from her. If he was desperate enough to get her involved in the first place, it was something very big. It was time she dug for some answers. She pushed back from her desk and poked her head out the door.

"Hey, do you have time to have dinner tonight?" Jihae asked.

"I'm not sure. Let me check my very busy social calendar," June replied, pretending to flip through a calendar.

"I would have to move a couple things around, but I can squeeze you in."

"Does Korean barbeque and soju at my place sound good?"

"Pork belly from that butcher on Third Street?"

"Hell to the yes."

"Meh," June said, deadpan. "I'm not holding back on the soju, so plan on making it a dinner-slash-sleepover."

"Done deal."

Jihae closed her office door and walked back to her desk. It would be wonderful to vent about her father to her best friend and figure out a way to uncover his secret. The only reason she wasn't grinning from ear to ear was that she had to cancel her date with Colin. They've been together for a few months, but she still couldn't get enough of him. But taking a break tonight was for the best. The mess with her father and her eminent return to Korea meant it was a bad idea to get more attached to him. She needed to create a cushion to protect her heart.

Despite her decision to distance herself a bit, it still hurt not to see him tonight. Rather than torturing herself more by calling, she texted him instead.

Hi.

The ellipses appeared on her phone immediately.

Hi.

I need to cancel our date tonight.

This time the ellipses took a while to pop up.

Is there a particular reason?

Yeah. Emergency girls' night in.

Is there something wrong?

Not really. Well, there's something. I'm just having some daddy issues that I need to vent about to June. She knows my history.

She stopped herself from explaining any further. She had every right to hang out with her friend. But Colin's answer brought a smile to her lips.

I hope it isn't anything serious and you could still have a fun time with her.

Not to worry. We'll have fun. It would be hard not to with pork belly and soju in the mix.

Don't do anything I wouldn't do.

I can't make any promises, she typed without thinking. There was another pause from him, and she realized that she'd inadvertently brought up their no-promises rule. She hadn't meant to fling that out like a defensive mechanism. While she wanted to maintain some distance, she didn't want to remind him that they weren't meant to last. Was she overreacting? Colin probably never even thought of having something long-term with her.

She wanted to tell him that she would miss him. She missed him so much already, but heartfelt confessions weren't conducive to not forming an attachment.

After they texted their goodbyes, she tried to focus on her game plan to dig in to her father's secret. Jihae had people she trusted within Rotelle Corporation, but she wanted to avoid asking them to outright spy on their own company. She would have to figure out a legitimate way to have them look for a connection between Rotelle and Yami Corp., no matter how minuscule. If she didn't know about it, it wouldn't be easy to find, but her people knew how to open doors.

If they found nothing then she would have to play a dangerous game, and get June involved in her mission. But that had to be the very last resort. It involved using June's connections in Rotelle's accounting department to follow the money. With her father, money was always the focus of any situation or problem. Whatever he was keeping from her had to involve payment of some sort, and no matter how deeply it was buried, someone from the inside should be able to unearth it.

But Jihae was terrified of what she would find. And it was the ultimate act of rebellion against her father. What if she discovered something bigger than she could imagine? She wanted the truth, but she didn't want to put any of her friends in danger of being disciplined by the company. Hopefully, her friends in high places would be able to sniff out some minor scandal, and she wouldn't have to get June involved.

She pressed the heels of her hands into her eyes. It was too much. She wanted to forget about her suffocating life, and the strangeness that was seeping into it. To forget that she would soon have to leave Colin. She wanted the world to fall away as she fell apart in his arms, where nothing mattered but the two of them being together.

A humorless laugh escaped her. She was the one who'd decided to cancel the date. She was the one who needed the reminder that their relationship was finite. But now all she wanted was to wrap herself around him and hold on. Hold on tight.

She stopped herself short. *Bloody hell.* How long had it been? How long had she been on the precipice of falling in love with Colin? The frightening part was that despite everything—including her guaranteed heartbreak when she had to leave him—she wanted to let herself fall.

Colin was becoming an expert at creating legitimate business reasons to spend alone time with Jihae. The latest and most brilliant idea was this location-scouting trip. It wasn't just an excuse to get away together. It was an important part of the production. They'd been discussing the possible location for a scene they both loved.

"I'd never been on a road trip," Jihae said in a singsong voice as she adjusted her sunglasses. She had her legs up on the dashboard and the sun glinted off her pink-tipped toes.

"So you've mentioned…about six times in the last couple hours," Colin teased. She leaned over and delivered a decent punch to his arm. "Hey, there will be no abusing the driver. I'm guessing you're new to road trips, so you may not be aware, but distracting the driver is a no-no."

"It is?" she asked in a suspiciously innocent voice.

"Yes. A big no-no." He shot a quick glance at her to see what she was up to, but she just gave him a wicked grin.

"So…let's say I unbuttoned myself, like so." She undid the top button of her thin, loose shirt. Then reached for the next button. "Then unbuttoned another one, like so. Would this be considered distracting the driver?"

"Not at all," he growled through clenched teeth. "By all means. Make yourself comfortable."

Her laughter felt like a caress down his body, and he frowned harder. How did he always manage to get into these situations with Jihae? She was relentless and he was helpless against her bold moves.

"Then I'll just undo one last button, so the top of my white lacy bra peeks out. Oh, look! It's your favorite one."

"You know I'll get you back for this."

"I don't know what you mean… I'm new to road trips and just don't know how to behave. Am I being bad?"

"As soon as we check into our hotel, and I hang the Do Not Disturb on the knob, I'm having you against the door."

"What the hell?" The top of her chest, exposed through her unbuttoned shirt, turned pink as color traveled up her neck. "It's all right for the driver to turn on and distract the passenger? That's a double standard. Who made up these ridiculous road-trip rules?"

Helpless laughter escaped him, affection tangled up with frustration. He reached out and patted her thigh, his fingers a hair's width short of the inseam of her pants. "Don't worry. You'll get the hang of it."

"Ugh. You're incorrigible," she said, squeezing his hand before she slapped it away.

Colin drove the next three hours with blue balls and anticipation rushing through his veins. When they at last entered Death Valley National Park, the sun had begun its descent, painting the sky and mountains with splashes of red, orange and violet.

"This is brilliant," Jihae breathed, leaning forward in her seat to look out the windshield.

"It is. The rest of the park is spectacular but you can't beat the sunsets against the mountains." He turned into one of Death Valley's two hotels. "So are you ready to rough it for two nights? We're on the same travel budget as location scouts, so the accommodations won't be up to your usual standards."

"I've stayed in *hostels* before." She crinkled her nose at him. "A standard room in a four-diamond hotel isn't roughing it."

"When did you stay in a hostel?"

"Around seven years ago."

"But what kind of accommodations do you usually have?"

"Presidential suites and penthouses. Fine. I get your point. You don't have to rub my nose in it. I never asked to live like a spoiled princess," she said glumly. "So how do *you* rough it, Mr. Self-Made Millionaire?"

"I usually camp when I come to national parks."

"Camp?" Her face held both horror and fascination. "Like as in camping? In the outdoors?"

"Wait a minute. You can't be serious." He turned to stare at her after parking the car. "You've never gone camping?"

"You probably don't know a lot about my family, but my father isn't exactly the type to load the family into the car and go camping," she said a little wistfully. Colin shrugged to hide his discomfort, because he did know quite a bit about her family. Before he could think of an appropriate response, she continued, "But I do want to try it."

"I'll take you someday," he said before he could think.

Did she think he was making her a promise? That they would be together long enough to reach *someday*? Maybe they *could* have their *someday*. He could come clean to her. Every moment he'd spent with her had been real. His every word and every touch had been true. But no. It was too late. She would despise him if she found out about his identity and how he'd betrayed her trust.

"Let's see if I could survive a couple nights in a standard room," Jihae said with a small, sad smile that broke his heart. "Besides, I don't think *Best Placed Bets* has a camping scene."

During the check-in, Colin requested adjoining rooms, so they could spend the night together without sneaking back and forth. When they got to her room, he was the perfect gentleman, opening the door for her and placing her suitcase just inside the entry.

"I'll see you later," he said, and left Jihae with her mouth gaping. Once he let himself into his room, he promptly found the entrance to hers and knocked. He heard shuffling and a muffled *oof* before she flung open the door.

"Hi." He grinned at her wide-eyed expression.

"Is that your room or the rest of my room?" she asked, getting on her tiptoes to look over his shoulder.

He laughed, and stepped aside to invite her in. "Welcome to my room."

"So this *is* the whole room," she said, excited about the new experience.

"Sure is."

Her eyes took in his room, identical to hers, in a quick sweep, then pressed herself against one wall. Then she took measured strides until she reached the opposite wall and burst out laughing.

"You could walk from one side of room to the other in less than twelve steps. It's so small and cute."

He walked over to her—in ten steps for him—and leaned down to nuzzle her neck. "I'm glad you like it."

"Mmm-hmm. I do. It's so fun." She leaned her head to one side to give him better access. "And I love our connecting door. We could finally have a sleepover."

He placed his hands on her waist and walked her backward until her back met the door that led to the hotel hallway. She gasped in surprise and stared at him.

"For real?"

"Hell, yes," he said before he crushed his mouth against hers.

Jihae's surprise was short-lived as she eagerly pressed her body against his and deepened the kiss, urging him to respond. He growled deep in his chest, his desire for her bursting into dangerous flames.

He reached between them and ripped open the blouse she'd carefully unbuttoned in the car. Impatient to taste her, he pulled down her bra until her breasts came free. He took her in his mouth until she moaned, digging her hands into his hair. He suckled deeply then moved greedily to her other breast, his hands reaching behind to cup her round backside.

Her hands tugged and tore at his shirt. He leaned back only far enough to pull it over his head, then reclaimed her lips. He shivered as she explored his chest and stomach, and smoothed her hand lower.

"God," he groaned. "I need to be inside you."

Rather than answering, she hurriedly unbuckled his belt and pushed down his jeans, then made short work of her own pants. He ran his hands over her naked body then stepped away to sheathe himself as quickly as his trembling hands would allow. Desperate beyond coherent thought, he wrapped her leg around his waist then lifted her up and brought her down on him, tilting his hip so he was buried inside her to the hilt.

"Colin."

"Yes, baby. Talk to me."

"Faster."

Her breathless demand pushed him over the edge and he pounded into her again and again without even a pretense of control. He was so damn close, he wasn't sure how much longer he could last.

"I need you to… I don't know if I can… Jihae, please."

He shifted her in his arms to give her more contact where she needed it and pumped harder, willing her to come. Just as he thought he wasn't going to make it, she screamed, tilting her head back against the door, eyes clenched shut. He joined her in climax and pushed into her one final time.

His limbs still trembling, he gently lowered Jihae's feet onto the floor and leaned against her.

"I've been dying to do this to you for hours," he mumbled against her warm, smooth neck. "You make me so crazy."

"And I can't get enough of you," she said huskily, her hands moving up and down his sweat-slickened back, both soothing and arousing him.

"We're going to shower first then I'm taking you to bed. Then we'll order room service to replenish ourselves, and go again. I'm not letting you out of my arms until tomorrow morning. Thoughts?"

"Oh, just that we're going to need to order a ton of food."

Eleven

Jihae opened her eyes slowly, savoring the feel of Colin's body wrapped around hers. Waking up next to him felt so right. She had never felt such warmth and security before. She wanted more, but this stolen night was the only chance they had to spend in each other's arms unless they could plan more location hunts without making everyone suspicious. Not only that, it also wasn't right using project funds to pay for their rendezvous.

She sighed, clutching at the arm Colin had wrapped over her. She shouldn't be worrying about having more of him, but making the best of what she had now. And right now, she had a hot hunk of a man, naked in bed with her. Letting go of her desperate hold on his arm, she reached behind her and wrapped her hand around him. *Mmm*. She smiled with her eyes closed. He was already hard.

"Hi, are you awake?" she whispered, slowly pumping her hand up and down his erection.

"You're insatiable, woman. Not even letting me rest after a long night," he growled, his hand sliding up to cradle her breast.

"From the state you're in, you've hardly had enough yourself."

"No, I haven't. I don't know if I ever will."

He flipped her to face him and swiftly took her mouth in a hungry, plunging kiss. They'd gone from zero to sixty in two seconds flat. She frantically swept his body with her hands, wanting to touch him everywhere at once. When he responded in kind with a pained groan, she had no room for anything in her mind but Colin and the way he touched her.

Their pleasure grew and consumed them, and soon their shouts of pleasure filled the room. They lay limp and satisfied while trying to catch their breath. Her lazy gaze drifted to the clock on her nightstand and she sat upright.

"It's eight o'clock! I thought you wanted to get an early start."

"You're right. Let's take a shower together to save time and get out there."

"You have to promise to behave in the shower otherwise we're going to lose more time."

"Scout's honor."

They hardly fooled around at all in the shower, and got ready in good time. After grabbing some coffee and muffins from the coffee shop in the lobby, they set out on the scouting adventure.

The proud peaks of the valley surrounded them as they drove from one point of interest to the next. South Korea was a beautiful country with four distinct seasons, each bearing its own fairy-tale charm. But she had never seen or experienced anything like the great vastness of Death Valley. One thing after another amazed her: standing in the

Badwater Basin, 282 feet below sea level, driving through the spectacular desert hills of Artist's Drive and the aptly named Artist's Palette, a geologic kaleidoscope of colors, and enjoying a handful of hiking trails. Each point of interest held its own unique charms, and she would never forget any of it. Especially since she got to experience it all with Colin by her side.

"I think we have the hiking trail we want." He took his eyes off the road for a second to glance at her. "Do you want to see one more spot? It's spectacular during sunset."

"What is it?"

"Have you seen *Star Wars*?"

"I beg your pardon?" she said with an affronted stare. "How could you even ask that?"

"Sorry. Sorry. So you must know what Tatooine is."

She rolled her eyes and didn't grace him with a response.

"Well, they filmed the Tatooine scenes for *A New Hope* and *Return of the Jedi* here in Death Valley. The Mesquite Flat Sand Dunes is probably the most recognizable of the locations."

"Shut. Up." She swiveled toward him and said in a near shout, "Are you bloody serious? Yes! I want to see Tatooine."

The sand dunes rose and fell in endless waves against the backdrop of the jagged, rocky hills and the bright orange-and-yellow sky. It was freaking Tatooine.

"Let's go, let's go," she said as she jumped out of his car. She took off in a run, not waiting to see if Colin was following her. Every person to themselves. They were on Tatooine, for God's sake.

She was out of breath by the time she reached the top of the first hill. But she got to enjoy the view of Colin climbing the hill with his backpack filled with their supplies.

Always prepared. When he reached the top, he handed her a water bottle.

"Drink, you nut. We're literally in a desert. Don't let the cool air fool you."

"Yes, sir." She winked at him and chugged at her water. She actually was very thirsty after the climb. "Let's keep going."

They were sandy and sweaty by the time they returned to the car, but Jihae didn't mind it one bit. That had been glorious. They even got a nice couple to take a picture of them together. It was the only one she had and it made her heart clench because she'd cherish it when this was all over.

They drove back to the hotel in serene silence, taking in the surroundings and the changing colors of the sunset. When they reached their rooms, Colin turned to her and bowed formally.

"May I take you out to dinner tonight?"

She giggled coyly into her hand and replied in her poshest British accent. "That would be an absolute pleasure."

"Excellent. I have reservations for seven. Is that enough time for you to rest and get ready?"

"Sure, as long as we take some alone time and take separate showers."

Colin laughed, dropping his silly formality. "I guess I could bear to stand an hour and a half on my own."

Jihae, on the other hand, felt a twinge of regret at not getting to spend every minute with him, but she needed to rest a bit. More importantly, she wanted to surprise him with the new dress she'd brought. She wanted to look beautiful for him.

"I'll see you soon," she said.

Their gazes held until she closed her door. Despite her best intentions, she was tempted to fling open the door and say *Just kidding. Of course I want to shower with you.*

After taking a shower *alone*, she sat down on her lonely king bed and switched on the TV, mostly for the commercials. She grabbed the brush she'd set down on the nightstand and methodically brushed out her hair. When her feet and legs felt a little less tired, she got up to blow-dry her hair. She planned on wearing it down for Colin. It went against the Princess Jihae rules, but they were far from home. No one was going to capture a picture of her and post it on social media out here.

Once her hair fell like dark satin down her back, she took time with her makeup, painting her eyes with dramatic colors. She kept her blush to a minimum and applied a deep pink lip stain to her lips.

She withdrew her dress from the garment bag and stepped into it. It was a rich, emerald-colored strapless dress with a fitted top and a tulip skirt that fell halfway down her thighs. She chose clear, crystal-dotted heels to complete the outfit. The mirror told her it had been worth the effort to dress up for Colin. She was still her, but she looked more like the fun, vibrant person she could be with Colin. It was an amazing feeling to see her outside appearance match the person she was inside. She couldn't wait to see the expression on Colin's face.

A quick glance at the clock told her she'd made it with five minutes to spare. She waited patiently for one more minute, then grabbed her clutch and headed out the door. There was no rule that a man had to pick up the woman, right?

When she knocked smartly on his door, she heard him walking toward it. She was holding on to the doorframe with one hand, arm raised high above her head, and leaning into it in her best Hollywood-bombshell pose. She felt a little silly but it was fun, and she wanted to have a bit of fun tonight.

"I… You…" Colin stared slack-jawed at her. His eyes heated as they traveled down her body then back up to her face. "Hell."

"Hmm. I was fishing for a compliment. But I'll take 'I… You… Hell,' I guess."

"If we didn't have a reservation, I would pull you into this room and make love to you with your hot little dress pushed up to your waist. You look so beautiful. I won't be able to undress you later."

She gasped softly, her own body warming and softening to his words. She coughed indelicately into her fist and fought for her composure. She had wanted to wow him, and had succeeded, but it was still a rush. As calm returned to her, she noticed he was handsome as hell in his blue suit and fine gray shirt. She could just about eat him up.

"Turn around," she said, biting her lower lip.

"What? Why?"

"Because I want to see what those pants do to your fine ass."

With a shrug, Colin turned in a slow circle for her. He raised an eyebrow with an arrogance that made her body burn. "Do I meet your approval?"

"Yes." She cleared her throat. "Top marks. Excellent bottom, that."

His low chuckle made her want to forget about the dinner reservations, but this kind of *real date* was not easy to come by. In fact, this was their first official date. She wasn't going to shortchange herself on it.

He stepped out of his room and offered her his arm. "Shall we?"

"Yes, please." She took his arm and smiled into his eyes.

The dining room was charming and intimate, and Colin had a romantic table by the fireplace reserved for them. He ordered them red wine—she was more of a craft-beer aficionado—then reached across the table and placed the tips of his fingers on her hand for a brief second.

"You're so beautiful," he said.

"Thank you," she said with a deep blush, suddenly feeling shy.

"I wish…"

"What? What do you wish?"

"I wish… I could have something I can't have."

"What is it? Tell me." She looked intently into his eyes, holding her breath. He seemed to be on the precipice of something monumental, and by the way his gaze bore into hers, it had to do with her. Did he want promises? A future with her?

He shook his head as though to clear it, and laughed lightly. "I wish we could fly to Lake Como and spend a lazy week there. Work has been so hectic for so long, I could really use a break. But alas, *Best Placed Bets* has no scenes set in Italy, so we wouldn't have any excuse to go."

He had been about to say something else. She knew it, and he wisely, but disappointingly, had taken the safer route.

She forced a bright smile and said, "Lake Como sounds wonderful. I always wanted to go there, but it was a bit far for my graduation trip."

The food was fresh and elegant, but she didn't taste much of it. The fun, romantic date she'd been hoping for now had an undercurrent of tension and melancholy. Colin was quieter than usual, too.

When they went to bed that night, he made love to her with an intensity that made her heart ache, like he was memorizing every single part of her. It felt as though he was preparing to let her go. In her head, she knew that it was for the best since she had to do the same, but everything in her being screamed that it couldn't be—that they had to be together.

It was hopeless. She was hopeless. She had gone and fallen in love with Colin.

"Are you well, Hal-muh-nee?" Colin said, as he kneeled on a *bang-suk* on the hard floor. He came to his grandmother because he was too lost to find his way back on his own.

Death Valley had been a few months ago, but he still dreamed of waking up with Jihae cradled in his arms, soft and warm in her sleep. He wanted to wake up beside her every morning. At some point along the way, he'd allowed himself to dream that she could be his forever. But now he wanted it to become reality.

"I am, but I don't think you could say the same," his grandmother replied, concern drawing her eyebrows together. "Sit comfortably, and tell me what has you so distressed."

Now that he was in front of his grandmother, he didn't know where to start. He had screwed up so royally, he didn't think even she could help untangle him from the mess of knots.

Colin had made himself a part of the investigation of Rotelle Corporation's espionage scheme. He'd helped rekindle a cold case by effectively spying on Jihae. Their relationship, at least on his part, was built on lies. But the lies and omissions had to stop. He had to find the courage to tell her the truth—all of it—and hope to God she would give him a chance to make it up to her. To make her happy.

"It's about Jihae," he said, rubbing his aching chest with the heel of his hand. "No. It's about me."

Grandmother gazed steadily at him with a calm countenance, patiently waiting for him to continue.

"I shouldn't have kept my identity a secret. It was cowardly and manipulative. I should have convinced her that she should work with me despite the fact that I'm a Song." He looked down at his fisted hands. "Now I'm in love with her, but everything we have together has been built on my lies."

"Does the girl know that you love her? Does she care for you?"

"I don't know. I think she cares about me, but once she finds out who I am and what I've done, she'll despise me for it."

"If that is truly the only outcome, then why are you here?" she asked with a shrewd glint in her eyes. "You are here because you want to correct the mistakes you have made."

"I do. I want to tell her the truth."

"What is really holding you back?"

"I'm afraid I'll lose her when I tell her the truth. Not only that, but I would be asking her to choose between me and her family. Her father would never allow her to be with me. If she stays me then she will lose her family and Rotelle Entertainment."

"Is it fair to ask that of her?" his grandmother said.

"It won't only be my deception I'll reveal to her. To tell her the whole truth, I'll have to tell her about her father's attempts to sabotage Hansol and destroy Garrett's marriage. Will she want to stay with her family knowing that? Maybe I won't have to ask her to choose between me and her family."

"Hmm. Don't you think she might use her knowledge of your deception against our family? To let her father know that we are on his trail?"

"No. Absolutely not. Jihae is honest, fair and principled. She'll never help her father, knowing what he had done. My gut told me from the beginning that she was innocent. And I have proof that she isn't involved, if you still have doubts."

"Yes, yes. I know what you overheard from her conversation with her father and how she refused to help Yami Corporation's CFO. Besides, you don't need to convince me of her innocence."

"But I do, Hal-muh-nee. I want you and Uncle James, and the rest of the family, to accept her. She is truly an amazing person, but so lonely. Her family…they aren't like us. They don't love her and appreciate her like family should. She's been neglected, controlled and used by them. I want her to become a part of our family and be loved as I have been. I want you to accept her as your own."

"Colin, do you want to marry this girl? Is that what you're telling me?"

"Yes. I want to marry her and make her happy. I want to beg for her forgiveness and make up for any hurt my lies will cause her when I tell her the truth."

"Then is it fear? Is it only fear that is holding you back from telling her the truth?"

"You're right. I'm so afraid of losing her, Grandmother. I can't bear to even think about living my life without her in it. If I tell her, she might leave me. Maybe I want to delay the inevitable."

"But you said you love her. Every day you continue to keep this secret, the more you are hurting her. Is that what you want? Is that the right way to love her?"

"I've been lying to myself that I'll be able to let her go when the time comes. That neither of us is emotionally involved, and we'll be able to walk away from each other without heartache. I've been so wrong." He wiped both his hands down his face, hating himself a little. "If I love her, I have to give her the choice to leave or stay based on the whole truth. If she wants to leave me after I've told her everything, she has the right to make that choice. If by some miracle, she is willing to give me another chance, then that is her choice, as well. Telling her the truth and respecting her decision is the best way I can truly love her at this point."

He pushed away the nagging thought that even if Jihae gave him another chance, her father wouldn't back down easily. If Colin ever reached that point, he would fight the world for her as long as she stood beside him.

"Colin, I know you. You are a good man. You made a difficult choice based on the difficult situation you were placed in. I know that my desire to have you join Hansol has been a great source of stress and guilt for you. In that, I feel partially responsible for your decision to spy on Rotelle Corporation. I understand you did that to pay me back a debt you don't owe me. You have done the best you can for our family."

"None of this is your fault. It's all mine. I had a choice and I made the wrong one. But now I understand what I have to do," he said with determination. "Hal-muh-nee, will you do something for me?"

"Anything, my dear child."

"If Jihae is willing to have me, will you promise to make her a part of our family?"

"If she will have us, then she will be family." She reached out to squeeze Colin's hand. "She will be my granddaughter."

Twelve

Jihae ended the call on her cell with shaky hands and placed it on her desk with a clack. She knew her father was a ruthless businessman, but she never thought it possible that he would be willing to break the law to get what he wanted.

Her friends from Korea had gotten back to her with disturbing news. They'd dug up some stale rumors among the highest executives that Rotelle Corporation might have planted a spy in Hansol Corporation the previous year. It didn't tell her how Yami Corp. was involved in the espionage, but her gut feeling said this was the secret her father had been keeping from her.

But why? Why would her father do this? He had more money than ten generations of his descendants could live off. Anything else he earned was superfluous other than for feeding his pride. Jihae froze. His pride.

She had a nagging feeling about the timing of the spy

being planted. The rumors had sprung up almost a year and a half ago. Close to the time that Garrett Song had broken his engagement to Jihae.

Oh, my God.

All that time, her father had blamed her for the broken engagement. That it had happened because word of her *unruliness* got out. He had blamed what she'd done as a college kid to guilt her for her broken engagement. And like a prat, a part of her had believed him. She'd believed that it was her fault. And she'd beat herself up for losing the chance to gain her freedom from her family. Soon, she'd regained her senses and was relieved the arranged marriage hadn't happened, but she still had carried her guilt inside her, trying to appease her father.

But behind all that censure, he had committed corporate espionage to get revenge for his humiliation. He couldn't stand that a mere nouveau riche family had dared to refuse his daughter's hand. So he'd taken out his frustrations on his jilted daughter and had gone after Hansol where it would hurt the most.

He hadn't been able to keep his crimes a complete secret, based on the rumors floating around among the inner circle. Her father, with his brilliant, conniving mind, must've known that his crimes could be revealed. And that was where Jihae came in.

He'd timed her business trip to the United States so she would be present for the commencement of his espionage plans. And his recent attempts to get her involved in dealings with Yami Corp. all seemed too perfect to be coincidences. Her involvement now would make her the perfect fall guy. That was why he'd been so adamant that she meet Sylvia Taylor and make the introductions she demanded. It might've even been her father who'd offered

Jihae's services to Sylvia Taylor to fabricate a direct connection between her and Yami Corporation.

All the evidence would point toward her—the woman scorned who'd sought revenge against her ex-fiancé and his family. She was the one in the United States. And if she'd blindly done what her father had demanded, she would be the one who went out of her way to help Yami Corporation. It would look like Jihae was trying to appease Sylvia Taylor because she had something on her. Then her father could claim to have no knowledge of the crime, and accuse Jihae of doing everything behind his back. There was no better scapegoat than his own daughter.

Devastation seared her heart black, and she shivered uncontrollably. She hugged herself tightly and clenched her jaws to keep them from chattering. She'd thought he loved her in his own way. She was his daughter, after all. But wasn't this proof of what she'd been denying all her life? Her father didn't love her. At least not enough to take the fall for his own crimes.

Her heart was breaking and her world was falling apart, and she could only think… *Colin.*

She needed him. Her shaking would only stop when his arms were wrapped around her. Silent tears were falling down her cheeks, soaking the front of her shirt. With jerky movements, she reached for her cell phone.

Colin. I need you. Please, she typed after several attempts.

What's wrong? What is it? Are you okay?

Just come. Please.

Are you at the office?

No, I worked from home today.

I'll be there in twenty minutes.

The mere fact that he was on his way eased some of her shivering, but she couldn't make her limbs work. So she sat very still at her desk, not bothering to stem the flow of tears. She didn't have the will to make them stop. She couldn't don her stiff upper lip, like Princess Jihae should.

In what seemed like both a second and a year, keys jingled and her door opened. Even though they were always together when they visited each other's places, they had exchanged their keys just in case. It was a good thing since her legs wouldn't hold her long enough to have stood up and opened the door for him.

"Jihae." Colin came thundering in, his hair standing in peaks and his eyes wild with worry. When he spotted her at her desk, he rushed to her side and kneeled beside her. He held her face between his warm hands as the tears continued to fall. "What is it? What's wrong, baby? Please tell me."

There was so much—so much that needed to be said. But now, she only wanted him and to forget everything else. By some miracle, she managed to whisper, "Hold me, Colin."

He wrapped his strong arms around her without hesitation, and he held her head tucked into the crook of his neck. He murmured soothing words while his hand drew reassuring circles on her back.

At some point, he lifted her into his arms and carried her to the sofa, then nestled her on his lap. The murmurs and the gentle touches didn't stop. She couldn't remember how long they stayed like that, but at some point, her tears finally ran dry and she clutched at the front of Colin's shirt.

She'd been abandoned by her father in the worst way, and she couldn't lose Colin, too. There was no family for her anymore. Even if her mother hadn't been part of her father's scheme, she would never oppose him for Jihae. She was alone and had no obligations, responsibilities or duties to make her return to Korea. Rotelle Entertainment was as good as lost since she'd disobeyed her father. But she had the experience and connections to start fresh in Hollywood. Losing Rotelle Entertainment didn't frighten her anymore. As long as she had Colin, she could face anything.

"I love you, Colin. I love you so much." She wanted promises. She wanted forever with Colin, and she didn't have to hold back anymore.

"Jihae." He tensed under her, his Adam's apple bobbing as he swallowed. "You can't say that. Not yet. Not right now. You're hurting, and there are things you should know…"

All she needed to know right now was that she loved him. That she'd finally found the courage to tell him she loved him. Talking could wait. She placed the tips of her fingers on his lips.

"Whatever it is, it doesn't matter. I don't want to hear it. In fact, I don't want to talk, either. All I want is you. Right now. Make love to me, Colin. Make me feel whole."

He gently pulled away her hand and looked at her with such sad eyes that it frightened her. "Jihae, I have something to tell you."

She didn't want to hear why he had such sorrow in his eyes. She couldn't handle any more bad news today, so she grabbed his face with both her hands and brought his mouth down to meet hers. He stiffened and tried to pull away, but she straddled him and swept her tongue across his bottom lip. When she swiveled her hips against him, he capitulated with a helpless groan and kissed her back with dark, stormy passion.

Their mouths met and dueled, and their teeth bit and teased. They frantically tore off each other's tops, and

Jihae spread her hands possessively over his broad, muscular chest, then leaned back to admire his beautiful body. While she was distracted, Colin threw her bra to the floor and palmed her breasts and massaged them.

She moaned and ground her center against his hard length until he echoed her moan and leaned in to kiss the sensitive spot behind her ear.

"Colin, please," she said, grinding her hips harder while hot moisture soaked through her panties.

He hiked her skirt to her waist and grabbed and tore her lacy lingerie in half. With fumbling hands, she helped him unbuckle his belt and unzipped him, pulling out his erection. She wrapped her hand around it and moved it up and down, drawing a groan from him.

"Condom," he rasped, lifting his hip off the sofa. "Back pocket."

The shift of his hips tore a high-pitched moan from Jihae, but she quickly reached down, pulled out his wallet and found the condom. When he grabbed for it, she shook her head. She tore open the package with her teeth.

"No, let me," she said.

As soon as she covered him with the condom, she pushed herself up on her knees then sank deep onto him. Colin made an attempt to check his passion and started out at a slow tempo. But she didn't want slow. This coupling was about her claiming him. Marking him as hers.

She pulled herself up and came down with a rotation of her hips. He scrunched his eyes shut and hissed, as though in pain. So she did it again. Faster and harder. She kissed him and her tongue mimicked the movement of her hips.

"I'm going to take you fast and hard, darling," she said against his lips. "And you're going to fall apart under me, screaming my name."

"God, you're killing me."

"Am I?" She emphasized her question with two hard pumps. "Tell me you're mine."

"I'm yours, Jihae."

"Tell me I'm yours." This time his response faltered, so she sank into him even deeper, circling her hips until he groaned. "Tell me I'm yours."

"You're mine. God help me. You're mine. Mine alone."

His eyes opened then and he grabbed her waist and lifted her up, tilting his hip into her. He filled her so deeply and fully that she whimpered, her smooth tempo falling apart. Colin took over with a fast, desperate rhythm, his movements hard and inelegant. Jihae was going to be sore later, but it felt so good. So right. There was nothing for her to do other than push him even harder.

She was so close, but she wanted to prolong this moment, so she hung on.

"Come on, baby. Come for me. Come for me, baby."

His pleading words were almost enough to push her over the edge, and when he sucked her aching nipple into his hot mouth, she came apart, atom by atom.

"Colin." Her scream echoed through her living room.

He was pushing faster and faster into her, his movements becoming more erratic by the second. A hoarse shout escaped his throat as he jerked into her one final time. They sat there cradling each other as they came back to earth. Her condo was still and quiet except for their harsh, shallow breaths.

Then, in a broken voice, Colin whispered, "I love you, Jihae."

"I love you more than anything, baby." His voice caught in his throat as his heartfelt admission tore free of him.

This wasn't how it was supposed to happen. As soon as he'd left his grandmother's house several days ago, Colin had gone to pick out an engagement ring. He was an optimistic son of a bitch. Knowing her kindness, her goodness, he'd let himself hope that maybe he had a chance of keeping her. That somehow she would forgive him and give him another chance. If she were to forgive him, he didn't plan on wasting a single second with her. He was going to propose to her.

But the timing hadn't been right the last few days. They'd worked long, hard hours, and by the time they were alone together, they were too exhausted to talk. And today she'd been so scared and suffering. When she'd told him she loved him, his heart burst inside him and set off beautiful fireworks of hope.

He was supposed to tell her that he loved her first. After he'd told her the truth, he was supposed to beg her for forgiveness and offer her his love. He didn't want her to feel humiliated by his duplicity any more than necessary. But now, with her love out in the open, she was going to feel doubly humiliated. Doubly betrayed.

He should have told her sooner. Much sooner. He had been a coward and now the little hope he had might be blown forever.

Once their breaths returned to normal, he gently sat her to the side and brushed her hair out of her eyes.

"I need to clean up. I'll be right back," he said.

She smiled tremulously and nodded.

He was a goddamn bastard. He went into the guest bathroom and stepped under the shower. He let the hot water wash over him, wishing it could wash away his guilt. But what was done was done. He couldn't change that, but he would do the right thing tonight.

Colin found her in the kitchen, holding a steaming mug of tea. Her hair was wet and tucked behind her ears, and she looked cozy in her pale blue pajamas. She glanced at him from beneath her lashes, suddenly shy.

"I made you some tea," she said, pointing to a steaming mug on the island.

He took a seat in front of it and motioned for Jihae to sit beside him. As he gathered his courage to reveal his secrets, she said in a soft, faraway voice, "I just found out today that my father was a criminal, and he had been planning to set me up to take the fall for his actions."

"He what?" Colin roared. She didn't deserve that. Her bastard of a father didn't deserve Jihae. He took a deep breath to calm himself. "Are you all right?"

"Don't worry. He *tried* to set me up, but failed. I acted out of character and didn't obey him down to the letter. I'm safe. Legally." She turned wide eyes to him, cocking her head to the side. "Aren't you going to ask me what this is all about?"

He attempted to swallow and failed, then answered, "I think I know exactly what this is all about."

"What are you talking about? How could you know any of it?"

"Will you promise to hear me out? Will you give me a chance to explain?"

"You could tell me anything. What's going on, Colin?" she asked, putting her soft hand on top of his trembling one.

"I'm Colin Song."

"Yes, and I'm Jihae Park," she said lightly, but unease crept into her expression.

"I am Colin *Song*, one of the heirs to Hansol Corporation, and Garrett Song's cousin."

She'd picked up her mug to sip her tea, but it came crashing down on the island, shattering against the marble. "What are you saying? I don't understand."

"Careful," he yelled. "You're going to hurt—"

She didn't hear him, or she didn't care. She pushed herself up to her feet with her hands on the counter. A jagged piece of the mug cut a bright line in her tender palm, but she didn't even flinch.

"Tell me!"

"Please, baby. You're hurt. Just let me stop the bleeding on your hand, and I'll tell you everything."

She backed against a wall and lifted her bloody palm to ward him off. "Stay where you are. Don't you dare come near me."

"Jihae—"

"Tell. Me. Now."

He needed to do as she asked if there was any chance of calming her down.

"I kept my identity a secret from you because I wanted you to see CS Productions on its merits. My team shouldn't suffer the burden of my connections. My family has nothing to do with CS Productions."

"You thought your cousin's jilted fiancée couldn't possibly know the difference between personal life and professional life?" Coldness seeped into her voice, but at least she appeared to be calming down. He suspected the next part would shatter that calm again.

"There was more than that. Rotelle had planted a spy in Hansol Corporation that could have derailed Garrett from becoming the CEO. Despite our PI's best efforts to figure out the extent of the espionage so the family could bring a legal case against Rotelle, the trail had run cold. And I wanted to find out something helpful for the investigation. I wanted to help my family find justice."

"So you lied to me to avenge your family. In your eyes, I was already guilty by association."

"The spy your father recruited through Yami Corp. was

Garrett's wife's former lover. He had set it up so Natalie would take the fall for the espionage. Garrett nearly lost his wife and daughter because of that. Because of the way your father attacked Garrett and Natalie so specifically, we didn't doubt you were involved."

Blood drained so completely from her face that her lips matched her pale skin. "That's because my father is very thorough in his deviousness. If evidence of the espionage attempt somehow led to him, he set it up so that I would take the fall for it. He'd even timed my arrival in the States to match the commencement of his scheme."

"Did you find that out today? God, that bastard. How could he do that to you? I'm so sorry—"

"Shut. Your. Mouth. You have no right to be sorry for my father's betrayal when *you* betrayed me so thoroughly. You *used* me."

"I was an idiot. I thought I was doing it for my family. To pay them back for their love and support." This was a nightmare. He was drowning in fear, and he couldn't see the light above. "But from the day I started working with you, I knew in my gut that you had nothing to do with the espionage scheme. Then you confirmed in your conversation with your father that you didn't even know who Yami Corp. was—"

"You actually spied on me? You listened in on a conversation I was having with my father? Which conversation was this? Since you discovered I didn't know who Yami Corp. was then…that was my first conversation with my father about Yami and the whole mess. That was the night we first made love." She gasped and speared him with a look of such accusation and heartbreak that he had to look away. "Did you make love to me—have this relationship with me—to earn my trust? Was all this your way of using me to get information out of me? Or was it your plan to break my heart all along? To avenge your precious family?"

"Jihae, no. God, no." He took a step toward her and she flinched, turning her head away as though his proximity would hurt her. He stopped. "I made love to you because I couldn't hold back anymore. No matter how hard I fought it, I wanted you more than my next breath. Not being with you would have burned me into ashes."

"So the part where you had sex with me was just to satiate your lust then."

"No. Please. I knew in the depths of my soul that you were innocent, and by relaying Sylvia Taylor's move to Hansol's PI, my involvement in the investigation was over. I didn't know then, but I was already so deeply in love with you. I fooled myself into thinking that I would be happy with whatever you gave me. I didn't deserve forever with you, but I thought we could have a short time together without you getting hurt. I was an idiot and none of it makes sense now."

"No, it doesn't. You were selfish, and you were cowardly."

"I was, but I will make it up to you if you would only give me a chance. I will become the man you deserve. I love you with every cell in my body—more than life itself. I'd made up my mind to tell you, but I was waiting for the right time. Again, that was my cowardice. But I wanted to tell you everything and beg for your forgiveness. I never meant to hurt you. Please give me another chance."

"You broke my heart, Colin. I have no forgiveness or hope left in me, because you ruined me. You stole my chance to choose you, and I'll never forgive you for that."

"I love you, Jihae. I'll never stop loving you."

Even if she didn't believe him, he had to try to convince her that she was loved and cherished by a foolish man. A fool's love was still love, and he hoped that it could provide her with a little salve for her pain. Colin got down on his knees in front of her, pulled out the ring from his pocket and held it out to her without opening the box.

"I won't insult you by even dreaming that you could accept my proposal, but once I told you everything, I was going to propose to you so I could spend the rest of my life loving you and making you happy. My love wasn't planned, but it's the greatest truth I know. And even if you can't accept me, please know that you are loved most deeply. Truly. Your father betrayed you, and I added to that hurt on the same day. My past mistakes are unforgivable, but causing you such pain today is beyond reprehensible. Please forget about me. Don't let your memory of me cause you any further pain. I'm not worth it."

Jihae didn't say a word, but tears were streaming down her face again, every drop like blood seeping from her heart. He got to his feet and placed the engagement ring on the counter.

"This is yours. There is no one else who will wear it. Do with it what you will." He turned from her then and took his first step toward the door and out of her life. But the burning pain in his heart made him turn around and look at her one last time. "I love you so very much. I'm sorry I couldn't be the man you deserve to be with."

It was only when he put his shaking hand on the doorknob that he heard her first broken sob. He held back the tears that rose to his eyes. He didn't deserve even a speck of relief from his anguish.

Thirteen

Time had passed. The cut on her palm had faded away into a thin white line, and Princes Jihae was able to pour herself into work without feeling much of anything. The production of *Best Placed Bets* was running toward the finish line. She was damn proud of what Rotelle Entertainment, CS Productions and the staff, crew and talent had accomplished.

Rule Two—they must finish the film no matter what—remained firmly in place, because she always kept her word. While she avoided Colin as much as humanly possible, her team continued to work with his to make the most of their partnership.

Every day she went to work and pushed herself to exhaustion, then came home and collapsed into a restless sleep. Every day. That was how she had survived the last few months.

In the rare moments that her guard came down and

she remembered she'd lost Colin, pain too monstrous to describe came crashing into her, paralyzing her. But that just motivated her to fall deeper into character and become Princess Jihae down to her soul. It was a good thing. Everything she was—her face, body, hands and heart—all felt numb from the cold. She was frozen solid, and her true self remained locked behind the thick, icy walls.

The old Jihae had trusted, hoped and loved, but Princess Jihae knew better. Trust, hope and love only led to heartbreak. Her childish hope that her parents loved her despite their distance, censure and neglect... It was so stupid of her. Her dream that she could belong to someone and have that someone belong to her. To love and be loved. A complete joke. She was alone. She had always been and always would be. Alone.

"Hey, girlfriend. Do you have a minute?" June asked as she stepped into the office.

"For you. Anytime." Jihae did her best to smile for her friend. Her confidante. But it felt foreign and awkward on her face. "Come have a sit."

June held out a bag she had been hiding behind her back. "Ta-da."

A rusty, unnatural laugh rattled from her. "What is it?"

"*Nigiri*, baby. One of the staff went to Little Tokyo for lunch and was sweet enough to bring some sushi back for us."

Jihae's stomach roiled, but she smiled her distant, stiff smile again. "How nice of them."

"Jihae-ya," June said, switching to Korean. "You really need to eat. You're going to make yourself sick pushing yourself like this."

"And since when do I not push myself?"

"I know. You always ask a lot of yourself, but not like

this. I could tell you're not sleeping well, and you're wasting away. I hardly ever see you eat."

"I eat." When she remembered, which was seldom. "Okay, okay. Give me those *nigiri*. I'll eat them."

"Thank you, Your Majesty, for condescending to eat the gourmet sushi presented right in front of your face."

June's trademark sarcasm pulled free a real smile from Jihae. "Thank you for the sushi. And thank you for taking care of me."

"You're very welcome." She smiled back, relief shining on her face.

They ate in companionable silence, June piping up to make random, funny comments here and there. The sushi surprisingly wasn't dry and flavorless, like all the other food she'd attempted to eat. She could actually taste the fresh fish and the perfect texture of the rice, and it was delicious. A thin string of warmth penetrated her icy wall, and an impossible thought occurred to Jihae.

Maybe, just maybe, she would come out of this okay. Not whole and strong, but at least, as a *living* person. She had lost so much of herself from her father's betrayal and from Colin's... She'd lost Colin. She'd begun to think that she would never be herself again. That the real Jihae would never emerge from behind the wall of Princess Jihae.

But this could be the first step. The first real smile. The first enjoyable meal. The first time she enjoyed someone else's company since her world had collapsed. Maybe from this point on, she could take little steps to find herself again. To find satisfaction in her work, and to find whatever happiness she could find in her life.

"Thank you, June," she said with affection.

June's eyes widened in surprise and she smiled warmly at Jihae. "My absolute pleasure."

"We should do this again soon."

"Lunch? Nah. The next step to rehabilitation is getting you drunk."

"I like that idea. We could get plastered and go kill it at a karaoke."

"Now you're talking." June paused and looked straight into Jihae's eyes. "Welcome back, friend. I missed you so much."

The wrap party was one occasion when Jihae couldn't avoid Colin. They'd done the film together. He had as much right to be there as she did. She chose a loose, draping column dress to hide her weight loss and wore her hair down in thick, shiny waves. Possibly the only good thing that came out of the whole mess was that she didn't give a damn about what her father thought anymore.

He continued to threaten to fire her from her position for disobeying him, but he wasn't going to risk the financial success he stood to gain from *Best Placed Bets*. Her guess was he would push her out of Rotelle Entertainment as soon as the project was over. Jihae huffed a humorless laugh. Too bad she was leaving before he could have the satisfaction of firing her. She'd stuck with Rotelle Entertainment to see this film through, but she had plans to start her own production company.

The moment she entered the party, she was surrounded by people, so she didn't get a chance to see if Colin was there. It was for the best since she didn't want to spend the whole evening wondering if and when she would bump in to him.

Everyone in the grand hall was in high spirits. From the direction to the acting, everything had been superbly done in the film. They were filled with confidence that it would really be something to behold once the editing was finished. In her years in the industry, Jihae had never quite seen anything like it.

While she held herself to rigid standards, working on *Best Placed Bets* had been an absolute pleasure. They'd all worked together as a team through the rare minor hitches, but most of the production process had fallen into place like well-carved puzzle pieces. It was an uncommon but satisfying experience. And being part of it all had truly been an honor.

"Jihae," Ethan said, coming up to her with Kimberly beside him. "Congratulations. It has been an absolute pleasure to work with you."

"Ditto." Kimberly leaned in to hug her, and Jihae embraced her warmly.

"You guys did such wonderful jobs," Jihae said. "I can't tell you how proud I am, and how grateful I am that I had a chance to work with you both."

"Thank you, Jihae," Kimberly said with a watery smile. Then she cleared her throat. "Colin said he had a meeting, but he should be here any minute now."

"Oh?" Jihae couldn't think of anything to say beyond that.

The three of them weren't able to continue their conversation much longer as Jihae got pulled this way and that. When she was able to disentangle herself from the throngs of happy, celebrating colleagues, she made for the bar like a woman on a mission. Despite her mental preparations and determination, she was a nervous wreck at the prospect of seeing Colin.

"Dirty martini. Extra olives, please," she said to the bartender as she took an empty seat.

The others sitting at the bar seemed like the introverts of their group, seeking some alone time, which was perfect for her. She wanted to be alone with her beautiful martini for a few minutes. She took a sip of the bitter, briny cocktail and bit into the flesh of a salty olive. Her eyes closed shut. It was heavenly.

"Hennessy straight," said a voice she recognized from her dreams.

Why had he approached her? She'd expected an awkward hello, but she hadn't prepared herself to actually talk to Colin. She wasn't ready, so she kept her eyes closed and silently chewed her olive.

"Jihae."

Oh, God. She hated his beautiful voice. She hated the reflexive shiver that ran down her spine. She hated the thump of her broken heart. *Get a grip, Princess. You can do this.* She opened her eyes and slowly turned around. Colin was standing a few feet away, leaning against the bar.

"Congratulations on the wrap." She forced her words through stiff lips. He had worked hard and deserved the compliment.

"Thank you. Congratulations to you, too."

"Sure." She took a significant gulp of her martini.

Meanwhile, she was trying very hard not to notice anything about him. How striking he looked in his slim, black suit and open-necked dress shirt. How elegant his long fingers looked wrapped around his glass. He'd lost weight. His boyishly handsome face was now sharp and edgy. The face of a man who had known pain and survived. She tried to notice none of it. He wasn't hers anymore. Was never hers to begin with.

But she had something to relay to him, so she calmed her churning emotions.

"I want you to know that I've found some evidence connecting Rotelle Corporation to Yami. There were some suspicious activities in an overseas account belonging to one of Rotelle's shell companies. My father hid his tracks well, but some forensics showed the money being transferred to an account here. It isn't enough to put my father away, but it'll be enough to keep him from coming after Hansol Corporation and your family again. I'll make sure of that."

"Thank you, Jihae."

"No need to thank me. It's the right thing to do." Having said her piece, she was ready to find a dark hole to crawl into. She couldn't bear to be near Colin anymore.

"You look lovely," he said, his voice low and hesitant.

"Don't." Her numb frozen heart cracked and bled.

"Jihae, I just want to know that you're okay."

She froze as fury leaped to the surface. She couldn't believe what she was hearing. And she didn't want to believe the tenderness in his eyes.

"No, you don't get to see if I'm okay. What you get to do is stay away from me. I'm barely beginning to live again. You can't pop back into my life and ask after me. You forfeited that right when you destroyed me."

"I'm sorry. God, I didn't mean to... I'm an idiot. I'm sorry."

Enough. Jihae drained her drink and shot to her feet, but before she could storm off, Colin gave her a curt nod and strode off toward the opposite end of the hall. *God help me.* She wanted to run after him. Because despite everything, she still loved him with all her broken heart.

It was the night of Adelaide and Mike's wedding rehearsal. His cousin held a special place in his heart and she was marrying a man who actually deserved her. Colin was happy for them but the feeling was dull and faded.

His world was devoid of Jihae, and he was hollowed out. Life had lost its vitality, and he merely endured and survived it. Not that he deserved anything more. He'd betrayed her and broken her trust so completely, he couldn't even try to apologize to her again. He didn't deserve her forgiveness. For months, he'd tortured himself with thoughts of should've, could've, would've. He should have done a million things differently. Maybe then, he'd still have Jihae in his life.

But it was too late for regrets. He had poured all his energy into finishing the production of *Best Placed Bets*. At the very least, he'd kept that promise to her. Now he would have something they'd created together to hold on to. To keep him afloat in an existence he could hardly stand.

Colin was Mike's groomsman so his presence was mandatory, and there was no way he would ever let them down. Garrett and Natalie were the best man and the matron of honor respectively, so they had made the trip home from New York with their two daughters in tow. Colin's sorrow and anguish were his to bear, and it was time to take care of the people who loved him.

The wedding party bustled around the small chapel like tiny figurines in a shoebox. While everything seemed chaotic, Adelaide's wedding coordinator had the situation under tight control. If he remembered Garrett and Natalie's wedding correctly, the woman was a genius at what she did.

He found Natalie standing near the edge of the commotion, holding an infant in her arms.

"Hey, there," he said, giving her a one-armed hug and a peck on her cheek. Then he stole a peek at the sleeping angel, just three months old. "Does she have superpowers? How is she sleeping through this ruckus?"

"Riley sleeps through anything as long as I'm holding her. But the moment I put her down in her car seat, she'll wake up in a second."

"May I hold her for a bit?"

"Oh, my God. Yes, please. My arms are burning," Natalie said as she gingerly transferred the little bundle into Colin's waiting arms. "You're a saint. Truly."

"And where is my dear cousin while you carry his daughter to the point of exhaustion?"

"Why, he's on the more difficult task of toddler duty." She laughed lightly and pointed past his head. "Look over there."

He spotted Garrett's tall, broad form easily, made all the more prominent by the three-year-old on his shoulders. His cousin was leaning his head toward Mike to hear what was being said, but the bellowing commands of his preschooler seemed to make it difficult for him. Colin chuckled quietly, shaking his head.

"So Sophie still rules the household, I see."

"Hey. That's only because I allow her to."

"What about Garrett?"

"Oh, no. He doesn't get to rule. He's putty in us women's hands."

Surprised laughter escaped his lips, and he worried he'd disturb the sleeping baby in his arms. Thankfully, Riley really could sleep through anything.

The rehearsal dinner was held on the Song family's garden terrace. After the harried wedding rehearsal, the setting was perfectly intimate and peaceful. When Adelaide's bridesmaids and Michael's bickering parents left, the cousins relaxed into the evening. His grandmother finally stood and bid everyone good-night after a long, pointed look at Adelaide.

Garrett had put his two girls to bed at some point in the evening, and sat with his arm around his wife's shoulder. And Adelaide and Mike held hands on the table and cast blushing glances at each other. Never had Colin missed Jihae more than he did now.

"Will you please stop making those lost-puppy-dog

eyes, Colin?" Adelaide said. "It makes me want to fuss over you and shower you with affection."

"Yeah. It's pretty damn heartbreaking," Garrett added.

"Screw you, dear cousins," Colin replied mildly. But he was panicking inside. Of course, his family would know. They could see his suffering as clearly as he could see their happiness.

"Hal-muh-nee debriefed us on your truly mucked up situation. I can see why she enlisted all of us to help. You're a mess, dear cousin," Adelaide said gently. "I think it's a Song family trait. When we fall in love, we love deeply. We love forever. You have to find a way to win her back."

"That's not possible. She would never forgive me. Nor should she." Colin gave up trying to maintain a light mood. They would see through him, anyway.

"Just look at me and Garrett, man," Mike chimed in. "We both messed things up so royally, we shouldn't be sitting at this table with these amazing women by our sides."

"But their capacity for love and forgiveness is greater than what we could possibly imagine," Garrett said, his voice rough with emotion. "And I don't know where I would be today if Natalie hadn't taken me back."

"Oh, honey." Natalie kissed Garrett softly on his mouth and leaned her head against his shoulder. "It was the best decision I ever made."

"Sometimes you have to forget about weighing things out, and just trust your gut instinct." Adelaide linked her fingers through Mike's. "If I hadn't taken a leap of faith, I wouldn't be the happy bride that I am."

"Are you happy, baby?" Mike asked her with such tenderness in his eyes. "Because that's all I ever wanted."

"I am. So happy." Adelaide cupped Mike's cheek in her hand and he leaned into it. "And I can't wait to start the rest of my life with you."

"God, could you guys all stop being so goddamn happy for a second?" Colin raked his fingers through his hair. He was pleased for his cousins, but it reminded him of what could've been. It hurt to think about Jihae. "I thought you guys were doing some kind of intervention for me. Not rubbing salt into my wounded heart with your love fest."

"We're just showing you what you could have if you got over your guilt and focus on your love," Adelaide said.

"What we've learned is that love makes us stupid brave. Maybe a little reckless, but mostly brave." Garrett smiled as though being stupid in love was the greatest thing in the world. "That bravery could help you do anything."

"What about the investigation?" Colin said, feeling terrifying hope spark to life inside him. "Aren't we going to bring charges against Rotelle Corporation and Chairman Park?"

"Bring charges against the devious devil himself? I wish," Garrett said. "But he was so thorough in covering up Rotelle's involvement that our PI ran out of leads again. And Sylvia Taylor hasn't made a peep. Jihae made it pretty clear that there will be no introduction to the talent agency, so she wisely gave up."

"Besides, Hansol discovered the espionage scheme before permanent harm could be done. And Natalie and Garrett are doing great. Right, guys?" Adelaide said, giving her brother and sister-in-law a big thumbs-up. "We could leave the past in the past, Colin. If you love Jihae, we'll stop the investigation against Rotelle Corporation. And I say this with Hal-muh-nee's stamp of approval. We don't need to go after her family and hurt her."

"Do you love her?" Natalie asked gently.

"More than life," Colin replied. He loved Jihae so much that every cell in his body ached to hold her again.

"Then go win her back." Adelaide kicked him under

the table. "Do the bravest, stupidest thing you can think of and overwhelm her with your love. She won't be able to think past her love for you."

"And we're all here to help you," Mike said. Everyone at the table nodded their support. "Just say the word and we'll do whatever you ask."

Emotion lodged itself in his throat, and Colin let himself weep for the first time after losing Jihae. But the tears were meant to cleanse away his guilt and regret, and prepare him to win back the woman he loved. Because if he knew anything, it was that he loved Jihae more than anything in the world and he would do everything in his power to make her happy. No matter what happened, he wanted her to know that he was hers and would always be hers. She deserved to know that his love was real.

Fourteen

Jihae checked into a hotel near the premiere location to get herself ready for the red carpet. Her stylist was scheduled to come in an hour. After a quick shower, She wrapped herself up in a plush bathrobe and dried her hair, absent-mindedly running her fingers through it.

She'd chosen a warm, rose-and-gold dress for the occasion. She now only wore white when she damn well felt like wearing white. After the wrap party, she realized that if she wanted to survive, then she had to move on. And the first step had been to break free of her father's hold on her. Hiding behind Princess Jihae's persona was what was expected of her. She was not Princess Jihae. The princess belonged to her father. She had been a puppet controlled by her father. Never again.

She was Jihae Park, film producer and business executive. She was the one who had brought Rotelle Entertainment to the next level. That took skills, intelligence, perseverance and plain old hard work. After the premiere, she was going to submit a formal resignation letter to her father. It was time to devote herself to getting her production company off the ground. And with the evidence she had against Rotelle Corporation, her father wouldn't be able to do a damn thing to stop her.

The hollow, cold feeling where her heart used to be showed no signs of diminishing, but she couldn't let her life and happiness depend on another human being. It was no one's job to find happiness for her. It was hers and hers alone. She was still too ragged to feel whole, but she would find joy in her life, and make something of herself.

She wasn't a nobody just because her father saw fit to discard her like a used paper plate. She had been fooled by a man who claimed to love her, but she wasn't a fool for it. Someday, these things would make her stronger. It was too soon, but she would rise above everything she'd gone through.

There was a smart knock at the door, and she glanced at the clock. There were still at least forty minutes left until her appointment. Jihae walked to the door and looked out the peephole. It was June.

"June," she said, hugging her friend. "What are you doing here?"

"I pushed back your appointment for half an hour, so we have a good hour to talk."

"Talk? About what?"

"I don't know if this is going to change anything, but watching you put on a brave face every day hasn't been easy. You can't exist as a numb shell." June dragged Jihae to the settee and plopped both of them onto it. "You're a strong woman. You can fight. You can thrive. But will you ever be truly happy without Colin? Because I've never seen you light up from the inside out like when you were with Colin."

"Was it that obvious I was in love with him?"

"Honey, please." June waved her hand dismissively. "The way the two of you looked at each other fogged up the office windows."

"Why didn't you say anything?"

"About you two being together? Because you would have told me if it was something you wanted to share."

"It wasn't going to be anything permanent. I never thought—" A sob broke out against her will. She took deep breaths through her nose. She promised herself she wouldn't shed a single tear for Colin ever again.

"You never thought you would fall in love with him."

Jihae could only nod.

"Oh, hon. I think you guys fell for each other the first time you met." June reached out to squeeze her hand and held on to it in quiet support. "It's my job to be observant. I wouldn't be a good executive assistant if I wasn't. It was hard to ignore how lovesick you guys were."

"Colin doesn't love me. He—he was just using me."

"I know. You told me he kept his identity a secret from you and eavesdropped on your conversation with your father. That was a dick move on his part, but at least he was doing it for his family. And that gets me to the part why I rushed over here."

"What is it?" Jihae asked, unable to quell her curiosity.

"It's about Colin's relationship with his family. It wasn't only you. No one knows about his connection to the Song family and Hansol. He has kept it a tightly held secret all his life."

"How did you find that out?"

"Colin's cousin Adelaide called me a few days ago. She said she didn't know if you would take her call, so she reached out to me. Colin must've told her I was your friend. Someone you would listen to."

"But why are you telling me this now?"

"You're trying so hard to put your life back together. I didn't know if telling you would only make things harder for you. But no. You love him, and you have a right to see the whole picture."

June explained that his father had coasted through a life of privilege and entitlement on his family's money and good name. He was hardly a father to Colin. It was his grandmother, Grace Song, who had raised him.

But as he grew older, Colin was desperate to make his name and succeed on his own outside the shadow of Hansol. He didn't want to be anything like his father. In order to become a self-made man, he closely guarded his identity from the public. He refused to benefit from his connections. But in order to stand on his own, he had to disappoint his grandmother and refuse to join Hansol.

"I know this doesn't excuse him from not telling you he was Garrett Song's cousin, but everything in him must have rebelled against revealing his secret. He didn't even know if he could trust you to keep his identity a secret, so he had gone with his default. Just like in any situation, he would have wanted to be judged based on the merits rather than his connections and his family name."

Jihae didn't need to hear this right now. She didn't want to know that he was an honest, honorable man. That he had to bear the guilt of disappointing the person who'd raised him to be true to himself. When the opportunity arose to allow him to help his family, how could he refuse? No. She couldn't do this right now. She couldn't feel her heart wrench for the little boy Colin was, and for the man he became. She didn't want to feel the tears streaking down her cheeks.

"I'm not telling you this to hurt you, Jihae. You are fierce and amazing, and I'm so proud of you. But I don't want you to have any regrets. His motivations don't make his actions right, but maybe it'll help you look at what happened in a less punishing light. Maybe it'll help you hurt less to know that what he did wasn't a coldhearted scheme."

Jihae abruptly stood from her seat, and wiped her tears away with both hands. "June, thank you for rushing here to tell me all this. You're a good friend, and I love you for it."

"But?"

"But I'm going to kick you out now because I have a premiere to get ready for and I don't want my face to be a swollen mess. I can't deal with this right now."

"You know he'll be there tonight."

"Of course, I know. All the more reason I can't show up with puffy, red eyes. I don't want him to think that I'm still crying over him. Let me keep a scrap of dignity in all this. I won't have to see him ever again after this."

"That. I just needed to make sure *that* was what you still wanted after learning the full story." June gathered her jacket and got on her feet. "I think my work here is done, and I will bid you adieu."

"Thank you, June."

"Have a wonderful night. You earned this, and *Best Placed Bets* is going to blow everyone away."

After one last hug, June left Jihae to her thoughts. But she kept her mind carefully blank even as her heart pumped and churned inside her, water raining down from her heart as the ice around it melted.

Jihae arrived near the end of the line for the red carpet. The stylist had chastised her repeatedly for her tears, and it had taken ages to make her look presentable. When she stepped out of the car, flash bulbs burst around her, and she gave them her real smile, rather than her signature Princess Jihae half smile. Despite everything, she was proud to be there, and proud of the film she'd produced.

She heard the expected chatter over the color of her dress and her free-flowing hair. Even her makeup was warm and stormy, unlike her former icy, elegant looks. Appearing before the public as herself was incredible. It freed something inside her. The insecurities and resentment she carried deep within unchained themselves and flew away. She was here as her own person, and she was fiercely proud of who she was.

She stopped and smiled for the cameras for what seemed like the hundredth time when she heard a commotion behind her. From her perch on the stairs, she saw a small group of people walking toward her and the crowd parted like red curtains to allow them through. At that moment, she spotted the tall, broad-shouldered man wearing a velvet, royal blue tuxedo. She thought anyone would have been able to single him out of the crowd, even the Hollywood red-carpet crowd.

He looked exquisitely handsome with his slightly unruly hair slicked back from his forehead. He was even thinner than when she'd last seen him, but he looked sharp and sophisticated…and full of determination. Colin had always been a confident man with an air of authority about him even as his usual, lighthearted self. But the man who stood on the carpet looked like he was ready to take on the world, exuding power from every part of him.

When he came to stand at the bottom of the short staircase, Jihae realized she'd been holding her breath. She let it out in a rush and stretched out her hand to steady herself on the rail.

"Jihae." His voice was low and tense, but hearing her

name from his lips sent a thrill down her spine. "You look so beautiful."

"Colin, what are you doing?" she said, glancing around at the gathering crowd.

"I just wanted you to know how much I love you." His voice broke. "I know I've hurt you—so much—because of my guilty conscience and hang-ups. I've betrayed—"

"Stop that." Jihae rushed down the steps and tugged him to the side until they were a few feet away from the red carpet. It didn't exactly give them privacy, but the reporters had now turned to the next celebrity walking down the carpet.

"I've betrayed your trust," he continued as though there was no interruption. "I've invaded your privacy by eaves-dropping on you. And most of all, I should've believed in you and trusted you with my truth."

"Colin, we're done. You've apologized already and I've declined to accept." She tried to sound aloof and disinterested, but her voice shook.

The thought of him as a little boy without a father he could look up to, and of him as a young man, disappointing the woman who raised him to become the man he was today… It tore at her heart.

"I love you so much and I was so afraid of losing you that I was slowly losing my mind. I fooled myself into thinking that I could let you go when the time came. I tried to convince myself that what we had was a brief affair and no one would get hurt. I told myself to cherish every day with you because it was bound to end. That telling you the truth was only bound to hurt you."

His confession made her realize how she had tried to fool herself in the same way. She'd told herself she could keep herself from falling in love with him. She had always planned on leaving him. Foolishly believed that she would be able to leave him. She lied to herself to protect her heart, but Colin had still given his heart to her. He had loved her all along, and had fought with the fear and guilt inside him.

"I don't know if I could believe you. You broke my heart, Colin."

"I know I did. God, I know. But losing you broke me. Nothing has meaning to me anymore. Please give me a chance to love you. I will dedicate my life to making it up to you. To making you happy. Without you, my world is colorless."

A sob escaped her. Her life as Princess Jihae had been colorless. *She* had been colorless, lifeless, until she met Colin. He had filled her life with color, and she was finally able to bring out all the beautiful, powerful colors within herself. And she wanted so much to forgive him. To grab the happiness he was offering her. But she was so afraid.

"I don't think I could endure another broken heart. I won't be able to survive next time." Tears ran down her face, probably undoing all the hard work of her stylist, but it was hopeless. There was no way she could stem her tears.

"I swear to you there will never be a next time. I will never keep a secret from you again. I'm far from perfect, and I may hurt you at times in my stupidity, but I will always own up to it and work harder to be the man you deserve. Please." Colin kneeled before her on the cold asphalt. "Please give me a chance to love you. Let me cherish you for the rest of our lives."

Jihae was so entranced by Colin's words that she didn't see the group of people who came to stand behind him for a second. Then she drew back in shock. It was the Song family. She recognized Garrett Song and Grace Song from the business papers, and Adelaide Song from the fashion magazines. James Song was also there. Another man and woman stood beside Adelaide and Garrett, and seemed to be their significant others. They all wore warm smiles and earnest expressions. All but Grace Song, who stood in the middle with calm dignity.

"Please forgive him," James Song said. "He's so entertaining."

"We'll personally kick his ass if he misbehaves again," Garrett said as though he meant it.

"He's an idiot but we love him." Adelaide shrugged. "Could you, too?"

Then Mrs. Song finally spoke. "Will you be a part of our family?"

"Will you give me another chance?" Colin asked, still kneeling in front of her with tears brimming in his eyes.

He had always kept his connection to his family a closely guarded secret. But he had enlisted all their help to win her back. Her tears fell furiously. He had done this for her. Despite the scar in his heart left by his father, Colin wanted to open himself up to her, and in doing so, revealed to the world that he was Colin Song of the Hansol Song family.

"You just revealed your secret in public." She stated the obvious, too awed to be clever.

"I know. I don't care who knows. This secret I'd held on to for so long was merely a form of my pride. I wanted to be seen for the man I was, and I wanted to claim my success as my own. But all my life, my family has been there for me, and I couldn't have done anything without their love and support."

"Oh, Colin."

"And I offer you not only my love and support, but my family's as well. Will you marry me and grant me—us— the privilege of being your family?"

"Yes," she whispered then said with more strength, "Yes, I will marry you, Colin Song. Please stand up."

He stood and pulled a small box out of his pocket. It was the one she had messengered back to him. He carefully withdrew the diamond ring, and asked, "May I?"

"Yes."

He lifted her hand and pushed the ring onto her finger. It fit perfectly. When she glanced toward the Song family, Adelaide and Garrett's wife were wearing tremulous, watery smiles, and even the men's eyes were red-rimmed. She looked toward Grace Song and she gave her a solemn nod with a gentle smile on her face. They were going to be a family.

"You're mine now, you know." Colin raised her hand and kissed her softly on the knuckles, smoothing his thumbs over the ring. "And you can't back out because we have a ton of witnesses."

Jihae had been so focused on Colin and his family that she didn't realize that they were again surrounded by cameras…and applause.

"Oh, well." She cupped his cheek, all her love shining in her eyes. "I guess I'm stuck."

"You bet you are." Colin dipped her back to the roar of their audience and kissed her thoroughly, marking the beginning of their happily ever after.

* * * * *

HOT HOLIDAY FLING

JOSS WOOD

One

Adie Ashby-Tate was done—for this evening at least.

In a small but exquisitely decorated conference room in the iconic Grantham-Forrester hotel on 5th Avenue in the heart of Manhattan, Adie waved goodbye to her last guest and allowed her smile to fade.

She gripped the edge of her main display table, thankful for the empty room now that all the millionaires and billionaires who'd attended her "Christmas Indoor Market" had left. She loved interacting with clients and showing them her carefully chosen wares, but keeping the charm flowing for four or more hours was exhausting.

Because her feet were aching, Adie kicked off her heels and sank her feet into the expensive carpet. She looked around, pleased she'd managed to capture the essence of a snowy European Christmas market in the small ballroom. She'd strung fairy lights, the ten-foot

Christmas tree in the corner was draped with fake snow and a diffuser released hints of hot chocolate, pinecones and cider. She'd dropped the temperature to just this side of chilly to echo the sharp bite of a snow-tinged winter's night and she'd propped a snowboard and skis against a papier-mâché replica of a horse-drawn buggy.

The room suggested wealth, but more importantly, romance and the spirit of Christmas. The costs involved made her eyes water, but setting the scene, drawing in her clients and then transporting them to a simpler time was worth every penny and the hours of back-breaking work.

Still holding onto one of her display tables—covered in an expensive rich red velvet—Adie stared down at her burgundy-tipped toes and rotated her head from side to side. In a moment she'd move to the bar and pour herself a much-deserved drink, a reward for a job exceptionally well done.

An evening that ended with a book full of orders could be termed only successful, and her artisanal, superbly talented suppliers were going to be very, very pleased with her work tonight. More orders would come. Her gifts were one of a kind and the very rich liked nothing more than rarity and exclusivity.

After this event, Adie was spending the run-up to Christmas in New York City to see whether there was scope for her to open a branch of Treasures and Tasks in Manhattan and to ascertain whether she and Kate—a new friend she'd met through one of her clients—could work together. She needed more than a few orders before she decided to sink a lot of cash into expanding into one of the most expensive cities in the world. So she'd spend the next three weeks working out of New

York, testing the market while juggling requests from her existing clients in London and all over the world.

As an exclusive, private concierge who dealt only with very high net worth individuals, Christmas was Adie's busiest season. But she wanted, and needed, every moment of her days filled, especially at this time of year. This was the time of the year when the ghosts of the past—Christmas and his friends—decided to drop by and harangue her and she'd prefer to be too busy to pay them any attention.

She'd be exhausted in January, but being distracted was worth the price.

Adie looked at her tables. More than half a million pounds worth of inventory sat on the exquisitely decorated tables—from jewel-encrusted bottle stoppers to gold plated memory sticks—but because some of the richest people had the stickiest fingers, she needed to count the inventory and then pack everything away. It would take a few hours.

Tomorrow she had a series of meetings with potential clients, but the one guy Kate never stopped talking about—an old friend of Kate's whom she called "the most reluctant influencer" on Earth—hadn't pitched. Turned out, Adie hadn't needed his support. Tonight had been a raging success.

Adie heard the rap of knuckles on the partially open ballroom door and swiftly turned. This was an upmarket hotel with good security, but being burgled was always a possibility.

The man in the doorway was doing a damn fine job of stealing her breath.

Adie placed her hand on her sternum and told herself she was an idiot for feeling lightheaded. He was just a man, flesh and blood…

But…*what* a man!

He was so tall he had to duck his head to walk through the door. Wide shoulders, long muscular legs and what had to be a washboard stomach under the mint green button-down shirt tucked into a pair of plain black pants. He held a battered leather jacket in his clutched fist. His body was off the charts hot, but it was his face that held Adie's attention.

A young Cary Grant, maybe… But then she quickly decided he wasn't classically handsome enough for the comparison to work. He had the broad forehead and the strong chin, but his nose was a little too hooked, his stubble too thick to carry off Grant's urbane, man-about-town look. No, this man belonged in action, like her all-time favorite Hollywood hotties, Gerard Butler and Tom Hardy.

"Ma'am, he was on the guest list so I let him up. I hope that's okay?"

Adie pulled her eyes off Mr. Delicious to look at the security guard. When she processed the amusement in Dan's eyes at her slack-jawed reaction to her guest, she straightened her spine and told herself to act her age. Many billionaire princes and A-list movie stars were her clients. She was not normally this easily impressed.

Meeting those light eyes—fog blue or silver?—under those straight thick brows, a shade lighter than the burnt sugar color of his hair, she felt pinned to the floor, but finally managed to pull a polite smile onto her face. "Good evening. You're a couple of hours late, but you're welcome to take a quick look if you don't mind me packing away behind you."

"I should've been here earlier, but I was unavoidably detained."

His voice was as rich as the dark chocolate tart she'd

consumed in a tiny restaurant in the French Quarter of New Orleans last year. But within the richness, Adie heard exhaustion. Frankly, the man looked like he needed a drink. She gestured to the small bar tucked into the corner. "Can I offer you a drink?"

"God, yes. Please. Whiskey if it is available."

Adie smiled at his enthusiasm and walked, still barefoot, to the bar. She glanced down at her feet and shrugged. He was four hours late, she was packing up and her three-inch slingbacks were beautiful but torturous so he'd have to live with her bare feet.

And judging by the glance he'd directed at her legs, bare under the edges of a red cocktail dress hitting her legs midthigh, he rather liked what he saw.

It had been a while since she'd come across a man who made her feel both hot and shivery. It was a delightful feeling but, she cautioned herself, also a dangerous one.

Be careful, Adie.

Adie held two bottles in the air. "Bourbon or Scotch?"

"Scotch, please. On the rocks, if there is ice."

Appreciating his choice of a twelve-year-old whiskey, Adie poured a healthy amount into two glasses and lifted the lid on an ice bucket. Using silver tongs, she picked up ice cubes and dumped a couple each in the crystal tumblers before walking back over to him. Without her heels, the top of her head reached only his collarbone and next to him she felt dainty and deliciously feminine.

Adie handed him the glass and his fingers slid over hers, sending a delicious stream of "oh, yeah" up her arm and causing her nipples to contract. Heat pooled between her legs and she felt both languorous and hyped.

Adie stared down at her fingers, still wrapped around the glass, bracketed by his darker ones. She wanted to see, and feel, his fingers cupping her breasts, to look down and see his head between her…

Holy Christmas crackers! What was going on here?

Yanking her hand away, Adie stepped back and lifted her own glass to her lips, hoping he didn't notice. She didn't like feeling so out of control. Even in the old days, back when she'd used men and their attention as a distraction, she'd never experienced such an intense reaction. Back then, she'd been more concerned about what a man could do *for* her—mentally and emotionally as opposed to physically and financially—rather than what he did *to* her.

He stopped in front of a faceless gold mannequin wearing a tiny camisole and panties and cocked his head to the side. Tucking his jacket under his arm, he reached out and rubbed the silk between his thumb and finger.

"It's from one of the most exclusive and talented designers in the world. It's made from Lyon silk edged with Chantilly lace and comes in every color you can think of," Adie gabbled, her face heating. "Obviously she has other designs, if that's not your thing."

His lips quirked and those gorgeous eyes flashed with amusement. "It's not *my* thing at all. I'm more of a take-it-off than a try-it-on guy."

Adie smiled at his joke.

He cleared his throat and Adie forced her eyes to connect with his. Those eyes darkened, turned intense.

"Gorgeous," he stated, his eyes not moving off hers. Adie wasn't sure whether he was referring to her or the lingerie or both. "I'd like to see it in its more natural setting…"

And she'd have no problem wearing it for him. She

could easily imagine a huge bed, luxurious, sweet-smelling cotton sheets, a bottle of Moët in a silver ice bucket, fado music—expressive, passionate and melancholic—playing in the background.

And the late afternoon sun falling on the bed, turning his hair to burnished gold…

Adie quickly lowered her eyes, took a fortifying sip of whiskey and placed her glass on the table, grateful when he resumed his slow stroll down the tables, those light, intense eyes darting over her inventory. He picked up a hand-blown glass Christmas tree ornament, holding the gorgeous peacock design up to the light.

"It's mouth-blown and hand-painted. The crystals on its plumage are diamonds."

He didn't react but simply sipped his drink and looked down at the open box displaying Christmas crackers. "And these?"

Adie looked at his profile, wondering whether his wavy hair was as soft as it looked. She inhaled his woody, sunshiny smell. It took all her processing power to make sense of his question.

"Uh…handmade in the UK from eco-friendly luxury paper. They are tailor-made and the prizes can be anything you want. I had a client who bought each of his children a new car for Christmas and we inserted the car keys inside."

His lips quirked up in a half smile and Adie desperately wanted to know whether his mouth was as skilled as it was sexy. She really should have sex more often; this reaction was ridiculous. But, like relationships, random sexual encounters weren't her thing.

But she was seriously considering making this man the exception to her rule.

"I take it those kids didn't receive entry-level models."

Of course they didn't, her clients didn't understand the word *entry-level*. "Porsches and Lamborghinis."

He whistled and moved on.

"Are you in the market for something special?" Adie asked him, trying to judge whether he was a serious spender. His pants were quality, his shoes were expensive, but she couldn't tell if he was a billionaire or a millionaire or just rich. Unfortunately, if he was just rich, he wouldn't be able to afford what she was offering. Her products were aimed at the multimillionaire to billionaire section of the marketplace.

"Just looking."

Those words, she'd come to learn, were often code for I-like-it-but-I-can't-afford-it. Oh, well, he might not be good for business, but he was lovely to look at. Adie glanced down at her watch and noticed that it was past eleven and she still had a couple of hours of work ahead of her. She had a long day packed with meetings tomorrow and it was time to hustle Mr. Delicious along.

"No way!"

At his outburst, Adie's eyes flew to the object in his hand and she grinned. The centerpiece of the object was a 3.5-carat heart-shaped diamond, and more round diamonds studded the crocodile leather band.

"Is this a dog collar? For three hundred thousand?" he demanded, sounding and looking outraged.

"Gorgeous, isn't it?" Adie took the collar from his hand and examined the intricate work.

"How can anyone spend so much money on a dog? I'm mean, don't get me wrong, I love animals, but this amount of money?"

"My clients adore their animals," Adie explained.

She put down the dog collar and stacked the boxes of handmade chocolates and moved them to the side, giving her enough space to sit on the heavy table, her legs swinging. It felt so good to get off her aching feet. Picking up a sample dish of chocolates, she held it out to him.

He shook his head. "I rarely eat chocolate."

"You'll want to eat this," Adie assured him. "Have you ever tasted bacon and Mexican chili in chocolate?"

"That would be a no."

"It's rare, rather wonderful and…"

"Ridiculously expensive," he finished her sentence and smiled.

Adie snapped her fingers and pointed her index finger at him. "You're catching on." She watched as he slid the chocolate into his mouth, wishing it were her lips making contact with his, her tongue sliding against his. Adie wiggled in place and released a frustrated breath. Needing to do something with her hands, she picked up another chocolate truffle, looked at it and bit down on the bittersweet treat.

Gorgeous…rich, creamy and, hell, *hot*!

Adie chewed, swallowed and waved her hand in front of her mouth. She looked into his laughing, fog-colored eyes, and blushed. "Wasabi. Not what I was expecting…"

"Want some of mine?"

Adie looked at the half-eaten truffle in his fingers and wondered if he was going to feed her the rest of his chocolate. Suddenly desperate for some contact with him, any contact, she slowly nodded.

He seemed to hesitate, his eyes skimming her face. It was obvious to her that he was testing the waters, wanting to make sure he was interpreting her signals correctly.

He was.

His eyes held hers, fascinating and mysterious, as he placed the chocolate in his mouth and his hands on her knees. Heat skittered up her spine as he gently pushed her legs apart, stepping into the space he'd created. Adie held his eyes and her breath as he lowered his head... closer and closer until his lips were a whisper from hers. Unable to bear the suspense—she wanted his kiss more than she needed to breathe—she lifted her hands to his chest and placed her lips against his. Soft, hard, both at once and when his hot tongue on the seam of her lips cajoled her to open up, she willingly followed his lead. But instead of his tongue entering her mouth, she tasted bittersweet chocolate, a hint of chili, the rush of salty bacon. She moaned in delight.

Adie, wanting more—wanting everything—curled her hand around the back of his neck and held him in place, enjoying the chocolate-covered strokes of his tongue against hers, the way his fingertips pushed into the skin on her hips, his other hand cupping her jaw.

Adie heard him moan and then his hands were on her waist, hauling her closer so that the vee of her legs connected with his rigid erection, her feet curling around the backs of his knees.

Adie felt like she'd dived off a cliff into a warm, deep pool of delight. She ran her hands down his strong, muscled back, over his spectacular butt—and it felt as good as it looked. Her fingers danced over the backs of his thighs. She wanted this, she wanted more...to see him naked, to taste every inch of his hot, masculine skin.

It had been so very long...

He pulled back to drop kisses on her jaw, over her cheekbone, on her temple. His breathing was harsh in her ear and Adie reveled in the notion that he wanted her as much as she wanted him.

Had there ever been such a perfect kiss? Adie didn't think so…

Needing him, needing more, Adie gripped his jaw with one hand, seeking his mouth. Oblivious to where she was, she picked up his hand and placed it on her breast, groaning when the pad of his thumb brushed over her nipple. Tipping her head to the side, he changed the angle of the kiss, taking more, going deeper, silently demanding that she give him everything…

Adie pulled his shirt out of his pants and sighed into his mouth when her hands found hard muscles. She explored the bumps of his spine and when her hands moved over his sides and across his stomach, heading south, she felt his hand on hers, stopping her progress.

He stiffened, stopped kissing her, and after a moment lifted his mouth off hers.

He stared at her for the longest time, his eyes now steel gray with passion, his breathing ragged.

"You're beautiful," he muttered.

"Kiss me again," Adie begged, pleasure overwhelming her pride.

He shook his head. "If I do, I won't be able to stop."

Adie, knowing that this was wrong, that she was taking a massive risk, and not caring, lifted her shoulders in a small shrug. "So, don't stop."

A part of Adie hesitated, wondering what her real motivations were. Was she acting like this because it was that time of year? The season of doubts and regrets and over-thinking. During the festive season she always, always second guessed herself…

Was she making the right choices? Was she really happy with her life? What if this, what if that…

But no one had ever made her feel so much, so soon. It had been a long, long time since she'd used a man, and she'd never jumped into bed so quickly, but nobody had ever made her feel like this. She wanted more. She wanted one night of wild passion and if his kisses were a prelude to the main event, she was in for the treat of a lifetime.

She was a grown woman and she was allowed to explore her sexuality so, tonight, she wasn't going to second-guess herself, to wonder if she was falling back into old, destructive patterns. In the morning she could analyze her actions and deal with her regret, but she wasn't going to do that tonight.

Not with him.

"I have a room, upstairs," Adie whispered, her heart in her throat.

His thumb drifted over her bottom lip, tense and expectant. As he opened his mouth to speak, her phone jangled from across the room. Not interested in anything anyone else had to say, she stared at him, waiting for his answer. Why was he hesitating? Was he playing hard to get?

"I—" Her phone rang again and Adie, through her lust, recognized the ring tone. It was Kate. If she didn't answer, her friend would keep calling. She was pain-in-the-ass persistent.

Adie pushed him back and jumped to the floor. "Sorry, if I don't answer, she'll keep calling."

He nodded and Adie brushed past him to walk over to her bag, yanking her phone out of the side pocket. Annoyed and frustrated, she scowled at the screen and jabbed the answer button.

"What?"

"I just realized that I left you to pack up. I'm on my way back to help you..."

Seriously? Nooooo!

"I don't like you being on your own with so many valuable items. I mean, the security there is good, but anyone could con his way in..."

Adie's eyes darted across the room to where he stood, hands in his pockets, pulling the fabric of his pants against his still-hard erection. Who was he and what was he really doing here? As blood returned to her brain, Kate's words sank in and Adie bit her lip, her eyes flying over the table. Had he kissed her to distract her, so he could slip something valuable into his pocket? The dog collar was too big but the diamond-encrusted bottle stoppers and the gold memory sticks were easily hidden.

And had she really invited him up to her room? Would she have walked away with him without securing the room? Possibly.

Probably.

Oh, God...what the hell was wrong with her? He was a stranger and she'd been about to risk her body and her safety and her business? She was acting like she had when she was a young adult, impulsively and without thought, looking for attention, a distraction.

She refused to go back there, go back to that person she'd been. She'd worked too hard to jeopardize everything she'd work so hard to achieve, to become the person she was.

No man, no matter how attracted she was to him, was worth her backsliding even an inch.

Adie disconnected her call with Kate and folded her arms across her chest, forcing herself to meet his eyes. Passion had fled and his gaze was now concrete gray and hard.

"I see the moment has passed and your offer has been withdrawn."

Adie bit her bottom lip. She jerked her head toward the door. "I think I got a bit carried away," she said, her voice low. "If you'll excuse me, I have work to do."

He walked over and stopped an inch from her. Adie refused to move—her pride was back—and she kept her folded arms as a barrier against him coming any closer.

She stiffened as he dropped a kiss on the corner of her mouth. "Don't hurt yourself counting stock, I didn't steal anything." He dropped another kiss on her cheekbone and then her temple. "Thanks for the chocolate. And the drink."

"It was nice meeting you." He gave her a sexy smirk but Adie noticed his smile didn't soften his eyes. "But kissing you was better."

Adie said nothing as he turned away. She watched him walk to the door, biting down on her bottom lip to keep herself from calling him back, from begging him to take her up to her room and show her how good sex could be.

Because she knew with him it would be too bloody fantastic.

Christmas was a pain in the ass, Hunter Sheridan decided, leaning back in his chair and placing his feet on the corner of his desk.

After Thanksgiving, productivity went down, laziness went up and it felt like every one of his employees was distracted by thinking about, planning for and chatting over holiday festivities.

If Hunter had his way, the entire holiday would be canceled. But, while Christmas meant less than nothing to him, there were people out there obsessed with the holiday and who were, judging by what he'd seen last night, prepared to spend a lot of money celebrating.

Three hundred thousand for a dog collar? Wow.

Hunt leaned back in his chair and dug his fingers into his eye sockets, reluctantly admitting that dog collars and wine stoppers and bittersweet chocolate weren't foremost on his mind.

Adie Ashby-Tate was.

Oh, he'd known who she was the moment he stepped into the ballroom of the Grantham-Forrester. He instantly recognized her from Kate's incessant social media posts. And who else but the owner of the company would be the last to leave?

With her shaggy, short espresso-colored curls cut close to her head and her delicate features, she reminded him of a young Audrey Hepburn. Her skin was a deep shade of cream, and her eyes...

He ran his hand through his hair and blew out a long stream of air. Those eyes... Jesus, they were gorgeous. Against her luminous skin, they were the color of dark coffee beans tipped onto winter snow.

Her body, slim but curvy, had been a revelation and she'd fit him perfectly, as if she were a puzzle piece he hadn't known he was missing.

Puzzle piece, luminous skin, the action in his pants... How old was he, thirty-five or fifteen?

Hunt rubbed his hand over his jaw. He'd been immediately attracted to her looks, but catching her at the end of her event, he'd seen the woman beneath the salesperson, a woman more down-to-earth than he'd expected for someone completely immersed in their world, *his* world.

It was a place laced with over-the-top opulence, fantastic service and unforgettable experiences. It was a world of excess and bling, instant gratification, pride and arrogance. According to his online research, her fa-

ther was a British lord, her mother an American tobacco
heiress and she was their only child. Adie's mother was
a former famous model, her father was once—before
inheriting a fortune from his parents—a professional
polo player. These days, her father didn't seem to do
much of anything, choosing to hop from superyacht to
superyacht, mansion to mansion in the pursuit of pleasure, accompanied by a variety of young, busty women.

Their daughter was very much a product of that rich,
aristocratic world. Adie's dress, a shorty frothy number,
had been designer, and fat diamond studs had glinted
in her pretty earlobes. Her perfume was expensive and
her accent was upper-class British, thoroughly classy.
She was the real deal, a proper aristocrat and, although
he hadn't seen her working the room, Hunt knew she'd
done it with grace and charm.

He should've introduced himself, that much was obvious, but if he had, he wouldn't have gotten to kiss her,
hold her slim body against his, feel her sleek curves
under his shaky fingers. He'd been surprised at her
offer to go upstairs—because she hadn't seemed the
type—but he'd wanted to accept her unexpected offer,
because, hell, that kiss blew his socks off.

Knowing that she needed to know who she was going
to bed with—a potential client, one of the most influ-
ential business people in the city, according to Kate—
he'd been about to introduce himself when her damn
phone rang.

He'd watched as a frisson of fear and wariness replaced lust in her eyes and he'd seen his chance slipping away.

By the time she'd finished her conversation, it was
obvious she was having second thoughts about what

she'd proposed. So, he'd kissed her goodbye, knowing he'd see her again in less than eighteen hours.

And that they'd soon be picking up where they'd left off.

Hunt massaged the tight knot in his right trapezius muscle, thinking that he had work to do, lots of it. But, because he was acting like an adolescent, he couldn't stop thinking about Adie's sweet and sensuous kiss. It had been the sexiest of his life and, had they gotten to the really good stuff, Hunt thought there would have been a good chance of them setting the hotel on fire.

It had been that hot.

He couldn't remember when last, if ever, he'd had that same take-her-to-the-floor reaction to a woman. He'd been busy lately and hadn't slept with anyone but Griselda for more than a year, not because he was committed to her or their arrangement—he wasn't—but because he'd been too busy to bother.

Right now, he'd ditch everything…

EVERY.

THING.

…to take Adie Ashby-Tate to bed.

Hunt released a frustrated growl, annoyed that he couldn't move his focus and concentration onto anything other than a gorgeous woman with big brown eyes and a pixie face.

This wasn't who he was, wasn't what he did. He was never distracted by women and he never allowed them to affect his productivity. Work was all that was important.

He had several companies to run, a legacy to create, goals to reach. People—women, friends, acquaintances—sucked up time when he could be working. But here he was, completely distracted.

God.

Help.

Him.

Hunt heard the door to his office open and looked up as his long-time assistant approached his desk, staring down at his tablet. "So, Griselda is off the list of people for whom I must purchase a Christmas gift? Is that correct?"

Very. "Yep."

Hunt noticed the curiosity in Duncan's eyes, but didn't explain that he'd broken off his two-year—Fling? Liaison? Affair?—with Griselda a few days earlier when she'd asked him to consider co-raising a child with her. His "hell no" had been rather emphatic and his ending of their fling/liaison/affair had been the vehement exclamation point on that subject.

Honestly, people exhausted him.

He'd thought he'd hit the jackpot with Griselda. Thanks to his bouncing between foster families and group homes as a kid, his short but drama-filled marriage, and his best friend and business partner's death, he'd deliberately chosen a woman who made no demands, financial or emotional. And Gris never had. Until the other day when she'd asked him to father her child.

And all thoughts of his ex faded on meeting Adie last night…

Duncan pursed his lips. "Well, not buying Griselda an expensive piece of art or jewelry should save you a pretty penny."

Hunt swallowed his smile and hoped his expression remained inscrutable. Even after so many years as his PA, Duncan still acted as if Hunt were on the knife-edge of slipping into debt. Since he had enough money for a hundred lifetimes, even if he chose never to work another day in his life, Duncan's penny-pinching and cost-cutting attitude was a constant source of amusement.

Leaning back in his chair, Hunt looked up and noticed a deeper worry in Duncan's eyes, something more intense than the cost of gifts. Duncan was almost as stoic and implacable as Hunt so seeing his stressed face was a surprise.

"Everything okay?" Hunt asked, sitting up and leaning forward.

Duncan gripped the back of the visitor's chair and shook his head. "I just got an email… Uh, my first partner, the man I thought I was going to marry, is in the hospital after suffering from what they are calling a brain episode. For some reason, and although we haven't been together for more than fifteen years, he designated me to make any medical decisions if he's incapacitated. And, he's incapacitated."

Hunt heard the surprised confusion, and the intense fear, in Duncan's voice. "I'm sorry."

Duncan's head bobbed up and down in a terse acknowledgment of Hunt's sympathy. "I know it's not a good time for me to take a leave of absence, there's so much that needs doing concerning your foundation's annual fundraiser."

Honestly, Hunt had mostly forgotten about the yearly Christmas fundraiser. This year they were trying something new—an urban treasure hunt race. All the funds raised would go to support the Williams-Sheridan Foundation, named in honor of his and best friend, Steve's friendship.

Duncan quietly and efficiently organized everything, and Hunt's involvement was to show up at the cocktail party and hand out prizes to the winning teams.

Duncan also purchased Christmas gifts for Hunt's biggest clients, his favorite suppliers, for the sports players who acted as his brand ambassadors. As his right-hand man, Duncan made Hunt's life run smoothly. Duncan not only managed his office with aplomb, he also booked theater tickets, made reservations, dealt with Hunt's housekeepers and interior designers and made suggestions for and booked Hunt's infrequent holiday breaks.

And Duncan made Christmas bearable by shielding Hunt from the chaos of the season. But Duncan needed personal time and Hunt had to put his assistant's needs first. He'd survive Christmas…

Maybe.

"Call Jeff and tell him to file a flight plan and leave as soon as you can."

Gratitude at the casual offer to use his private jet flashed across Duncan's face. "I can book a commercial flight, it will be so much cheaper…" Duncan protested.

And jam-packed and stressful while Hunt's plane and pilot were just sitting there, doing nothing. "Use my plane, Duncan," Hunt told him, using his don't-argue-with-me voice.

Duncan nodded his thanks. "Concerning work, I'm pretty sure I'll be just sitting around at the hospital so I can still be productive. I'll have my laptop and phone with me."

Hunt stood up and walked around the desk to briefly lay his hand on Duncan's shoulder. "Work if you want to, Duncan, but not because you have to. Be with your friend."

Because, God knew, Hunt would do anything for a couple more hours, days, with Steve.

Duncan looked down, sighed and then he straightened his spine and blinked back the sheen of moisture in his eyes. "Thank you, Hunter, I appreciate it."

Duncan picked up a couple of folders, straightened them and placed them on the corner of Hunt's desk. He picked up a couple of pens and dusted some used staples off Hunt's desk into his hand. Hunter smiled at his assistant's fussing.

"Kate and Adie Ashby-Tate will be with you in five minutes."

Hunt was looking forward to seeing Steve's twin Kate. It had been a while, although she had called earlier in the week to ask him to attend the Christmas market last night.

"I'll finish up a few things here, but I'll be in touch, as soon as I can, with a plan on how I'm going to manage my duties regarding your Christmas schedule, your functions and the treasure hunt race."

God, Hunt hoped he would. He was lost without Duncan.

Seeing the time, Hunter stood up and buttoned his suit jacket, smoothing down his designer tie. Hunter walked over to his massive floor-to-ceiling window overlooking Central Park and scowled at the dark gray clouds. Snow was predicted for that evening, just a light dusting, but that wouldn't stop Hunt from his daily run around the park. Keeping fit kept him sane and he needed to spend a little time each day outside. If he didn't, he felt like the walls of his office and apartment were closing in on him, pulling to the surface memories of being locked up in group houses.

After his meeting with Kate and Adie, he'd walk toward the park and back. That would do him until he could pull on his exercise gear. Hunter turned at the brief knock on his door and saw Duncan pushing it open.

"Your four-thirty is here, Hunter."

Hunter looked at the slim woman walking into his office, immediately taking in her tousled brown hair and bright red, sensuous mouth.

There she was…

And it terrified Hunter to realize that he'd missed this woman he didn't know.

Two

Stepping into an enormous light-filled office—thanks to the floor-to-ceiling windows framing a helluva view of Central Park—Adie pulled a professional, happy-to-meet-you smile onto her face. This meeting was important. Hunter Sheridan was Kate's friend, her hotshot influencer and the one Adie needed to snag if she had any chance of making fast inroads into the crème de la crème of Manhattan society.

Kate, as she'd explained to Adie, didn't understand why Hunter Sheridan wielded so much influence, but maybe it was, per Kate, because he didn't give a damn what society thought about him or whether they accepted him or not. Hunt, Kate said with a smile, was a true individual, and while he could be charming if he tried, he could also be rude, demanding and impatient.

He was a hard man...

Adie, laying eyes on the man standing near the window knew just how very hard this man could be.

Stopping suddenly, her eyes clashed with his. She understood, somehow, that he'd known exactly who she was last night...

While she hadn't known anything about him at all.

She'd thought him to be anyone other than Manhattan's Most Magnificent. Though today he did look the part, Adie reluctantly conceded.

He was a natural clotheshorse and she loved his black Italian designer suit. His shirt was white, his tie silver and, if she'd had any doubt about his wealth last night, she had none this morning. He looked like what he obviously was—megarich and powerful.

And she'd asked him, without knowing his name, to come upstairs with her, to see her naked.

God, she couldn't be more humiliated if she'd walked through Knightsbridge naked with her hypercritical mother pointing out all her flaws to pedestrians passing by.

Adie had spent many hours since their encounter cursing him, but mostly cursing herself. Falling into a man's arms wasn't what she did, not anymore at least. In her teens and twenties, she'd been addicted to attention, throwing herself into the arms of any man who would catch her. She'd fall in love easily and completely, convinced that this guy would be the one to give her what she so desperately craved: love, time, attention, a family.

Most of the guys ran, scared by her intensity. But a few stuck and because she was completely messed up, when they offered to take the relationship to the next level—handing her an "I love you," a "let's move in together" or even a "will you marry me?"—she was the one who galloped away.

Because the thing she wanted the most also terrified her to death.

And really, she now knew that it was better to be alone than to be rejected.

Because nothing lasted forever.

Five years ago, soon after turning twenty-five, she'd wised up and realized that her behavior was destructive and demeaning. After a lot of self-reflection, she accepted the fact that she constantly sought attention because she'd never received any from her parents as a child. She accepted the fact that she used guys and relationships as a distraction to fill the holes in her heart. After years of chasing love, she'd decided that she no longer wanted it. She needed to learn to be happy on her own.

By keeping busy and living an over-full life, she'd become strong and independent, totally career focused and committed to providing her clients with six-star service. She never allowed any romantic relationships to develop, terrified she'd revert back to being that demanding, clingy woman she'd been.

And sex was a vague memory.

But Christmas was always a bad time of year for her, and Adie knew the stress of the holiday season triggered sadness and depression in lots of people. She wasn't immune. As the festive season rolled around, and images of perfect people, families and situations bombarded her, she was reminded of her ugly childhood and neglectful parents. Seeing Kate with her mom last night at the Christmas market had rubbed salt into that particular wound…

It was obvious that mother and daughter took great delight in each other and adored being in each other's company. Rachel, despite being a successful attorney, took her role as a mother very seriously. Her kids, as Kate told Adie, were the reason Rachel's sun rose every morning. Losing her twin brother, Steve, had devastated Kate, but Rachel was the one who took a year off work, who'd been unable to function for months after Steve's death.

Adie had no doubt that should something happen to her, her mom would hold a very tasteful funeral and cry prettily. Lady Vivien Ashby-Tate had the emotional depth of a puddle and after a week, she'd become bored with playing the mourning mommy.

Adie pushed her hand through her short-cropped hair, wishing she could chide herself for being harsh. But the reality was that her mom didn't love her, never had, and Adie was a burden her parents wished they'd never been saddled with.

Seeing Kate and Rachel together had made all those old feelings of neglect and need float to the surface. She'd berated herself for not being in a relationship, for not pursuing her dream of having a family. She'd felt herself slipping back into neediness. And that was before the sexiest man she'd ever laid eyes on walked through the door.

She was mostly happy. For most of the year, she was content with being single and having a kick-ass career. But as December edged closer, the Christmas blues made their arrival and she routinely started to question what she wanted, what she needed.

Every year, the fight to stay the independent, strong woman she was became harder.

All she could do was distract herself, to run herself ragged in order not to think. Christmas was her busiest time so keeping up with her clients' last-minute requests kept her to-do list full. For the past couple of years, she'd also fitted in as many hours as she could as a volunteer. Last year, she'd helped organize a London-wide food drive for homeless people. The year before, she was the stage manager for a local pantomime production.

This year her distraction of choice was trying to establish a new business in New York.

It was not giving in to more kisses from Hunter Sheridan.

"Kate, Adie."

Adie felt the confused look Kate sent her way, but she couldn't drop her eyes from Hunter's compelling face. She'd kissed those lips, had her hands on the bare skin of his stomach, felt his erection pressing against her…

Please, world, open up a portal and drop me into it.

"Have you two met?" Kate demanded, throwing her bag onto the couch in the corner of Hunt's office.

Hunt walked, gracefully for a man of his size, over to the couch, picked up Kate's Birkin tote, and pushed it into her arms. "We need a minute, Kate. Maybe more than a minute. Go talk to Duncan, he needs someone right now."

Kate frowned at him. "But we have a meeting…"

"Katherine. Go."

Kate's frown deepened at the command in Hunter's voice and turned her eyes in Adie's direction. Adie, convinced she was as red as a beetroot, gave her friend a quick nod. Kate didn't need to be here while Adie sorted out this mess. She was embarrassed enough.

"Give us ten, Katie," Adie said, finding her voice.

Kate threw up her hands, obviously exasperated. "Okay, then."

Adie waited until the door closed behind Kate before

making eye contact with Hunt again. "You're Hunter Sheridan."

Hunt's mouth twitched at her pronouncement and Adie closed her eyes, cursing her stupid statement. Who else would he be?

Adie tried again. "So, this is awkward…"

Hunt folded his arms across his chest, revealing the face of his watch. Adie, because it was her job, instantly recognized the timepiece. It was one of only ten from a renowned Swiss maker who was so in demand there was a decade-long waiting list. If she'd seen that watch last night, she would've instantly placed him in her can-afford-anything-anywhere box. Him being a potential client might've made her act with more propriety but she couldn't swear to it.

The wretched man was that compelling.

"Last night I thought you were someone else…" It was a weak explanation but the only one she had.

Amusement flashed in his eyes. "Who?"

"Well, not *you*, obviously," Adie crossly replied. "If I knew you were Hunt Sheridan, I would never have suggested…"

"Taking me upstairs?" Hunt lifted his thick eyebrows. "Really? How…novel. Normally, it's the other way around."

Adie looked at his mouth, remembered how skilled he was at kissing her and calculated the distance between them. A couple of steps and she'd be in his arms…

No, she wouldn't allow him to be her Christmas distraction, her festive fling… She didn't play those games anymore. He wasn't the way to deal with her feelings of abandonment, of being unloved and neglected. He wouldn't help her forget about cold Christmases spent with strangers who ignored her or her grandmother who detested her. That was when she was young. After she turned ten, it was normal for her to spend most of the festive season alone.

Christmas had never been a fun time of year.

Hunter couldn't change that.

But he *could* make or break her Manhattan business.

She had to keep him at arm's length…

Adie stared at a point behind his shoulder and forced out her apology. "I do apologize. I wasn't very professional last night."

"No, you weren't," Hunt agreed, his tone measured and calm. "You weren't wearing any shoes—you have pretty toes by the way. You tossed back superb whiskey like it was juice, fed me chocolate and invited me into your bed."

Yeah, she remembered. She'd been there.

"I'll completely understand if you don't want to proceed with this meeting," Adie said, her words stiff.

Hunt had the temerity to flash a megawatt grin. "No, you're here and I'll listen to your pitch. But…"

Adie held her breath as he walked across the room to stand in front of her, hands in his pockets, completely at ease. He stared down at her, his eyes an enigmatic color between gray and blue. "But, at some time in the future, rain or shine, hail or hellfire, we will pick up where we left off last night."

Adie saw the heated desire in his eyes and knew he was thinking of how he'd held her in his arms, his hand on her breast, his other hand under her skirt, down the back of her panties. He'd rocketed her from zero to a hundred in seconds and, had Kate not called her last night, this meeting would be a hundred times more awkward.

And it was plenty awkward already. Mostly because she still really, desperately, wanted to strip him naked and do wicked, wicked things to him.

Without giving her a chance to respond, Hunt sidestepped to the right and walked over to the door, yanking it open. "Kate, come back in, we've got work to do."

Adie stared at his broad back, bemused, confused and—dammit—wholly turned on.

Thank God Adie'd done this pitch a hundred times before and could recite the words by rote. There was nothing too big, too costly or too complicated for her to fulfill. She touched on what she could offer him as a concierge in terms of travel—luxury villas and upmarket hotel suites, adventure holidays and reservations at the best restaurants wherever in the world he happened to be.

Hunt's face remained impassive and, worse, unimpressed. She mentioned backstage passes to sold-out music and culture events. He finally showed a hint of interest when she mentioned the best box seats at sports stadiums. The purchasing of personalized gifts for employees, friends and family raised another flicker of interest and she ended by reassuring him that, by employing Treasures and Tasks, he'd enjoy white-glove service in every aspect of his life.

Hunt picked up her glossy brochure and thumbed through it. Adie gently bit the inside of her lip, wishing she could read him. She'd never met anyone with such a poker face. This wasn't the man she'd met last night, the one with passion in his eyes. No, this Hunt was all business. Adie thought they might be wasting their time. He didn't seem impressed by anything she'd said.

She knew that some people called her a glorified

personal assistant, but she didn't care. She loved arranging personal experiences, like over-the-top wedding proposals and anniversary dinners, private meals cooked by fabulous chefs, wine tastings in galleries and private viewings of museums and art galleries by world-renowned curators. She loved facilitating experiences that would create lifelong memories...

But, to be honest, buying another diamond bracelet or superbike for a spoiled child didn't excite her.

Maybe it was because her parents thought luxury gifts were an adequate substitute for their time and affection. Instead of the Victorian mini-mansion playhouse she'd received at eight and the pony she was given at ten, she would've far preferred for them to read her a story, drive her to school or—novel idea—live in the same house with her.

Or at the very least, be there on Christmas morning.

Hunt pulled a writing pad toward him, picked up a fountain pen and dashed words across the page. After ripping off the sheet and passing it to her, Hunt leaned back in his chair and linked his fingers over his flat stomach. Adie looked down at the list he'd handed her and quickly read through the bullet points. They ranged from buying Christmas gifts to organizing a couple of cocktail parties, decorating his apartment and booking a surfing holiday in Jeffrey's Bay sometime in the New Year.

The last item on the list was the one that intrigued her the most: to help with the final arrangements for his foundation's urban treasure hunt race... Now, that sounded interesting.

Adie placed the paper on his desk and crossed her legs. Hoping her expression matched his inscrutable one, she lifted one eyebrow, waiting for an explanation.

"Duncan takes care of most of what you provide. And he does his job exceptionally well."

She wouldn't be getting any business from him, Adie thought. Why would he pay her when he had his own personal concierge on staff? Now all she could hope for was that his fondness for Kate would prompt him to mention Treasures and Tasks to his rich friends. If Adie didn't sign up some new clients on retainer, she couldn't justify the costs of setting up a satellite branch in Manhattan.

Hunt continued, "However, Duncan is leaving shortly for a family emergency. I doubt he'll be back before Christmas and while he says he's going to carry on working, I don't want him to feel torn between his duty to someone he loves and his job." Hunt held Adie's eyes and she caught the flash of emotion in his expression, there and gone too fast for her to discern what he was feeling. He leaned forward and tapped the paper she'd placed on the desk. "I'm prepared to hire you to fill in for him. I presume you can handle all of this?"

Adie internally scoffed. Was he kidding? Compared to arranging a Michelin chef to cook in an igloo so her clients could have dinner under the northern lights, this was child's play.

"We can," Adie replied, picking up the list again. She frowned at the last item. "Can you give me a little more detail about the urban treasure hunt race?"

"It's my foundation's primary fundraising event of the year. Teams of two—one a professional sportsperson and one an underprivileged teen from one of the sports programs the foundation runs—race through lower Manhattan, looking for clues. The sports stars raise money for the foundation by asking people they know to pledge an amount for every leg completed. We receive a lot of corporate donations, as well."

"And when is it?"

Hunt grimaced. "This coming weekend. The hunt happens on Saturday, culminating in a cocktail party where we give out prizes."

"That sounds like so much fun," Kate said, smiling. "And Duncan arranged it all himself?"

Hunt returned Kate's smile and it was pure affection. "Duncan handled the entrants and matching the sports stars with the kids. There's a company that handles all the race details, they set up the route and place people along the way who hand out clues. The contestants just run around Manhattan, searching for clues and the first team to arrive at the designated endpoint earns money toward the teen's college fund. The professional team-mate wins triple matching funds from the foundation for the money they've raised. Everyone wins prizes at the evening event, as well." Hunt shrugged. "Duncan will know the details."

Adie's mind was running at warp speed. "What still needs to be done regarding the race?"

Hunt looked at her. "I know there are some outstanding issues. I'll ask Duncan to send you the list of what hasn't been confirmed. Expect it sometime later this evening."

"Is Duncan still on the premises?" Adie asked Hunter.

He looked at his watch and nodded. "My driver will be collecting him in five minutes to take him to the airport. He's flying out shortly."

"On your Gulfstream?" Kate asked him.

Hunt nodded. "Yeah."

Adie turned in her seat to face Kate and handed her

Hunt's list. "Can you go with Duncan to the airport and get all the information you can about how far he's got with regard to the various bullet points on this list? We might have to call him later, but I'd prefer not to disturb him after he's gone unless we really have to."

"I've already asked him to email you the file on the urban treasure hunt," Hunt interjected.

"Okay, good. Then go through all these other bullet points. I bet there are at least twenty things not on this list. Get those too."

Kate nodded and stood up. "I'm on it."

Adie smiled up at her. "Thanks, honey. I'll see you back at your place later, there are just a couple of points I need to iron out with Mr. Sheridan."

Kate sent her an uncertain look at the formal use of Hunt's name, but Adie gave the tiniest of head shakes and Kate nodded. After walking around the desk, she dropped a kiss on Hunt's cheek and sauntered from the room, moving easily on her spiky heels.

Hunt watched Kate leave and when the door closed behind her, he spoke again. "I think Kate is going to like working as a private concierge. It will suit her vibrant personality."

It wasn't what Adie had expected him to say. "I think it will too, but we need to pick up some clients before I can afford to employ her on a long-term basis. Kate, with her connections, will be expensive."

Hunt pushed his chair back and stood up, walking over to the state-of-the-art coffee machine in the corner of his large office. He offered her a cup and when Adie declined, he fixed himself a cup of coffee—unsweetened and black—and carried it over to the large window, leaning his shoulder into the glass.

Adie followed him and echoed his stance, folding her arms across her chest.

"I need help, at least until Duncan comes back." Hunt sipped from his cup, his gray eyes looking at her over the rim. "How does it work and how much do you cost?"

Adie ran over the financial implications, gave him a ballpark figure, and suggested that she send over a quote and a contract later.

"Well, it's not like I have much of a choice. Duncan's unavailable and I don't want to organize cocktail parties and decorate trees and go shopping."

"Well, Kate and I are happy to take care of all that for you," Adie told him, trying to sound brisk.

"Good." Hunt placed his cup on the bookcase nearby and turned to face her, moving closer until she could feel the heat radiating off him. He smelled so good, of soap and man and something expensive but understated. She wanted to bury her face in his neck and just inhale…

He can't be your Christmas caper, Adie. You've got enough on your plate without indulging in a festive fling.

And, as she'd reminded herself earlier, distracting herself by jumping into the arms of a man wasn't something she did anymore. It had been years since she'd been tempted to engage in that sort of behavior—

Hunt trailed his fingers over her cheek. "I haven't stopped thinking about kissing you. You've been on my mind all day."

—but, damn, Sheridan was temptation personified. Adie turned her cheek into his open palm.

"I don't sleep with my clients, Hunt." Was she informing him or reminding herself?

Both.

"That's sensible," Hunt said, bending down to nibble his way up her jaw. Adie tipped her chin up and to the side to give him better access.

From a place far away, sensible Adie spoke. "Seriously, Hunt, I don't sleep with my clients." Even back in the day, sleeping with a guy was a very big deal and most of her relationships imploded long before they got to that point.

"Haven't signed the contract yet…" Hunt muttered.

"But you will."

"Later," Hunt insisted, his lips moving over hers. Adie, knowing she should resist him, opened her mouth anyway, and when his tongue touched hers, she groaned. This was better, if at all possible, than last night. He seemed harder, tougher, sexier and she wanted him with every atom pulsing in her body.

And because she'd never felt this way, with anyone, ever, Adie pulled out of his arms and stepped back, her hands raised in a "back off" gesture. Whatever was zinging between them felt too intense, too powerful. He was a tsunami of soul-and-breath-and-thought-stealing lust.

Hunt, thank God, got the message, and instead of reaching for her, jammed his hands in his pockets. Adie, having noticed the very impressive erection tenting his pants, kept her eyes on his face. Yeah, the implacable distant businessman was gone, and a frustrated man stood in front of her. But Adie knew, soul-deep, that he wouldn't push her down a road she wasn't one hundred percent happy to walk.

"This isn't a good idea, Hunter."

"You thought it was an excellent idea last night," Hunt pointed out.

"I didn't know who you were last night and our mutual attraction caught me off guard," Adie replied. Off guard was an understatement, but he didn't need to know that.

"I don't date," Adie blurted out, needing to end this conversation.

Hunt barely reacted. "Neither do I."

That wasn't the reply she'd been expecting. "Why not?"

"I enjoy uncomplicated, no-strings-attached sex." It was an answer, but not to the question she'd asked.

With Hunter Sheridan, nothing was uncomplicated. Not their mutual desire, nor her desperate need to get her hands on him nor the flustered way he made her feel. Oh, she'd very much enjoy what he'd teach her sexually, but a roll around a big bed with him wasn't worth sacrificing the hard work she'd done to get to this point.

She no longer needed to chase attention, to look for validation in all the wrong places.

But what if she just wanted sex from him, her inner voice wheedled. Well, tough. It was Christmas and because the season made her feel emotional and vulnerable, she couldn't take the chance.

No, it was better not to take any risks.

Hunt swiped his thumb over her bottom lip before dropping his hand to his side. "I'm not going to push you, Adie. But anytime you want to change your mind, you know where to find me."

Adie straightened her shoulders and her spine. "I'm not going to change my mind."

Well, she'd *try* not to.

Hunt smiled his devastatingly sexy half smile, half smirk. "Oh, I think you will. Hopefully sooner rather than later."

Adie's mouth fell open at his arrogance, but before she could form the words to slap down his ego, he looked at his watch. "I need to get back to work. Send me your quote and the contract and I'll look it over."

Adie blinked, dizzy from his rapid change of subject. "Okay."

Hunt walked over to his desk and slid a card from a silver box on his desk. Flipping it over, he scribbled on the back before handing it to her. "That's my private phone number, you can reach me on it anytime, anywhere. Feel free to use it."

Adie didn't need him to draw her a picture. "I won't."

"Yeah, I think you will," Hunt replied, amused. "And I expect to see you here, twice a day, once in the morning and again in the evening, to keep me updated."

Adie glared at him. "I could just send you an email!"

Hunt picked up her bag, gestured for her to walk over to the door. He opened it and dropped her bag over her shoulder. "Yeah, you could, but that wouldn't be any fun."

"I didn't think you were the fun type," Adie told him, feeling cross and outmaneuvered.

"I'm not, but I'll make an exception for you." Hunt bent down and dropped a kiss on the corner of her mouth. "See you back here at nine tomorrow morning. Unless…"

"Unless what?"

He nodded to the card in her hand. "Unless you call me between now and then."

Adie, not knowing how to respond or what else to do, stomped away.

Three

After a few days in Manhattan, and at Kate's insistence, Adie had moved into the guest room of Kate's Chelsea apartment.

She was mostly house trained, Kate laughingly informed her when making the offer, but she wasn't great at mornings. She'd been telling the truth. Adie, dressed to make her way to the Upper East Side and Hunt's building, shook her head at Kate's bedhead and dopey eyes.

Knowing that she needed some answers from her friend, Adie hastily poured Kate a cup of coffee, fixed it the way she liked it and shoved her into a seat at the small table in the kitchen. Then Adie pushed the cup into Kate's hands, hoping her return to reality wouldn't take too long.

The first sip did nothing, neither did the second. Kate's eyes remained foggy.

Adie picked up her tub of yogurt. "Come on, Williams, I need to go, and I need you to wake up and focus."

Kate lifted up a finger and took another few sips of her coffee. When she stood up to refill her cup, Adie knew she was on her way back to the land of the living.

Picking up her tablet, Adie opened the list she was working on and fired a couple of questions at Kate. Jotting down her responses with her stylus, she nodded. She asked Kate whether she'd contacted caterers for Hunt's annual Christmas cocktail party and received a laconic reply.

"So what's going on between you and Hunt?" Kate asked, looking at Adie over the rim of her cup.

"Nothing," Adie replied, turning around to throw her plastic yogurt container in the trash. And that was the truth. Nothing was happening and nothing was going to happen between her and Hunt. No Christmas, or any other type of, flings for her.

"Pfft! I don't believe you."

"Why wouldn't you?"

"We've had a couple of meetings with Hunt and the room feels ten degrees hotter whenever you are together and the chemistry between you crackles," Kate said, lifting her feet to rest her heels on the edge of her seat.

"Yeah, we're attracted to each other, but nothing is going to happen." She'd give Kate that much.

"Why not?" Kate demanded. "Is it because of Griselda?"

Who? Adie shook her head, confused. "Who is Griselda?"

Kate pulled a face, looking uneasy. "Uh…she's well, uh… I don't know how to describe her."

"Try," Adie snapped. When Kate didn't reply, she

repeated the question, pushing the words through gritted teeth. Okay, she was totally overreacting here. She had no right to be jealous. She and Hunt had only shared a couple of kisses and he wanted to sleep with her...

But if he had a girlfriend, she'd be not only furious with him, but she'd be disappointed in him too. Her parents openly flaunted their affairs and, as a result, Adie deeply respected commitment and fidelity. If she did indulge in flings, affairs or brief relationships, men involved in relationships would be strictly off-limits.

And her questions didn't mean she was going to have a fling with Hunter Sheridan! But there was nothing wrong in gathering intelligence...

"Is she his girlfriend? Partner? Significant other?" Adie demanded, conscious of a tiny ache in her heart. No, she refused to feel disappointed or hurt. She'd met Hunt Sheridan a few days ago; she had no right to feel possessive...

They'd kissed, twice. She was totally overreacting. Totally.

Kate wrinkled her nose. "Nah..."

"You don't sound convinced," Adie stated, folding her arms against her chest.

"I don't know how to describe what they are, Ades, and no, I'm not avoiding the question."

Adie glared at her, picked up her tablet and accessed the internet. She typed "Hunt Sheridan + girlfriend" into the search bar and cursed when her screen filled with dozens of results. Adie opened a popular online magazine and felt her heart sink at the photographs of Hunt at a prestigious gala, his strong arm around an exquisite woman's tiny waist.

As a child, Adie desperately wanted to be taller,

blonder—more of a Cinderella than a Cinders. Griselda was exactly who Adie wanted to be when she grew up. Like Adie's mother, Vivien, Griselda was a tall, skinny, elegant, cool blonde who owned her own string of dance studios. She'd been a prima ballerina before injury cut her career short, and she and Hunt, according to the website, had been an item for two or so years.

Adie lifted her head to look at Kate. "The press calls her his girlfriend."

Kate waved her comment away. "Hunt doesn't. As far as I know, their relationship is…undefined." Kate shoved her hand into her hair, obviously uncomfortable. "Just ask Hunt if you want to know."

"I'm not interested."

Kate laughed at her ludicrous statement. "Of course you are, you're nuts about him!"

"Am not."

Kate's smile grew wider. "Oh, honey, you can lie to yourself but not me." Kate ran her finger up and down her coffee mug, her expression turning serious.

"I can't talk about her, Adie. I won't talk about her and Hunt's relationship. Just like I wouldn't talk to Hunt about your relationships."

Adie had to appreciate Kate's loyalty and her disinclination to gossip.

"Of course, you'd have to have a love life for me to talk about it," Kate pointed out.

Adie stuck out her tongue at her friend. It was a childish gesture, but effective.

Kate's grin slowly faded. "If you really want to know, ask Hunt."

"Kate!" Adie wheedled, pride taking a beating from her curiosity. "Don't leave me hanging, tell me about Grisella."

"Griselda," Kate corrected her, "and no, I won't. Besides, you said there wasn't anything happening between you and him so why do you care?"

Kate walked away, leaving her words hanging in the air. Adie resisted the impulse to wrestle her to the ground and beat the information out of her.

And Kate, damn her, was right. Adie had no intention of having any type of fling, Christmas or otherwise, with Hunter and she didn't care that he had a girlfriend. Market research in Manhattan was this year's distraction of choice and so far, it was doing a pretty crap job.

She had to up her game. Immediately.

Hunt missed his early morning meeting with Adie as he'd flown to Chicago at the ass crack of dawn to deal with a wage dispute at one of his distribution centers, but she'd been on his mind all day. He'd tried to work on the way to Chicago, but he kept checking his phone for an acknowledgment of the text he'd sent telling her he'd see her back at his office around six.

It was now six fifteen and fully dark as Hunt left his car and crossed the wet sidewalk to walk into the lobby of his building. Stepping into his private elevator, he tapped his foot irritably, wishing the damn thing would move faster.

If she wasn't sitting in his office waiting for him, he'd be seriously annoyed. So annoyed, in fact, that he might have to track her down at Kate's apartment. He needed to see her, dammit.

Need...

He didn't like that word. He'd trained himself as a child not to need or rely on anyone, not his mom or any of his foster parents. In his twenties, divorce and death reinforced the idea that he could only ever rely on himself. No, he *wanted* to see Adie. There was a huge difference between the two emotions.

Hunt rarely kept his staff working beyond five and when he stepped onto his floor, he saw that all the office lights were turned down low. The place was deserted, and he doubted Adie would stay in a strange, empty office.

Hunt stepped into his dark office and tossed his briefcase in the direction of his leather couch. Instead of the familiar *whoomp* he expected to hear, a low scream hit his ears, quickly followed by a curse. "Ow, ow, ow!"

Hunt's fist hit the light switch and he immediately looked toward the couch. Adie half lay on the couch, her long-sleeved black dress hiked to show off a very lovely leg. His briefcase rested in her lap and she rubbed her shoulder and glared at him.

"Why the hell did you do that?" Adie demanded, her eyes round and wide.

Hunt quickly crossed the room to reach her. He sat down on the edge of the couch, his thigh pressed into her hip. "Because I didn't expect you to be in my office, sitting on my sofa in the dark. Are you okay?"

Adie winced and prodded her shoulder with her fingertips. "I'm going to have a bruise."

"Do you need some ice?" Hunt asked, trying to think of a way he could move the tight round neck of her dress to inspect her shoulder.

"No, it's fine."

Damn.

Hunt lifted his briefcase off her lap, placed it on the floor and noticed Adie's heels were also on the floor, tipped on their side. His eyes flew over her—still gorgeous—but there was a head-sized indentation on the green throw pillow next to her. He looked at her, amused. "Were you asleep?"

Adie looked like he'd caught her rifling through his desk drawers. "I've been working long hours for weeks and weeks. Christmas is the busiest season for me. I was up at two this morning, dealing with a Japanese client who has bought a very rare, very expensive Samoyed puppy from a breeder in California."

"I've never heard of that breed," Hunt stated.

"I hadn't either and I asked my client about it, which was a huge mistake. He spent twenty minutes telling me about the puppy's bloodline and how much it cost."

"Give me the one-minute version."

"White, double-layer coat, originally from Siberia, intelligent, sociable and inquisitive. Very, very rare and this puppy cost the equivalent of a medium-sized car."

Hunt raised his eyebrows. "And you have to get it from California to Japan? How? In a crate?"

Adie's wide mouth curved and her smile hit her eyes. Hunt felt like he was witnessing the birth of a new star, the rearrangement of a faraway galaxy.

He sucked in a breath, looking for air.

"My clients' pets don't go in crates, Hunter. No, I found a dog walker who was prepared to collect the puppy and fly with him, on a private jet hired for the occasion, from Los Angeles to Osaka."

"Wow."

Adie pushed her hands through her hair and tugged at the hem of her dress. "Anyway, I didn't get much sleep last night so I thought I'd just close my eyes for a minute. I didn't expect to get brained by a briefcase."

"I didn't expect you to be here," Hunt replied. Her hand went down to the hem of her dress and he captured the fabric between his thumb and index fingers, idly rubbing the soft material. "And, trust me, I have no problem looking at your legs."

Adie blushed, then sucked her bottom lip between her teeth. Her eyes, staring into his, were filled with a mixture of lust and confusion. He wondered which emotion would win.

"This is crazy, Hunt."

"Can't argue with that," Hunt agreed. "I take one look at you and all the blood in my brain heads south. All I can think about is getting you naked and making you mine."

Adie covered her face with her hands, but through the cracks in her fingers, he saw her complexion turn pink. He couldn't remember when last he'd seen a woman blush. It wasn't something that happened much anymore.

And Hunt was super curious to know how far down her blushes extended.

"I want you, Adie. You want me too."

"Well, duh," Adie muttered. "But it's not that simple, Hunt."

Hunt could see her looking for an excuse and knew she was going to say that he was her client, that they should be professional, that this could get complicated. Hunt decided to cut down her arguments before she could voice them. "We're old enough and smart enough to keep work and our attraction separate, Adie. One has nothing to do with the other."

"Theoretically," Adie replied. "But it never quite works out that way, does it?"

"If we want it to, it will," Hunt assured her. But instead of looking more relaxed, Adie's shoulders were up around her ears and she twisted a funky, vintage ring around the middle finger of her right hand. Something was really bugging her...

Oh, hell. Somehow Hunt knew she must've heard, or read, about Griselda's presence in his life and that she'd added two and two and reached pi.

Dammit.

Adie's next words confirmed his suspicions. "You have someone in your life, Hunt. And I don't like the idea of being the other woman."

Okay, he was going to strangle Kate with his bare hands because she was the only one who would've mentioned Griselda, the only person with the temerity to interfere in his business. The little brat!

"I don't have a relationship with Griselda."

Adie's eyebrows lifted, silently telling him not to BS her. "Not that there was anything to end, but I called it off a couple of days before I met you."

Adie cocked her head to the side. "How can you end something that is un-endable?"

Hunt smiled at her made-up word. And how could he explain Griselda to Adie without sounding like a complete dog? Griselda had been convenient and Griselda considered him equally convenient... They were each a resource the other used. So much so that Griselda had propositioned him with the idea of being her sperm donor.

God, he'd barely given that idea, or Griselda, any thought since he'd met Adie. In fact, Adie was currently occupying all of his mental energy. It was a very unusual situation.

"It's over and done. Can we stop talking about her now?" Hunt demanded, sounding irascible.

Adie scooted down the couch behind him and found some space to swing her legs off. Her feet touched the floor and she stood up. Hunt stared at her as she slid her feet into a pair of bright orange heels.

Okay, when they made love she could keep those sexy shoes on…

"What do you want from me, Hunter?" Adie asked, walking over to his desk and sitting on the edge, her legs swinging.

Sex, maybe a couple of laughs, a fun way to end the year. Hunt believed in being upfront and honest, he didn't want to deal with hurt feelings or confusion. Sometimes, he was convinced that casual sex required more negotiation and emotional awareness than entering into a long-term relationship.

Hunt felt his nerves prickle and the moisture disappeared from his tongue. He felt ridiculous. He was a man in his thirties who had the right to just want some fun. Provided that Adie felt safe and was on board, they could have a great time.

Keep it simple and free of ambiguity.

"I was married once and it didn't work out." Okay, that wasn't where he'd planned to start his explanation and it wasn't relevant to the present situation. What the actual hell? He never discussed Joni, with anyone. He didn't like explaining to people that he'd been a fool.

"I'm sorry." Adie tipped her head to the side, obviously curious. "What happened?"

He wouldn't tell her. It was his business and not pertinent to this discussion. "She screwed around on me and was addicted to using my credit card."

God, now his mouth was operating without his brain's permission.

Adie winced. "She was a shopper."

That was like saying Usain Bolt was quite quick. Feeling like he had hands squeezing his neck, Hunt yanked his tie down and undid the button holding his collar closed. "I don't talk about her, about what happened."

Except that he had just expressed far more than he'd ever expressed before. To anyone. Hunt dismissed that thought and pushed his suit jacket back, his hands on his hips. "She's not pertinent to what we were talking about."

"That you have a girlfriend."

"I told you I ended it! I do not have a goddamn girlfriend! Jesus!" Hunt gripped the bridge of his nose, hoping to squeeze his frustration away.

"Does Griselda live in Manhattan?"

Why was she asking? Did it matter? "She lives in the city but she's currently on the West Coast, she'll be there until Christmas. And none of this has anything to do with me wanting to sleep with you!"

Adie's huge round eyes met his. She put her thumbnail between her teeth and flicked it against her front tooth. Hunt wished she would end the torture and put him out of his misery. It wasn't difficult, he just required a yes or a no.

"I'm not sure, Hunt," Adie eventually told him.

Ah, well… *Hell.*

Adie gripped the desk on either side of her hips and Hunt fought the urge not to go to her. "I presume you are only offering a one night stand or a couple of one night stands, right?"

For some reason, his throat felt thick and tight and he couldn't force a yes up his throat. So Hunt nodded instead.

"Thought so." Adie hauled in a deep breath, then another. "Look, this is a pretty difficult time of year for me and sometimes, for complicated reasons I don't intend to explain, I've been known to look for a distraction, for something to help me through the season of love and goodwill to all men. That's the reason I am here, in Manhattan, during the busiest time of year for me…because I'm hoping to be so busy I can't think."

Hunt wanted to know what demons were nipping at her heels. What compelled her to keep herself so busy?

"But I don't use men to get me out of my head and between the work you've given me, my existing clients and trying to meet and sign up new clients, I am slammed."

Hunt watched her dark eyes and while she wasn't lying, she wasn't telling the complete truth either. Man, she fascinated him. On a deeper, darker and more dangerous level—a level he preferred to avoid.

Yet, he couldn't help thinking that she'd yet to say no.

"Are you saying no?" It was, after all, vital to be clear.

Adie nodded. "I'm saying no."

Hunt felt his stomach sink to his toes. Was that disappointment he felt? God, he'd been rejected before—not often, but it had happened—but it had never stung like this before. What was it about this slight, quirky woman who pulled unidentified and strange feelings to the surface?

One long kiss and she'd be begging for more…

So would he.

But he didn't want Adie like that. He wanted her to have no reservations, no second thoughts. He wanted her to be fully, utterly, wholly in the moment with him. Nothing less was acceptable. For that brief time, he wanted all of her and he wouldn't get it if she had the smallest doubt niggling at the edges of her mind.

Hell.

Adie jumped off the desk and walked over to the sofa. "It's been a long day and I have a bit of a headache. Do you mind if we get to work?"

Hunt was frustrated. He supposed he was spoiled. He'd never had to work this hard with Griselda, or any other woman. Once a man obtained a certain level of power, things usually came easy. Adie was anything but.

And, admittedly, she did look tired. Hunt could see the fatigue in her eyes, the strain around her mouth. He'd worked through fevers and migraines, and back when he'd been a professional ballplayer, he'd played with a cracked ankle and a concussion. Long story short, he never allowed anything to get in the way of what he needed to do. Maybe Adie was the same. But she obviously needed rest, an early night. If he suggested that she take off, he knew she'd insist on working.

Adie, he was coming to realize, had a helluva work ethic and a mile-wide stubborn streak.

"Look, I'm really beat and I've had a horrible day," Hunt lied. "Can we pick this up in the morning?"

As he knew it would, relief flashed through Adie's eyes. "Sure. I need to go over the final arrangements for the urban treasure hunt race with you tomorrow so I'll see you in the morning."

Hunt remembered that he had an early breakfast meeting and that the rest of his day was equally busy. "Sorry, I'm going to have to miss that. What about tomorrow evening, the same time again?"

Adie shook her head. "I promised Kate I'd go to her folks' house and be the referee as the Williams family argues about the best way to decorate Christmas cookies."

A long, hard shudder hit Hunt. Icing cookies plus memories of being with Steve and the Williams family was a combustible cocktail. "And you think that's a fun way to spend an evening?"

"I'm staying with Kate and it seemed rude not to accept the invitation," Adie replied. "Are you going?"

"I was invited, but no. You should know that Kate's clan is nosy and noisy and competitive and loud—"

Adie smiled. "Will there be wine?"

"Lots of wine. And Richard's eggnog, which is, I have to warn you, strong enough to strip the enamel off your teeth."

Adie clapped her hands, excited. "I love eggnog!"

It wouldn't take much for Adie, who didn't weigh more than a feather, to become intoxicated. Maybe he should go along to keep an eye on her...

"You're connected to Kate through her brother Steve, right?" Adie asked before Hunt could examine why he was feeling protective over this English girl who would be leaving the States in a couple of weeks.

Hunt nodded. "Yes, Steve and I played ball together. He was my best friend and business partner. He died a while back."

Hunt remembered attending the Williams clan's Christmas cookie bakeoff for years before Steve died. It had always been one of the happiest nights of his year. He'd enjoyed listening to the raucous, loving family argue and tease each other. They were the family he'd always dreamed of as a child. Many years had passed since Steve's death, but Hunter still received an invitation every year. He hadn't been back. He'd attended other functions with the Williams family, but he always found an excuse to miss the Christmas cookie bakeoff. And most of their other Christmas festivities too.

"I should make an effort to see them since it's been a while. But I prefer to meet them at restaurants or at neutral venues."

"Because being around them, in the place where you can visualize Steve, hurts too much?"

Exactly so.

Hunt expected her to dig for more, to put her fingers into the small crack he'd presented and widen the fissure, but Adie surprised him when her only reply was an understanding smile. Good. Because he had no intention of talking to her about Steve, about how gutted he still felt, how much he missed his friend, especially at this time of year.

Adie had dropped into his life, and in a few weeks, she'd drop out. One didn't talk about best friends and how much one missed them to people who wouldn't be permanent fixtures in one's life.

Okay, that meant not talking to anybody about Steve, but that was okay. Hunt wasn't a heart-to-heart-conversation kind of guy. What was the point of talking, anyway? Steve was gone and talking wouldn't bring him back, wouldn't replace what Hunt had lost.

A friend, a brother, a strong connection.

And the only conversation he was really interested in having with Adie consisted of whether or not she'd spend the night with him. Or a couple of nights. However, he phrased it, he just wanted a hell-yes, take-me-to-bed answer.

But he couldn't push, wouldn't.

"Can you look at your schedule and maybe carve out an hour for me sometime tomorrow afternoon?" Adie asked, breaking the silence between them. "I do need to get your input on a couple of issues."

Hunt did a mental review of his day and nodded.

"Meet me here at five and I'll have you out of here by six, in plenty of time for the great cookie contest."

Adie nodded, dropped her head and stared at the floor. Then she looked past him to his view of Central Park and he saw the indecision on her face. What was she wrestling with? Whether to sleep with him or not? But her words, when they came, had no connection to what he wanted.

"I know this is none of my business but you should go, you know. To the cookie contest. No matter how hard it is. Kate talks about her twin a lot, Hunter, and how she and her family miss him," Adie continued, her smile sad. "As Kate told me, they not only lost Steve when he died, they also, sort of, lost you."

Hunt pushed back the lapels of his jacket to shove his hands into the pockets of his pants. His instinct was to snap at her, to tell her to mind her own business, that he was her client. That the only "getting personal" he wanted involved them shedding their clothes. And he could do that; he was enough of a bastard to get his point across. But, instead of pushing back, Hunter considered another response.

"He was the closest thing I had to a brother. And while he was alive, they were my family." He looked away, knowing his voice was close to cracking from the grief that was still, after so long, a living, breathing entity? Why was he telling her things he'd never been able to tell Kate or anyone else? Why was she able to pull his words to the surface?

"I think it's obvious they still consider you part of the family." Adie ran her hand down his arm, gripped his hand and squeezed. "Make cookies with them, Hunt. Even if you don't want to renew that close connection, it's a small thing that would give them a lot of pleasure. And it's the season to do good."

How could he resist those big brown expressive eyes? And, let's be honest here, if Adie was going to spend the evening with the Williams clan, then Hunt wanted to be there too. Something about her, more than lust and attraction, drew him.

Hunt, uncomfortable with the emotion swirling between them, mock shuddered. "Ugh, Christmas."

"Scrooge," Adie teased him. "I'm going to go." Pulling her hand from his, she walked toward the door and Hunt's eyes dropped from her luscious ass to her shapely legs. He could easily imagine his hands underneath her butt, those legs around his hips as he pushed into her.

He wanted her. Worse than that, he needed her.

Dammit. There was that word again.

"Adie?"

Her hand on the handle to the door, she turned. "Yeah?"

"Give my proposition some thought, okay? We'd be good together."

"Okay, I'll think about it."

Hunter squinted at her departing back, knowing that was as much as he was going to get from her.

For now.

She'd think about it?
Was she nuts?

Adie hailed a cab outside Hunt's building and gave the driver Kate's address. Then she asked herself why she hadn't flatly refused Hunt's straightforward offer. Oh, she knew why she wanted to say yes—he was volcano hot, she melted every time she got within thirty feet of him and she couldn't stop thinking about how good they'd be in bed—but no was the only possible answer.

Okay, she'd propositioned him the other night and, while it was completely out of character for her, it was still different from his offer fifteen minutes ago. On the night of the market they'd been two strangers. She'd hadn't known who he was. She'd thought it would be a "ships passing in the night" type of deal.

Uncharacteristic, sure but also uncomplicated. And instinctive...

She should've stuck to her guns, kept her no a no. Adie was mentally backtracking like mad. Sure, there were good and obvious reasons why she shouldn't sleep with him: he was her client, she wanted to do business with him in the future, she wanted him to recommend her to his rich friends and associates and she did not want to give the impression to him, or anyone, that she sealed the deal with sex.

And he'd recently ended his relationship with his long-term girlfriend. Adie wasn't interested in being the Band Aid to fix his dented ego.

Adie sighed and banged the back of her head against the seat of the taxi, reluctantly admitting that those were all valid excuses, even though they weren't the main reason why she should categorically refuse his offer.

Her hesitation was with Christmas. The feelings that bubbled up to the surface this time of year were so much stronger than at other times. From the middle of November until the New Year, these few weeks magnified and exacerbated all her fears and insecurities. The season was a trigger for her to indulge in excessive self-reflection about her past and to compare herself to other people who seemed to have more and do more.

She'd taught herself to drop her bad habits of looking for attention and validation in all the wrong places. For ten and a half months of the year she celebrated her single status, her commitment to her career, her ability to dash around the world and not have to explain to anyone where she was going or how long she'd be away. For roughly three hundred and thirty days a year, she reveled in her freewheeling lifestyle, completely content to be a wealthy, single woman with no pets, husband or children. For most of the year, she didn't give a thought to being partnerless or childless. She was content, happy even, to be on her own.

But at Christmastime…

God, the season slapped her silly. As soon as she saw the first decorated tree, the first string of Christmas lights, heard a favorite carol, the ghosts of Christmas past, present and future dropped by to say hi…

And soon they were whispering in her ear…

You should be looking for love. Wouldn't you like a child someday, someone to buy gifts for, to watch his face light with joy when he sees the presents Santa left on Christmas morning?

Look at this lovely advertisement of a family having fun together. And—look!—they even have a dog! Don't you want a family like that? What about a dog? You'd like a dog…

Adie stared out the grimy window of the cab, oblivious to the Christmas decorations and the sleet touching the shoulders and heads of the pedestrians on the sidewalk. At this time of year, she tended to obsess about her parents and wonder why they couldn't love her, or show any interest in her, why her mom was so completely disinterested in being her mom. At Christmastime she had many "what if" thoughts—what if she had a husband, what if she had kids?

Would she feel happier, lighter, more fulfilled? Would having a family erase the hurt her parents caused? Did she really want to live the rest of her life being single? How long would flying all over the world, making her clients' lives easier, fulfill her?

Would she ever experience a love-filled, cozy Christmas?

She never felt like this in March or September, in August or at the beginning of spring. No, her descent into being maudlin and morose was directly linked to the festive season so right now, she had to stay objective, practical and unemotional.

Adie didn't want to backslide into bad habits so dating was out of the question. And having a festive fling when she wasn't as emotionally strong as she could be… It wasn't wise. She was a careful woman and she had no intention of walking through that minefield. She was vulnerable. This wasn't a good time of year for her and her usually impenetrable, keep-the-hell-out wall was a little cracked.

Sleeping with Hunt—with any man, but especially with Hunt—would be like handing him a sledgehammer and pointing out the most brittle, easily broken bricks.

Nope, not happening. Not today, tomorrow or anytime soon. Not with Hunt or with anyone else.

Four

The next evening, Hunt found himself in Carnegie Hill, seated at the Williams' long dining table covered in a bright red tablecloth festooned with Santas, Christmas music playing in the background and a glass of whiskey was in easy reach.

In front of him was an oversized cookie in the shape of a Christmas tree; and multicolored bowls of frosting, sprinkles and sweets littered the length of the table.

Rachel Williams, bright-eyed and thoroughly excited, stood at the head of the table, the wine in her glass sloshing with every gesture she made. Kate looked more like her mom than ever before, Hunt noticed.

"Quiet! Quiet!"

Hunt looked around the table and smiled as ten faces turned in her direction. Mike, the youngest was flying single at tonight's Christmas event—he was, per Kate, an even bigger player than Steve had been and that was saying something. But Grant, the oldest brother, was married and had a two-year-old girl, Bella, and a four-year-old boy, Cayden. Cayden was sitting on Kate's lap and nobody but Hunt seemed to notice the kid was sneaking pieces of his already-broken Christmas tree cookie to Rachel's Maltese poodle sitting under the table.

Hunt's eyes moved to Adie. Like him, she was still dressed in her work clothes, a white button-down shirt and black pants, severe but oh-so sexy. He ran a hand over his face. Sitting across from her, being here, felt right, like this moment was long overdue.

That being said, it was still overwhelming. He wasn't used to so much noise: people talking over each other and the Christmas carols in the background. To Hunt, it felt like someone had dialed up the volume on his life, and he couldn't help looking around for Steve, convinced his friend was in the kitchen or just around the corner. Then Hunt remembered Steve was dead and it was a gut punch.

Hunt had made a habit of distancing himself from this much emotion. He'd made a habit of forcing it down, pushing it away, and at work he could easily do that. He and Steve might've started the company shortly after they both retired from professional sports, but Hunt had managed and grown the business over the past ten years without his friend. The memories of Steve at work weren't strong.

In this house, they were everywhere.

His being here tonight had to be hard for the family too, but they weren't acting like it. When Rachel opened her front door and saw him standing there with Adie, tears leaked from her eyes. She'd pulled him into a hug, not letting go for the longest time. Richard, a little more stoic, shook Hunt's hand and clapped his shoulder, and Grant and Mike greeted him like they'd seen him yesterday. Hunt felt guilty for avoiding this particular tradition, all their Christmas functions, and felt equally guilty for not spending more time with them than he had.

He'd missed them and they'd, apparently, missed him back. It felt good. Weird. But good.

Rachel banged her spoon on the table to make her noisy family stop talking and Richard reached up and gently removed the glass of wine from her hand. He placed it on the table and looked at Hunt, who was sitting to his right.

"She's the clumsiest creature alive and this carpet frequently looks like a crime scene."

Rachel tapped his shoulder with her spoon. "Hush now."

Richard rolled his eyes at Hunt and turned his attention back to his wife. Rachel made eye contact with everyone at the table individually before speaking. "I've changed the Family Cookie Contest rules—"

"Are you allowed to do that without our consent?" Kate cheekily asked her.

"Yeah, Mom, can you do that? Isn't this family run as a democracy?" Grant asked, purely, Hunt decided, to wind Rachel up. Grant was braver than he could ever be. Rachel was tiny but she was fierce.

"This family is not, in any shape or form, a democracy. Since I spent twelve or more hours in labor with every one of you, I am your supreme ruler," Rachel retorted, but Hunt heard the affection in her voice.

"That's pretty accurate actually," Richard commented, his tone dry as dust.

Rachel narrowed her eyes at him. "In front of you

is a giant tree cookie and participation is mandatory...
everyone has to decorate one."

"And how do we judge the winner?" Kate demanded.
Hunt heard the competitive streak in her voice and
smiled. God, she and Steve were so alike.

"We take photos of our trees and we share them on
social media. The tree with the most likes is the winner."

"That's not fair, Hunt has a pretty big fan base," Kate
whined. "He's famous."

After much discussion about the rules and deadlines
and how to count the likes—and after giving him a
handicap—Rachel finally gave her family permission
to start decorating their cookies. Hunt, not having a
creative bone in his body looked at the bowls of frosting and the piping bag at his elbow and shook his head.
With Duncan out of the office, Hunt was incredibly
busy and yet he was sitting here about to pipe icing on
cookies.

But, honestly, there was no place he'd rather be.

Adie flashed him a smirky smile and expertly
twisted her piping bag so that the white frosting filled
one corner of the bag. "Watch and learn."

Hunt followed her directions and soon had his cookie
covered in white frosting. He reached for a bowl of
chocolate buttons and placed them around the edge of
the tree, pleased by his efforts.

He popped a button into his mouth, caught Adie's
eye and instantly remembered the exceptional one-of-a-
kind chocolates he'd tasted a few days back. "Well, it's
not chili and bacon," he told her when she met his gaze.

Adie blushed, but before she could respond, Grant directed a question at him. "Kate's been telling me about
your foundation's urban treasure hunt. It was an in-

spired idea to team celebrities with teenagers from the foundation's sports programs. And running through the city sounds amazing. You're going to have such a good time."

Hunt shook his head. "Oh, I'm not running."

Everyone turned to look at him and he frowned at their perplexed faces. He lifted his hands in the air. "What? Why are you all looking at me like that?"

"I thought you were part of a team. Why on earth aren't you participating?" Adie voiced the question they all, obviously, wanted the answer to.

Actually, that was a damn good question. Why wasn't he running in his own damn race? Running was something he enjoyed but, like so much, it was way down his list of priorities. Work, and more work, filled positions one to five.

Work was all he did.

Hunt wriggled, uncomfortable with the way the Williams clan, including the kids, were looking at him. Adie just sat in her chair, smiling at his discomfort.

He didn't have a decent excuse and he didn't want to tell them that the thought of running hadn't occurred to him. "I'm too busy, even more so than normal because Duncan is out of the office and my workload is intense."

"It's a couple of hours on Saturday, Hunter, and everybody, including you, deserves some downtime," Adie told him, resting her forearms on the table, her elbow precariously close to her glass of eggnog. He reached across the table and moved the glass to a safer spot.

"Even if it was something I wanted to do—" and to be honest, he kinda, sorta, did want to "—I can't enter because I don't have someone to run it with me. The kids involved have already been matched with the athletes and have, hopefully, started to develop a relation-ship with their mentors."

"It's your race, you can add someone to the regis-tration roll or you can run with whomever you want to," Kate said.

True. He mentally thought through some of his ac-quaintances and ex-teammates and realized they were either already partaking in the race or had previous commitments. "Steve would be my go-to person," Hunt quietly stated. There, he'd mentioned Steve's name. For the first time in a decade, he'd brought Steve into the conversation. Hunt felt Richard's hand on his shoul-der, the manly squeeze. Talking about Steve was hard, but damn, he deserved to be part of the conversation.

Hunt looked at Rachel and, on seeing the tears in her eyes, quickly looked away. God, if she started crying, he wouldn't be able to bear it.

"Since the foundation is named after Steve, what about one of Steve's brothers running with Hunt?" Adie's brisk question cut through the tension.

Grant shook his head. "I'd love to but we're leaving to go out of town tomorrow."

Adie looked at Mike, who shook his head. "Sorry, I'm unavailable too."

Kate pouted. "I see nobody asked me."

Adie patted her back. "Honey, your idea of exercise is binge-watching a series on Netflix."

"Funny," Kate retorted.

When their laughter died down, Hunt shrugged, ig-noring his spurt of disappointment. "It's not a big deal and I really should work. I'll be at the start and then I'll see everyone at the cocktail party later."

"I'll be your partner."

Hunt's eyes flew back to Adie, as did everyone else's. "What? Why?"

"It sounds like fun," Adie told him. "I get to run around Manhattan chasing down clues in odd places. It'll be awesome!"

"It's a seven-mile race," Hunt pointed out.

"I used to run cross-country as a kid and, at university I loved running marathons. I still, occasionally manage a five-mile run on the treadmill. Pfft, I'll be fine," Adie said, brushing off his concerns over her fitness.

"But won't you be busy organizing the day?" Hunt asked her.

Kate answered for Adie. "Nope, the events company is in charge from the moment the teams arrive at the morning start. And Adie's already delegated the awards dinner and dance following the race to me so I'll be around and able to deal with any last-minute problems."

Hunt looked at Adie and saw the challenge in her eyes. Laughter tipped up the edges of her mouth. "What, Sheridan, are you scared that one of your old teammates, or one of the younger kids, might beat you, a New York native?" she teased.

No, he wasn't scared because that was never going to happen. He pointed his piping bag at Adie. "You'd better not slow me down."

"Pfft, you'd better not slow *me* down. And my tree cookie is way better than yours."

Hunt looked down at his tree and saw that the white frosting had slid off, taking six chocolate buttons with it. He scowled at Adie, who just grinned. Unable to resist her impish face, he flicked a button across the table in her direction.

"Hunter Sheridan, we do not throw food!" Rachel

scolded him and Hunt felt like he was nineteen again. It was both terrifying and reassuring.

"Yes, ma'am."

As the conversation moved on, Hunt looked around the table at the large, loving family and contrasted their affection, their obvious enjoyment in being with each other with what Griselda had proposed—loveless co-parenting with their child being raised more by a nanny than by them. If he ever had a child, he wanted to raise it within a tight, loving, noisy, affectionate family and that would require him to make a commitment, to relinquish his freedom, to give up control.

He couldn't do it, not now, not ever. He'd worked so hard to create a world where he felt comfortable operating. He preferred keeping women, all people, at a distance.

Hunter briefly wondered how Griselda's West Coast trip was going and shrugged away his curiosity. Their road together had split into two forks, one for him and one for her. He was okay with that. Everything had its season after all.

Hunt looked across the table at Adie, who was deep in conversation with Rachel. If he had to equate women to seasons then Griselda was winter, but Adie was spring. Bright, vibrant, interesting...*new*.

But still just a season, and his time with her, when he finally got her into bed, would pass quickly.

She'd move on and so would he because nothing lasted forever.

When Adie suggested she be Hunt's partner for the Amazing Race–style treasure hunt across Manhattan, she'd thought it would be a small event, with them mostly running through Central Park.

Choosing to concentrate on buying Hunt's gifts for his business colleagues, staff and friends and organizing his corporate Christmas events, and keeping up with the never ending requests from her existing clients, Adie had handed most of the race related work over to Kate and had minimal input into the foundation's event. As a result, she hadn't taken in many of the details.

The race, she'd quickly realized when she arrived at the starting point, was bigger and bolder than anything she expected. There were reporters and news crews, and crowds of onlookers were contained behind the tape. And while they were starting the race in the park, they'd be winding their way through Midtown before heading for lower Manhattan.

So far today she'd seen an Olympic figure skater, a world-class swimmer, lots of famous basketball players, golfers and many baseball players. Their teenage running mates looked wide-eyed and excited.

While she'd been a runner in school and was naturally fit, she'd forgotten that Hunt had once been a world-class athlete. She'd also forgotten to take into consideration that Hunt's legs were a lot longer than hers. And, as he'd told her at the starting line, he regularly ran ten miles.

And competitive, dear Lord, he was competitive!

They were in Chelsea on the fourth of seven legs and Adie, breathing heavily, was dodging tourists and residents, trying and failing, to keep up with Hunt's long-legged stride. They were, as far as they knew, in either second or third place and Hunt was determined to be first. He was the head of the foundation, he'd reminded her, he needed to lead by example.

His leading by example might just kill her, but whatever.

It wasn't in his nature to trail behind anyone, Adie thought, keeping her eye on his broad back in the insulated lime green running tops they both wore. He hadn't created a massive business empire by allowing other people to take the lead. No, he was determined and driven and he fought for what he wanted. And today he wanted to win, and if he had to drag Adie to the finish line, half-dead, then that was what he'd do.

Adie was starting to think that death was a distinct possibility.

Hunt stopped and waited for her to catch up, his hands on his hips. Damn but his running tights should be declared illegal, she decided. The material clung to his muscled thighs and running behind him, catching glimpses of his perfect ass, was one of the few high points of this freezing day.

She wanted coffee, she wanted her parka, she wanted to lie down and sleep for a week. Really, she was too old to run at such a fast pace without much training.

She wasn't sixteen anymore.

"Can you see the sports memorabilia store?" Hunt demanded when she reached him.

So that was what they were looking for. She'd forgotten. Looking around the quaint shops, her attention was caught by a vintage jewelry shop across the road, its window filled with the unusual and the quirky. Knowing it was her type of shop, Adie instinctively stepped off the sidewalk to cross the road but Hunt grabbed her top and hauled her back to his side.

"That's not a sports memorabilia store."

Well, no, but this store was more her style. She needed five minutes, just to see whether it was worth another visit. Hunt scowled at her suggestion. "We're running a race, Ashby-Tate!"

"Five minutes can't hurt," Adie said, using her most cajoling tone.

"I know those eyes of yours could convince a monk to give up his vows of celibacy but they won't work on me, not today," Hunt told her, looking past her to scan the street. He lifted his arm and pointed. Adie saw a half-concealed sign showing just the first four letters of *Sport*.

Adie felt Hunt tug her down the street and she sent a look over her shoulder, mentally committing the name of the shop to memory because Mr. Competitive couldn't give her five minutes.

Hunt allowed her to walk for about ten yards and when they could see all of the sign saying they'd found the right store, he broke into a fast jog. Adie, trailing behind him, leaped over a small dog on a leash in her haste to meet Hunt, who'd found the event company staffer. He stood next to a huge vertical banner advertising Hunt's foundation and wore a red-and-green elf hat and pointy ears. A few feet from him a Santa Claus held a transparent bowl and collected donations from the Christmas shoppers and pedestrians. A small crowd had gathered in the hope of seeing some of their favorite sports stars.

Hunt greeted the young man and held out his hand for the next clue. The staffer, wearing a lime green Williams-Sheridan Foundation sweatshirt similar to their running tops, gave them a genial smile. "Hey, there, are you having a good run? Let's take the photograph and get you on your way."

Hunt removed his phone from the pouch on his bicep and prepared to take a photograph of the three of them, proof that they'd made the stop and at what time.

"Uh, where's your bobblehead?"

Hunt frowned at the young man's question and looked at Adie. Adie lifted her hands in an I-don't-have-a-clue gesture. "What are you talking about?"

"Each team was given a bobblehead figure at the start of the race and you are supposed to have the figure in every photograph. If you don't, you'll get disqualified."

Adie recalled the bobblehead figure someone handed to her and remembered Hunt saying it was Babe Ruth and he'd bring them luck. She'd left Babe, as far as she knew, on the table next to the young woman at the second stop, which was way back on the Lower East Side.

Hunt released a series of curses and placed his hands behind his head, gray eyes frustrated. "You are god-damn kidding me."

"Sorry, I'm not. If you don't have the bobblehead, you'll be disqualified."

"Why the hell didn't the other guys giving clues tell us that?" Hunt demanded.

The kid shrugged. "They might be new or maybe they just forgot."

They'd been doing so well so far and, because she'd left the bobblehead, all their efforts were in vain. Adie placed her hand on Hunt's chest and stared up into his light eyes. "I'm so sorry, Hunt, I messed up."

Instead of yelling at her as she expected him to do, he just lowered his arms and dredged up a smile. "It's just a race, right?" He looked at the kid. "Can we carry on without the bobblehead?"

"Yeah, but you're technically disqualified. But you know, you are the main dude so you'd probably still be in the running." The kid smiled. "I mean, it's not like they're going to boot you out, right?"

Adie instantly knew that didn't sit well with Hunt. He

wanted to win, but he wanted to do it on a fair playing field. He didn't want any special favors. She respected the hell out of him just for that. As much as she wanted to hail a taxi, get out of this freezing wind and stop somewhere for a hot cup of chocolate, she knew they had to finish the race, as a point of pride. He was representing a foundation that was founded on hard work, fairness and equity and he had to lead by example.

"Let's carry on. We'll tell them we're disqualified, but at least we will have finished." Adie suggested.

Hunt looked down at her and shook his head. "I'm going back."

Adie's mouth dropped open. "What do you mean?"

"I'm going to run back, get the bobblehead and then we'll finish the race." He shrugged. "I need to show the kids that you can't cut corners, that a job worth doing is worth doing properly." He looked at the young man, who'd pulled his elf hat over his pink ears. "Can I leave my partner here? It'll be faster if I do it on my own."

He shook his head, regretful. "Either you both do it and get the photos, or you'll be disqualified."

Hunt winced, obviously disappointed. He cursed again, his shoulders slumping. After a minute he looked at Adie. "Okay then, we'll do it your way. Ready to run disqualified?"

Adie, knowing she'd regret this later, shook her head. "Nope."

It was impossible to miss the disappointment in Hunt's eyes. "You want to give up?"

Adie shook her head. "Nope, we're going back, both of us, together. I'm going to bitch and whine but if it means finishing the race properly, then that's what we do."

The tender expression in Hunt's eyes nearly dropped

her to her knees. "You've already run four miles, Adie, and the temperature is dropping. We don't have to do this. By the time we're done, we would've run nearly ten miles."

Dear God, no. They could run disqualified, Adie thought. It was a stupid mistake, people made mistakes, even brilliant, driven CEOs. Or their personal concierges. People would understand.

But instead of begging him to carry on, a different sentence came out of her mouth.

"Would you be going back if you were on your own?" Adie asked him, her tone challenging.

Hunt slowly nodded. "Yeah, I would."

Dammit, she'd known that was exactly what he'd say. Adie stamped her feet and blew on her hands. "Well then, the quicker we turn around, the quicker we'll get to the finish line. Last, I'm sure, but we'll do it properly." She smiled at Hunt. "There had better be hot chocolate at the end, Sheridan or I won't be happy."

Hunt dropped a quick openmouthed kiss on her lips. "I'm sure there will be. But if you want something special, I'll call ahead and arrange that. Wasabi or bacon and chili?"

"Plain is fine, but there had better be a vat of it."

Hunt gave her a quick hug and Adie soaked up his warmth. Taking his hand, they broke into a slow jog and headed back in the direction they came.

Oh, she was so going to regret this in the morning. Or in fifteen minutes.

Five

Hunt, standing within a group including the Monarchs' manager and captain, looked across the art deco music hall. With the arrival of the celebrities and sports stars and their significant others, the hall was filled to capacity. A DJ shared the stage with a huge Christmas tree and the dance floor was crowded.

The buffet-style food had been demolished and the bartenders were hopping. It had been a long day, one that would be talked about for a long time to come and Hunt had had as much fun as everyone else. Okay, he and Adie, thanks to their stupid mistake, had taken forever to complete the route, but they'd been only ten minutes behind the last competitor. Frankly, considering they'd run another half race, they'd kicked ass.

Of course, that hadn't stopped the teasing from his ex-teammates and sports colleagues. They'd been, as he expected, ruthless. But under the teasing, he'd heard respect and that meant more to Hunt than anything else.

And he wouldn't have been able to do it without Adie.

Adie had immediately picked up on his need to do the race right, and she'd been at his side, or a few steps behind him, the whole way. Despite her threat to bitch and whine, she'd done neither, just put her head down and got the job done.

His respect for her was through the roof.

Griselda would never have considered running; it would've been beneath her. In fact, when he'd first proposed the urban treasure hunt race as a way to raise funds for his foundation, she'd told him he was better served overseeing the event and micromanaging the event coordinators to make sure nothing went wrong. Griselda, he'd recently realized, fed his appetite for control while Adie, well, with Adie he simply had fun.

God, he couldn't remember when last he'd felt so light around a woman. Or smiled so much. She was easy to be with; Adie didn't make small talk but when she spoke, he was immediately interested in everything she had to say. She was, in every way he could think of, the exact opposite of Griselda.

Griselda...

Hunt pushed his hand inside his jacket to pull out his phone and abruptly stopped, telling himself he didn't need to read the message again. He knew the words by heart.

While I didn't think your follow-up call confirming the end of our relationship was necessary, thank you for the courtesy. I hope, someday, we can resume our friendship.

So stiff and so formal, just like their relationship.

Hunt briefly closed his eyes and knew the strange feeling pumping through him was a sense of relief. Griselda was, officially and definitely, part of his past. And, while he'd always considered himself single, nothing bound him and Griselda together. He felt lighter, brighter, happier, like a snake who'd shed too tight a skin.

Maybe it was time to make more changes, to reevaluate his life, to start looking outside of work for ways to fill his hours. He'd loved today, being outside, exercising but also interacting with the volunteers, teenagers and sports celebrities. He should start doing more races, maybe a triathlon or two. Or maybe the foundation could organize urban treasure hunts in other cities.

He should brainstorm his idea with Adie and Kate, see whether they could translate his vague idea into an actionable plan. His excitement dropped several levels when he realized that Adie would be leaving soon, that she wasn't going to be in the city for more than a couple of weeks. Dammit.

Ignoring the cold fingers squeezing his lungs, he looked around the room. Speaking of his sexy teammate, where was she?

Hunt searched for her and eventually found her standing in the corner opposite him. She wasn't hard to spot, in a room of women mostly wearing neutral shades, her wide-legged green pants and matching wraparound top were the exact color of a Christmas tree. The brilliant green highlighted her creamy, flawless complexion and dark, ruffled hair. He normally liked long hair on a woman, but Adie's short hair suited her pixie face.

God, she was gorgeous.

And he wasn't the only one who noticed...

Thirty minutes ago, she'd been deep in conversation with Maxwell Green, a newly retired basketball legend. Before that he'd caught her laughing at whatever Blake, soccer's hottest player this season, had been telling her. Now she was leaning against the far wall, and his brand ambassador's hand—the man whose salary he paid to promote Sheridan Sports—was flat on the wall above her head as he loomed over her...

But Adie wasn't objecting. If anything, she was enjoying Liam Pearson's attention far too much. Yeah, not happening.

Hunt didn't bother excusing himself from the group, he just pushed his way through the crowd and within minutes stood behind Pearson, his arms crossed. Adie was the first to notice him and, instead of moving away from Pearson, she just raised her eyebrows. "Something I can help you with, Hunter?"

Hunter rocked on his heels and gritted his teeth as Pearson took his time lifting his hand off the wall and creating distance between him and Adie.

"Boss," Pearson murmured.

Hunt saw irritation flicker through the man's eyes at being interrupted and he narrowed his eyes at Pearson. In ten seconds, hopefully less, Pearson would realize that Adie wasn't another of his many conquests, that she wasn't someone who'd be another notch on his extremely scarred bedpost.

Hunt held his eyes.

Ten seconds passed, then fifteen and Hunt saw Adie eyes jumping between his face and Pearson's and after twenty seconds—Pearson liked to push boundaries—the man lifted his hands in defeat. Turning to Adie, he sent her a regretful smile. "It's been lovely talking to you, Adie."

Adie tossed a puzzled look at his back and when her eyes met Hunt's, she scowled. "What just happened?"

If she didn't know, then he wasn't going to elucidate.

"Hunter?"

Oh, okay, then. Hunt jammed his hands into the pockets of his soft black pants. "He was chatting you up and was about to ask you out on a date."

"That much I understood," Adie retorted.

There! That! Her going out on a date was not going to happen.

When he told her so, fury—hot and wild—sparked in her eyes. "And why would you think, for one bloody minute, that's your decision to make?" Adie demanded, her voice cold.

Because dates lead to intimacy and the only person he could imagine getting naked with Adie was *him*. Yeah, call him a Neanderthal or overbearing or ruthless, but he was the only man who'd kiss that wide mouth, explore the dip of her waist, slide his fingers between her feminine folds.

Adie slapped her arms across her chest and tapped her foot in annoyance. "Waiting for an explanation of your high-handedness, Sheridan. I might be working for you, but your authority over me does not extend to who I date!"

Hunt realized their argument was garnering attention. Looking around, he noticed a dark passageway to the right of them, clearly marked Staff Only. Judging by the lack of light, it wasn't being used, but it would be a perfect place to get his point across.

Conscious of his strength, he gently gripped Adie's narrow wrist and tugged her down the passageway, stopping when the hallway turned and they were out of sight of the party. Hunt placed his hand under Adie's elbows and easily lifted her off her feet, turning so his back shielded her from anyone who might amble down the hallway. Lowering her to her feet, he watched as she pushed her back into the wall, her eyes dark and mysterious in the low light spilling in from the music hall.

Adie, because she was as feisty as hell, lifted her chin. "Still waiting for an apology, Sheridan. Or an explanation as to why we are here."

Hunt slapped his hands on the wall on either side of her head, his eyes bouncing from her eyes to her red mouth. "You're not going to get an apology. And you know damn well why we are here."

In the small space he'd left between them, Adie gestured to the hallway. "I'm in the dark, literally and metaphorically."

He'd seen the flash of awareness in her eyes, noticed that her gaze kept dropping to his mouth.

"Stop being coy, Adie. You know I want to kiss you, I've been wanting to kiss you all damn day. And I'm sure you want to kiss me back."

He expected a sarcastic retort, a denial, for her to play hard to get, but Adie's hand moved up his arm, onto his shoulder to curl around the back of his neck. She further surprised him by reaching up onto her tiptoes and placing her lips against his, sighing as their mouths connected.

Hunt dropped his head and pushed his hand between the wall and her slim back, pulling her into him so that her breasts pushed into his chest, her stomach into his hard-as-hell erection.

He wanted her with a desperation that bordered on irrationality.

Unable to delay gratification for a millisecond longer, Hunt lifted his thumb to the adorable dip in the middle of her bottom lip and pressed down gently. "Open up, sweetheart, I need to taste you."

Adie's gentle breath drifted over his thumb, hit his lips and Hunt covered her mouth with his, seeking her tongue. She tasted of chocolate and white wine, smelled of hyacinths and heaven. Hunt's senses went into overdrive: his nose filled with her delicious scent, her mouth was a gourmet's paradise, he heard every sigh she uttered. Her body, under his roving hands, was feminine and slim, with subtle curves begging him to explore more.

In that moment, Adie was everything he needed or could ever want.

Hunt's hand curved around her bottom and she tilted her hips up to rub against the rod in his pants and Hunt felt a little lightheaded, probably because every drop of blood was heading south. After skimming his hand over her butt and down again, he bent his legs and easily lifted her off her feet.

Pushing her into the wall, Hunt groaned when his cock rested against her mound and watched as she tipped her head back to rest against the wall, exposing her elegant neck. "You are so very beautiful," Hunt told her, dropping his lips onto the cord on the right side of her neck. He nibbled gently, not wanting to leave a mark on her, and allowed his lips to move up to that sensitive spot where her jaw met her ear before tugging her earlobe into his mouth.

"Damn, I'd really like to take you to bed."

Adie tensed in his arms and Hunt winced, knowing his words had broken the spell. He never spoke without thinking but Adie had him tied up in knots.

Adie slid down the wall and when she stood on her feet again, Hunt took a small step back, but kept his hand on her waist. He couldn't not touch her—after a soul-melting kiss, that was asking the impossible.

Adie pushed a trembling hand through her hair before placing her fingertips on her lips, closing her eyes.

"Dear God, Sheridan, you know how to kiss."

Did he? Or had he just upped his game because he was kissing her? "Right back at you, sweetheart."

Adie took a tiny step and placed her forehead on his chest, the top of her head fitting under his chin. She gripped handfuls of his shirt in both hands and Hunt waited for their breathing to even out. It could take minutes or days, he didn't care, he was just happy to be standing here with her in his arms.

Of course, he'd be far happier if they were in a bed naked…

"We should get back, people will be wondering where you are."

"Don't wanna," Hunt replied, dropping a kiss in her hair. He wouldn't push her, this still had to be her decision.

He sensed Adie's lips curling into a smile. "Now, be a big boy, Hunter."

Hunt gripped her hips and pulled her into him, pushing her stomach against his still-impressive erection. "I am a big boy."

Adie's laugh was low and sexy and sparks ignited over every inch of his skin. Then, dammit, she placed her hands on his chest and created a foot of distance between them. But her hands, Hunt noticed, remained on his chest. She seemed to be having as hard a time letting him go as he was releasing her.

Good to know. They could be home in thirty minutes, naked in thirty-one… "Come home with me, Adie."

Adie stared down at the toe of her black shoe peeking out from under her wide-legged pants. "It's not a good idea, Hunter."

Hunt felt irrationally angry and deeply disappointed. They weren't feelings he was accustomed to. As a ballplayer, he'd never been short of offers and when he'd had his fill of stranger sex—it got old quicker than he thought it would—he hooked up with friends who knew the score: a good time, no commitment and no drama. Then he met Griselda. Over the last few months, their sexual encounters had been sporadic at best. And uninspiring. It was no more her fault than his, but the truth was that, at the end, the spark between them was already dying.

Unlike the roaring wildfire burning between him and Adie.

"Please don't give me that tired excuse of us working together. Give me a decent reason because I know you want me and I sure as hell want you." Hunt rubbed her cheekbone with the pad of his thumb. "What can I say to change your mind?"

Adie fiddled with the bow at her waist and Hunt, knowing that a small tug would be the starting point to undressing her, wished she wouldn't. "Honestly, I'm sure there are a dozen things you could say that would change my mind—"

Now, this was interesting. "Like what?"

Adie wrinkled her nose and ignored his hopeful question. "Can I be honest with you?"

Sure, honesty was one of his favorite things. "Go ahead."

"Christmas is a bad time of year for me," Adie said, her voice low. "For most of the year, I'm a badass…"

He had to smile at that, he couldn't imagine Adie taking names and kicking ass.

Adie placed her hand on his waist and he flinched when she lightly pinched him. "Don't you laugh at me! I really am! I'm strong and confident and happy. I enjoy going out and having a good time."

Hunt tensed, not liking the idea of Adie having a good time without him. And what exactly was that good time comprised of? Sleeping with guys? Yeah, the thought did not thrill him.

Hunt ran his fingers through his hair, irritated with himself. He wasn't a hypocrite, if men could enjoy themselves in the bedroom so could women, without any guilt or stigma. He knew that, intellectually, but the thought of Adie having random affairs made his teeth slam together.

Yet, a quick affair was all he could offer her. Ironic, right?

"I'm committed to being single, to not being answerable to anyone, to not being married, having a partner or having kids."

Despite her tough words, Hunt thought he heard wistfulness in her voice. "You sound like you're trying to convince yourself not me."

"Ah!" Adie drilled her finger into his chest and Hunt captured it. "In July or February, we would probably be in bed together but it's Christmas…"

Okay, he'd lost her. "What does Christmas have to do with us sleeping together?"

"It's *Christmas*, Hunter!"

"I need a bit more of an explanation than you telling me over and over that's it's Christmas, Adie."

Adie's shoulders reached her ears. "When I was a lot younger, I had a history of using men to satisfy my need for attention and validation. I'd jump into relationships fast and, inevitably, would end up with a broken heart."

Hunt didn't know where she was going with this but he'd listen. Listen, and try to understand—that was all he could do.

"I cured myself of doing that and I've been celibate for a long, long time."

"How long?" Hunt asked.

"Five years."

"Hot damn," Hunt replied. "But I'm still not seeing the connection between you saying no to me, your past and Christmas."

"I'm not sure if I'm attracted to you because, you know, chemistry." Adie pushed her hand through her hair, looking miserable. "Or if I'm looking for attention or if I'm using you as a distraction to push away a lot of bad memories. They always seem to float to the surface at this time of year."

"Can you share those memories with me?" Hunt asked, curious.

"I'm sorry, I can't. I'm scared that, by sleeping with you, I'd be jumping back into an old habit and that I might start confusing attraction for attention again."

Hunt immediately understood the subtext to her words. "You're worried you are going to confuse sex and affection?" He wouldn't say the word love—it had no place in this conversation.

Or in his life.

Adie stared at the floor, her arms crossed over her chest, her mouth thin with embarrassment.

Hunt lifted her chin and waited for her to meet his eyes. "I'm not the guy you want to fall in love with, Adie. I don't do love, commitment, happy-ever-after. I don't believe in the concept."

Adie threw up her hands, frustrated. "Yeah, I understand that. I don't either, Hunter! That's why I'm trying to figure out what I'm feeling, why I need to keep saying no to sleeping with you."

"Look, I know myself really well and, frankly, this has little do with you and everything to do with me," Adie added.

He heard her "get over yourself" subtext as clearly as if she'd spoken the words. Oh, and that was something else he found so damn attractive about her—he didn't intimidate her. Neither did he put stars in her eyes.

"You're an attractive, successful, interesting guy but I'm also leaving soon and we are working together and it's all too complicated."

Adie rested her forehead on his collarbone. "Trust me, Sheridan, I'm wickedly tempted but I learned, a long time ago, that nobody is going to look after me. It's up to me to protect myself. This is me, protecting myself."

I'd like to protect you.

Hunt lifted his hand to rub his lower jaw, feeling a little unbalanced from that very unusual and left-of-center thought. But for the first time in his adult life, he wanted to stand between a woman and whatever caused her pain. He wanted to protect Adie from whatever threatened her, whether it was self-doubt or her past or some existential threat.

He wanted to wrap her in his arms and hold her tight, putting his back to the world and taking the hits for her.

Holy crap.

Hunt didn't recognize himself. This wasn't who he was, this wasn't who he wanted to be. Adie had him tied up in knots; around her, he was the human equivalent of an intricately tangled ball of Christmas lights.

The real Hunt, the Hunt he was comfortable with—free, decisive, commitment-phobic—never spent this much time talking to or thinking about a woman.

But Adie, whether she was with him or not, was always front and center and...

He didn't like it.

Not one bit.

But, dammit to hell and back, he really liked her.

Adie patted his chest before stepping back. "Let's just take a deep breath here, Sheridan. Hell, in a day or two you might find me bloody annoying and you'll be desperate to get rid of me."

"I doubt that," Hunt murmured, not being able to visualize feeling that way.

"Or I might find that you are actually a huge jerk under that gorgeous body and hot face."

Now that was much more likely.

On Sunday morning, and after a night reliving Hunt's truly excellent kiss, Adie stood under the portico of The Stellan, which was one of the most iconic apartment buildings in Manhattan. Like the Eldorado, it was constructed in the thirties and was an art deco masterpiece.

Adie found it hard to believe that Hunt owned not one, but all the apartments in this building. Most he used as office space, the penthouse was his living space and the floor separating his work and personal space was an apartment used for visitors. His view of Central Park, while not as wild as the vistas from Ashby Hall overlooking the sandy beaches of western Wales, had to be amazing.

Adie rocked on the heels of her over-the-knees brown suede boots and wished Hunt had invited her up to his apartment instead of offering to meet her outside. She would love to see where he lived, but knew that if she stepped into his apartment, she had a very good chance of becoming intimately acquainted with his bedroom.

Which wouldn't be the worst place to be on a Sunday morning...

Had she been in her early twenties, that was exactly where she'd be this morning. Lying there naked with stars in her eyes, mentally redecorating his bedroom, wondering what to cook him for dinner or whether they'd have a boy or a girl first.

Yeah, she'd gotten that carried away before. To be honest, she'd been, on the odd occasion, worse than that. She'd once, okay, maybe a few times, flat out begged her boyfriend not to leave her.

It had not been pretty.

Looking back on the desperate, sad, intense girl she'd been was difficult. It made her cringe, but it was necessary because she refused to be that needy, weak person again. Because her parents had withheld love and affection, she'd craved attention and she'd looked for it in all the wrong places. It had taken her a long time to wake up and become emotionally independent but, since her midtwenties, she'd been too scared to test those sexual waters again.

What if those *I-think-I-might-love-him* and *does-he-like-me* and *I'll-do-anything-to-keep-him* feelings came roaring back again? It had taken her so long to find herself, to be at peace with who and what she was, that she couldn't take the risk of backsliding, of letting Hunt crawl under her skin and into her heart.

She couldn't, wouldn't, take the risk of reverting back to that scared, insecure person she'd been.

The combination of Christmas and Hunt could do

that to her. No, she was right to refuse his offer of a quick affair.

But what if she slept with him and managed to stay emotionally detached? What if she trusted herself a bit more, trusted that the five years since her last broken heart had healed her? What if she was perfectly capable of handling a quick affair with Hunter? What if she was cured of her attention-seeking habit?

If that had happened, was she refusing Hunter for nothing? Was she missing out on some spectacular sex with Hunter for a no-longer-valid reason? If she was cured of her youthful folly, she could not only embark on a blistering affair with Hunter but she could also, when she returned to London, start to date again.

Was she making a huge mistake by simply assuming she was still weak?

"Adie."

Adie hauled in a deep breath, grateful oversized sunglasses covered her eyes because, damn, Hunt tempted her to rethink her no-sex stance. In designer jeans, desert boots and a gray-and-blue-flecked sweater worn under a battered bomber jacket, he looked relaxed and younger than usual. And she liked the thick stubble on his jaw and his messier-than-usual hair. Hair she wanted to run her hands through, hair she wanted to grip as he kissed his way down her stomach, over her hipbone…

"Hi."

"Hi back. Thanks for giving up your morning," Hunt told her, blowing on his hands.

His fantastic eyes searched her face. "Everything okay?" he asked.

No. Because every time I see you, I want to shed my clothes and seduce the hell out of you.

Adie pulled a fake smile onto her face. "Sure. Everything is fine." She stamped her feet. "Damn, this weather is ridiculous."

"Yeah, I wish I could blow off work and head for the islands," Hunt told her, placing his hand on her back and directing her to walk south. "Hot sand, pretty girls in bikinis, big surf."

Icy mojitos, warm water…bliss. "Do you surf?" Adie asked him.

Hunt nodded. "Whenever we could, Steve and I used to head to Hawaii to catch some waves. We'd spend our days surfing and our nights partying, drinking and chatting up girls."

Wanting to dig a little deeper, Adie tossed out another question. "You and Steve were pretty close, right?"

Hunt stared off into the distance and took a moment to respond.

"He was my best friend and my brother, in every way that counted. When I lost him, I felt…adrift. When you don't often connect with people, you treasure the people with whom you do experience that connection."

She'd tried to connect with everyone when she was younger. Hunt, it seemed, hadn't tried at all. Different people, different paths.

"Kate and I are relatively new friends, but I tell her more than I do most. Or maybe I end up telling her stuff because she won't let me keep any secrets," Adie admitted.

Hunt laughed. "Steve was like that, as well. He'd push and push until you eventually realized it was easier just to tell him. But he was a great secret keeper."

She trusted Kate, as well. "Were Kate and Steve very alike? I mean, I know they looked alike but were their personalities similar?"

"Peas in a pod," Hunt replied, dipping his hands into the pockets of his jacket and shortening his long stride so she didn't have to hustle to keep up with him. "Steve knew all my secrets and if you are not careful, Kate will soon know all yours."

She already did. Not that Adie had any great and dark secrets; her parents were selfish and being around them hadn't been fun. She worked too hard and because she'd been so in love with the idea of love, she no longer dated, especially at Christmas. She might be a workaholic but her life wasn't that complicated.

"Around this time of year, and after days like yesterday, I miss him the most."

Adie's step hitched at his unexpected statement and she darted a look at his face. Under his scruff, the muscle in his jaw was rigid with tension as were the cords in his strong neck. He also looked slightly paler than he had minutes before. Yeah, this was a very tough, touchy subject and Adie knew he wouldn't appreciate any sentimentality or trite expressions of understanding.

In fact, she was amazed they'd gone this deep, this quick. After all, Hunt kept telling her he didn't do emotional connections.

Adie felt the intense desire to comfort him, to wrap her arms around his waist and bury her face in his neck. Hunt, she was sure, wasn't familiar with the restorative powers of a hug, with how good it felt to lean on someone else.

Knowing she needed to take baby steps, Adie pushed her hand into the pocket of his jacket, sliding her fingers between his. She ignored the look of surprise he sent her and just squeezed his hand, hoping he understood that, just for this moment, he wasn't alone.

Hunt's hand tightened around hers and she laid her

head on his shoulder, grateful for his big body sheltering her from the icy wind. Reminding herself that they were associates and not lovers, she reluctantly straightened and tugged her hand from his.

Hunt, however, refused to let her go.

Well, okay then.

Trying to ignore thoughts of how wonderful she felt snuggled up against him, she reminded herself they were just colleagues—even if they were holding hands—and asked him why he'd wanted her company this Sunday morning.

Hunt pulled a folded piece of paper out of his back pocket with his free hand and shook it open. He handed it to Adie and she scanned the typed notes.

"It's a list of names, denoting age and sex." She looked at Hunt and saw the hint of red blooming on his neck. Hunt was embarrassed? She didn't think he had it in him.

"An explanation, Sheridan?"

They approached a crossing and stopped behind a young couple pushing a toddler in a pram. Adie was about to tell him to hurry up with his explanation, but he gave her a small shake of his head. Frowning, she looked around and saw that his presence was gathering interest. The young father nudged his wife and mouthed "Hunter Sheridan," and another man surreptitiously pulled out his phone to snap a photo. The young mom and the other women standing around were content just to look at him, their eyes filled with female appreciation.

Adie couldn't blame them; he was eye candy.

Hunt took the paper from her, folded it up and placed it back into his pocket. Ignoring his admirers, he placed his hand in the middle of Adie's back to usher her across the road.

Adie turned around and looked back at the crossing and noticed that people were still watching. "I know that you are a Manhattan mover and shaker, but I didn't realize you were so recognizable."

"I played for, and now co-own and sponsor, one of the greatest baseball teams in the country," Hunt explained, "My face is out there."

And it didn't hurt that it was such a stunning face too.

"Yeah, all that ugliness is very memorable," Adie said, her tongue firmly in her cheek.

Hunt's hand moved up her back to squeeze the back of her neck. "Brat."

"I am," Adie cheerfully agreed. "And you still haven't told me about the list and why I am walking around Manhattan with you instead of drinking coffee in my pj's and thinking about breakfast."

"Yeah, that." Hunt twisted his lips. "It's a list of the kids currently in residence at a foster home situated in Albany…"

Hunt stopped talking and Adie knew that if she pushed him, he might clam up or, worse, change his mind about this morning.

"Most of those kids will be spending Christmas there. Their foster mother is one of those amazing people who step up, every single time. The social workers know that when they are up against the wall, they can call Miss Mae, and she'll make a plan to take in another kid."

Adie had always admired people like Miss Mae. Not wanting to repeat what her parents put her through, and now that she was older and smarter, she couldn't imagine having kids of her own, never mind taking in kids who'd walked through several levels of hell already.

Hunt quietly continued his explanation. "I've been confidentially supporting the home for years, working through a social worker who deals with Miss Mae. Normally, I channel the funds through her and at this time of year, I give her extra money to buy presents for the kids and Miss Mae gets them what they need. But Miss Mae has been ill, and the social worker broke her foot so neither can get out to buy presents and I don't want the kids to go without."

"Surely there are other social workers, someone on your staff who could help you? Or, here's a novel idea, a concierge?"

Hunt pulled a face at her mild sarcasm. "I considered all those options, but it's really important to me that I keep this particular contribution under the radar. The only person, besides you, who knows what I am doing is the social worker. Secrecy is imperative."

Okay, Adie was now confused. "But you have a foundation, you give away money all the time. Why the need for secrecy?"

Hunt ran his hand over his face. "Ah, that. Well, because Miss Mae wouldn't accept it."

Adie jerked to a stop and faced him, puzzled. "I don't understand. Running a foster home has to *be* expensive and I'm pretty sure the state doesn't cover all the bills. Why wouldn't she accept your help?"

Hunt rubbed the back of his neck, obviously uncomfortable.

Adie wanted to tell him she didn't need an explanation but her curiosity kept her from forming the words. She wanted to know.

"Miss Mae was my foster mother and I lived with her for two years."

Oh, Hunter.

"Where were your parents?" Adie gently asked him, trying to keep her tone as conversational as possible. Pity, she knew, would make him retreat.

"My mom had quite severe mental health issues, she was in and out of psychiatric facilities."

"And your dad?"

Hunt shrugged. "He's just a name on my birth certificate."

Adie listened intently, knowing he was giving her a little insight into his past and his thinking. She felt... well...it was an old-fashioned word but... *honored* fit the bill. Hunt, she was pretty sure, didn't often speak about his past.

And he still hadn't explained why he needed to secretly support Miss Mae. "Tell me about your highly classified mission," Adie said, lightening her tone to ease some of his tension, "and why Miss Mae won't take the help you seem to think she needs."

"Uh, that would be because, years and years ago, I waltzed into my old home full of sass and importance, with a truckload of stuff—furniture and appliances and clothes—and flung it at her, expecting her to throw her arms around me and tell me how wonderful I was. I hadn't seen her for a couple of years and wasn't very good at keeping in touch and she was already pissed at me for my silence.

"My intentions were good, but my enthusiasm ran into her pride. She lost it and ripped into me, told me that I was too arrogant by half, that she wasn't a charity case and she'd survived for a long time without my help. I yelled, she yelled. I called her ungrateful, she called me a patronizing brat..."

He shrugged. "I handled the situation badly but she has more pride than Lucifer."

So, she suspected, did Hunt.

"So now you support her quietly, through the social worker."

"Lauren tells me what she needs, I provide it. Quietly. That's why it can't go through the foundation, I don't want to risk her getting wind of who her benefactor is and getting all huffy again."

There was something so touching about a tough guy, hard and determined, with a soft center. Hunt came across as a driven, hard-as-nails businessman, but he hadn't forgotten where he came from or who helped him along the way. And, she might be wrong, but she suspected that Miss Mae was more of a mother figure to him than his own mother had been. The rift between them still seemed to have the power to scorch him.

And, if Miss Mae was as fond of Hunt as he was of her, she had to be hurting too.

"How long ago did this happen?"

Hunt wouldn't meet her eyes and Adie knew he didn't want to answer her question. "Hunter?"

"Twelve years ago," Hunter reluctantly admitted. When she stopped and just stared at him, he lifted his hands. "She's stubborn!"

"You haven't spoken to her in more than ten years?" Adie demanded, her voice rising.

"Oh, we've spoken, we're not that bad. We lunch every couple of months—at her favorite diner—and she always insists on paying for her half." Hunt scowled, obviously irritated. "But she won't hear of me paying for anything else because she promised me, over a decade ago, that she'd never take a cent from me. I've offered to buy her a bigger house and a new car but she keeps refusing."

"Wow, that's taking stubborn to a whole new level."

"Tell me about it," Hunt grumbled.

"Come on, she must know you are paying for the kids' Christmas presents," Adie protested.

"I'm sure she suspects, but since the social worker won't discuss the donation or tell her where it comes from, her pride will let her accept the help." Hunt looked frustrated. "Damn, she's a handful."

"But you love her."

Hunt's shrug was as much confirmation as she was going to get, but actions said so much more than words. It was obvious he absolutely adored Miss Mae.

"So, it looks like we are going to spend the morning buying Christmas presents for a bunch of kids," Adie said, tapping her foot on the sidewalk.

Relief softened Hunt's mouth and the tension in his body eased. "I'll pay you for your time, of course, but I'd like to keep this separate from the concierge business."

Please, she wasn't going to take payment, not for this.

Touched by his willingness to do what was right, Adie slowly nodded. "I am very happy to spend loads of your money and I'll even help you wrap the presents but it's going to cost you."

"I just said that I'd pay you," Hunt pointed out, but his mouth twitched at the corners, indicating his amusement. Funny how she was learning to read him.

Adie placed a hand on her stomach. "That's not the type of payment I was talking about..."

Humor touched Hunt's eyes. "What are you thinking? Flowers, dinner, a helicopter ride over Manhattan?" He flashed her that sexy half grin. "A night of unbridled passion?"

Adie rolled her eyes. "Nice try, Sheridan. Nope, you need to feed me. A girl can't shop on an empty stomach."

"That I can do," Hunt said, placing his hand on the

small of her back and steering her down a narrow street. "I know a place where they serve the best bagels in the city. But feel free to change your mind. Especially about the night of passion."

"Don't tempt me, Sheridan," Adie muttered.

When Hunt laughed, Adie realized she'd spoken out loud. *No, Adie, don't even think about it!*

But how could she not?

Six

Hunt, in the middle of composing an email, felt the car stop. He lifted his head to look out the window. Pete had parked in his usual spot next to the portico of The Stellan and was leaving his seat to open the door for Hunt.

Hunt saved his work, closed the lid to his laptop and shoved it into his briefcase. He shook his head when his car door opened. Pete was in his seventies, it was cold enough to freeze nitrogen and the rain was turning to sleet, but despite telling him a hundred times that he was more than capable of opening his own car door, Pete was old school and refused to listen.

It had been a day from hell, Hunt thought, as he left the car and thanked Pete. The assistant Hunt was sharing with his CFO was out sick and he'd spent the day tracking documents and files, searching for emails and answering his own phone.

Hunt heard the ding of a message arriving on his

phone and pulled it from the inside pocket of his jacket. Griselda? Now what?

If I sign all the releases and legal documents in the world, would you consider giving me your biological matter for me to use to get pregnant?

Hunt read the message, then read it again to make sense of her request. It sounded like Griselda wanted his sperm...

What the actual hell? Hunt didn't hesitate, his fingers quickly typing a reply.

That would be a hard no.

What was Griselda thinking? He didn't want kids, but there wasn't a chance in hell of him handing over his genes and not having any contact with his child afterward.

And really, if there were a test to prove their suitability as parents, Hunt doubted he and Griselda would pass.

Hunt didn't know a lot about raising children but he knew they needed love and affection and time. Neither he nor his ex had it in them to provide anything their offspring needed. He didn't know if he ever would. So why did the image of a little brown-eyed, dark-haired baby keep drifting in and out of his mind, a cute toddler sitting on Santa's lap, squealing at the sight of presents under the tree?

Those images didn't stop at babies and toddlers. He could also see himself spending hours in the batting cage with his son, walking his daughter down the aisle...

Hunt rubbed his hands over his face and cursed. What the hell was wrong with him? There had to be a logical explanation. Hunt pondered the problem and decided it had to be a combination of Christmas and viewing the storyboard earlier for the summer advertising campaign for Sheridan Sports featuring happy families engaging in sporting activities. He was overreacting, a natural response to facing what he didn't have, what he'd once desperately wanted.

He no longer wanted kids, didn't want a wife or a family to call his own. His work was all that was important, work he could control. Work, unlike his mother, wasn't a constant disappointment. Work, unlike his first wife, didn't betray you by spending all your money and sleeping around on you. Work couldn't die and leave you without your best friend.

Work was simple; relationships weren't.

Hunt sighed, conscious of a headache building at the back of his skull. All he wanted was a whiskey, a couple of hours of silence and some time to decompress. He couldn't wait to get up to his quiet, empty apartment and unwind. After a busy weekend and a long day of meetings, he was peopled out.

He needed space to breathe and to think.

That being said, he still, inexplicably, wanted to see Adie, to be with her. She hadn't come into the office today and he'd missed her, looking up eagerly every time someone knocked on his door. He'd then spent the next ten minutes feeling annoyed at his disappointment.

Despite wanting to be alone, he wouldn't mind seeing her wide smile, to look into her dark eyes, to hear her say…well, anything in her classy, British accent. Kissing would be great, taking her to bed would be friggin' fantastic, but he'd reluctantly settle for laying eyes on her.

Needing her, wanting her more than he needed solitude to decompress, irritated the hell out of him.

"Mr. Sheridan? Are you coming in?"

Hunt jerked at the sound of his doorman's voice and looked over his shoulder to see Glen holding open the door to his building.

Hunt strode inside, desperate for a drink and to slump back on his couch. He'd watch the city lights and try not to miss Adie or Steve and he'd make an attempt to relish his time alone. To banish those images of things he no longer wanted…

"Mr. Sheridan—"

Hunt ignored his doorman's call, waving his words away. Stepping into the private elevator that would take him directly to his penthouse, he slapped the button to close the door and saw Glen's shocked face.

"But I need to tell you—"

He'd had enough of people today and whatever Glen had to say could wait. Hunt rested the back of his head on the shiny metal skin of the door and closed his eyes. If he were normal, if he had any skill at relationships, he would be coming home after a crap day and stepping into the warm embrace of a partner, a wife, a significant other. She'd hug him, rub his back, pour him a whiskey and maybe take him to bed to distract him.

He wanted that tonight and for the person waiting for him to be Adie. He so wanted her to be standing in his space when the doors to the elevator slid open, seeing her wide smile and messy short hair.

Hunt shifted from foot to foot, annoyed that he kept pulling thoughts of her front and center. She was getting under his skin. In the middle of his meeting today, he remembered Adie having a long conversation about a skateboard with the hipster clerk at a famous surf and skate shop yesterday, asking him about the width of the deck and low, high and mid trucks. During a call to his accountant, he remembered her spending a half hour debating between two very lifelike, almost creepy-looking baby dolls, her face intense and animated.

She was fun to be around and he could do with her dry sense of humor and quick smile. He also wouldn't mind getting her naked.

Nope, he wouldn't mind that at all.

Hunt tapped the back of his head against the elevator wall, mentally and physically frustrated. Adie was someone who worked for him, someone who would be in Manhattan for only the next couple of weeks. He shouldn't be thinking about her, wishing she were here, missing her.

He never gave women, anyone, this much mental attention and it was time he stopped.

Hunt felt the elevator slow and then the doors soundlessly slid open. Music, hot and loud, assaulted his ears and his headache immediately intensified.

Stepping into the hallway, he dumped his briefcase onto the hall table and rubbed his fingers across his temple. This was an ultrasecure building and the only person who had unrestricted access was his cleaner. Since he'd caught Flora using his stereo system before—which he normally didn't mind—Hunt immediately assumed that her college classes had been switched and she was working late.

Exactly what he *didn't* need.

Thinking that he needed to kill the music before his head exploded, Hunt stepped into his living area and blinked. He closed his eyes and pushed his forefinger and thumb against his eyelids, hoping the mess would disappear, but when he opened them again, it was still there. His handcrafted, stainless steel and glass-top coffee table was pushed to the side and was piled high with ribbon and festive too-bright wrapping paper.

Sheets of it were scattered across the wildly rare and expensive navy-and-cream carpet made in the ancient city of Tabriz, and piles of presents, all wrapped, were scattered across the room.

Hunt stepped over a heap of Christmas presents for Mae's kids and picked up the universal remote buried in the detritus on the coffee table. He punched the power button and silence, welcome and warm, fell. Thank you, Jesus, he could finally think.

And God, what a mess. He hated chaos, physical and mental; it reminded him of his less-than-stable childhood, of sharing rooms with far too many boys, of not having any privacy, of feeling out of control.

This was his home and, obviously, Adie had come around sometime today, started on wrapping the presents for Miss Mae's foster kids and left, shutting the door on the disorder.

Not what he expected…

"Hunt? Is that you?"

Hunt turned at the feminine voice coming from the direction of the kitchen. His heart sighed with pleasure, irritating him further. He wanted to be alone, dammit.

Or he *should* want to be alone.

And how dare Adie think she had a right to be in his space when he got home, had a right to make a shamble of his very orderly and exquisitely decorated living area?

He heard movement behind him and Hunt's entire system sighed and settled in a silent, but potent, *there she is* as Adie walked into his living room, dressed in faded jeans and a thigh-length cream jersey, thick socks on her feet. She held a glass of wine and...

And she looked right.

She looked like she belonged.

And that terrified Hunt.

And because he was scared stupid at how right she felt in his life and in his space, he lashed out. Rationality be damned.

"What the hell are you doing?" he roared.

Adie's bright smile faded and she followed his eyes to the paper and presents on his floor.

"Uh—"

"You don't have any right to be here, messing up my place, making yourself at home!"

The glass in her hand wobbled and her complexion changed from warm cream to cold milk. Her eyes turned to burning coals and her lips thinned.

"You told me you'd be done by five!" He tapped the face of his watch. "It's after nine!"

"I know what time it is, Sheridan," Adie calmly replied, placing her wineglass on the wooden trunk that served as a side table for his long buffalo hide couch. Hunt strode over to her, picked up her glass and whipped a coaster under the foot to capture the condensation rolling off the glass. The trunks were also antique, made from rare wood and would be impossible to replace if they got water stained.

Adie raised her eyebrows at his actions but Hunt didn't care. He'd grown up with nothing so he protected and looked after what he had.

Resisting the urge to take a sip from her glass, he strode over to the drinks trolley in the corner and dumped a healthy amount of whiskey in a crystal tumbler. He noticed a dirty glass next to the decanter and irritation rose again. "You're drinking my wine *and* my whiskey? And could you have not taken your dirty glass to the kitchen?"

Adie folded her arms across her chest and the look she handed him was pure disdain. "Wow. Who spat in your cereal?"

Hunt gritted his teeth. "I've had a day from hell and all I wanted to do was to come home, zone out in my uncluttered, peaceful home and chill. But it looks like a war zone."

Adie walked over to his red leather chair and sat down on the edge, bending sideways to lift up a flat-soled, knee-high boot off the floor. She slipped her foot into the shoe and pulled up the zip. Before reaching for the other boot, she looked at him, her pale face annoyed. Annoyed? No, her eyes were blazing with banked fury and held a healthy dose of hurt.

Hunt felt a wave of remorse, a tide of humiliation breaking over his head, but he couldn't apologize.

"Well, all I wanted to do tonight was go with Kate to a gallery in Greenwich Village because one of my favorite artists is having a one-night exhibition. But because you needed these presents wrapped as soon as possible, I came over here after I finished work—my day was also tough, thank you very much!—to get it done."

Fair point.

"Did you or did you not tell me to come over at any time, that Glen would let me in?" Adie asked, her voice slicing through him.

He had. And maybe that was what Glen had been trying to tell him… He should've listened and he could've ignored this ugly scene.

"I've been here for four sodding hours. I have paper

cuts and a backache. I put on some music because I was bored, had a glass of whiskey to take the edge off the fact that one of my new clients thought it was okay to ask me to organize her a boy toy for some extramarital entertainment when she reaches St. Bart's. After explaining to her that I am not a pimp, I then spent the next three hours wrapping these presents, thinking that you'd never, not in a million years, begrudge me a glass from the open bottle of wine in your fridge, while I debated what pizza to order!" She hadn't lifted the volume of her voice at all but he could tell her anger and temper levels were rising fast.

Zipping up her other boot, she picked up her oversized scarf and wound it around her neck. Slinging her tote bag over her shoulder, she stomped into the hall and looked around in frustration.

"Where's the damned button to summon the lift?"

Lift? Right, that was what the English called an elevator. Before his brain could catch up and form his answer to her question, Adie was crossing the carpet toward him to snatch the remote out of his hand. Scanning the buttons, she saw the icon for the elevator and jabbed it, throwing the remote onto the sofa when she was done.

He'd messed up. Badly. God, how could he salvage this situation? "Adie—"

Hunt followed her into the hall and walked straight into the elevator, its doors open. "Don't you dare talk to me right now, Sheridan, I'm seriously cross at you and I don't want to say something I'll regret."

Hunt placed his hand on the door to keep it from closing. "Like what?"

"That you're selfish and rude and unappreciative.

And though you are hotter than a trip around the sun, right now you are being a dick."

She was right, but he didn't know how to apologize or explain. That wasn't something he did. The only word he managed to form now was her name so he said it again. He wanted to tell her not to go, to pull her out of the richly decorated elevator and take her to bed. He wanted to lose himself in her, for her to lose herself in him.

"Back off, Sheridan!" Adie flicked his hand with her finger and because she caught him by surprise, he lifted his hand off the door and it immediately slid closed. Adie's furious and hurt face disappeared. Hunt rubbed the lower half of his face before linking his hands behind his head and cursing.

He'd thought he wanted to be alone, but he was wrong.

So wrong.

Adie, who'd been staying at Kate's Chelsea apartment, was ridiculously grateful Kate was in Boston, reconnecting with an old college friend. She'd left on the three o'clock flight and intended to catch the red-eye home. Or, as she'd informed Adie, if said friend had retained his college good looks, she might not be returning home at all.

Adie hoped for the latter, because she really, really needed to shore up her defenses and reassert her mind's control over her heart.

She paced Kate's lounge in men's style pajamas, a glass of red wine in her hand, conscious of her bruised heart banging away in her chest.

Hunt shouldn't have the power to hurt her, in any way. He was her client, a gateway to picking up more business in this closed-off, cliquey world. And she had the proof of that. Since she'd started working for Hunt, she'd had many inquiries from Manhattan A-listers for her concierge services. People she'd normally have to spend months, if not years, courting, were coming to her because Hunt had tossed some business her way.

He was her *client*…

But—ack!—he was more than that.

She'd genuinely started to believe that, despite the sexual tension between them, they'd become friends. She'd stupidly thought he not only wanted her, but he also liked her and respected her. His behavior tonight cast that in doubt.

She hadn't been friends with a man for a long time so she couldn't be sure of the whole man/woman friendship dynamic. But Hunt had told her a little about his life with Miss Mae, had opened up about his past. They'd had fun buying the kids' toys—although she frequently had to drag him away from the tech stuff—and she'd thoroughly enjoyed his company.

Judging by his ready laughter and relaxed attitude, she thought he'd enjoyed hers, as well.

That was why his actions tonight had been such a slap in the face. Especially when she'd been giving up her personal time to help him.

And, let's be honest here, the out-of-the-blue attack reminded her of her childhood, of being her mother's verbal punching bag, for being blamed for stuff that wasn't her fault. In her head, she heard her mom accusing Adie of ruining her marriage, telling her daughter that it was her fault her dad spent time with his mistresses and that carrying a baby ruined her mother's body.

Adie took a large sip of her wine and rested the glass

bowl against her forehead. Was she mad at Hunt or was she mad at her mother?

Oh, she was always mad at Vivien, Baroness of Strathhope, but she was also really angry with Hunt.

And he deserved her anger.

So, she could either continue to pace the carpet and wonder if Hunt would apologize—probably not—or she could do something constructive with her time, like reading through today's emails, something she'd yet to tackle.

Action was always better than brooding so Adie flopped into the nearest chair and reached for the laptop sitting on the coffee table in front of her.

There were at least ten requests from clients for additions to their Christmas shopping lists, another client wanted her to have her Knightsbridge apartment decorated for Christmas and another wanted a meeting in January to discuss a fiftieth birthday present for her husband.

Adie, forcing herself not to think about Hunt, replied and sent an email to her assistant in London to help facilitate the requests.

Adie heard an incoming message on her phone and picked it up, grimacing when she saw the message from her boy-toy-seeking client.

I'm sorry, did I go too far?

That would be a yes...

Adie started to type a reply, a gentle suggestion that the woman consider working with another concierge company, when the intercom buzzed.

Thinking it was the pizza she ordered, Adie hit the

button to open the downstairs door and looked around for her bag to pay the delivery man.

When the knock came on her door, Adie wrenched it open and in one practiced movement, reached for the pizza box and held out her other hand for him to take her money.

That's when she recognized that pale, pale pink button-down, the tanned skin between the open collar of his shirt, the geometric black-and-white pattern of the tie hanging below his open collar.

Adie raised her eyes and her heart took flight as she met Hunt's light, almost tender eyes.

"I met the pizza guy downstairs," he stated, lifting up the box.

"Thanks." Adie tucked the money into the top pocket of his coat and tried to tug the pizza box from his hand. "You can go now."

Hunt kept his grip on the box. "Aren't you going to share?"

Adie narrowed her eyes at him. "Are you going to apologize?"

Of course he wouldn't. Men in his wealthy and powerful position never did. She'd seen it over and over again, had experienced it...

The privileged and powerful could mess up but they expected people to either ignore their mistakes or to clean them up.

Adie had no intention of doing either.

"I'd prefer not to do it in the hallway, but if that's the only way I can get you to listen, I will."

Adie blinked at him, confused. "You will what?"

"Apologize," Hunt said, his tone terse. "Can I come in— Okay, the hell with it. I was a jerk, Adie and I'm sorry."

Wow, he'd actually done it. Holy Christmas cupcakes. Adie tipped her head to the side. "Did that hurt?"

Hunt's mouth twitched. "A little."

"Pity, it should've hurt more since you behaved so badly." Adie stepped back into Kate's small hallway and gestured him inside. Hunt, still carrying the pizza, walked from the hall into the kitchen and placed the box on the island in the center of the room. Then he turned to a cupboard and pulled out a glass. Gesturing to the open wine bottle on the counter, he lifted his chin. "May I?"

"Sure. Unlike some people, I'm happy to share my alcoholic beverages."

Hunt winced. "Yeah. That wasn't my finest moment."

Hunt poured and sipped before turning to pull plates out of a cupboard. He also found flatware in the drawer under the counter. He knew Kate's apartment better than she did, and Adie commented on the fact.

"Steve and I shared this apartment over ten years ago," Hunt explained. "Steve bought it and Kate bought it from his estate."

Adie had not known that.

Hunt looked down at the pizza box, his hands gripping the counter. He eventually lifted his eyes to meet hers and Adie sucked in a hard breath at the turbulent emotion she saw rolling through all that ice and smoke.

"I had a shitty day and I was annoyed that I missed you today. I don't miss people, Adie."

Everything inside Adie warmed a couple of degrees at his terse admission. She'd missed him too, and she'd thought about him all day, wondering what he was doing. She'd spent thirty minutes talking herself out of heading for his office for a late afternoon catch-up session. There wasn't anything important she needed to discuss with him; she'd just wanted to see his face. Adie compromised by going to his apartment and she'd taken her time wrapping the presents they'd purchased, desperately hoping he'd come home before she was finished.

"I was trying to convince myself that I wanted to be alone and that I needed some time on my own. I also had a bitch of a headache. I walked into my apartment and there you were and I was both confused and so damn happy to see you and I didn't want to be either. So I got pissed.

"And then I shouted," he added on an embarrassed shrug.

"You did shout."

"I'm sorry," Hunt said, looking miserable. "You make me irrational."

It was the nicest, grumpiest compliment Adie had ever received and her internal temperature rose another degree or two. If he carried on this way she might spontaneously combust.

"I don't like the way you make me feel," Hunt admitted, his knuckles white as his grip on the counter tightened.

Adie picked up his half full glass of wine and took a sip. Despite knowing she shouldn't and that she was playing with fire, Adie asked the question anyway. "How do I make you feel, Hunter?"

"Confused, excited, out of control… So damn horny I don't know which way is up. Or if I'm even breathing."

Oh, God, so she wasn't the only one dealing with some wild emotions. It was such a relief to know that Hunt—unemotional and distant—also felt unsettled and unbalanced.

Adie took another sip of wine, conscious of his eyes

drilling into her. Meeting his hot gaze, she saw the desire in his hot, stormy gray eyes and saw how fiercely he wanted her. Men had wanted her before—as a notch in their belt, as a conquest, out of mild attraction, as a way to pass time—but, with Hunt, she didn't feel like she was his way to alleviate boredom.

He wanted *her*.

Nobody else.

And she felt the same. She shouldn't, it was dangerous—but she did.

Don't do it, Adie, don't take the risk.

Because it was Christmas, she was feeling more vulnerable than usual and she didn't want to slide back into the bad habits of her youth. But, on the other hand, she wasn't the desperate girl she'd once been, she knew her faults and her weaknesses, she wouldn't allow herself to feel more for him, to confuse sex with love. She could do this, maybe she *had* to do this, to prove to herself she was stronger than she thought she was.

Maybe she should trust herself, after all. What harm would one night do? And maybe, if they were lucky, a night long on sex and light on sleep would burn this need out of their psyches.

They should give into it so they could get over it.

It made sense to her...

Still holding his glass of wine, Adie took his hand and told him to grab the bottle of wine.

Hunt gestured to the box of pizza. "I thought we were going to eat."

Adie lifted herself up onto her bare toes and brushed her mouth against his. "Later. Right now, I can think of something else I'd rather do. Can you?"

Hunt's thumb slid over her bottom lip and his eyes deepened to the color of wet concrete. "I can think of several things I'd rather do and all of them involve you getting naked."

Adie turned her head so she could nip the pad of his thumb. "Well then, what are you waiting for?"

Adie turned away, but Hunt tugged on her hand and she turned back to him, feeling a little exasperated. If he kept delaying, she'd start thinking and she might end up talking herself out of this...

"Are you sure?"

Yes, no...*yes*.

Definitely yes. Because, when she was seventy, she didn't want to regret not having a Christmas caper with one of the hottest men she'd ever encountered. She wanted this one night and tomorrow she'd shore up her defenses and play it safe.

Tonight, she just wanted him.

"Yeah, I'm sure. Now, are you coming or not? Or do you still have a headache?"

Hunt's laughter was low and wicked, and oh-so-sexy. "Like I'd use that feeble excuse. As for coming, I intend to, but only after you are two or three ahead of me."

Adie grinned at his quick wit until she saw that, under the joke, he was very serious. Yowzer, two or three? Holy hell.

"I'll settle for just one, Sheridan."

"I won't," Hunt told her, placing his hands on her hips and lifting her so that her eyes were at the same height as his. "With my fingers and my tongue, then again when I'm deep inside you."

Adie swallowed, sighed and placed her mouth against his. She let him carry her to the bedroom, anxious to get started.

Seven

Sex was the last thing he'd expected tonight, but since he was a guy—a guy who'd fiercely wanted this woman from the moment he first laid eyes on her—he'd take it.

He wasn't an idiot.

Easily carrying Adie through to what used to be his bedroom, Hunt feasted on her mouth, relying on muscle memory to get them to where they wanted to be. Habit had him kicking the door closed and he allowed Adie to slide down his body to stand on the floor.

He cradled her lovely face in his hands, wondering if he should ask again if she was sure this was what she wanted. But he could see the desire in her eyes, the flush of excitement on her cheekbones, on her neck. Using one finger, he pulled the material of her collar away from her neck and saw her pink-tinged creamy skin. When she closed her eyes, obviously enjoying his touch, he swallowed down the need to reassure himself.

This was something they'd been heading toward for the past ten days, it was inevitable. And in the morning, they'd be as they were before...

She didn't want more, neither did he. She'd confessed to being the type who felt too deeply, who got carried away, but that was when she was younger. She was older now and he'd keep them on even ground—he never lost his head and he wouldn't start now.

They were colleagues, friends having sex, they didn't need to complicate the hell out of this situation.

Then why did he feel a little nervous, like he was taking a step off a high cliff into a churning pool of dark seawater? He'd had lots of sex before. He knew what he was doing...

But making love to Adie would be different. That unwelcome knowledge had him hesitating.

What price would he have to pay for indulging in his need for her? What would he lose? He didn't know and Hunt didn't like taking a risk without knowing all the possible outcomes.

Adie's small hand came up to hold his cheek. "Hunt? Everything okay?"

Hunt blinked and shook his head. He focused on her suddenly hesitant expression. "Um, if you've changed your mind, that's okay. No hard feelings," she told him.

He hadn't changed his mind; he couldn't. "Only the world ending, and you telling me to stop, would make me walk away, sweetheart."

Relief jumped into her eyes. "Oh. Then why are you just standing there, not touching or kissing me?"

Now that was a damn good question and something he intended to rectify immediately.

Not having an answer, Hunt lowered his head to hers, tasting her lush, sexy lips. Adie arched her back and wound her arms around his neck, lifting her hips and moving closer to push her stomach into his erection.

Needing to taste her fully, needing everything, Hunt placed both hands on her breasts, immediately noticing how her nipples hardened in response. Finding them with his fingers, he took advantage of her sigh to push his tongue into her mouth, tasting the red wine she'd been drinking.

For a moment, the world stopped turning. They were the only two people on earth and their passion not only ignited but detonated, sending spikes of lust scampering along every neural pathway in his body.

He wanted her, more than he'd wanted anyone or anything before.

Needing to see her, wanting to know whether his imagination came anywhere close to reality, Hunt lifted her pajama top up and over her head and pushed her bottoms over her hips. The fabric pooled at her feet as Hunt looked down, sucking in a harsh breath at her gorgeous, naked body.

She was pale, but her skin was lush, as if she were covered in a layer of clotted cream. Her breasts were small but firm, her nipples the rich pink of a pomegranate. Her stomach was flat, her belly button delightful and the small patch of hair between her legs was darker than the hair on her head. Her long, shapely, runners' legs were a delight.

"Hunt, you're staring," Adie whispered, trying to tug her hands from his.

"That's because you are so worth staring at," Hunt roughly replied, "I suggest you get used to it because I could do it for—"

Biting off the word—the *forever* nearly slipped out—

Hunt told her to turn around, and when she finally did, Hunt took in her slender back and her world-class ass.

Man, if he lasted two seconds after pushing into her it would be a friggin' miracle.

"I'd like to look at you too," Adie told him, sending him an impatient look over her shoulder.

If he got naked, he wouldn't be able to hold back. Besides, there was something incredibly sexy about being dressed while your lover was naked...

After toeing off his shoes and socks, Hunt pulled Adie so her back was to his front and crisscrossed his arms over her torso, his hands on her breasts. Needing to see her, wanting his eyes on hers, he dropped his arms to her waist and gently lifted her, walking her across the room to where a free-standing mirror stood in the corner of the room. Her head dropped back to rest against his collarbone and her eyes were on his hands, watching their reflections as he gently pinched her nipples, making them harder than before.

"Look at me, Adie."

Adie's eyes lifted and clashed with his, dark brown slamming into gray and Hunt felt his erection jump. Adie pushed her butt into him and he groaned, grinding himself against her. He'd wanted to take more time to explore her but one hand, by its own volition, skated over her stomach and he bent his legs so that he could push his hand between her legs to cup her mound.

"Open for me, sweetheart," Hunt commanded and Adie spread her legs. Hunt sighed when her feminine heat hit his hand. Sliding his fingers between her folds he smiled when her juices covered his fingers. So responsive... Moving up, he rubbed his index finger against her clitoris and Adie stiffened in his arms, her eyes growing wide.

Initially, he thought she didn't like his touch, but when she held his hand against her and lifted her hips, he released a soft laugh.

Yeah, she liked his touch. Very much.

"Hunt, God, this..."

Hunt touched his mouth to her neck, moved his lips across her skin to nip the ball of her shoulder. He removed his hand from between her legs and dragged his wet fingers across her stomach and up and over her nipple, making it glisten. "I can't wait to taste you, to be inside you. I can't wait to make you mine."

Adie's eyes were foggy with lust and she surprised him by picking up his hand and placing it back between her legs. "Touch me, Hunter."

He laughed, happy to oblige. Hunt watched as pleasure tinted her skin a deeper shade of pink. Needing to see every bit of her, needing for there not to be anything between them, he lifted her right foot onto the seat of the chair next to the mirror, exposing her to his gaze.

Hunt saw the momentary flash of embarrassment cross her face, but before it could take hold, he spoke in her ear. "Every inch of you is lovely. So feminine, so responsive. I knew it would be like this..."

"Like what?"

"Fan-freaking-tastic."

Hunt, needing to know more of her, pushed one finger into her hot channel, felt her clench around him and smiled. His thumb brushed her bundle of nerves and she pushed down on his fingers, wanting more. Hunt slid another finger into her and watched as her mouth opened, her breath coming in excited, shallow gasps. He knew she was close, knew that with a little pump, another flick, she'd fall apart in his arms.

Adie, insensible to anything but her rising pleasure,

tried to push her fingers between his and her happy place, but Hunt took her hand away, holding it against her stomach. "Let me do this for you, Adie."

"Then do it!"

Bossy. Hunt, wanting to hide his smile at her impatience, dropped his head back to her neck. After a moment, he rested the side of his head against hers, their eyes clashing again in the mirror. "Kiss me, Adie."

Adie half turned, stood on her toes, and her mouth found his. Hunt nearly staggered at the passion he tasted, blown away by her need for him and what he could give her.

Her tongue pushed into his mouth and he let her take control of the kiss as he decimated her control down below. Bending his fingers, he found that special spot deep inside and tapped it while, at the same time, he increased the pressure on her clitoris. Adie arched her back and yanked her mouth off his, breathing heavily as she tensed in his arms.

He waited for a second, tapped and swiped again and she released a harsh cry as she contracted around his fingers, her body shaking as her orgasm hit her. Hunt pushed for more and she convulsed again, a deeper, longer spike than her initial orgasm.

Hunt held her as pleasure consumed her, enjoying the gasps and groans of a completely fulfilled woman.

It didn't matter that he was rock hard, feeling like he was about to rip open, he could wait, he *would* wait. This was about Adie and about what he could give her, how he could make her feel. About learning about her body and what made her fall apart.

Hunt watched as Adie came back to earth, her eyes foggy with pleasure and surprise. She allowed him to hold her weight, and Hunt knew he'd never seen anything sexier than Adie standing naked in his arms, slumped against him, his hand still between her legs, his other covering one breast.

She met his eyes and smiled softly. "Wow."

"Good?" he asked, even though he knew that it had been. It was in her eyes, reflected in the satisfied tilt to her lips.

"No, amazing." Adie yawned and lifted a hand to her mouth, her eyes widening with embarrassment.

"Tired?"

Adie nodded. "Sorry, I haven't been sleeping well lately."

"Me neither," Hunt told her, turning her around to face him. "And I'm afraid that tonight won't be any better."

Adie arched her eyebrows as her hands started to undo the buttons of his shirt. "Why, do you have other plans for us?"

"I promised you at least another two orgasms," Hunt reminded her, his fingers exploring her wonderfully round, smooth backside. "And I always, always keep my promises."

"Oh, well," Adie said on a happy sigh, "I can always sleep when I'm dead."

"Did your client really ask you to find her a boy toy?"

Adie, half-lying across Hunt, nodded. She was physically wiped and mentally wired. Moving was an impossibility and that was fine because Hunt was an exceedingly fine mattress...

Adie wanted to frown but didn't have the energy. "She did and I'm so disappointed in her. She knows my rules."

"Which are?"

"Well, obviously, I don't arrange people's sex lives… *Ick*. Also, even more obviously, drugs are out of the question."

Hunt's hand stroked her skin from her shoulder to hand and back up again. "Good to know since I'd hate to see you in orange."

"Animals are tricky too. I will arrange for the transport of a pet, accompanied by a human, provided I have proof that the dog has been bought from a breeder with exemplary credentials. My clients want only the best, so they normally deal only with decent breeders anyway, so that's not a problem." Adie traced patterns on his pec with the tip of her index finger. "I'll source dogs, cats and horses—I once had to find a client a polo pony for his son—but I won't deal in exotics, I learned that lesson very early on."

"What happened?" Hunt's voice rumbled over her.

"One of my very first clients wanted a capuchin monkey. I felt uneasy about it, right from the beginning. I don't like the idea of primates being kept in captivity, I'm not a fan of animals in cages…"

"But?"

Adie wrinkled her nose, remembering the fear in the tiny primate's eyes. God, she still felt guilty. "I needed her money. She was my first client and as rich as Croesus. It was a choice between taking the commission or making rent that month. I found her a monkey but someone reported her to the RSPCA, the UK equivalent of your Humane Society. They visited my client and asked where the monkey came from. Apparently, the dealer I got it from was running a smuggling operation bringing exotics into the country."

"Damn."

"Yeah. The officer laid into me, rightly so, and gave

me a huge wakeup call. The monkey was relocated to a zoo and is thriving. Since then I'm very, very careful with requests that involve animals."

"How long have you had your business?" Hunt asked, changing the subject.

"Since I was seventeen, eighteen?"

Hunt lifted his head to look down at her in surprise. "Really? That long?"

"Yeah, though obviously on a lot smaller scale. The seeds of the business were planted at school." Adie folded her arms across his chest and rested her chin on her fist. "My ridiculously wealthy parents, and I say that not to brag but to make a point, sent me to a very exclusive boarding school but frequently forgot to pay the fees. My mother wouldn't give me an allowance, I had to ask her every time I wanted something and since our relationship wasn't great and I was stubborn, I refused to ask her for a damn thing. So I found ways to earn my own cash. I ran a little shop, selling chocolate and energy drinks and odds and ends. Someone would mention they wanted pizza and I would order ten in, charging by the slice. I became known as their go-to girl, if they wanted something but were too lazy to look for it, I would find it, buy it and add a hefty markup for my trouble. They'd pay."

"Impressive." Adie wanted to roll around in the warmth and admiration in Hunt's eyes. "You're obviously a natural entrepreneur."

"Yeah, when I'm feeling generous, I can almost be grateful to my parents for pushing me into my career."

Hunt stroked her hair and pushed his fingers into her hair to massage her scalp. God, that felt fabulous. "I'm discerning a little bitterness. Why?"

Adie shrugged. "My parents shouldn't have pro-created."

Hunt frowned. "Well, I disagree with that statement because you are here and lovely. But why do you say that?"

"I wasn't a welcome addition to their world. I am, apparently, the reason their marriage fell apart, why they fight, why my father has affairs. Children change the makeup of a relationship."

Hunt's hand on her hip tightened and she picked up the new tension in his long, hard body. "They told you this?"

"My mother mostly but my father didn't disagree with her."

"Holy shit. My mother had her issues, she was in and out of state psychiatric facilities all her life, but I never doubted her love for me."

"My mom doesn't love anyone but herself," Adie told him before waving her words away, "My parents are the reason why I was an attention hound for far too many years. Any attention was good because I received none from them."

Adie sat up and rolled away from Hunt. She sat on the edge of the bed, her back to him. "Why are we talk-ing about this? Are you hungry? There's still pizza in the kitchen."

She stood up and pulled an oversized rugby shirt off the chair next to her bed. Slipping it over her head, she looked at Hunt, who was watching her through hooded eyes. He was utterly at ease in his nakedness and he had every right to be. Big arms, a ribbed stomach, strong muscled thighs and sexy, broad feet.

Maybe getting dressed wasn't such a good idea; pizza could wait. She wanted to run her hands down those legs, tongue her way over that washboard stomach, moving downward to his most intimate area…

Hunt waited until her eyes returned to his face before smiling at her. "I like what you are thinking but after two rounds of spectacular sex, I need pizza and a glass of wine and a little time to recover."

Adie blushed, shocked he could read her that easily. Rocking from foot to foot, she watched him roll to his feet and walk around the bed in the direction of the bathroom. But Hunt surprised her when he stopped in front of her and gently pulled her into his embrace. It felt like second nature to wrap her arms around his waist, to lay her cheek on his chest.

She felt his kiss in her hair, his broad hand raking her shirt up to rest his hand on her naked butt.

To Adie, it felt like Hunt had taken her apart sexually, exposed her and left her feeling vulnerable and off balance. But his hug put all those shattered pieces back together again. It was a physical promise of safety and acceptance.

She could've stood like that forever, soaking in his strength, leaning into him, feeling his tender lips in her hair, on her temple. It was, by a long way, the best hug she'd ever received and Adie wanted to stay there for the longest time…

Possibly forever.

You are doing it again, Adie, you are acting the way you used to. You are running into a deep pond instead of tiptoeing around the edge. Stop, right now!

She was not going to fall in love with him or start fantasizing about a future with him. Her stay in Manhattan was temporary. Hunt was a one-night stand and she would not let herself weave dreams around him.

She dealt only in reality these days, and all that was real was the attraction burning between them.

Hunt pulled back and Adie immediately allowed her arms to drop to her sides. "What's wrong, sweetheart?"

Adie wrenched a happy smile from somewhere deep inside and tossed it his way. "Nothing at all."

This was just sex and she wasn't about to repeat her old cycle of "sleep with him, immediately fall in love with him, get your heart broken."

She was older and better than that.

"So… I'm going to heat up the pizza, find some more wine."

You have to establish boundaries so just get it done. Because you know he can't stay the night.

Having him stay after such excellent sex, would be tempting her heart a little too much.

"And then we can say goodnight. It's been a long day."

Hunt frowned at her. "You're kicking me out?"

She couldn't wake up to his sleepy smile in the morning, didn't want to find herself under him, with him pushing into her while she was still dreamy and half asleep. Well, she did, but it was too much too soon. She needed to rebuild her barriers.

If she didn't put some mental and physical space between them, she might slip back into the destructive patterns of her teens and early twenties. And that was a risk she would not take.

Please don't insist on staying. I might not be able to say no. And while I'm stronger than I used to be, I don't want to test that strength.

Adie forced her lips into a cheeky grin. "I know you like to call the shots, Sheridan, but my bed, my rules," she told him, turning away.

Hunt's hand shot up to catch her wrist and Adie stopped, sighed and looked at him. Releasing his hold on her, he cupped her face in his hands, his lips drifting over her mouth in a devastatingly tender kiss. "Relax, Adie, it's all good. If you don't feel comfortable with me staying over, I'll leave. You might not realize this, but you hold the power here."

"I do?" Adie asked, surprised. She'd expected a lot more pushback.

Hunt stroked the line of her jaw. "Of course you do, you always did and always will. I'm not gonna lie, I want to do this again, as many times as we can before you leave the city, and to that end, I'd like to make love, sleep with you, wake up and start all over again.

"But if you need some time to wrap your head around what's happening between us, then I'll go home and try and get some sleep," Hunt added.

"Nothing is going on with us!" Adie squeaked. "This isn't going anywhere. This is just us having some fun in bed!"

Oh, God, how embarrassing it would be if he thought she was falling for him, the most elusive man in Manhattan! That would be a disaster.

Hunt pulled back at her ferocious statement and lifted his hands as if to ward off an attack. "Adie, relax! I didn't mean to imply that either of us wanted something serious!"

"Then what did you mean?" Adie demanded, her heart thumping and her breath ragged.

"Look, you told me that you haven't had sex in a while—five years, you said? Maybe you need to work through what happened between us, I don't know, I'm just speculating here because I know that women think about sex differently than men do."

"And what do men think?" Adie sarcastically asked, eyebrows raised.

"Mostly that we're so damn grateful to have gotten some," Hunt replied. His easy grin doused what was left of her simmering temper. "While you do whatever you need to do tonight, on your own, know that I'll be lying awake thinking of you. Then I'll have to take a cold shower and then I still won't be able to sleep and then I'll be as irritated as hell at work—"

Adie laughed at his overexaggerated whine, realizing he was teasing. "Nice try, Sheridan, but you're still going home."

Hunt dropped a kiss on her lips and tapped her butt. "You're a tough cookie, kicking me out into the cold night."

She was just walking away from temptation-on-broad-feet. And because she was, she refused to think of Hunter Sheridan as anything more than a temporary fling, a bit of fun, a way to pass the time.

He was her Christmas fling and she would not, *would not*, fall in love with her sexy client.

And, what was obvious, he wouldn't let her fall in love with him either. Good thing.

But he was still, Adie decided, going home.

Because, really, there was no point in tempting Fate.

Adie, having done a final inspection of Hunt's apartment before his guests arrived for his much-anticipated Christmas tree–trimming cocktail party, dashed down his hallway and skidded into the master bedroom, whipping off her sweatshirt as she barreled across the room toward the en suite bathroom.

She was running late. After she punched the keypad on the wall next to the door, the shower heads instantly responded and hot water and steam filled the huge shower enclosure. Adie knew she'd miss Hunt's luxurious bathroom when she returned to London. She would also miss his massive bed, the way everything in his apartment was controlled by an electronic tablet, the incredible views of Central Park…

Most of all she'd miss Hunt.

Adie stripped and, leaving her clothes on the floor, stepped into the sophisticated shower, sighing when the double-headed jets pounded her body with hot water. By mutual agreement, and because they were both aware that they were on limited time, Adie had all but moved into Hunt's apartment, wanting to spend as much time as she could with him before she flew back to London at the end of the week.

They'd been sleeping together for two weeks. Christmas Eve was a few days away and their time together was nearly over, but she didn't regret one moment she'd spent with Hunt. This had been the best three weeks of her life. In between joining the Williams family for a weekend of skiing in Vail, she and Hunt went ice skating at Rockefeller Center and window shopping down 5th Avenue, gently arguing about which store had the best Christmas windows.

They ate at little-known diners and Michelin-starred restaurants and they had, once or twice, appeared in the social columns, with the reporters speculating about whether his relationship with Griselda was over and whether the private concierge had captured Hunt's elusive heart.

No hearts were involved—she hadn't let hers out of its cage—but Adie's business brain couldn't help feeling pleased for the publicity as she received quite a few inquiries for her concierge services after those articles appeared online.

It was definitely starting to look like she could open a branch of Treasures and Tasks in Manhattan, and before she left, she needed to have a meeting with Kate to thrash out the details.

Although Adie was pretty sure Kate was on board, if she changed her mind Adie would pick and choose her New York–based clients carefully and manage their requests from London. Distance wasn't an issue; she had clients all over the world and could manage their needs from the moon, if necessary.

But presently, she had to get ready for Hunt's stupendously exclusive and very formal tree trimming party. Right now, the eight-foot tree in Hunt's living room was stringed with lights, and boxes of handblown glass ornaments, ones she'd purchased through her supplier in Poland, were resting in their velvet cases, waiting for the guests to hang them on the branches.

Having organized these types of parties before, Adie was fairly sure Hunt's guests, apart from one or two, wouldn't bother with the tree, they'd be far more interested in drinking, socializing and eating the canapés provided by the exceptionally expensive chef she'd hired for the evening.

She'd do the bulk of the decorating, either during the party or later.

Adie washed her body, wishing she could dry off, slip into a pair of soft jeans and a pretty sweater and socks and curl up in a comfy chair with a glass of wine. Or she wished that instead of entertaining strangers she didn't know, she could open the door to the Williams clan.

Instead of expensive ornaments and fancy food, they

could order Chinese and sing along to Bing Crosby and Frank Sinatra as they argued about where to put a papier-mâché Santa or a string of tinsel. She wanted to watch Kate and her brothers argue, see the soft smiles Richard and Rachel exchanged, sneak into the kitchen to kiss Hunt senseless.

She wanted simple and meaningful, a Nativity scene and red candles and gaudy decorations. She wanted colorful rugs on his neutral couches, badly wrapped presents under the tree, greenery over the door frames, mistletoe hanging in every room.

She didn't want rich—she worked all day with rich—she wanted *normal*.

Adie placed her hands on the shower wall and looked down at the tiles beneath her feet, rolling her shoulders as the hot water loosened the tension in her neck. In a few minutes she'd climb out, dry off, and then she'd apply some makeup and slip into the sexy designer dress she'd picked up earlier in the day. Comprised of black Chantilly lace, beaded and embroidered, over a nude fabric, it was both sexy and demure, with its scalloped V neckline and A-line skirt. She loved it and she hoped Hunt would too.

But she'd still prefer to be dressed in jeans, drinking red wine, trying not to think of the call she'd taken earlier…

Think about something else, Adie.

Adie went over her mental to-do list, hoping she hadn't forgotten anything. A Dubai client wanted a last-minute gift from Tiffany, and she'd sent Kate to buy the bracelet he'd seen online, a complicated design featuring diamonds and sapphires and costing a little shy of half a million dollars. She'd received the photographs from the floral designer who'd decorated her client's

Knightsbridge flat. He'd done a fantastic job. But the client wouldn't get to enjoy her festive house after all, because—after telling Adie that her payment had been processed—they'd changed their minds and wouldn't be visiting London this year.

She agreed with Adie's suggestion that the flowers and the exquisite tree be donated but Adie was furious that Gid had worked his butt off during an already busy season, to fit in her request to decorate the house only to have her clients change their minds at the last minute.

Sometimes her clients could be real jackasses.

Like most people, there were days when Adie hated her job, and today had been one of those days and Adie couldn't help but focus on the negative.

How many more private chefs would she organize for marriage proposals to later hear that the couple had split up just a few years later? How many more holidays would she organize that would not be enjoyed because her clients changed their minds? How many more diamond-and-sapphire bracelets would she buy and ship, how many would be worn?

But she was dancing around the real reason for her distress.

Her day had spiraled only after she received a request from her client, a German businesswoman, the CEO of a perfume company. The call had rocked her, and for the first time in a long time, she'd had no idea how to respond to her client's blithe, this-isn't-a-big-deal request.

Sadness overwhelmed her, and Adie placed her hand on her stomach, pushing the sensation away. She couldn't afford tears now, or to remember the past. Her childhood was over and she wasn't that neglected child, nor was she a lonely teen, looking for affection.

Change your thoughts, Adie. Now, immediately. Switch gears and focus on the positive.

She was a successful businesswoman having a brief affair with a gorgeous, smart guy. It was Christmastime, but she was managing the blues, her emotions and her expectations. Maybe she'd finally grown up and could handle a no-strings affair. And she deserved an extra pat on the back for doing it at Christmastime, when she was, historically, more likely to slip back into those destructive patterns of looking for love in all the wrong places.

And maybe that was why she felt so very comfortable with Hunt, relaxed about where they were and what they were sharing. They'd spoken about their pasts and their expectations and it was a relief to know that Hunt didn't do relationships. He was as anti-marriage, anti-commitment and anti-children as she was.

They were on the same page, reading from the same book. He liked her, loved her body and in a couple of days, he'd kiss her cheek, hug her goodbye and send her on her way.

There would be no tears or regrets. In time he'd become a pleasant memory.

And maybe Hunt was her gateway man, the one who would show her how to be with a guy without any expectations or projections. That she could have a sexual relationship with a guy and remain unaffected.

She'd handled herself, and Hunt, well, Adie decided. She'd thoroughly enjoyed his company and his lovemaking and she'd managed to ruthlessly shut down any dreamy thoughts or wacky ideas of having a long-distance relationship, or any kind of long-term relationship, with Hunt.

She liked him, adored his body, would miss him when she left—but she'd resisted falling in love with him.

Thank God.

Adie rubbed her eyes with the balls of her hands, wishing she could crawl into Hunt's big bed and go to sleep.

Despite her mental pep talk, she still felt a little overwhelmed and a lot tired. Christmas was always the most stressful time of year for her and she generally worked ridiculously long hours. She was not only working hard, but when she did finally collapse into bed, Hunt was always there.

And because she was on limited time with him, and because she couldn't resist him, she'd always spend a few hours tangling the sheets with him.

Adie released a huge yawn, closed her eyes and rested her forehead against the tiles. She just needed a little nap...

Eight

Adie heard footsteps and then the shower door opened. She groaned when Hunt's thumbs applied pressure to that spot at the base of her skull, enjoying the sweet, sweet pain of tension releasing. Reaching back, she tapped his bare thigh, murmuring a quick hi, and a "man, that feels so good."

Hunt dropped a kiss onto her shoulder before massaging her shoulder blades. "You looked sad earlier. Everything okay?"

How long had he been watching her? Adie wanted to look at him but his hands on her back, thumbs digging into her spine, kept her facing forward.

"Adie, is everything okay?"

Oh, right, he'd asked her a question. "Yeah, fine. Just tired." Not wanting to lie, she added, "And a little pissed."

"Why?" Hunt asked, strong hands working her glutes.

"A client told me today that she was leaving for the Seychelles, and that her eight-year-old daughter was staying home with her nanny and housekeeper. Then she tells me that she supposes she should—her words not mine—buy the kid some presents." Adie snorted her displeasure. "Her daughter was such an afterthought. It was like she was making arrangements to kennel her dog. I guess it just struck a very big nerve."

"Tell me why?"

Adie turned to face him, placed her hands on her hips and lifted her shoulders to her ears. She had the brief thought that she was as naked as a newborn but immediately dismissed it, feeling completely at ease with Hunt because he'd told her, over and over again, how much he loved her body.

And, because she was sure they were friends as well as lovers, Adie felt comfortable enough with him to explain.

"To understand, you'll need a little backstory." Adie pushed her hair off her face. "When I was four, my mother left my dad and took me to Europe, where we moved from castle to villa to apartment, living off her trust fund and her friends' charity. My mom was vivacious and pretty and entertaining and people were always happy to have her. Me, not so much. And, not wanting to piss off her hosts, my mother kept me hidden away from the action. She was there to party, to entertain and be entertained, so I rarely saw her. In fact, most of my childhood memories are of my mother's back, watching her walk away."

Hunt didn't speak, but his eyes radiated empathy. Empathy she could deal with, if she'd seen pity she would've stopped talking.

"My father demanded custody of me, mainly because

he mistakenly thought it would anger and irritate her. He was shocked when my mom agreed, very quickly it had to be said, and I was shipped back to England. Not wanting to look after me himself—I'd disrupt his life too much—he decided I should stay with my grandmother, at Ashby Hall, the family seat."

"That must've been quite an upheaval."

"It wouldn't have been so bad if they'd allowed my nanny to come with me, but no, my grandmother said she'd look after me." Adie pulled her bottom lip between her teeth and bit down hard until Hunt tapped her lip with his finger and told her to stop it.

"There's more," Hunt stated.

There was.

"It turned out that my grandmother wasn't thrilled to have me. They hired me another nanny—she was okay—and my dad did come back to Wales occasionally, mostly on the weekends, to see me. But then he met the first of many mistresses and I was forgotten."

"Jesus, Adie."

"When I was eight, my grandmother died and my mother came back to Ashby Hall to live—she and my father never divorced—and that's when the blame game started… I was the reason why my dad never came home, the reason their marriage disintegrated. She should never have had me."

"If I ever meet your mother, I might just choke her," Hunt growled, his gray eyes incandescent with rage.

"You think that now, but within five minutes of meeting her, I guarantee she'll win you over. My mother is the most charming person you'll ever meet," Adie told him, placing her hands flat on his chest.

"Anyway, the reason why I'm telling you this is because you noticed I was sad and I am. Somewhere in

Germany, there's a little girl who is feeling lonely and unwanted at Christmastime and, because I know how hurtful that can be, I want to choke the life out of her mother, my client."

"Don't work with her again," Hunt told her, frowning. "Drop her."

"I can't do that!" Adie protested.

"Sure you can…" Hunt's thumbs slid up and down her hipbone. "You're in demand, Adie and that means you can pick and choose your clients. You don't have to do everything for everybody. Choose the people you want to work for, hike your prices so you become even more exclusive and ditch the people you find annoying. Or offensive. Or who irritate you.

"Trust me, the more exclusive you become, the more in demand you'll be. Rich people like what we can't have," Hunt told her, bending his head to kiss the side of her neck. "And talking about wanting…"

How was he always able to make her feel better, to settle her? Hunt was able to push away the harsh memories and lighten her spirit. He was dangerous…

Hunt's finger skated over her lower lip and Adie glanced at his waterproof watch and winced. "You have guests arriving in forty minutes, Sheridan and I have to dress, do my hair and slap on some makeup."

"I've seen you dress in a hurry and know it will only take fifteen minutes," Hunt told her, moving his hand to her breast, his thumb gliding over her nipple. "There's plenty of time for what I want to do."

"And what's that?"

"Instead of telling you, let me show you."

Hunt tugged her out of the blast of water and sat down on the ledge spanning the width of the shower enclosure. Pulling her down so she straddled his thighs, he lifted his hand to her neck and pulled her head down to ravish her mouth. After a few minutes of intense, hot, skin-melting kisses, Hunt pulled back, his eyes dark with passion.

"I can't get enough of you. I think about you constantly, especially when I shouldn't," he muttered, sounding annoyed. "How the hell am I going to let you go?"

Adie, knowing it was the sex talking, knowing nothing that was said when two people were naked was admissible later, didn't answer.

Instead, she touched her lips to his jaw, dragging her mouth over his two-day stubble, up to his ear to tug his earlobe between her teeth. Hunt replied by pulling her closer, lifting her so her mound was pressed against his thick erection. Adie couldn't help lifting her hips, sliding against him to create a little friction, sending ribbons of pleasure shooting through her system.

Hunt dipped his head to take her nipple into his mouth, his tongue rolling over her bud. He managed to walk that very fine line between pleasure and pain and Adie wanted more…

When she forgot to regulate her thoughts, sometimes she wanted everything: the good sex, the conversation, early morning coffee, making love as often as they wanted…

Now, who was letting the sex talk?

She'd been so good keeping her feelings out of it, she wouldn't slip now, not when she was so close to leaving with her heart intact…

She knew of one way to stop thinking of Hunt in terms of forever and that was to stop thinking at all. When Hunt was inside her, rocketing her away, she thought of nothing but the pleasure they shared, the thrill they gave each other.

Impatient with herself and with him, Adie wrapped her hand around his shaft. His low growl of approval ignited her nerve endings. Without giving him time to move, or even think, she positioned herself and sank down onto him, groaning as he filled and completed her.

Adie hooked her ankles behind his back, placed her hands on his shoulders and rocked, loving the feeling of his intimate flesh connecting with hers.

"We need a condom, honey."

But he felt so good and she didn't want to stop. But he was right; this was how babies were made. And God knew, a baby was exactly what she didn't need.

The image of a black-haired little girl with Hunt's gray eyes flashed on the big screen of her mind and Adie could smell her baby girl scent, feel her soft hair and was blinded by Hunt's smile on that pixie face. She could see the little girl, touch her, smell her…

Adie shuddered, causing desire to course through her.

Right now, she wanted Hunt's baby. She wanted Hunt. She wanted a lifetime of sex, of sleeping beside him, of arguing about whose turn it was to make coffee. She wanted everything.

No, she *didn't*.

She was confusing lust with love, intimacy with intercourse.

Adie felt a tremor pass over her again and she moved her eyes to Hunt's face and clocked his worried expression.

"You okay? You turned a little pale."

Adie nodded, needing to reassure herself as much as she needed to reassure him. "I'm fine. Really."

Hunt lifted his hips and she felt him grow bigger inside her, setting those exquisitely responsive nerve endings on fire. "God, Adie, you feel amazing. I'll grab a condom now. I just want to enjoy you a little more."

This was intimacy, Adie thought, this was the truth. Skin on skin, heat on heat. This was real.

Adie rode him gently, swept away by pleasure, riding a wave of need. When he demanded more, she increased her pace. She stared down into Hunt's eyes, knowing that she'd see his face in her dreams for the rest of her life. He was going to be the man she judged all other men against and she knew, without a shadow of a doubt, they would all fall short.

Hunt wasn't perfect, but he was perfect for her. He shouldn't be, but he was.

Hunt gripped her chin and forced her to look at him. "Stop thinking, Adie. Whatever keeps pulling your attention away can wait. Be here, be with me."

Adie nodded, wishing she could tell him that she was with him, that she always would be. But instead of speaking, she slammed her mouth to his, trying to pour all her regret, all her distorted, useless need for him into a kiss. Hunt's hard, strong arms wrapped around her and he surged to his feet. Adie moaned when he slipped out of her.

Hunt carried her out of the shower and, ignoring the still pounding water, walked out of the bathroom toward his California king, tossing her onto the smooth comforter. Adie scooted up the bed as Hunt opened the drawer next to his side and pulled out a condom. He took the thin rubber from its covering and rolled it down his shaft.

Lowering himself to the bed, Hunt gently separated her thighs and looked down at her most secret spot. Instead of sliding inside, Hunt dropped his head to lick her, and then he licked her again.

Adie placed her forearm over her eyes, convinced she'd expire from an overload of pleasure. Hunt teased her with his tongue, with his fingers, lifting her up to where she was sure she'd come, only to take her to the edge and leave her hanging.

Finally, when she was sobbing, begging for release, Hunt pushed into her. She was so close she needed nothing more than his gentle command to come and she did, pulsing and shattering and flying and sobbing.

Adie was dimly aware of Hunt's hoarse cry, him calling her name, but all she could do was grip his shoulders as the world shattered, realigned and shattered again. This was the essence of pleasure, the origins of the cosmic bang. This was where light started, dreams were conceived and stars collided.

This was the majesty of the universe in action.

Nine

Hunt looked across his elegantly decorated apartment to where Adie stood by the Christmas tree, her head bent over the velvet-covered box containing Christmas ornaments. Deep in conversation with a tech giant's wife, Adie lifted an ornament to the light, her finger spinning the glass.

The bauble shimmered and sparkled. As did Adie.

Hunt sipped his whiskey, his attention on her and not on his guests. He couldn't believe that three weeks had passed so fast and that Christmas was just a few days away. Adie would be leaving soon and his apartment, and his life, would go back to normal...

If working fourteen-hour days, being empty of colorful conversation—being empty, period—could be called normal. He didn't want her to go. Yet he couldn't ask her to stay...

For the first time in his life, Hunt wasn't sure what

he did, or didn't, want. He didn't want Adie to leave his life, but neither could he ask her to stay in it. He didn't want to stop sleeping with her, but how could they maintain a physical relationship when she was six thousand miles away?

He was in no-man's-land, not wanting to lose her but not prepared to love her either.

They'd had fun, Hunt thought, but nothing lasted forever. He had proof of that. For the first few weeks or months after his mom left the psychiatric hospital, she was a decent mom, but being strong wore her out. Her inner demons always made a reappearance and sent her scuttling back to where she felt safe and protected. And him back to a new foster family or group home.

His friendship with Steve had ended with a car accident and Hunt's marriage had burned hot and died as quickly. Nothing lasted forever...

Even if Adie was based in Manhattan, even if they gave it their best shot, it would eventually wither and die. It was how things happened and there were no exceptions to the rule.

But, crap, he wanted there to be.

He wanted to end every party he ever hosted or attended by taking her back to his bed, their bed, only to wake up with her curled up against him. He wanted to share showers and meals, space and time, conversation and children. His wealth and his world.

But if wishes were horses and all that...

He could wish up a storm, but those wishes didn't translate into anything concrete. Dreams and hopes and wishes were for people who were optimistic and a little foolish. Pragmatists like him—and Adie—knew that everything ended and some endings were more painful than others.

The end of his marriage had stung, mostly because he didn't like to fail. Steve's death eviscerated him, and Hunt never wanted to experience grief like that again.

But if he let himself love Adie, only to lose her, he'd never recover. So it was simple. He couldn't let this relationship continue and he most certainly would not allow himself to fall in love with her.

And if he did, he had no one but himself to blame.

He didn't know why he was even thinking about this because Adie had told him she had no intention of deepening their connection. She'd chased down love and affection as a young adult and she'd been disappointed time and time again. She was now emotionally and financially independent, of her parents and of a man, and she didn't need anyone else to make her happy or to give her life meaning.

Like him, she was just fine on her own.

In those quiet, early morning hours when his defenses were down and his heart spoke louder than his brain, watching her as she slept, if he had the odd thought of wanting to be the one who made her happy, forever, then that was his problem, not hers.

"You haven't taken your eyes off her for a moment."

Hunt turned his head to look at Kate and scowled. "If that was true then I would've face-planted a hundred times or more."

"Stop being so literal," Kate retorted, "you know what I mean."

Unfortunately, he did. And it was true, his eyes were constantly seeking Adie, needing to know where she was, and once he caught sight of her in that black lace dress, he fought the urge to kick out his guests and take her to bed.

Or leave the guests to their own devices and take her to bed. Either would work.

Kate thumping his biceps muscle broke into his fantasies around middle-of-a-party sex. "What?" he demanded.

"Sometimes I'm too damn smart for my own good. Or rather, your good."

"Meaning what?"

Kate snagged a full glass of champagne from a passing tray and stared at the pale yellow liquid for a long time before answering his question. "Look, it's not a secret that I never liked Griselda and when I met Adie, the first thought that popped into my head was that she'd be perfect for you. That's why I asked you to attend her Christmas market."

Hunt stared at her, trying to wrap his head around Kate's words. And her matchmaking. "I thought you wanted to use me as a way to break into Manhattan society, to pick up some new clients."

Kate's snort was in direct contrast to her elegant red Vera Wang gown and the classy diamond-and-ruby hairpin in her blond hair. "I am the daughter of Richard and Rachel Williams, who have been part of that world since before I was born. I am stupidly rich and invited to all the best parties. I didn't need your help to pick up clients or for you to introduce her to potential clients, Hunter."

Wow, talk about being slapped back.

Kate smiled at him. "Don't get me wrong, my connection with you doesn't hurt and Adie working for you has definitely impressed a lot of people, but neither of us needed you to establish her business."

Hunt sipped his whiskey and narrowed his eyes at Kate's smirking expression. "Okay, got it. Message received. Can we talk about your matchmaking scheme now?"

Kate slipped her hand into the crook of his arm and rested her head on his biceps as they both watched Adie. "I thought you were well matched but I never expected you two to have such hectic chemistry and be so well suited.

"I see you two together and you gel. You are both so close, this close," Kate lifted her hand, a tiny gap between her thumb and index finger, "to falling in love."

Hunt stepped back and folded his arms across his chest. "How much champagne have you had?"

Kate ignored his question, her eyes going back to Adie. "But I'm scared for her, Hunt. Hell, I'm scared for both of you. I know her better now and, while I don't want either of you hurt, I do know how resilient you are. You're a survivor, you can cope with anything, but Adie isn't as strong. She's worked so hard to become who she is today. If she falls for you and you don't fall for her back, it'll hurt her, Hunt.

"For Adie, love has been…elusive. If you don't plan on keeping her forever then you need to end it, Hunt, before she falls deeper and can't get herself out."

Hunt couldn't speak. He could hardly breathe. He wanted to argue with Kate, tell her she was allowing her imagination to run away with her, but he couldn't utter the lie. Kate, as observant as ever, had hit the nail on its head and demolished it in the process.

He either had to go all in with Adie or end it. And since he didn't want a relationship, didn't want more than what they had, couldn't deal with more, that meant cutting ties…now, immediately.

Well, as soon as possible. His skin prickled and ice invaded his veins. No, it was too soon. He hadn't had enough of her yet.

They had three days left together. They could be together during the remainder of her stay in the city and then they'd say goodbye.

"She's leaving in three days, Kate. Nothing much can happen in so short a time." Was he trying to convince Kate or himself?

Kate didn't even try to hide her enormous eye roll.

"It's the most romantic time of the year, Sheridan!" Kate gestured to his window and Hunt noticed gently falling snow and the way it covered his balcony in a pretty layer of white. "This is the season of magic and miracles and, let's be honest here, stupidity! Babies are made, proposals are issued, I-love-yous seem to fall more easily. Don't get caught up in the hype, Hunter!"

"Have you ever known me to be unduly influenced, Kate?"

"Well, no," Kate admitted, a stubborn look on her face. "But there's a first time for everything."

Hunt rubbed her arm. "Relax, Katie, Adie and I know what we are doing. We're adults and very much have this under control."

Kate stared at him for the longest time and Hunt resisted the urge to squirm. Maybe this situation with Adie was a little out of control, but he intended to rectify that, to make sure they kept their intense chemistry corralled. He had no intention of getting hurt, but he could handle it if he did—Kate was right, he was a survivor—but he had no intention of allowing Adie to be affected in any way, at all.

Adie in pain was simply not an option. And if calling this quits three days before its expiration date meant avoiding that scenario, then that was what he'd do.

But in the morning, after he'd spent the night making love to her.

He'd give them both one last, glorious night to remember.

The next morning Adie opened her eyes to see big fluffy snowflakes floating to the ground as they passed Hunt's floor-to-ceiling bedroom windows. If she sat up, she knew she'd see the tops of the trees in Central Park dusted in powdered sugar, and Adie couldn't wait to find out if the busy city was the picturesque fairy-tale location she imagined it to be.

But for now, she was content to lie here in Hunt's huge bed, her bottom to his crotch, his big arm holding her close, his breath on the back of her neck, his big hand covering her breast.

Romantic, easy, lovely…yes, this was the perfect way to start a day.

Adie felt Hunt's hard erection pressing against her and heat rocketed through her. Why were they sleeping? They had only a few days left together, hours really, and they were wasting time when they could be making love. Rolling over onto her back, Adie turned her head to look at him and sucked in a harsh breath at the blazing heat in his eyes, the desire on his face.

She fell, and fell some more, unable to believe that such a masculine man could want her so much.

Adie tried to say good-morning but the words died in her throat, overwhelmed by the hot emotions she could see in his eyes. Yeah, tenderness was there, as was lust and was that regret? Or fear?

She didn't know; she couldn't tell. Neither could

she ask. She simply wasn't ready for a heart-to-heart conversation.

Besides, she didn't want to talk, she wanted to feel, to be, to love this amazing, sexy man as the snow fell behind them.

Gently pushing Hunt onto his back, Adie straddled his thighs, dragging her wet core over his ready-to-play erection. He felt so good, so intensely hard and hot, satin over iron. How was she supposed to give this up? How was she supposed to walk away from so much pleasure, from how he made her feel?

You can't think about that, Adie, not now—all you can do is enjoy him. Take the moment, the hour, the day...and mentally record every memory.

Adie, not wanting to end this before it started, leaned down to kiss Hunt, her tongue sliding into his mouth. Holding his face in both her hands, she stroked her thumbs over his cheekbones, her fingers over his jaw, trying to imprint these feelings into her psyche, hoping to burn the way he felt and smelled, the way he kissed and tasted, into her subconscious.

Hunt's hands moved up and down her back, over her butt, up her sides, and onto her breasts. His touch, like hers, was a little desperate, as if he were trying to commit her to memory, as well.

Hunt gripped the back of her head, fusing her mouth against his, taking the kiss deeper and then deeper still. His need for her fed her own desire and she tilted her hips, needing more, needing everything. She felt rather than heard his moan of approval and her hands streaked over his upper body, trying to touch him wherever she could. Oh, how she wished she could completely fuse their bodies together. Having him inside her wasn't enough—she wanted more...

And once she got it, she suspected it still wouldn't be enough.

Hunt, his hand in her hair, tugged her head back and when she looked into his eyes, she gasped at the passion and need in his eyes.

"Goddammit, you're exquisite." Tightening his arm around her waist, he flipped her over and entered her with one long, sure, perfect stroke. Adie's legs encircled his hips and she pushed her nails into his firm butt, groaning with approval as he sought her mouth, his tongue dancing with hers.

For the longest time, Hunt was content to stay inside her, kissing her with a ferociousness he'd never displayed before. Without leaving her, he kissed her throat, pushed her breasts up so her nipples could meet his mouth, nibbled her collarbone but always, always returning to her mouth.

Pleasure dipped and peaked but Adie didn't want to come. She didn't want this to end. And Hunt didn't hurry them along, seemingly content to make their encounter last, to drag out this experience for as long as possible.

Because they'd never do this again...

The thought hit her—a hot, hard, devastating swipe. This was it, as soon as they were done—probably after they'd had a shower and cleaned up—he'd call it quits.

And that was okay; she knew it had to end. And if he didn't end it, she would. She had to. Sure, she was supposed to stay only another three days, but her feelings for Hunt were growing at warp speed—when had that happened? She'd been so in control! And by the weekend she might be thinking about forever, about marriage and babies.

No, she couldn't let that happen. She needed to pack up her stuff and *go*.

There wouldn't be any promises to keep in touch, to see each other again…her fairy tale in New York was over and it was time for her to return to real life.

Because if she stayed, if they continued this, they would start saying words they didn't really mean, I-love-yous and I-can't-live-without-yous.

No, it was better to leave while they liked each other, while Hunt still liked her. She wanted Hunt to have only good memories of her.

"Stop thinking," Hunt told her. "Be with me."

Adie wanted to keep some semblance of control but Hunt's mouth was demanding. His hands were insistent and he was driving his cock deeper into her, demanding her response. Her nipples tingled, her skin flushed and her channel pulsed with need as she hovered on the edge of an earth-shattering climax.

How could she feel so good but so miserable at the same time? How could she be two people simultaneously, one begging him to push her over the edge, the other silently screaming that she had to leave, that she needed to protect herself, that her bourgeoning feelings for him scared the skin off her?

Then her orgasm hit, crashing over her head and she begged Hunt for more. He responded, shoving his hand between them to find her nub while his hips pistoned into her. Adie felt herself rocket upward and when she felt his release, she fell over that cliff again, falling, falling…exploding.

Tears streamed from her eyes and she tasted them on her lips, confused and upset and throbbing with the aftermath of concentrated pleasure.

He'd made her fly, sent her to the stars and back, but now reality was rushing up to meet her, cold and hard and oh-so-unwelcome.

* * *

He didn't love her and this had to end.

Maybe he loved her a little and this didn't have to end.

No, he knew he loved her. No way did he want this to end.

Hunt, running across Bow Bridge in Central Park, skidded to a stop and slapped his hands on his hips. His breath made a circle of mist in front of his face. He ignored the freezing wind plastering his running top to his chest.

What he knew for sure, deep down in that place where truth lived, was that he most certainly didn't want her to leave.

He'd thought he did, at the party last night he'd even resolved to break things off with her but thinking was easy. Doing, as he'd discovered, was impossible. His mind, determined to keep him safe, was convinced he needed to remain emotionally isolated and solitary.

His heart and soul, and body, couldn't conceive of a life without her in it.

Hunt placed his gloved hands on the edge of the cast-iron bridge and stared down at the frigid waters of the Lake. He'd vowed not to fall in love again, to have any emotional attachments, but Adie had snuck under his defenses and flipped that resolve on its head. He was scared of getting hurt, of course he was. He was terrified of losing her, but living his life without her scared him more.

He couldn't—he wouldn't—go back to the life he'd had before, an empty apartment, meaningless sex, his hours spent on work and more work.

He wanted something different, something meaningful...

And he wanted everything he could have with Adie.

He wanted that huge wedding, or a small wedding—whatever she preferred. He wanted to see her walking down the aisle toward him. He wanted to come home to her every day and wake up to her every morning. He wanted to see her rounded with a child—*his child*—to be there when she pushed a new life into the world.

She could be on her way to pregnancy right now. He hadn't remembered to use a condom this morning. But instead of feeling panicked and anxious at the idea, Hunt smiled, completely at ease with the notion.

His eyes drifted over the snow-covered landscape of his favorite park, and he could imagine a little boy with brown eyes playing in the snow, making tiny snowballs and throwing them at him, missing him by a mile. Or, if he inherited Hunt's pitcher's arm, snowballs that hit him square in the face. He could see his son's momma, another baby in a sling against her chest, the cold turning her cheeks pink, brown eyes sparkling with laughter.

It was easy to imagine his little family coming home to hot chocolate and coffee, Adie stepping over toys and books as she sank to the couch to lift up her shirt to feed their baby girl. He'd make them lunch, bathe the kids, then take his wife to bed and make love to her before one of the kids interrupted their sleep…

He suddenly and desperately wanted what Richard and Rachel had—a solid marriage, a lifetime of memories, children and companionship. Oh, he knew it wouldn't be easy—having tons of money wasn't a bulletproof shield against heartache, Steve's death being a case in point—but Hunt and Adie could work their way through it, love their way through it. They just had to stand together, shoulder to shoulder and face whatever came their way. They had to believe that love could conquer anything.

Hunt shook his head. He sounded like a greeting card, but it didn't make the emotion any less true. He'd sublimated his earliest dreams, pushed away his wish for a family because he'd been scared to feel loss and pain again, but a family was still what he wanted. And Adie was central to the family he imagined.

He'd never felt this way about Joni. Their relationship had been built on ego and pride. And his relationship with Griselda had been all about convenience. And, possibly, laziness. The thought of raising a child with Griselda now made him shudder. He and Adie wouldn't have separate apartments or nannies. He would be an active participant in raising their children. He'd take his son to the batting cages and little league practices, his daughter to ballet or cello lessons. Or, hell, vice versa if that was how his kids rolled. He'd be there.

Although he felt unsure and uncertain, he couldn't wait to dive in, knowing that he and Adie could do it all, together.

The only problem, Hunt thought as he started to jog back home, was convincing her.

Adie zipped her suitcase, grabbed the handle and pulled it off Hunt's bed. It hit the laminated flooring with a hard thump, narrowly missing her toe. Her eyes blurry with tears, Adie looked around his chocolate-and-aqua room, wondering how she'd find the willpower to pick up her bag and leave.

But she had to…

Because she was sliding into love, doing exactly what she'd promised herself she wouldn't do. So she had to leave while she still could, while she had the strength to walk away.

Hunt didn't want this either, Adie reminded herself. He hadn't offered her anything or suggested she stay in New York or asked her to delay her trip and spend Christmas with him. But something was different, something had happened between them last night and earlier this morning. They hadn't just had sex—they'd made love.

Sex was easy, but lately, she and Hunt hadn't engaged in the biomechanical act. No, they'd made love, dammit, in every sense of the words.

Using their bodies, he'd pulled her into his mind and him into hers. There was a shocking intimacy in the way they touched each other that went beyond the prosaic act, it was as if Hunt knew her, could see inside her. They'd *connected*.

But she had to sever that connection, now, immediately.

Because if she didn't, if she allowed this to grow, there were only two possible outcomes. She'd start weaving fantasies around him and he'd soon become frustrated with her and call it quits. Or, if for some weird reason his feelings grew faster than hers and he wanted something permanent from her, she'd run.

Adie wrapped her arms around her waist and walked over to the big window, looking down at the snow-covered streets and trees. She would not do that to Hunt, would not allow him to think they had a future when she knew she was the ultimate runaway lover.

It didn't matter that Hunt had said he wasn't into commitment, that he was as anti-relationships as she was. She'd seen something in his eyes last night and it had scared her. Whether she was right or wrong, whether he was falling for her or not, it didn't matter, she was bailing before this situation got more complicated, before their feelings strolled into the party and ruined everything.

But damn, if there was one guy in the world who could tempt her to stay, persuade her to take a chance, then Hunt Sheridan was that guy, the only guy...

"Coffee?"

Adie furiously blinked away tears—she would not let him see her cry!—and hauled in a deep breath, testing a smile. She slowly turned to see him standing in the doorway, the two cups dwarfed by his big hands. Hands that had held her, stroked her for the last time.

It's better this way, dammit! You're walking away with your heart, without silly expectations, having had three weeks of the best fun, in bed and out of it.

And Hunt, Adie fiercely reminded herself, didn't "do" love. He wanted freedom, to remain unentangled, to give all his focus to his work. And that was why his relationship with Griselda had lasted for so long. She'd made no demands on him and had been happy to take as little as he offered.

Oh, God, maybe he'd restart whatever he and Griselda had...

The thought made Adie want to throw up. But it made sense—Griselda lived in the city, she made no demands on him and their whatever-they-had had worked for a long time.

Hunt stopped in the doorway to his bedroom and Adie looked at him, wishing she could freeze time. He was still dressed in his running gear and expensive sneakers. His solid black running pants molded to his muscular legs. He'd ditched his parka, but his light blue running top skated over his broad shoulders and over his wide chest to fall in a straight line over his stomach. His hair looked messier than usual and she knew her fingers running through those silky strands had contributed to his tousled look.

Despite his lack of sleep, he looked fit and healthy, and yeah, so sexy he stripped her of her breath. Hunt wasn't conventionally handsome but had the masculine face that made a woman look, and then look again. From this moment on, heavy stubble, hair the color of burnt sugar and gray eyes would always be her favorite color combination…

Hunt walked across his bedroom and placed Adie's cup on the bedside table closest to her. Moving closer to the window, he pushed his shoulder into the glass, staring down at the park he'd just run through, the trails now slick with sleet.

"I see you're all packed," Hunt quietly commented and Adie searched his face, and his words, for subtext. She found none.

"Yeah, I thought I should go."

"Want to explain why? I thought you were flying tomorrow."

"I was, am." Adie twisted her hands together. "I thought that we should, you know…"

"I really don't," Hunt said, after sipping his coffee.

The "end this" stuck in her throat, she couldn't make herself say the words. Adie rocked on her heels. God, she hated this part. Saying goodbye was never fun.

"When do you think you'll come back to the city?" Hunt asked.

"I have to be back sometime in the New Year," Adie replied, her hands wrapped around her mug as if she were looking for warmth. "Kate and I plan on opening up a Treasures and Tasks by the end of February. Once the legalities are in place, I'll leave Kate to run the Manhattan branch and I'll only be making the trip back every six months or so."

"Since you have yet to mention contacting me, I presume that's not in the cards?" Hunt asked, his tone low and hard.

Adie forced herself to say the words. "No, I won't be contacting you."

"Would you like to clarify why? I thought we enjoyed each other."

Adie shifted from foot to foot and told herself to stop fidgeting. "We did—I did."

Hunt raised his eyebrows above suddenly icy eyes. "Care to explain, Adie?"

No, not really. It hardly made sense to her...

"I just think we've run out of road."

"Bullshit," Hunt snapped. "Tell me the truth."

Adie put her coffee down, jammed her hands into the back pockets of her tight-fitting jeans and lifted her shoulders to up around her ears. She went for the most valid, easiest-to-explain response. "I live in London, Hunt, you live here. Neither of us wants anything permanent so I'm easing my way out of your life."

"Easing? You're full-out galloping!"

Well, yeah. But he wasn't supposed to have picked up on that.

Adie forced a smile onto her lips and attempted to look jaunty. "Once I'm out of the picture, I'm sure Griselda will be very happy to take up where you left off."

Hunt's eyes flashed with anger and Adie grimaced. God, why did she have to bring up his ex? Oh, maybe because she wanted to know whether he intended to reinitiate contact with the blond ballet dancer.

Hunt stared at her, his expression suggesting she'd

grown two heads. "Do you really think I'd go back to her? After what you and I shared?"

"We shared your bed, Hunt. That's about it."

"I thought we enjoyed each other as much out of the bedroom as we did inside it," Hunt replied.

And what did he mean by that?

"I'm only going to say this once... Griselda will never be a part of my life again," Hunt said, his words clipped. "We're done. She wanted something I couldn't give her."

Adie cocked her head to the side. "Love? Commitment? A proper relationship?"

"No, Griselda didn't want that from me. What she wanted was for us to co-raise a child together," Hunt explained, keeping his eyes on hers. "I told her no."

Holy hell, really? "And why didn't you tell me this before?"

Hunt's eyes narrowed. "Maybe because we were only sharing a bed, Adie."

Oooh, touché.

Despite knowing that she was dragging out this goodbye, Adie wanted to know more. "Did you say no because you don't want to be a dad?"

He was anti-commitment, anti-relationships, so his not wanting to father a child, to tie himself to a woman through a baby for the rest of his life, made sense.

Hunt held her eyes, his expression enigmatic. "I didn't think I did. I've changed my mind about quite a few things since you dropped into my life, Adie.

"I don't want a cold relationship, Adie, with a cold woman. I don't want a nanny to raise my child, to visit my child in the apartment downstairs. I want my child to run down the hall and climb onto our bed, snuggled down between us, nag us to get up because he wants to play. I want to do the midnight feedings and bath times, read stories to our kids, take them to their sports games and ballet lessons and play in the snow. I want to be a dad, not their sperm donor or bank manager.

"Be my unborn kid's mom, Adie," Hunt added.

"What?"

Had he lost his freaking mind?

Adie looked at him, looking for the hint of humor that would tell her he was joking. But she didn't find it.

What was happening here? Instead of going up one level—let's try and keep this alive, let's see where this goes—he'd skipped five or six and went straight to the highest floor, the scariest level.

The urge to fling herself into his arms, to plaster her mouth against his and utter a series of yes's in-between kissing him senseless, was strong. Because joy flooded her system and her heart took flight, she forced herself to take a step back and hold up her hand. God help her, she needed to leave before she threw caution to the wind and said something stupid.

Like yes.

"I—I… Hunt, God. Where is this coming from?" Adie demanded, her voice turning shrill. "We've known each for three weeks and now you're asking me to be your baby mama? This was just supposed to be a three-week fling, Sheridan! No commitments, no strings, a good time and then we walk away. What the hell are you doing?"

"I'm trying to keep you in my life, dammit!"

"Why?" Adie shouted back.

"Because what we have is amazing. Because this can be something special, a once-in-a-lifetime thing!"

His words bounced off his walls, off the glass of his expansive windows and Adie felt them pummel her skin. Oh, no, no, no, no! She didn't want this intensity, hadn't asked for it, couldn't trust it. This level was way out of her comfort zone.

He hadn't mentioned the *L* word, but it was there, hovering between them. But love, expressed or not, would die. It always did. Maybe not by his hand but in time, by hers. She couldn't be loved, didn't want to be...

Love was a myth. Wasn't it?

Adie stared into his eyes, saw the tenderness under his frustration and felt herself leaning toward him, wanting to believe that this was it, that love could last, that she could change. But that wasn't fair, not to him and not to her.

She saw his face soften, watched as his hands reached for her, but before they could physically connect, she jerked back.

She couldn't allow herself to be sucked into a relationship, a relationship that had no chance of lasting.

One of them had to be sensible.

"This is unrealistic thinking, Hunter, it really is. We've had a nice time but, deep down, you know we are both too screwed up to have the big house, kids and white picket fence. I'm the product of two of the most dysfunctional people in the world and you, when you recover from this rush of blood to your brain, you'll regret your words. In time you'll feel frustrated at having to balance a girlfriend and your work. You'll start to resent me and I'll start to hate you and if we have a kid together, it'll be a hundred times worse. And we'll screw up a child who didn't ask for any of this. You haven't thought this through."

"I'm thirty-five years old Adie, and I run a multibillion dollar company. I know my own mind," Hunt said, sounding annoyed. He reached out to take her hand and sighed when Adie hid her hands behind her back. She couldn't let him touch her. If she did, she'd sink into him and that would be disastrous.

"Give it a shot, Adie. Give us a chance. I know we live in different cities, but we'll figure it out. We'll take it step by step if that makes you feel more comfortable."

Adie shook her head, walked over to the bed and picked up her bag, slinging it over her shoulder. Then she grabbed the handle of her suitcase and tipped it onto its wheels. "I can't, Hunter. I mean, I could stay, we could try and make it work but we both know it would fall apart eventually. I'm not good at relationships. I don't believe in love and I don't trust it. I know that I will never let myself love you because I'm terrified of giving myself over to something that won't last. And because my fear is bigger than anything, I will kill what we feel and you will end up hating me.

"And I can't live my life knowing you hate me, Hunt."

Hunt jammed his hands beneath his armpits and rocked on his heels. He looked away, and when he spoke again, he sounded miserable. "Don't walk out, Adie, don't go. Let's work this out."

Adie simply shook her head and pulled her bag out of the room, heading straight for his elevator. She glanced at the big Christmas tree in the corner of the sitting room, the hand-painted ornaments glinting in the morning light.

Happy damn Christmas to me.

This one, she decided, would probably be more miserable than all the rest put together.

Unfortunately, there was no one to blame but herself.

Ten

Adie had heard about receiving signs from a higher being but had always thought the universe had better things to do than send messages to inconsequential humans. But, sitting on the steps leading up to her flat in Notting Hill after a twenty-hour trip through hell, she was, maybe, starting to believe the New Agers might be onto something.

Because, damn, her flight from JFK had been a series of rolling disasters from start to finish. On her arrival at the airport, there had been, inexplicably, confusion about her ticket, with the computer not being able to find her booking. After finally receiving her boarding pass, she'd gone to the wrong gate and she'd heard only one call asking her to report for boarding, causing her to sprint to the other side of the terminal to make her flight. The airline attendants, and the passengers, hadn't been shy about expressing their irritation.

In the air, she'd thought her problems were over, but turbulence over the Atlantic had been brutal and then her plane had circled Heathrow for an hour before the pilot landed in a violent crosswind. On landing, she'd couldn't locate her luggage and, on finally reaching her flat—tearful and tired—she realized she'd lost her keys.

Well, not lost precisely, she recalled tipping out the contents of her bag in Hunt's apartment to swap bags and her keys must've fallen to the floor there.

She had a spare set of house keys in her desk drawer at work but the keys to her office were on the same ring as her keys to the flat. She needed her assistant, Kaycee, to let her into the office, but Kaycee was en-route to Dublin to spend Christmas with her family. She could call a locksmith but finding one would be near on impossible and if she did, she'd have to pay a king's ransom for his services. Another, less stressful option would be for her to find a hotel…

Or to go back to Manhattan…

The thought popped into her head, as it had done every minute since she'd stormed out of The Stellan. But this time she couldn't push it away, neither did she want to. She wanted to be in New York. Hunt, apparently, wanted her there…

Adie felt a drop of rain on her nose, then another. She glared up at the heavy sky. "Can you give me a break? I'm sitting, I'm thinking, I'm trying to work it out!"

Miraculously, someone upstairs was listening because the rain held off. Adie wrapped her arms around her knees and considered Hunt's proposal.

Okay, let's deal with the easy stuff first, she decided. Moving to Manhattan wouldn't be an issue, Kaycee was fantastically efficient and the majority of Adie's work was done over the internet. She'd have to fly back to London occasionally but that was why planes were invented.

Her parents wouldn't care where she lived, neither did they care what she did. They weren't a factor in her decision-making process.

Right, now she had to confront the thorny issue. Hunt...

No, Hunt wasn't the problem, *she* was.

He'd told her he wanted her to stay, that they had a chance of creating something amazing—a Christmas miracle in itself—and her first inclination was to dismiss his statement. Because, really, who fell in love in under a month?

Especially two people who didn't believe in love.

But Hunt, as he'd pointed out, was in his midthirties and he was a guy who knew his own mind. He wasn't one for overstating, for exaggeration. He meant what he said and said what he meant so, yeah, maybe he did want to make this work.

He hadn't said the words, but Adie thought he might love her. He wouldn't have given her false hope, mentioned her staying or having his babies if he didn't.

And falling in love with her was a helluva thing, given his history of loss and hurt and disappointment and his anti-commitment stance. If she weren't a yellow-bellied scaredy-cat, she'd be thrilled that a man like him—successful and powerful—had lowered his guard to let her into his life. He'd taken a chance, been brave, handed her his heart and his dreams and she'd stomped all over them in her high-heeled boots. Because she was scared.

She'd lived her life being scared—scared to be loved and have that love ripped away, scared to put her faith in someone to have them disappoint her time and time again. She didn't have enough courage to take a chance...

Your childhood is behind you, Adie...

How many times had she repeated those words to herself? But had she ever said them with any meaning? Her past, and her parents, were still dictating her actions today. She was still running instead of facing her problems. Her childhood was long over but she still let it influence her life. Her parents had been useless, neglectful and self-absorbed, but she didn't have to follow in their footsteps. She could do better, be better...

If she drilled down to the core of her feelings, if she pushed away her many excuses, denials and rationalizations, she knew she was utterly in love with Hunt. And yes, maybe they wouldn't last forever, maybe everything would fall apart in two or three months because that was what was destined to happen. But it wouldn't be because she created drama or found a way to leave.

She was done with self-sabotaging.

She could only try.

Try, with everything she had, to be happy, to be happy with Hunt.

Trying was all she could do. And that started with getting back to New York...

Adie stood up, about to call for a ride, when a ubiquitous London cab pulled to a smooth stop beside her. The window came down and the driver, who looked remarkably like one of Santa's elves leaned across the seat to give her a friendly grin. "Where to, luv?"

"Heathrow?"

"Sure thing."

Adie climbed into the car and slammed the door shut. Dragging her phone out of her bag, she quickly jumped on the internet and saw that the next flight to

New York left in a few hours. She booked her ticket and immediately got a message asking if she was interested in being upgraded—free of charge—to business class.

Uh, yes, please.

"You do know it's Christmas Eve, right?" The driver asked her, looking at her in the rearview mirror. "The traffic is going to be hectic."

Adie smiled at him and shook her head. "We'll be fine. In a matter of ten minutes, I've found you, booked a ticket, got an upgrade and look, the traffic is flowing freely."

"Well, huh. Guess the universe is looking out for you."

Adie smiled. Yep, maybe it was.

It was after midnight on Christmas Eve and Hunt walked down 5th Avenue with his hands jammed into his coat pockets and scowled at a couple taking a selfie in front of an overly decorated Christmas window. The woman lowered her phone, kissed her boyfriend and held up her phone again to catch their smooch.

He and Adie hadn't taken one photograph together. Hell, their relationship was over before either of them could think about keeping a memento of what they'd had.

And what was that? Hot sex over a few weeks…

Hunt tried to duck around a group of tourists standing in front of another window, but the crowd moved, forcing him to choose between staying where he was or stepping off the sidewalk into a puddle. Choosing to keep his feet dry, he looked over their heads into the window and immediately saw why it had captured the attention of the crowds.

It was a window within a window, posed mannequins

looking at an old-fashioned winter wonderland scene, perfectly capturing Christmas. Even he, morose and sad and pissed, could appreciate the artistry in the window. The models were modern and stylish, sporting trendy clothing and accessories and the second window harked back to a simpler time, of tobogganing and snow, candy canes and enormous Christmas trees.

Adie would love the detail, the link between old and new.

Hunt turned away, wishing he could stop thinking about her, stop missing her. While only a day and a half had passed since she'd walked out, he could barely breathe because he missed her so much. He hadn't slept much last night, dozing off somewhere close to dawn only to wake up and reach for her…

To find she wasn't there. Hell of a thing to feel sucker punched as he opened his eyes, the air rushing from his lungs, feeling weak and shaky and so damn miserable.

Would he feel like this every morning for the rest of his life?

It'll fade, Hunt told himself. *It always does. This is just grief, you have to get through it, one day at a time. You've done it before, remember?*

As Kate said, he was a survivor.

His shoulders hunched against the icy wind, Hunt recalled Kate's words from his Christmas party a few nights ago.

"For Adie, love has been…elusive."

Hunt jerked to a stop, ignoring the "Watch it, dude" of a man who had to dodge him at the last minute.

Had he even told her that he loved her?

God, he couldn't remember.

He'd asked her to have a baby with him, to stay in New York, all but demanded it in fact. But had he told her that he loved her, that she was his world? Had he really, completely, fluently explained what she meant to him?

Would it have made a difference? Might she have considered...*more* had he uttered those three important words? Hunt preferred actions to words, but they'd had so little time together before they'd parted. Adie really didn't have time to realize that, while he was slow to commit, when he did commit, he went all in.

He didn't like to fail.

Even back in the day, as a young adult, when Joni had asked for a divorce, he'd wanted to stick it out. He'd worked his ass off, both as a player and in business, and success was always a certainty, not an option.

Did Adie realize that when he made a promise, when he set his mind on a task, he always, always gave it his all? Adie had no idea that his love wasn't conditional, that his loyalty was unshakeable. That he would love her through all her insecurities, that he was the one place where she would always and forever be adored, accepted? She hadn't had that as a child. Her parents had emotionally neglected her, but he wouldn't. It simply wasn't in his nature.

When he worked, he worked; when he loved he loved. And he did love her. With everything he had, he was, with everything he could be.

Did she even have the faintest idea?

But how could she? They'd known each other for three weeks and the time they'd spent together outside the bedroom was minimal. He was a good lover but not that good, unfortunately.

He needed to tell her, now, *tonight*. Well, as soon as possible. He needed to explain, to lay all his cards on the table, to completely expose himself. He had to give everything he had to get her back.

She was worth it. She was worth anything.

Hunt yanked out his phone and scrolled through his phone, looking for the number of his pilot. Had Duncan filed it under *Pilot*, his name or the name of the airport where the plane was parked?

Forget it, he'd call Duncan. Hitting the one key on his keypad—idly noting that Duncan would soon be bumped to number two on his speed dial—he looked around and tried to get his bearings. Heading back in the direction of the old-fashioned window, he mentally urged Duncan to answer his damn phone.

"Hunter? It's late. Is everything okay?"

Hunt released the air he'd been holding. "Sorry, I know. But can you get hold of my pilot, tell him to file a flight plan to London? I want to leave first thing in the morning.

"And can you get Pete to collect me as soon as possible?"

"I'm on it," Duncan reassured him. He hesitated. "Is everything okay?"

"I'm not sure. Ask me that question in twenty-four to thirty-six hours," Hunt replied. Obstructed by the crowd by the window, he stepped off the sidewalk and his foot landed in a puddle, soaking his shoe and the bottom six inches of his pants.

Hunt winced at the cold before shrugging it off. It was only then that he remembered why Duncan wasn't in the city. "How's your friend?"

Duncan hesitated and then Hunt heard his long sigh. "Unchanged. I'm going to have to make a decision about whether to take him off life support or not."

"Jesus." Hunt rubbed his hand over his jaw, ashamed

that he hadn't checked in on his assistant before now. "I'm so sorry, Duncan. Is there anything I can do?"

"No, but thank you," Duncan replied. "I might need some more time, Hunt. I thought I was over him, but I'm not, not really."

"You've got it," Hunt told him, his voice thick.

"Saying goodbye is hard and I'm regretting the things I said and so many of the things I didn't say."

Hunt heard the tears in Duncan's voice and tried to swallow the lump in his throat. He desperately looked for something to say that might offer comfort. "You were the person he trusted enough to make the big decisions for him, Duncan. He obviously loved you a great deal."

Duncan was silent for a long time and Hunter was okay with that. Sometimes it was simply enough to be connected, to have someone listen. Hunter heard him sniff but when Duncan spoke again, Hunt could tell he was back to his efficient self. "Flight plan, pilot, London, pick up ASAP. Got it."

"Merry Christmas, Duncan. I wish you...strength."

Duncan cleared his throat. "Merry Christmas, Hunter. And I hope she says yes."

How the hell did he know that? Hunter looked at his phone, but when he put it back to his ear to demand to know if his assistant had developed psychic powers, Duncan was gone.

And, yeah, Hunter hoped she said yes too.

Hunt brushed snow off his shoulders and stamped his feet as he stepped into the lobby of The Stellan, grateful for the blast of warmth. He looked toward the night doorman who'd lumbered to his feet.

"Mario, working Christmas Eve?"

"Yes, sir," Mario replied. "It's not a big deal, the family is only flying in later this morning."

"Nice," Hunt replied, wishing he could be certain of the reception from the only person—apart from the Williams clan—he considered his family.

Well, he'd soon know. In ten or so hours, he'd know whether Christmas would be his favorite holiday or if he'd be hating the holiday for the rest of his life.

"Pete will be here soon. Will you buzz me when he arrives?" Hunt asked, striding toward the elevator.

"Sure. But, Mr. Sheridan, you have a visitor."

Hunt sent him a sharp look, convinced that Mario had been at the Christmas eggnog when no one was looking. It was Christmas Eve, he lived alone and nobody would be visiting him at this time of night—or morning—at this time of the year.

Mario grinned at him, lifted his thumb and jerked it to the side. Hunt turned slowly and saw a small figure curled up on the visitor's couch in the lobby. Hunt's breathing turned shallow as he recognized that pale face, that messier-than-usual hair.

Adie.

Holy hell, she was back.

Hunt couldn't take his eyes off her. "When did she get in?"

"Shortly after you left," Mario replied. "She asked me not to call you, said that she'd wait for you to come home. I was about to call you when I noticed that she'd fallen asleep."

"She's been to the UK and back," Hunt said, trying to work out why she was in his lobby, back in his life. Did it matter? She was here.

Hope, warm and tentative, bloomed in his chest.

Mario chuckled. "So, are you going to just look at her or are you going to get her out of my lobby?"

"Out. But give me a second," Hunt answered, whipping out his phone. He quickly contacted Duncan and told him to cancel the flight plan and his driver.

Then Hunt bent over Adie, slid his hands and arms under her and gently lifted her to his chest. She stirred, her eyes fluttering open. "Hunt? Where am I?"

Hunt dropped a kiss in her hair. "Home, sweetheart. You're home."

"Good," Adie replied, before closing her eyes and falling back to sleep.

Adie opened her eyes and sat up. It was snowing again. Big fat flakes drifted past Hunt's huge bedroom window, one or two splattering against the glass. Dark heavy clouds told her that more snow was on the way, and the trees swaying in Central Park suggested the wind was howling.

Lying back down again, Adie decided it was a perfect day to drift back to sleep. She patted the bed next to her, but Hunt wasn't there. Maybe he'd gone to work…damn.

What was the time? Her watch was always where she left it, on the bedside table, and Adie picked it up and squinted at the face. It was past ten…

Well, huh. It had been a while since she'd slept so late. Adie peered over the side of the bed to see what she'd knocked to the floor when she picked up her watch and saw a bunch of keys, *her* bunch of keys. The ones that opened her flat and her offices…

She was back in New York…

Adie scampered out of bed, realizing that she was dressed in one of Hunt's T-shirts. She glanced around the room to see her clothes piled up on the wingback chair next to his side of the bed.

Adie rubbed her forehead with the tips of her fingers as memories of the past thirty-six hours slapped her, hard and fast. It had been a smooth flight from London and she should've slept in the comfort of business class, but she'd been too hyped and far too nervous. It was only when she got to The Stellan and sat down on the couch in the lobby that she started to relax and she must've fallen asleep.

She presumed it was Hunt who got her upstairs, undressed her and put her to bed.

Where was he? Adie started to walk out of the bedroom to find him but then she caught a glimpse of herself in the mirror on the far wall and let out a tiny shriek. Her hair lay flat against her head on one side and stood up on the other, her face was creased from the pillow and her mascara dotted the tops of her lids and made tiny stripes under her eyes.

She looked like someone who'd been traveling for a couple of days. Oh, wait, she had been...

"God, get in the shower before he sees you," Adie told her reflection, grimacing.

"Too late," Hunt drawled from the doorway. "And I think you look amazing."

Adie whirled around and stared at him, drinking him in. He wore stone-gray chino pants and a white shirt under a crew neck sweater the color of a tangerine. Trendy sneakers covered his feet but it was his expression that captured her attention, part hope, part expectation, a little amusement.

She wanted to launch herself into his arms and was about to do that when she remembered that she needed to shower and brush her teeth. She placed her hand over her mouth and spoke through her fingers. "Hold that thought!"

At the door to his bathroom, she turned to look at him again. "Any chance of a coffee? And something to wear? Because I've lost my luggage. And can we talk?"

Hunt smiled at her erratic speech and nodded to the bedside table. "Coffee." Then he pointed to the dressing room. "Your bags arrived this morning. The airport had them delivered here because you put down my address as your primary residence. All your stuff is in the closet, your toiletries are in the bathroom."

Adie looked at the closet and then back at him. "You unpacked for me?"

"And I made a hell of a noise doing it." Hunt smiled. "I can't tell you how many times I nearly woke you up, but I couldn't, you were obviously exhausted."

Adie swayed from foot to foot, torn between wanting to get clean and stepping into his arms. Choosing to get her coffee, she took a huge sip, then another, sighing with pleasure.

Hunt slid his hands into the pockets of his pants. "Take a shower, Adie, and then we'll talk. But, if you are longer than ten minutes, I'll join you in there and trust me, no talking will be done."

It was tempting to linger but, Adie thought as she brushed her teeth, the next time they made love she didn't want any misunderstandings between them.

Hopefully, she'd be in his arms, in his bed soon because, really, how long did it take to say sorry, I was wrong, I love you and please can I stay?

Hunt heard her footsteps coming down the hallway and turned away from the window in his sitting room. She couldn't have been more than fifteen minutes, but it seemed longer, an age. God, she looked amazing and he couldn't believe she was here, in his apartment.

He took a moment to study her, pleased she hadn't taken the time to apply makeup or dry her newly washed hair. She'd pulled on yoga pants and a thigh-length sweater and her feet were bare. Her lack of fussing suggested she was as eager to get things settled as he was.

And he couldn't wait so he jumped straight in.

"Why did you come back, Adie?"

Adie perched on the edge of the cushion of his leather couch, placing her hands between her knees. Hunt sat down opposite her, his forearms on his knees, his eyes locked on hers.

"I had a nightmare trip back to London, everything went wrong. I got back to my apartment and realized I'd lost my flat keys."

"I found them next to the bed," Hunt replied.

"I thought about going to a hotel but quickly realized that wasn't where I wanted to be."

Hunt, desperate to pull the words out of her, forced himself to be patient, to wait for her to explain in her own way. They had only one shot at this and he wanted to get it right.

Adie sighed. "My default setting is to run when a guy tells me I'm important. Normally I run only after things are a little more established, after I've driven him to distraction and found an excuse to bail. I don't trust myself when it comes to love, Hunt. And, normally, I find it impossible to trust a man when he says that he loves me. I guess that's because my parents blithely and frequently told me they loved me, but I knew they didn't because their actions didn't match up to their words."

She said normally, *hang onto that word.*

Hunt linked his hands together, riding the waves of

emotion. Anger at her parents, love and tenderness and protectiveness for her.

Adie looked at him as if expecting him to say something, but he just rolled his index finger in the air, silently telling her to continue.

It took a little time for her to speak again. "When I got to London, I realized that it's not you I don't trust, it's me." She pulled in a deep breath and met his eyes. "I'm hoping you are in love with me. I know that I'm in love with you—I have been since that night I first met you."

"Thank God," Hunt muttered.

Adie held up her hand. "I'm so damn scared, Hunt." She stared down at her intertwined fingers, which were as white as his own. He flexed his fingers and felt blood rushing back to his digits. Standing, he walked around the coffee table that separated them and sat down on its glass top. Adie released an agitated squawk and swatted his knee.

"Get off, it'll break. That's a limited edition table."

"It's strong and it will hold me and I don't give a damn how expensive it is," Hunt stated. And it was true, she was all that was important.

And taking that fear out of her eyes was also imperative. Hunt placed his hands on her knees and squeezed. "Love is a scary emotion. And because I'm very much in love with you, I'm equally terrified."

"You are?" Adie asked, obviously surprised. "I didn't think anything could scare you."

"You terrify me. Losing you terrifies me. Confession time, when I found you in the lobby, I was heading upstairs to pack a bag. I was going to follow you to London."

Adie's big eyes slammed into his. "You were?"

He lifted his hand to stroke her cheekbone. "I was prepared to beg you into coming back with me." He needed a clear answer, then he could breathe easily again. "Are you back, Adie?"

Adie nodded, tears in her eyes. Hunt was about to grab her, to haul her to him, when she held up her hand again. "You should know that I'm not good at being in a relationship, Hunt, but I'm going to try. I love you too much not to try and you've got to promise not to give up on me."

He'd never give up on her. He started what he finished, as he now informed her.

Adie smiled at his reassurance, but he could tell that she still wasn't convinced.

She hesitated before speaking again. "I'm not opposed to having a family, to kids, to making a solid commitment, but can we take it one step at a time? We've only known each other such a short time and it's all gone so fast."

Hunt considered her question and was about to tell her he'd give her as much time as she wanted when a small voice deep inside him told him not to. Trusting his instinct, he shook his head. "Nope, that's not going to happen. I'm not going to give you any time to talk yourself out of this, to let your head override your heart.

"I want to get married, now, immediately. By New Year's Eve at the latest. And then I want us to ditch the contraception," Hunt added.

Adie's mouth dropped open and she was the loveliest goldfish Hunt had ever seen. "No, Hunt, we can't!"

Hunt smiled at her. "We can and we will. Come on, Adie, jump all in with me, take this massive leap of faith. Be bold, be courageous."

Adie started to laugh. *"Hunter..."*

"Adie. Yes or no? Will you marry me immediately?" Hunt made sure she heard the serious question behind his smile. "Love me, sweetheart, and let me love you as you've never been loved before."

Adie rested her fist against her lips. "You're being serious."

"Deadly," Hunt said, desperate for an answer. "Well?"

He saw her haul in a breath and for one second, just one, he thought she might say no, but then her smile bloomed, her eyes danced and she lifted her shoulders in a carefree shrug. A low chuckle rumbled out of her. "What the hell…okay. Tie me up in knots, Sheridan, tie me up so tight that I can't run. So tight that all I can do is love you."

Hunt leaned forward and his lips brushed hers. "That's all I want, Adie, is for you to love me."

Adie draped her arms around his neck and looked into his eyes, love and desire and relief rolling through hers. "I do. So much."

Hunt rested his forehead against hers, his hands still gripping her knees. "And I love you, darling. Welcome home."

And, judging by her tender expression, Hunt knew she finally accepted that he—not this building or this city—was her home, with him was where she was meant to be.

Just like she was his soft place to fall.

It was, he decided, going to be an exceptionally good Christmas after all.

* * * * *

COMING SOON!

We really hope you enjoyed reading this book.
If you're looking for more romance, be sure to
head to the shops when new books are
available on

Thursday 10th December

To see which titles are coming soon, please visit
millsandboon.co.uk/nextmonth

LET'S TALK
Romance

For exclusive extracts, competitions
and special offers, find us online:

- facebook.com/millsandboon
- @MillsandBoon
- @MillsandBoonUK

Get in touch on 01413 063232

For all the latest titles coming soon, visit
millsandboon.co.uk/nextmonth

MILLS & BOON

THE HEART OF ROMANCE

A ROMANCE FOR EVERY KIND OF READER

MODERN

Prepare to be swept off your feet by sophisticated, sexy and seductive heroes, in some of the world's most glamourous and romantic locations, where power and passion collide.
8 stories per month.

HISTORICAL

Escape with historical heroes from time gone by. Whether your passion is for wicked Regency Rakes, muscled Vikings or rugged Highlanders, awaken the romance of the past.
6 stories per month.

MEDICAL

Set your pulse racing with dedicated, delectable doctors in the high-pressure world of medicine, where emotions run high and passion, comfort and love are the best medicine.
6 stories per month.

Celebrate true love with tender stories of heartfelt romance, fro the rush of falling in love to the joy a new baby can bring, and a focus on the emotional heart of a relationship.
8 stories per month.

Indulge in secrets and scandal, intense drama and plenty of sizzl hot action with powerful and passionate heroes who have it all: wealth, status, good looks…everything but the right woman.
6 stories per month.

HEROES

Experience all the excitement of a gripping thriller, with an inte romance at its heart. Resourceful, true-to-life women and strong fearless men face danger and desire - a killer combination!
8 stories per month.

DARE

Sensual love stories featuring smart, sassy heroines you'd want as best friend, and compelling intense heroes who are worthy of th
4 stories per month.

To see which titles are coming soon, please visit

millsandboon.co.uk/nextmonth

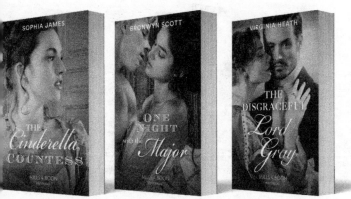

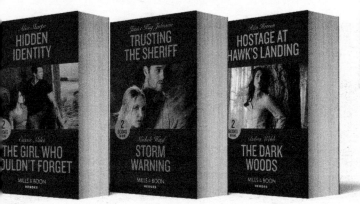

MILLS & BOON
True Love
Romance from the Heart

Celebrate true love with tender stories of
heartfelt romance, from the rush of falling
in love to the joy a new baby can bring,
and a focus on the emotional
heart of a relationship.